Flowers of Fire

THE EAST-WEST CENTER—formally known as "The Center for Cultural and Technical Interchange Between East and West"—was established in Hawaii by the United States Congress in 1960. As a national educational institution in cooperation with the University of Hawaii, the Center has the mandated goal "to promote better relations and understanding between the United States and the nations of Asia and the Pacific through cooperative study, training, and research."

Each year about 2,000 men and women from the United States and some 40 countries and territories of Asia and the Pacific area work and study together with a multinational East-West Center staff in wide-ranging programs dealing with problems of mutual East-West concern. Participants are supported by federal scholarships and grants, supplemented in some fields by contributions from Asian/Pacific governments and private foundations.

Center programs are conducted by the East-West Communication Institute, the East-West Culture Learning Institute, the East-West Food Institute, the East-West Population Institute, and the East-West Technology and Development Institute. Open Grants are awarded to provide scope for educational and research innovation, including a program in humanities and the arts.

East-West Center Books are published by The University Press of Hawaii to further the Center's aims and programs.

Flowers of Fire

Twentieth-Century
Korean Stories
edited by

Peter H. Lee

AN EAST-WEST CENTER BOOK
THE UNIVERSITY PRESS OF HAWAII
HONOLULU

Copyright © 1974 by The University Press of Hawaii
All rights reserved
Library of Congress Catalog Card Number 73–90853
ISBN 0–8248–0302–7
Manufactured in the United States of America
Designed by Dave Comstock

To My Students

Contents

Preface

THIS anthology evolved from my courses in Korean literature given at several universities in the United States. Some of the stories were read in the original, but most, in translation. I have benefited from lively discussions in the classes.

A word about the choice of material: compared to a somewhat scanty coverage of earlier decades, the post-liberation years, especially those after the Korean War, are generously represented. No attempt has been made to excerpt novels as most of their plots are too extensive for such treatment. Because it was not possible to include all major writers active today, I have drawn a line at 1968. The stories written thereafter are quite numerous and would require another collection. Although not intended to be historical, the present anthology is offered in the hope that it may give some notion of the diversity of twentieth-century Korean fiction.

I am grateful to living authors and translators for their cooperation; to Paek Ch'ŏl of the Korean P.E.N. Club and Paek Sŭnggil of *Korea Journal* for their encouragement; and to the Center for Korean Studies at the University of Hawaii for typing the manuscript. I wish to acknowledge the kind permission to reprint of *Encounter* for "Shower"; the *Korea Journal* for " A Third Kind of Man," "The Heir," and "The Portrait of a Shaman"; and Praeger Publishers for "A Stray Bullet," which appeared in *Listening to Korea,* edited by Marshall R. Pihl. Michael E. McMillan read the translations and offered useful suggestions. I wish also to express my thanks to Glenn F. Baker of The University Press of Hawaii for his editorial help.

Introduction

TWENTIETH-CENTURY Korean fiction has matured in a most turbulent setting: Japanese occupation (1910–1945), collapse of the independence movement (1919), the Second World War, the liberation (1945), the Korean War (1950–1953), and revolutions (1960, 1961). Few people have experienced so many political and spiritual crises in a span of fifty years. But what is important is that these crises were occasions for the emergence of a new generation with a new voice. Each time, new writers subjected the ruling literary fashions to a fresh evaluation. Each time, they succeeded in reshaping the literary medium appropriately to contain the quality of new values and new visions. Indeed, these cultural and moral crises not only fostered the experimental movements but effected the modernization of the language and the liberalization of techniques.

The advent in Korea of a literature that can be considered essentially modern in spirit was preceded by a transitional period, the so-called period of new literature, in the first decade of the present century. The first task of this new movement was the forging of a new literary language, one that would permit freer and more varied expression in verse and prose. Poetry attempted the simple "new style" free verse, breaking away from the limitations of the traditional prosody, while fiction adopted a prose style which approximated the everyday language of the common people. The spirit of the new movement was, therefore, antitraditionalist and dynamic, but the stories, which dealt chiefly with enlightened pioneers who longed for the new science and civilization, still followed the conventional theme of the "reproval of vice and promotion of virtue." They presented types rather than individuals and were chiefly concerned with how the characters fared in a story on the theme of reward and retribution. In defiance of the contemporary use of literature as a political and social means of persuasion and enlightenment, a new generation emerged in search of new modes of expression shortly after the independence movement.

Inspired by President Woodrow Wilson's doctrine of national self-determination, a peaceful demonstration took place on March 1, 1919, in Seoul and throughout the country. The "Declaration of Independence," signed by thirty-three representatives of the Korean people, proclaimed to the world that Korea had the right to exist as a free, independent nation. Participated in by an estimated two million people, the demonstration revealed to the world the nature of Japanese rule in Korea. Although the movement kindled the national consciousness and saw the establishment in Shanghai of the Provisional Government of the Republic of Korea, an appeal to the goodwill of Western powers fell on deaf ears. Some surface conciliatory moves on the part of the Japanese military administration notwithstanding, the colonial policy remained unchanged.

The land survey (1910–1919) established modern land-ownership rights and deprived the peasantry of the basis of their livelihood. The land hitherto tilled communally by farmers became either government property or was turned over to the Oriental Developmental Company, Japanese land companies, and immigrants. A single-crop agriculture, established to increase rice production to meet food crises in Japan, brought about the disintegration of the self-sufficient Korean rural economy. By 1932 half the farmers had become tenants, but Korea provided half of her total rice production to Japan. High rents (50–80 percent of the annual farm income) and taxes, usurious loans (75 percent of the farmers were in debt), and low wages forced 46 percent to drift to cities or emigrate to southern Manchuria and Japan. Nearly 80 percent of urban dwellers were classified as lower-income families.[1] The rigors of poverty and the impotence of the common people are mirrored in the stories written in the twenties and subsequent decades to the sixties.

The movement for literary naturalism was launched in the twenties by a group of young writers who rallied together with a new definition of realities and universals to emancipate fiction from defects in form and content. In his essay "Individuality and Art," Yŏm Sangsŏp defines naturalism as an expression of awakened individuality. Its purpose is to expose reality, its sordidness and darkness, especially the sorrow of disillusionment resulting from the negation of authority and the shattering of idols. In the name of realism and in defense of individuality, Yŏm thus attempted to displace his predecessors. Yŏm's first story, a version of the chronicle of despair, reflects the educated man's skepticism and despair after the unsuccessful independence movement.

Many examples of the so-called naturalist fiction are

personal stories, exercises in the first person singular. Desire for the real led writers to expose problems, but these were the problems encountered by the intelligentsia, offering themselves as the subjects of case studies. Most stories written in this vein deal with the miseries of life of the poor in the city or with attempts to escape from socioeconomic pressures. The disharmony between the writer and the society often drove him to nature, where the earth and the simple people furnished him with themes and motifs for some of the better stories in the Zolaesque tradition. "Fire," the first of its kind, has as its heroine a helpless girl of fifteen who was married off to be brought up by the husband's family. Kim Tongin's "Potato" is a clinical study of a fallen woman, Pongnyŏ, who was sold for eighty wŏn[2] to a widower twenty years her senior. Driven by poverty and the incompetence of her husband, she begins to lose all sense of decency and dies violently at the hand of her Chinese lover, whom she tries, but fails, to kill.

But perhaps the most persistent theme in these stories is the assault on taboo. The ethical and moral order that prevailed in traditional Korea was Confucian; the assault on that orthodox moral code began less than twenty years before the introduction of realism into Korea. Unlike European masters of realism who were eager to claim that their works were fact, not fiction, Kim Tongin, when he dealt with morbid subject matter, prefaced his works with an apology that they were fiction, not fact. Often writers are anxious to abjure the traditional values. At one point, Yŏm Sangsŏp exclaims that man is "a slave of wrong ideas" and that conscience is "a devil named idea." But their works oscillate between negation of and affirmation of traditional values.

Also, ostensibly the most objective clinical studies are

strewn with lyrical outbursts or parables. In "Fire," the heroine Suni goes to a stream to get water; there she sees a group of minnows that in the past had always eluded her attempts at capture. Finally, she catches one that at first leaps around in her cupped hands but soon loses its strength. She then throws it on the ground and looks closely to see whether it is still alive. After a short while, it stops wriggling; she has deprived a living thing of its life; its death is a symbol of the fate that awaits her at home. Such a parable appears seldom, but is a part of the naturalist's technique not only to render the deadly weight of facts less burdensome to the reader, but also to drive home the truth the stories intend to transmit.

Naturalism in Korea was never a unified literary movement. The writers represented here were productive over a span of several decades and wrote works which, though labeled naturalist, diverged somewhat widely in their treatment of themes. "Wings" by Yi Sang, which traces the unending flow of the hero's mind, is a stream-of-consciousness story. Others wrote panoramic novels, or case studies of emancipated women. Also, no writer has remained naturalist throughout his career: Kim Tongin and Hyŏn Chin'gŏn wrote both naturalist stories and historical novels.

The contributions by writers of literary naturalism to modern Korean fiction are many. Emphasizing the originality and the autonomy of literature, they defined for the first time the nature and function of writers in the modern world. Their introduction of the realistic method furthered the development of a colloquial prose style and the refinement of techniques. Their iconoclastic tendency led to the search for morbid subject matter, thus broadening the scope of themes treated in Korean fiction. Startled by the ugly, terrifying truths unveiled by their method, however, they reverted to the elements of the fabulous and the romantic from which they had struggled to free themselves. They were forced to grapple with the dialectic of dream and reality, wonder and truth. The triumph of the naturalist outlook over those based in tradition was not quite as complete as it was in the West. But the naturalists have taken modern Korean fiction further on its path.

With the occurrence of the Manchurian "incident" in 1931, Korea's role as a source of strategic raw materials increased. Hydroelectric power, and chemical, mining, and other heavy industries were developed with Japanese capital to meet the needs of Japanse expansion on the continent of Asia. The program for increasing rice production, abandoned in 1934, was reinstated after the Japanese invasion of China in 1937. The national mobilization law imposed wartime conditions. In order to assimilate Korea as an integral part of the Japanese empire, the unity of the two countries and the transformation of Koreans into Japanese subjects were emphasized. Monthly worship at Shintō shrines were enforced, teaching of the Korean language at school was prohibited, and two major Korean dailies were abolished. Civil servants donned the Japanese khaki uniforms—Günter Grass, we recall, compared the brown color of Nazi uniforms to dung in *Hundejahre* (*Dog Years*). Every day, school children recited the "Oath of imperial Japanese subjects," sang patriotic songs, and bowed to the east where the emperor resided. Soldier Tanaka reproached the emperor for his crimes against mankind before he was shot. But such defiance was possible only in a German play.[3]

The grinding poverty of the lower class at home and abroad, especially in the Korean settlements in southern Manchuria, was the chief concern of the writers of the "new tendency" movement, which later became proletarian. Excoriating the contemporary disregard of the masses in fiction, writers of the class-conscious Korean Artist Proletariat Federation (KAPF), organized in 1925, emphasized the importance of propaganda, and regarded literature as a means for the political ends of socialism. The movement also attracted fellow travelers, who emerged from the world of twilight and dreams to shout "V Narod" ("To the people"). The controversy between the socialist and the conservative, however, stimulated lively debates over the function of literature.

Produced in the teeth of military encroachment upon every literary activity, fiction in the thirties emerged in the void created by the compulsory dissolution of KAPF in May 1935. Already, in 1928, some KAPF members had relapsed into liberalism and humanitarianism, affirming that art was not propaganda, that craftsmanship was more important than message, and that the nationalist cause was more urgent than the victory of dialectical materialism. Repeated arrests of the members, however, dealt a final blow, and upon the collapse of an intricate organization with a fervent ideology, the literary world lost a catalyst that had stimulated debates, and writers scattered. The publication boom also contributed to the dispersion of writers, who no longer felt the need to belong to a coterie with its own credo and organ.

In the absence of a possibility of sociopolitical involvement, writers proposed the purity of art and perfection of techniques, an action that was also a protest against the reduction of literature to journalism by influential omnibus magazines and against historical and other popular novels written for a wider public. Unable to find a father, each member of the younger generation sought to explore his own world in his ivory tower, aloof from society. Some returned to nature and sex (Yi Hyosŏk); others retreated to the labyrinth of shamanism (Kim Tongni); still others fondly portrayed characters born out of their time, defeated and lonely. All in all, they were oblivious of historical forces and of social changes at work. Narrative sophistication and subtlety were achieved by a negation of the writer's commitments and his responsibility to his art and himself. While exiled patriots were engaged in heroic resistance, the flabby younger generation laid bare the vulnerabilities of an escapist and, at times, opportunist outlook. A notable exception was Yŏm Sangsŏp, formerly a staunch opponent of KAPF, who produced in 1932 a document of the time in his novel *Three Generations*—a dialogue between liberalism and socialism, and a study in the disintegration of traditional values and social classes.

The early forties were a dark period in all branches of Korean literature, owing to the Japanese suppression of all writing in the Korean language. In February 1940 Koreans were ordered to adopt Japanese names, and those who spoke the Korean language in public were seized and imprisoned. When in 1941 the Sino-Japanese war developed into the Pacific war, the Japanese army ceased relying on volunteers, as it had since 1938, and began conscription. A massive mobilization resulted in the conscription of more than 3.3 million Korean workers, sent as far as Sakhalin and Southeast Asia. A quota delivery system was enforced in 1941, and food was rationed. While some maintained a loyalty to the spirit of the independence movement, others collaborated with the Japanese. Some joined the Korean Writers Patriotic Association and Korean Press Patriotic Association; some went to improve the morale of the soldiers in northern China in 1939; some took part in the meetings of the Greater East Asia Writers Congress (1941–1942 in Tokyo; 1943 in

Nanking); some even poured out unctuous rhetoric in Japanese extolling the military cause.[4]

Liberation came to Korea on August 15, 1945. Already the Cairo Declaration of November 1943 and the Potsdam Declaration of July 1945 had announced that "Korea shall become free and independent." But the hastily drawn military lines along the thirty-eighth parallel soon hardened into a political boundary across which the armies of the United States and the Soviet Union confronted each other. The meeting of foreign ministers in Moscow in December 1945 decided on a trusteeship for Korea by the United States, England, China, and the Soviet Union. The subsequent Russo-American conferences in Seoul to discuss the establishment of a provisional Korean government failed, and a general election was held in the South in May 1948 under U. N. supervision. The constitution was promulgated on July 17, and the Republic of Korea was born on August 15, 1948. In the North, the Supreme People's Assembly ratified the constitution in September 1948, and the Democratic People's Republic of Korea was thereby established.

Some of those who had barely survived the last years of Japanese rule emerged from imprisonment. Notable among them were members of the Korean Language Society, and intellectuals who had refused to acquiesce in the monstrous war. The Language Society had been established in 1921 to preserve the language, to standardize orthography, and to compile a standard Korean dictionary. On the literary scene the Left/Right controversy that had raged in the late twenties and early thirties revived. There were furious groupings and regroupings, and some collaborators, in order to atone for their past offenses, espoused communism. The advocates of pure literature since the late thirties, most of whom had not had the

moral courage to posit a question or to unmask brutal
reality, opted for the restoration of the Korean traditions
and the continuity of a literature unencumbered by
ideology. In the midst of movements and countermove-
ments, which appeared with bewildering rapidity, a
genuine reappraisal of Korea's literary heritage during
her "dog years" went undone. Little attempt was made to
explore such issues as knowledge and action, literature
and responsibility, and art and freedom, or to probe the
uncertainty and bafflement besetting the country after
liberation. And as soon as a semblance of calm set in—
most of the hardcore Leftist writers had gone north by
1948—the Korean War broke out on June 25, 1950. Seoul
was abandoned for the second time on January 4, 1951
(the "January 4 Retreat"), when the Chinese army intervened.

Perhaps the most important change that took place in
the postwar Korean literary world was the emergence
in the fifties of a new generation. Most of them, born
between the twenties and thirties, experienced the horror
of war as students and later as soldiers. The freedom and
peace that appeared to return to Korea in 1945 proved not
to have returned at all. Far from being able to enjoy the
fruits of the liberation, Korea faced a more formidable
and insoluble problem than ever before in her history: the
division of the country. Less than two years after the birth
of the First Republic, war erupted. The armistice, in failing to bring about unification, only added a new set of
problems. Conscious of the political, social, and moral
chaos caused by the war and its aftermath, a group of
young writers rose to repudiate this chaotic world, and to
challenge the ruling literary fashions and conventions.

Literary moods, modes, and themes popular in
Korean fiction till the early fifties were merely the tag-

ends of earlier literary movements in Europe. Untroubled by current anxieties that faced the new generation, and uninformed about modern innovations in fiction—such as in form, sequence, and point of view—established writers still wrote in the realistic and naturalistic tradition. To them the novel was still a mere fictional narrative of characters, following closely the rules of plot, character, and setting. Shut off from the outside world and under the vigilant surveillance of the Japanese military police, Korean writers felt that realistic and naturalistic techniques, with an emphasis on moods and anecdotes, were then perhaps best suited to their works. Their chief concern was plot, conceived in chronological terms. What the new generation discovered was the inner world of the protagonist, his psychological and philosophical dimension, his stream of consciousness.

Skeptical of inherited techniques and established reputations, the new writers evaluated anew the leading names and achievements of modern Korean fiction. They freed Korean fiction from its strict formalism and reshaped it better to contain the quality of complex, contemporary experiences. What the young writers have in common is a fierce concern with the exploration of the new condition of man. Their material may be the untidy, shabby, and incoherent pattern of everyday life; but they are not afraid to delve into the most secret chambers of the unconscious and to communicate their findings. They may vary in point of view or approach, but they affirm their function as writers in a contemporary society to make us a little more aware of the world we live in and to convey to us a new reality and a new vision.

The single most important reality in postwar Korean fiction is probably the partition of the country. One outcome was the war, a war of fratricide, of man against himself. The historical actuality, calling for an authentic response to man's new situation, favored the emergence of engaged literature. In their eagerness to testify to engagement, some writers took a stand on the shifting political issues and portrayed the victims of a malicious, repetitive history that denies individual freedom and personal fulfillment. Eyewitnesses to the enactment of an absurd history, they contemplated the ambiguities of action and man's fate. Some have explored the division as the existential source of their fiction. As a symbol not only of Korea's trials but of the division of man, his alienation from himself and the world, the Thirty-eighth Parallel torments the conscience and consciousness of every hero in search of his destiny. Some accept it voluntarily as retribution for Korea's guilt; some refuse to relinquish hopes of reunion; but others go insane, driven by the hopelessness of ever reaching home. But two Koreas are fated never to meet in literature, and a work such as Uwe Johnson's *Two Views,*[5] a candid appraisal of two Germanies, has remained an impossibility in Korea. Ever since the birth of the First Republic, South Korea's political ideology has been anticommunism, and until very recently, opposition to any negotiated settlement for reunification. Only during the short-lived Second Republic did Koreans talk freely of peaceful settlement and even neutralism. Furthermore, unlike other ideological or political boundaries, the DMZ at the Thirty-eighth Parallel is a no-man's land where only wildlife and guerrilla activities thrive. No South Korean and North Korean ever exchanged a word in fiction, much less fall in love and move freely across the border.

Further innovations made in the fiction of the mid-sixties include a new definition of the imagination and self, and a new approach to character, plot, and dialogue.

This fiction of representation, characterized by an emphasis on phenomenological time and the external world, has, as elsewhere, become an instrument of knowledge, man's search to understand himself and others. Those entrenched in the traditional narrative are likely to be anachronisms. Some like Hwang Sunwŏn and O Yŏngsu, though removed from the current trend, have deftly mediated between realism and lyricism; while others, refusing to make concessions to a hypocritical and savage society, have retreated into a world of symbols, emblems, and parables. The novel, W. J. Harvey says, is the distinct art form of liberalism. "Its state of mind has as its controlling center an acknowledgement of plenitude, diversity and individuality of human beings in society, together with the belief that such characteristics are good as ends in themselves."[6] Indeed, the novel "cannot be written out of a monolithic or illiberal mind. . . . Because of the range of his subject matter, because he must see life as *divers et ondoyant,* because he must accept his characters as asserting their human individuality and uniqueness in the face of all ideology (including his own limited point of view), the novelist must tend to be liberal, pluralistic, foxy."[7] Nurtured in a most perverse atmosphere, twentieth-century Korean fiction has struggled to assert its freedom and autonomy. Its vitality and versatility will be a measure of the continued possibility of the liberal imagination in an uncertain age.

by Hyŏn Chin'gŏn

Fire

uni, who was barely fifteen years old, had
been a bride for little more than a month.
In her half-awake state she felt she was suffocating, as if a boulder were pressing down
on her chest. A boulder is usually cool, but what pressed
on Suni's chest, which was tender as a dove's, was damp
and sticky, stuffy like the monsoons, and must have
weighed more than a thousand pounds. She was panting like an animal. Then came an excruciating pain,
stabbing, tearing, maiming, and pounding her loins.
Her hips throbbed and twinged. When an iron club
pushed her innards aside and thrust into her chest, her
mouth fell agape, her body convulsed. Normally this
much pain would have wakened her, but her daily rounds
of labor—carrying a water crock on her head, pounding
grain, treading the watermill's wheel, carrying meals to
farmhands in the rice paddies—wore her out, and she
could not wake up, much as she tried. But she was not

Translated by Peter H. Lee

in a coma. "I'll probably die this instant. I will die, if the pain keeps up. I must open my eyes," she said to herself, but she could not open them, for they were closed as if glued. She could not push back the muddy flood of slumber. Meanwhile, mouth still agape, her body convulsing, she began to gnash and grit her teeth to endure the violent pain. After a while she was able to open her eyes, heavy with nightmare. Then she saw her husband's face, like the lid of a rice kettle, above her own. His dark face, large as a big round wooden tray, matched the surrounding darkness, but the glaring whites of his eyes, the half-open lips coated with a string of saliva, the yellowish teeth exposed by the crooked grin—these she could discern clearly. Then his large face kept on growing, along with the dark brown shoulders, which appeared as large as a bunch of bean stalks and then as the house itself. Overwhelmed by the terror rising from her navel and the pain twisting her bowels, Suni now trembled, now floundered, fighting the persistent slumber that seized her by the nape of her neck, and finally realized what had happened.

When she was at last released from pain, the brief June night was already finished. The gigantic frame of the man moved around in the room and then left. He must have gone out to work in the fields, she thought. Only then, with a long sigh of relief, was she fully awake. The paper window, dark as if painted with black ink, now turned to grey, and the yellow mats on the floor began to reveal their plaited surfaces. The glistening mirror on its rough stand, the tattered clothes hanging on the wall near her head—all told her that it was her enemy's room. Furthermore, there was a mattress under her. "What happened to me?" She tried to recall—she had fallen asleep last night in another place. In order to avoid the nightly assault, after washing the dishes, she had hidden herself in the barn. She had leaned against the two remaining bags of rice and spread empty sacks for a mattress. But no sooner had she stretched her legs than she fell asleep. How then could she have entered the enemy's room? He must have searched every corner of the house with his greedy, fiery eyes; he must have found her and carried her in his stout arms to the enemy's room; then he must have ministered to her the enemy's torture.

Before she could indulge further in such a reverie, her maimed body was engulfed again by another muddy flood of slumber.

"Aren't you up yet?" shouted her mother-in-law in a voice loud enough to make the house fly away. "You must boil the fodder."

Before the old woman's yell had subsided, Suni jumped to her feet. With one hand she rubbed her eyes, with the other she began to put on the clothes that her husband had stripped from her. Must I not have been sleeping until now? Her action recalled that of a soldier intently awaiting a commander's order. Therefore even in her sleep her mother-in-law's orders were frightening.

Whn she stepped out onto the veranda, day had not yet fully dawned. The pale white moon, ghostly as a dead man's eyes through the haze, was going down.

She walked straight to the fodder kettle she had prepared the night before and lit a fire. It was summer, but the early morning air was chilly; she enjoyed the way the fagots started to catch fire. She watched with interest the flame's red lips devouring dried pine twigs. A restless night had ended and another day of chores had started for Suni.

After boiling the fodder, she had to fetch water to cook the morning rice. While she held the water crock on her head with both hands, the misty air crawled in and chilled her armpits. By the edge of the brook she put down the crock and took a good stretch. The mountains and ridges, buried in the mist, seemed to wander in a dream. The heavy rain during the past days, to the delight of farmers, had filled the rice paddies; their surfaces, glistening in the white mist like congealed mercury, and the green freshly transplanted rice seedlings, were rubbing their sleepy eyes. In the midst of such a landscape, only the brook seemed to be awake, making tinkling sounds as it flowed. She approached the water to have a close look; the surface, she found, was as spotlessly clean as the pupils of fully awakened eyes. With a splash Suni dipped the gourd into the stream. The waters from all directions rushed in to cover the stream's wound, encircling the dipper. Realizing, then, that the wound was not serious, the waters began to form large rings and withdrew. Suni kept on ladling the water.

After delivery of the first crock, she returned for a second. She saw some minnows (how many times had she tried to catch them?) floating fearlessly on the surface. She was jealous of their playful gesture. Holding her breath, she tried to scoop them out, but they escaped easily. After several futile attempts, she got angry, picked up some stones and threw them recklessly. She only splashed water over her face and clothes. She felt like crying. The stones being unsuccessful weapons, she again put her hands into the water to scoop the fish out. This time an unfortunate one finally landed in her palms. As soon as the water dripped through her fingers, the fish, angry over its fate, started to jump in her palm. Suni was amused. Soon the poor, tired thing became still in her hand; Suni then hurled it cruelly to the ground. After offering a few wriggles, the little creature died, but Suni wanted to make sure and fingered it. It had been alive

and leaping a few moments ago, but now it had turned
into a corpse. When she finally realized what she had
done, she was seized with horror. The ghost of the dead
minnow seemed to hover before her. She hastily drew
water and headed back home, all the while with a sensation that someone was pulling her hair from behind.

No sooner had she finished her breakfast than she had
to grind barley. As she pounded the grain, her waist gave
out. She nearly hit her own head, drawn into the mortar
by the pestle's sheer weight. Then her arms gave out. But
she had to go on pounding.

It was noon, the time for Suni to prepare meals to
be carried to the farmhands (among them her own
husband) planting rice seedlings. The wooden tray loaded
with rice and soup pressed her head so hard she felt it
would sink like a turtle's. Her body seemed to contract.
Balancing herself with the load on her head, she emerged
out of the gate with heavy steps.

From a clear blue sky without a speck of cloud, the
sun was pouring down charcoal. In the rice paddies, the
white-clad sons of the earth moved about, planting seedlings on the earth's fertile breast, splashing water like
children. As they bent and stretched their backs, between
their upper and lower garments emerged a scarlike line
of sunburnt back. Their faces were smeared with mud
from attempting to wipe off the drops of sweat, as thick
as red bean gruel, streaming into their eyes. Determined
to transplant as many seedlings as fast as possible, they
kept on working, in spite of aching bones, without giving
a single sigh; rather, they happily sang improvised field
songs.

The burning sun was steaming the water in the
paddies. The tangled grass on the bank did not seem to
mind being trampled. The leaves would raise their heads

again and give a green laugh in the midst of glittering
lances of light. A will to have a sturdy, resolute life, a joy
of life reigned here, a robust effort to enrich life. In brief,
it was a world overflowing with health, a world that
scorned the existence of the weak and sick. Suni, however, was too weak to breathe the fresh air in the sea of
scorching sunlight. She felt giddy; her head swam.
Though her body was streaming with perspiration, she
felt a chill. As she was about to jump across a puddle, the
sun in the water glittered, its glare blinding her. All of a
sudden, the minnow that she had killed in the morning
loomed before her in the shape of a gigantic rockfish that
blocked her path. The moment she tried to escape, with
a scream within her mind, she felt herself fainting, as if
someone had grabbed her hair and was dragging her
around. As she heard a peal of thunder, she fainted.

After a while she revived, but her senses were unclear.
In a daze she vaguely recalled having left the house with
a tray of lunch on her head, the glitter of the sun in
the open fields, and the ghost of the minnow that had
blocked her path. What, then, had happened to her tray?
As she looked around her, she let out a scream and
started with fright. She discovered that she was lying in
the room of her enemy. She dashed out to the veranda like
one possessed. Her wide open eyes, still possessed by the
ghost, were terror stricken.

Her mother-in-law, who was raking level the wheat
grains spread out in the yard, cast a spiteful eye at her.
She could forgive Suni for spoiling rice and soup, but not
for breaking the few remaining china bowls. But she
could not very well scold a daughter-in-law who had
fainted and just recovered.

"You've come to, now? Why don't you stay in bed?

Go back to your room and lie down." She seemed to have a hard time trying to speak softly.

Suni nevertheless stepped down unsteadily and came down to the yard.

"Didn't I tell you to go back to your bed and rest?" This time her voice was louder than before.

"No, no, I'm all right," Suni replied.

She would rather die than go back to the room.

"You're disobeying me. You want to have your way again?" Unable to control her hatred, the old woman turned the rake around and rushed at Suni.

"You flighty little one, how dare you come out here after smashing my bowls? Shameless one! You smashed two bowls I bought last market day!" With the rake handle she began to beat Suni blindly on her head, back, and legs. Suni did not feel any pain. The beatings on her tired, aching frame only aroused in her a sense of weird pleasure.

"Look at this stubborn hussy. She doesn't even cry!" The old woman kept on flailing until she herself became too exhausted to wield the rake any longer. At last she threw down the rake and said, "Get out of my sight. Go to the kitchen and get the supper ready!"

Suni went into the kitchen and rinsed the rice, as she had been told.

Soon the sun set. The gloomy kitchen was so dark it seemed like night. Frightful night, unbearable night, was approaching her with its dark jaws agape. The fear she experienced at sunset assaulted her again. Her plan to avoid the terrors of the night had been a failure every time, but that hope wrenched her heart. With no new plan in sight, she lamented her sorry lot: how her parents were hundreds of miles away, how hard were her days and nights, how she had been beaten by her mother-in-law today. Endless sorrow choked her; tears welled up in her eyes. Her hands and even her arms were wet, as she wiped away the unending streams of tears. It was at that moment that someone shook her shoulders from behind. She turned around without thinking—she felt as if her liver had shrunk. It was her husband bending over her and looking her in the face. He must have returned from the fields. His sun-scorched, rugged face clearly took on a soft, compassionate expression, unbecoming of him. But the breathless Suni, like a chick grabbed by a hawk, had no room to appreciate his kind expression.

"Why cry? Stop, stop!" As he sat his stout body down, he comforted her and wiped her tears with a hand as large as the lid of a rice kettle. Then he left.

Upon seeing her husband, Suni felt even more frustrated. The boulder that pressed down on her chest, the iron club that tore her entire body to pieces—these thoughts dried the well of her tears; she racked her brains to devise a way to escape the night. No, night was not to blame. It was rather the room of her enemy. Were it not for that room, the husband would have simply disappeared after wiping her tears. Were it not for that room, he would have no place to torment her. Was there any way to get rid of that heinous room? She had so far been unsuccessful in avoiding the room, but she had to find a way. The rice in the kettle boiled over. As she was about to lift the lid, she spied a box of matches on the kitchen fireplace. A strange idea flashed through her mind. She seized the box, her hands trembling visibly, and, not looking around, hid it in her bosom. Was it not strange that such an idea had never occurred to her before? She smiled.

That night, fire broke out in the eaves at the back of

the room. Fanned by the winds, the fire spread in an instant all over the thatched roof. Just outside the hedge of the next house, Suni stood, her face never more radiant than now. Her heart bursting with delight, she stamped and jumped with joy.

The Author

Hyŏn Chin'gŏn was born in Taegu on September 9, 1900. He attended a high school in Tokyo and a university in Shanghai, where he studied German. He made his literary debut in 1920, and after the first six productive years, when he published most of his better stories, he wrote little, being busy in a long career in journalism. In 1939 he began serializing a novel about the Paekche loyalist general who put up a stout resistance against the T'ang invaders, but Japanese censorship prohibited its completion. He died on April 20, 1943.

A master of realistic style, tempered with a capacity for sympathy, his portrayals of such humble and dispossessed characters as a rickshawman, a psychopath, an immigrant to southern Manchuria, and a young girl married off at an early age according to the old Korean custom (as in this story) are most vivid. A witness to the trials of his people during the Japanese occupation, he aptly called his collection of stories Korea's Faces (1926), a chronicle of the spiritual temper of the twenties. "Fire" was first published in the journal Kaebyŏk in January 1925.

by Kim Tongin

Potato

Strife, adultery, murder, thievery, begging, imprisonment—the slums outside the Ch'il-sŏng Gate of P'yongyang were a breeding ground for all the tragedy and violence of this world. Until Pongnyŏ and her husband moved there they had been farmers, the second of the four classes (scholars, farmers, artisans, and merchants) of society.

As a young girl Pongnyŏ was reared strictly in a poor but moral farm family. Although the strict code of conduct of the scholar class was said to have disappeared in her family when it fell to the status of farmers, Pongnyŏ's family was of a slightly higher sensibility than the other farmers', and in the household her family canons remained in force as of old. Of course Pongnyŏ, though reared in this manner, regarded it as customary to strip in summer and go swimming in the creek like the other girls, or to go around the village half-dressed: but in her mind, however vaguely, she felt a certain concern with morality.

Translated by Charles Rosenberg *and* Peter H. Lee

At the age of fifteen, she was sold to a village widower for eighty wŏn and thus married off. Her bridegroom was twenty years her senior, and originally, in his father's time, the family had been farmers of considerable means and owned several plots of land. But by the groom's generation they were sinking and began losing their possessions one by one; the eighty wŏn with which he bought Pongnyŏ was the last of his estate. He was an extremely lazy fellow. The village elders, through their good offices, had obtained a sharecropper's plot for him, but after just throwing the seed about, he would neither tend nor weed the crop, but let it fall into neglect. Autumn came, and he harvested lackadaisically not taking anything to the landlord, but eating it all himself. ("This is a bad harvest year," he would say.) Because of such behavior, he never lasted two years running in the same field. He persisted in his ways, and within the compass of a few years, he lost credit and confidence so completely that he couldn't obtain any field space in the village.

After Pongnyŏ married him, they survived for three or four years, thanks only to her father's aid; but even he, the last of the old-time scholars, began bit by bit to regard his son-in-law with hatred. So they came to lose credit even in her family's house.

The couple discussed the situation this way and that, and subsequently, with nothing better to do, they came to P'yongyang as day laborers. However, because of his laziness the husband couldn't make the grade even that way. Carrying an A-frame[1] on his back all day long, he would go to the Yŏngwang Pavilion and moon at the Taedong River—how can one be a day laborer in this way? The couple worked as day laborers for three or four months, and then, through sheer luck, they entered a household as live-in servants.

However, they were expelled from even that house-hold within a short time. Pongnyŏ had looked after the house diligently, but could do nothing about the laziness of her husband. She looked daggers at him and pestered him but could not cure him of his slovenly habits.

"Why don't you put away the rice sack?"

"I'm getting sleepy; you do it."

"You expect *me* to?"

"You've been living your worthless life for only twenty years or so, can't *you* do it?"

"Ah, drop dead."

"What did you say, bitch?"

This kind of fighting went on unceasingly, and so, in the end, they were kicked out.

Where could they go now? So it was that, for want of anything else, they were forced into the slums outside the Ch'ilsŏng Gate. The main occupation of the people gathered there was begging, and their secondary pursuits were thieving and whoring among themselves. All the other terrible and sordid vices were practiced as well. Pongnyŏ started begging with the rest.

But who would give money to a young girl in the prime of her life?

"What's a healthy young person like you doing begging?"

Whenever she heard this kind of response, she made various excuses, that her husband was dying of a disease or something, but she failed to elicit the sympathy of the people of P'yongyang, hardened as they were to such excuses. And so it came to be that even in the slums they were among the poorest of people. In their circles a man with a good income was one who, starting out the day with a mere half chŏn² in coins, could return home with one wŏn and seventy or eighty chŏn in cash. In one exceptional case, there was a man who went out one evening to earn some money, and returned that very night with more than 400 wŏn, and soon started a cigarette business in the neighborhood.

Pongnyŏ was now nineteen years old, and was good-looking as well. If she were to follow the usual example of the other girls in the district and from time to time visit the houses of the prosperous, she could make then fifty or sixty chŏn per day, but given her upbringing, she couldn't bear to do such a thing.

The couple lived still impoverished; it became common for them to go hungry.

At that time, the groves of pines surrounding Kija's tomb[3] was alive with pine-eating caterpillars. The city government of P'yongyang decided to have the caterpillars caught by hand and, as if bestowing a benefice, allowed the slum girls to apply as laborers.

All the girls applied for the jobs; however, only fifty were accepted. Pongnyŏ was among them.

She caught caterpillars diligently. She placed her ladder against the trees and climbed; she grabbed the caterpillars with tweezers and put them in insecticide. She kept working steadily, and soon her bucket was full. In one day she received wages of thirty-two chŏn.

However, after working like this for five or six days, she noticed a strange phenomenon, namely that a certain group of girls never caught any caterpillars, but were always chattering and laughing below her ladder, just playing around. Not only that, but when it came to pay, the girls who were goofing off received eight chŏn or so more than the people who were really doing the work.

There was only one supervisor; he not only tolerated their loafing but occasionally joined in their frolic.

One day when lunchtime came, Pongnyŏ climbed down from her tree and ate, and as she was going to go back up, the supervisor called to her.

"Pongnyŏ! Hey Pongnyŏ!"

"What is it?"

She put down her bucket and tweezers and turned around.

"Come here a minute."

She went silently to the supervisor.

"Listen, Pongnyŏ, uh . . . let's go back over there."

"What for?"

"Well, you'll see . . . ."

"Okay. Hey, sis!"

Turning around, she shouted toward the place where the girls were gathered.

"Hey sis, let's go."

"Nah, I don't wanna. You two are going for kicks— why should I go?"

Pongnyŏ's face went crimson, and she turned to the supervisor.

"Let's go," the supervisor started off. Pongnyŏ lowered her head and followed him.

"Atta lucky girl, Pongnyŏ!"

Behind her, this kind of raillery could be heard. The downcast face of Pongnyŏ grew still redder.

From that day forward, Pongnyŏ, too, became one of those who worked not at all and yet were paid good wages.

As for Pongnyŏ's sense of morality and her view of life, from that day they changed. Until then, she had never even considered having sexual relations with a man other than her husband. She had considered such not as human behavior but as that of beasts, and she was certain that if she did such a thing, she would be struck dead.

But how can one account for what had come to pass? Since she herself, who was certainly human, had had this experience, it was by no means out of the range of human possibility. Besides, though she need not work, she got more money; there was a guilty thrill in it; and it was a lot more dignified than begging for a living. . . . If I were to describe it in other terms, it was "a waltz through life" . . . nothing could match this enjoyable experience. Was this not, then, the secret to human existence? Moreover, from the time this happened, she acquired, for the first time in her life, the self-confidence of a real individual human being.

From that time on, she began to powder her face.

A year passed.

Her savoir-faire enabled her to steer a smooth course through life. And as for her marriage, now the couple wasn't quite so destitute.

Her husband was usually at home lounging on the warmest spot on the floor and chuckling as if it were a fine thing after all.

Pongnyŏ was more beautiful than ever.

"Hey, man, how much did you make today?"

When Pongnyŏ saw a beggar who looked as if he had made a lot of money, she would solicit him this way.

"Today wasn't a very good day."

"Just how bad?"

"Only thirteen or fourteen nyang."[4]

"You did pretty well. Why don't you lend me five nyang?"

"Well, today I . . . "

When she carried on like this, Pongnyŏ invariably followed after the man, clinging to his arm.

"Now that I've caught you, you have to lend me the money."

"Christ, whenever I meet you, you make such a stink. Well, I'll lend it anyway. In exchange for something, huh? How about it?"

"I dunno. Ha, ha, ha!"

"If you don't know, I guess I don't hand it over."

"Well . . . you know I know what you want."

To this extent had her character advanced.

Fall came, and with its advent, the slum girls went about at night carrying wicker baskets, the better to filch sweet potatoes and Chinese cabbage from the vegetable fields of the Chinese living in the area.

Pongnyŏ also was adept at stealing her share. One night she was carrying a basket of stolen sweet potatoes and, just as she was going to make her getaway, a dark shadow loomed behind her and grabbed her tightly. It was old Wang, the Chinese owner of the garden. Pongnyŏ couldn't say a word, and just temporized, flirting, staring down at her feet.

"Let's go into the house," he said.

"If you say so, I'll go. Sure, why not? You think I wouldn't?"

Pongnyŏ, with a wag of her bottom and a toss of her head, swinging the basket, trailed after Wang.

About an hour later, she left the house of Wang. Just as she was coming out of the fields onto the road, suddenly someone was calling her from behind.

"Pongnyŏ, isn't that you?"

Pongnyŏ turned around with a start. There was her

next door neighbor holding a basket under her arm and groping her way out of the dark fields.

"Sis, is that you? Did you go in there, too?"

"You also went there?"

"In whose house, Sis?"

"Me? Nuk's. How about you?"

"Me—Wang's . . . How much did you get, Sis?"

"Nuk, that tight-fisted bastard. Just three head of cabbage."

"I got three wŏn."

She answered as if to boast.

About ten minutes later, after she set down the three wŏn in front of her husband, the two of them talked about old Wang and laughed and laughed.

From then on, Wang came over for her whenever he felt the urge.

When Wang paid his visits, he would sit and fidget for a time, and then her husband would acknowledge the situation and go outside. After Wang left, the couple would rejoice in their one or two wŏn.

Pongnyŏ gradually curtailed the sale of her charms to the village beggars. At such times as Wang was busy and couldn't come to her, Pongnyŏ would go to his house of her own accord.

By this time, she and her husband were among the wealthy of the slums.

The winter went by, and spring arrived.

Then it came to pass that Wang bought a virgin as wife for a hundred wŏn.

"Hunnh!" Pongynŏ just snorted.

"Pongnyŏ looks jealous."

When the village women spoke like this, Pongnyŏ humphed and laughed.

"Me, jealous?" She always denied it vigorously. But in her heart, she could not stay the dark shadows.

"You bastard, Wang. I'll get you for this."

The day Wang was to bring home his new bride drew even closer. Wang cut his long hair, of which he had always been so boastful. A rumor spread that it was at the suggestion of the new bride.

"Hunnh!" Pongnyŏ just sneered all the more.

Finally came the day when the bride, in all her nuptial finery, riding in a sedan chair, arrived at the house of Wang, which was out amid the district vegetable fields.

Later that night the Chinese who were gathered at the house plucked their curious lutes, sang their native songs, and merrily celebrated the wedding. All the while Pongnyŏ was standing in hiding around a corner of the house, a murderous intent gleaming in her eyes, listening to the merriment within.

The Chinese celebrated until about two in the morning, and when Pongnyŏ saw the last of them leaving, she entered the house. Powder was pasted whitely on her face.

The bride and groom stared at her in surprise. Glaring all the while with frightening eyes, she went over to Wang, grabbed his arm and hung on. A strange laugh bubbled from her lips.

"Come on, let's go to my house."

Wang could not say a thing. His eyes just bulged impotently. She shook him once again.

"Hey, come on."

"We're busy tonight. We can't go."

"Business in the middle of the night? What business?"

"Ours, all the same."

The strange laugh that had been flowing from Pongnyŏ's lips suddenly evaporated into silence.

"You low-life bitch." She raised her foot and kicked at the head of the finely attired bride.

"Come on, let's go, *let's go*." Wang was shaking all over. He shook free from her grip.

Pongnyŏ fell, but she got right up again, and when she rose, she was holding a glittering sickle in her hand.

"You Chink bastard, I'll kill you. You son of a bitch, you hit me, you hit me, you bastard, you're killing me!"

Screaming at him, she brandished the sickle. A violent scene ensued, its setting the house of Wang, that house standing alone in the desolate fields outside the Ch'ilsŏng Gate. However, even this violent scene soon stilled. The sickle that had been in Pongnyŏ's hand somehow got into Wang's and, blood gushing from her throat, Pongnyŏ fell dead on the spot.

Three days passed before Pongnyŏ's corpse could be taken to a grave. Wang went to see Pongnyŏ's husband several times. Pongnyŏ's husband in turn visited Wang a number of times. There was some manner of negotiation between them.

In the dead of night, they moved Pongnyŏ's corpse from Wang's house to her husband's house. And then, around the body, three people gathered. One was Pongnyŏ's husband, one was Wang, and the other man was a certain herbalist. Wang, without a word, reached into his moneybag and handed three ten-wŏn bills to Pongnyŏ's husband. Into the hand of the herb doctor, too, went two ten-wŏn bills.

The next day, Pongnyŏ, pronounced dead of cerebral hemorrhage by the herb doctor, was carried to the potter's field.

The Author

Kim Tongin was born in P'yongyang on October 2, 1900, and attended Meiji Gakuin and then Kawabata Art School, both in Tokyo. In February 1919, with a group of young writers, he launched a new literary magazine, Creation (publishing until September 1921), in which he published his earlier stories. His subsequent publication ventures with little magazines were not successful. In April 1942 he was imprisoned by the Japanese police on a dubious charge, but was soon released. He died during the Korean War, on January 5, 1951, in Seoul. His collected works were published in ten volumes in 1964. "Potato" was first published in the journal Choson Mundan *in January 1925.*

Often termed the pioneer of naturalism in Korean letters, Kim deserves recognition for his insistence on the pure art of literature and the modernization of the language. He contributed to the establishment of colloquial prose style as a literary medium by differentiating the tenses and even by incorporating dialectal and four-letter words. His iconoclastic tendency was quick to demolish traditional morality, but failed to offer an alternative. Hence the world of his stories is a world of ruins, and his morbid aestheticism finds expression in artist-heroes who obtain inspiration only through arson, rape, and murder. At the dead end of his struggles, he found an outlet in nationalism, as evinced by his historical novels.

by Yi Hyosŏk

The Buckwheat Season

o begin with, the summer market was known to be unpopular. While the sun was still in the middle of the sky, the market grounds had become nearly deserted. The sunlight scorched the backs of the vendors. Most of the villagers had gone, except for a few lingering fagot vendors who had not had a good day. There was no point staying longer just for those who were usually content with the purchase of a bottle of kerosene or a string of fish. Swarms of flies and village rogues were a nuisance. So the left-handed, pockmarked dry goods vendor Hŏ Saengwŏn finally broke the silence and asked the opinion of his fellow trader, Cho Sŏndal:

"Shall we close up?"

"A good idea. Have we ever sold enough here at Pongp'yŏng Market? Let's go. Maybe we'll have a better day at Taehwa tomorrow."

"We might have to walk all night."

Translated by Peter H. Lee

"The moon may come up, though."

Upon seeing Cho begin to count his earnings, making clinking sounds, Hŏ started to bring down the curtains from the stakes and gather up the goods spread before him. Rolls of cotton, silk, and satin filled two wicker trunks. Pieces of cloth lay scattered on the mat. Other vendors were also closing their stalls. Some impatient ones were already taking off. No trace could be found of the vendors of dried fish, rice candy, and ginger. Tomorrow markets would be held at Chinbu and Taehwa. To reach either one, the vendors would have to plod along twenty to thirty miles during the night.[1]

The marketplace, like a courtyard after a festival, was untidy. There was already some squabbling in a tavern. Shrill, unyielding cries of a woman mingled with the curses of a drunk. The evening of a market day would, without exception, begin with the high-pitched voice of a tavern woman.

"Saengwŏn, you play it cool, but I know all about your feeling for the Ch'ungju woman," grinned Cho Sŏndal, as if the woman's cry reminded him of the Ch'ungju woman.

"She's like a cake in a picture. You know we can't compete with young fellows."

"It's not always so. True, they are much attracted to her—take, for example, Tongi. He seems to have conquered her."

"What, that greenhorn? He must have bribed her with his goods. I thought I could count on him."

"You never can tell in this kind of affair. Let's stop guessing and go and see. I'll treat you."

Hŏ followed Cho reluctantly. Hŏ did not have much luck with women. With his pockmarked face, he had no courage to approach them; nor had they shown real interest in him. Half his life was lonely and uneven. However, at the mere thought of the Ch'ungju woman, he would flush like a child, totter, and feel numb, as if glued to the ground.

When he entered the Ch'ungju woman's tavern and found Tongi seated at the table, he got angry in spite of himself. Upon seeing Tongi flirting with the woman at the wine table, he could not contain himself:

"You're quite a playboy. What an ugly sight to see a fellow as young as you drinking and flirting with a woman while the sun is still out. You go around disgracing the name of traveling vendors, but still you plan to have a share in our trade." When his eyes met Tongi's bloodshot ones that seemed to retort, "It's none of your business," Hŏ could not resist an impulse to slap his face.

Tongi stood up indignantly, but Hŏ went on: "I don't know your origin, but you too must have a father and mother. They will be happy to see your ugly behavior, no doubt! Business is business; you've got to give it your whole heart. What use is a woman to a petty vendor like you? Now get out. Be off this moment."

Upon seeing Tongi leave the room dejectedly, without protest, Hŏ felt a sensation akin to commiseration. "He and I scarcely know each other; I must have gone too far." Hŏ was seized with remorse.

"You two are my customers, but how dare you berate that youth like that! He may be young, but he's old enough to sire a child," the Ch'ungju woman protested. She pursed her lips as she indelicately poured the wine.

"To a greenhorn, that sort of admonition is a remedy," Cho cut in, trying to patch up the situation.

"You are infatuated with him, aren't you? It's a sin to drain a kid."

After this scene, Hŏ began to acquire courage, as well as a bottomless urge to keep himself soused, and began to empty the cups offered him. As he began to feel drowsy, he thought more of Tongi than of the woman. What on earth would I do with that woman, even if I could snatch her away from him? He began to reproach himself for rebuking Tongi. Therefore, when, after some time had passed, Tongi came helter-skelter to call for him, Hŏ threw his cup down then and there, and rushed out of the tavern.

"Saengwŏn, the donkey has broken his rope and is raging."

"The rogues must have played a trick on him."

Hŏ was anxious about the animal, but was more moved by Tongi's concern. As he ran across the deserted market ground after Tongi, he felt moisture in his eyes, though he was laden with wine.

"What can we do about those incorrigible rogues?"

"I won't let them get away with being cruel to a donkey."

The animal was his companion half his life. They had traveled together from market to market, bathing in the same moonlight and lodging in the same inns. These twenty years had made them both old. The donkey's coarse mane was short as a stump broom like his master's hair, and his tail scarcely reached his legs, however hard he might brandish it to drive away flies. How many times had Hŏ removed the donkey's worn shoes and shod him with new ones. His hooves had stopped growing, and blood oozed from under the worn shoes. He could tell his master by smell and, at his approach, brayed and welcomed him as if to appeal his case.

When Hŏ stroked the animal's scruff, as if he were calming a child, the donkey's muzzle quivered and he heehawed, splashing saliva. Hŏ suffered a lot because of the animal. Unable to cool off, the animal's fatigued, damp body trembled—he must have gone through a lot. The bridle was loose, and the saddle was on the ground.

"You rascals," Hŏ shouted. Most of the boys had made off already; the remaining few, at Hŏ's yells, began to quaver.

"It's not our doing," a sniveling boy shouted back from a distance. "It's a mare that made him go wild."

"You talk like . . . "

"When your donkey saw Kim Ch'ŏmji's mare leave, it began to kick and foam like an enraged bull. We couldn't help watching the spectacle. Look at his belly!" The boy shouted again in a cocky tone and burst into laughter.

Hŏ felt hot in the face in spite of himself; he wanted to stand in front of the animal's belly just enough to screen it from their gaze.

"That old animal still wants a mare!"

At the boys' derision, Hŏ momentarily faltered, but was unable to take it any longer, and brandished his whip to chase them away.

"Go ahead and chase us, if you can. The left-hander tries to beat us!"

There was no hope of overtaking the market rogues. A left-hander cannot beat even a boy. He threw down his whip. He felt himself burning as the wine began to work on him.

"Let's leave. There's no end to squabbling with those fellows. The kids are more formidable than the adults, you know," Cho urged.

Then, Cho and Tongi saddled their donkeys and began to load. The sun seemed to have gone down considerably.

In his twenty years as a traveling vendor of dry goods, Hŏ seldom missed the market days at Pongp'yŏng. He traveled to such neighboring counties as Ch'ungju and Chech'ŏn, and even to the far-off Yŏngnam area; but now he seldom ventured out of his county except for a sortie to Kangnŭng to replenish his stock. As market days came every five days, he traveled from one town to another, constant as the moon in the sky. Though he would talk proudly of his birthplace, Ch'ungju, he seemed never to have visited it, much less gone for a prolonged sojourn. The beautiful hills and waters along the market towns were his home. Each time Hŏ and the animal approached a market town after a half-day's walk, the weary donkey would give out a fanfare of resounding braying, and Hŏ's heart would leap with joy, especially at dusk with lights swimming in the distance.

When he was young, Hŏ had economized and saved a fair amount of money; but once on the All Soul's Day Festival (July 15), he gambled extravagantly, and within three days lost everything he had. He had thought of selling his donkey—but his love for the animal intervened, and he gave up the idea. Thus he ended where he had begun, and had to resume his traveling vendor's career in search of a market. On the day he fled town with the donkey, he caressed the animal and cried, saying he had done well not to part with him. His debt compelled him to forgo the idea of making money, and he wandered from market to market, living hand to mouth.

He had once had a taste of luxurious dissipation, but he had yet to win a woman. To him a woman was a creature without feelings. "Am I fated to live this way?" Hŏ felt bitter. The only thing close to him was the faithful donkey.

Nevertheless, he could not forget the first incident in

his life, his only strange affair with a woman. It took place when he was beginning to frequent Pongp'yŏng market. He was young then—his life was not altogether meaningless after all.

"It was a night of a bright moon, but I still cannot figure out how such a thing took place." Hŏ Saengwŏn was about to narrate the story again. Cho had heard enough of it since they became friends, but he just could not show his boredom. Hŏ, on his part, feigned indifference and repeated what he wanted to.

"This kind of story goes well with the moon." Hŏ glanced at Cho Sŏndal, not because he felt sorry for his friend, but rather because he was moved by the moonlight. It was just after the fifteenth, hence the moon was a bit dented, but was still shedding a soft light, to his heart's content. Taehwa lies beyond twenty-five miles of night journey, over two mountain passes and one river, then a plain and a mountain path. The road appeared suspended from the hill's waist. It was past midnight, and in the stillness around him, he could catch the moon breathing like a beast within his arm's reach, and bean stalks and ears of corn, drenched in moonlight, appeared bluer than usual. The waist of the hill was all buckwheat fields, and the fresh flowers, as serene as sprinkled salt under the warm moonbeams, were overwhelming. The red buckwheat stalks were as frail as a fragrance, and the donkey's gait was refreshing. The road was narrow, and the three rode in single file. The jingle-jangle of the bells floated lightly over the buckwheat fields. With Hŏ at the head and Tongi at the tail, the former's narration hardly reached the latter, but Tongi, sunk in his own reverie, was not lonely.

"It was the night of a market day, just like tonight. The tiny room of the inn was stuffy, and I could not fall

asleep. So I got up about midnight and went out to have
a dip in a nearby brook. Pongp'yŏng was the same then as
it is now, buckwheat fields everywhere, as far as the eye
can see, with white flowers thick around the brook. I
could have removed my clothes in the river's stony bed,
but the moon was so bright I went into a nearby water
mill. Funny things do happen. There I stood face to face
with Sŏng's daughter, the prettiest in all Pongp'yŏng.
Luck must have favored me."

Responding to his own remark, Hŏ paused and
puffed on his pipe for a while, as if he begrudged his
story. Flavorful purple smoke wafted up and melted into
the night air.

"She had not been waiting for me, nor for anybody
in particular, for that matter. She was weeping. I could
guess what it was about. The Sŏng family was then in
sad straits, at the verge of ruin. She too must have been
worried about the family's affairs. They wanted to marry
her off to a suitable man, but she was dead set against
such an alliance. A girl is most attractive when she weeps.
At first she looked startled, but I suppose when one's in
trouble, one's mind softens easily. So we came to an
understanding. It was a fruitful, breathtaking night,
come to think of it."

"Then, the following day, she took off to Chech'ŏn
or some such place, right?" Cho chimed in.

"The whole family vanished before the next market
day. The market was astir with gossips. They chattered,
'the best for the family is to sell her off to a tavern.' In
vain I searched Chech'ŏn market, time and time again.
But not a shadow of the girl. Our first night was our last.
Since then Pongp'yŏng has caught my fancy. I cannot forget it even after half my life span has passed."

"You were lucky. Such a thing seldom happens.

Think of getting an ugly wife and siring children; your worries will only mount. The mere thought of it is enough to make me sick. But won't it be a strain to make the round of markets until I become an old man. I am going to change my career this fall. I'll open a little shop near Taehwa and send for my family. It's quite a job to move about the four long seasons around," Cho said.

"I may settle down when I find my girl again. I'll be plodding along this road and viewing the moon till the end of my life."

The mountain path opened into a main road. Tongi too came up front, and the donkeys trotted abreast in a row.

"Young man," Hŏ turned to Tongi. "You are in the prime of life. At the Ch'ungju woman's tavern, I went too far. I am sorry. Don't make too much of it."

"Not at all. It is I who am ashamed. There is no room for a woman at this stage of my life. Awake or asleep, I think only of my mother." Tongi's feelings having been dampened by Hŏ Saengwŏn's story, his tone was a shade subdued. "When you said, 'You too must have a father and mother,' I felt my heart break. I don't have a father. My only flesh and blood is my mother."

"Is your father dead?"

"I never knew him."

"What kind of father . . . "

Saengwŏn and Cho Sŏndal gave a hearty shout, and Tongi was all the more serious in his reply.

"I'm ashamed to tell you, but it is true. My mother gave birth to a premature child and was thrown out of her house. It may sound strange, but I've never seen my father's face, nor do I know his whereabouts."

A pass appeared before them, and the three got off their donkeys. The path on the ridge was rugged, and it was difficult for them to talk, so the conversation broke off for a long while. The animals slipped frequently. Short of breath, Hŏ had to rest his legs several times. Sweat washed down his back. Every time he crossed a hill, he revealed his age. He envied a young man like Tongi.

Beyond the hill was a brook. The plank bridge carried away by a flood during the monsoon had not been replaced, and they had to strip to wade across. Strapping their baggy trousers to their backs, they rushed into the water, half-naked and ludicrous. They had been perspiring profusely, but the chill of the night water soon pierced to their bones.

"Well, then, who on earth reared you?" asked Hŏ.

"My mother, compelled to take a husband, began to operate a tavern. A hard drinker, my stepfather was useless. Ever since I cut my wisdom teeth, there was never a day that he didn't beat me. When mother tried to intervene, he would kick and beat me, and even brandish a knife—a wretched household, you can imagine. I left home when I became eighteen, and here I am, a traveling vendor."

"I thought you were quite a man for your age. But your story tells me that you had a hard life."

The water was now waist deep. The swift current and the slick pebbles made the crossing hard. Cho Sŏndal and his donkey were on the other side already, but Hŏ Saengwŏn and Tongi, who had to support the old man, fell behind.

"Is your mother's home originally Chech'ŏn?"

"Not exactly. Though she never made it quite clear, I understand it's Pongp'yŏng."

"Pongp'yŏng? What is her maiden name?"

"I never heard her mention it."

"I suppose she is doing right," he mumbled as he blinked his weak eyes and missed his footing. As soon as he fell forward, he plunged into the water with a splash. The more he pawed the air, the more he lost control of the situation. Before Tongi could come shouting to his rescue, Hŏ had been carried away a good distance. His clothes dripping, he looked more miserable than a drowned dog. Tongi carried the old man on his back with ease. Though wet, the lean old body was light on his stout back.

"Sorry to trouble you so much. I must have been out of my mind."

"You needn't worry about that."

"By the way, did your mother look for your real father?"

"She wants to see him, even if only once, she used to say."

"Where is she now?"

"She is now separated from my stepfather and is in Chech'ŏn. I am planning to send for her this fall. If I work hard, sweating and grinding, I might manage to support the family."

"Certainly, yours is a laudable plan. This fall, you say?"

Tongi's broad shoulders seemed to warm his bones. When they had crossed, Hŏ wished to be carried a bit farther, and regretted having to dismount.

"You have been making blunders all day. What is the matter with you?" Cho asked.

"It's the donkey. The thought of it so engrossed me that I lost my balance." Looking at Cho Sŏndal, Hŏ burst into laughter. "Didn't I tell you? Old as he is, my donkey had a colt by the mare of a Kangnŭng woman. Could there be anything cuter than a colt with pricked ears prancing about? Just to see that, I sometimes go out of my way to tour the town."

"An extraordinary colt all right, for he nearly drowned a man," laughed Sŏndal.

Hŏ wrung out his wet clothes and put them on. His teeth chattered, his body shook, he felt chilly; but his mind was buoyant for some reason.

"Let's hurry to the inn. We'll build a fire in the yard and settle down to a warm rest. Boil water for the donkeys too. After tomorrow's market at Taehwa, Chech'ŏn will be my next stop."

"Saengwŏn, you too are going to Chech'ŏn?"

"Yes, I feel like visiting it after a long absence. Will you join me, Tongi?"

When the donkey began to trot, Tongi held his whip in his left hand. Though Hŏ's eyes were weak and dim, this time he could not fail to notice Tongi's left-handedness.

Their steps were light, and the tinkle of the bells resounded over the dark plain.

The moon went down considerably.

The Author

Yi Hyosŏk was born in P'yŏngch'ang, Kangwŏn Province, on February 23, 1907, and was graduated in English literature from Keijō Imperial University (now Seoul National University) in 1930. After a brief plunge into a proletarian literary movement (1928–1932), he became disillusioned by socialism and began to manifest escapist tendencies. His later stories, which represent flights from civilization, extolled nature and sex as sources of escape from the insoluble contradictions of society and self. Instead of probing the causes of the dissociation of self, he sought a peaceful life in the existing order. However, a fusion of his lyrical style and local color produced a story like "The Buckwheat Season" (first published in the journal Chogwang *in October 1936), which is generally regarded as his finest work. He died on May 25, 1942. A superb stylist, he contributed to the modernization of Korean prose. His collected works appeared in five volumes (1959–1960).*

by Yi Sang

Wings

o you know the "genius who became a stuffed specimen?" I'm cheerful. Even love is cheerful at such a time.

My spirit shines like a silver coin, even when my body is tired till my joints creak. My mind prepares a blank sheet of paper whenever the nicotine filters into my roundworm-ridden stomach. On the blank sheet I spread out my wit and paradoxes, as if placing the pieces in strategic positions in a game of chess. This is a horrible ailment of common sense.

Again, with a woman, I draw up a plan of life, a scheme of one whose spirit has gone mad after a glimpse of the ultimate of reason, a man whose skill in making love has become awkward. What I mean is that I plan to design a life in which I own half a woman—a half of everything. The two halves, like two suns, will keep on giggling face to face, with only one foot in life. I must have been fed up with all mankind. Goodbye.

Translated and abridged by Peter H. Lee

Goodbye. It may do you some good if you practice the irony of devouring food that you detest the most. Wit and paradoxes . . .

It is worth your trouble if you put on your mask. Your mask will feel at ease and noble—think of something ready-made no one has seen before.

Shut off the nineteenth century if you can. What is called Dostoevsky's spirit is probably a waste. It is well said (although I don't know by whom) that Hugo was a slice of French bread. Why should you be deceived by the details of life or of its pattern? Don't let disaster catch you. I'm telling this to you in earnest.

If the tape breaks, blood will flow. The wound will heal itself before long. Goodbye.

Emotion is a kind of pose (I suspect I'm pointing out only the elements of the pose).

The supply of feeling comes to a sudden stop when the pose advances to an immobile attitude.

I've defined my purport of viewing the world by recalling my extraordinary growth.

The queen bee and the widow . . . is there any woman in the world who has not become in daily life a widow? No. Would my theory of looking at every woman as a widow offend women? Goodbye.

This number thirty-three looks like a house of ill fame . . . eighteen families live in this compound labeled thirty-three, where all rooms are lined up shoulder to shoulder, their paper windows and furnaces identical. And everyone who lives in them is young, a budding flower.

No sun ever shines into the rooms, because they ignore the sun. On the pretext that they have to hang their soiled bedding on the clothesline in front of their rooms, they shield the sun from the sliding doors. They take naps in the dark rooms. Don't they sleep at night? I don't know, because I sleep day and night. The daytime for eighteen families is quiet in the compound numbered thirty-three.

But they keep quiet only in the daytime. At dusk they take the bedding down. And when the lights come on, eighteen families become much more brilliant than in the daytime. And then I hear the doors opening and closing all through the night. I begin to notice all sorts of odors: the smell of broiling herrings, the odor of women's makeup, the smell of water after washing rice, and the fragrance of soap.

What amuses me most here are the name plates posted on each door.

Standing all by itself there is a front gate that represents the eighteen families. But the gate, like a thoroughfare, has never been closed; so through it all sorts of peddlers come in and out at any hour of the day or night. None of the eighteen families bother themselves to go out to buy bean curd: they do their buying in their rooms, just by sliding the door open. It would be meaningless for the eighteen families to post their name plates at the gate that indicates number thirty-three. So they have devised a system of pasting their name cards on their doors, bearing such names as "The Hall of Patience" or "The Hall of Blessing."

On top of the sliding doors of my room—my wife's room, I mean—there is her small name card, a quarter the size of a playing card, just to follow the custom around the compound.

I do not play with anyone in the compound. I never greet anyone. I don't want to greet anyone other than my wife.

I think it would hurt my wife's reputation if I were ever to greet others or play with any of them. My devotion to her goes to that extent. The reason for my devotion is that she is, like her name card, the smallest and the most beautiful of the women of all the eighteen families. Because she is the most beautiful flower among all the eighteen flowers, she shines radiantly, even in this area with no sunshine under a galvanized roof. And I keep this most beautiful flower; no, I live clinging to her, and my existence has to be an indescribably awkward one.

I like my room very much. Its temperature is comfortable for me, and the semidarkness suits my eyes. I don't want a room cooler or warmer, brighter or darker. I have kept on thanking the room that keeps such an even temperature and darkness. I have been pleased to think that I was born to enjoy this kind of room.

But I don't want to calculate whether I'm happy or unhappy. I do not need to think about that problem. All went well as long as I spent day after day in idleness, with no reason. Wanting to be happy or unhappy is a mundane calculation. This way of living is the most convenient and comfortable condition.

This unconditionally suitable room is the seventh from the gate—"lucky seven." I love number seven like a decoration. Who would have guessed that the partition of a room into two with sliding doors was a symbol of my fate?

The lower part of the divided room sees sunshine. In the morning, it enters in the shape of a wrapping cloth; in the afternoon, it goes out the size of a handkerchief. I do not need to tell you that I live in the upper half of the room that sees no sun. I don't remember who decided that I should occupy the sunless part and my wife the sunny part. But I don't complain.

As soon as my wife goes out, I go into her room and

open the window to admit the sun. The sunlight on her dressing table makes the bottles display their colors. Watching the bright colors is my best amusement. I play by singeing tissue paper, which only my wife uses. If I gather the parallel sunrays into focus with a magnifying glass, the light becomes hotter and begins to scorch the paper. Presently a small flame accompanied by thin smoke begins to spread. The process is quick, but the anxious state of mind until that moment, akin to wishing oneself dead, interests me.

If I get tired of this game, I play with my wife's small hand mirror, which has a handle. A mirror has utility only when one looks into it; otherwise it is nothing but a toy. Soon I get fed up with the mirror. And my zeal for play leaps from the physical to the mental. Throwing the mirror down, I go to my wife's dressing table and look into the beautifully colored cosmetic bottles lined up in a row. These are more attractive to me than anything else in the world. Selecting and uncorking one, I bring it close to my nose and inhale it as softly as if I were holding my breath. My eyes close themselves at the exotic sensual fragrance. Surely it is a fragment of my wife's body fragrance. After corking the bottle, I reflect: from which part of her body have I detected this particular smell? But it is unclear, because her body fragrance is a composite of many odors.

My wife's room is always splendid. In contrast to my bare room, without even a nail on the wall, her wall has a row of hooks under the ceiling on which are hung her colorful skirts and blouses.[1] All sorts of patterns regale me. Dreaming of her naked beneath her skirts and of the various poses she would take, my mind loses its dignity.

However, I have no clothes to speak of. My wife doesn't give me any. The Western suit I wear serves at once as my Sunday best, my ordinary clothes, and my pajamas. My upper underwear through all the seasons is a black turtleneck sweater. The reason for black, I presume, is that it does not require washing. Wearing soft shorts with elastic bands around the waist and the two legs, I play without complaint.

Without my knowing it, the sun went down, but my wife has not returned. Tired playing my own games and knowing that it's time for her return and that I should vacate her room, I creep back to my room. It is dark. Covering myself with a quilt I take a nap. The bedding, which has never been stowed away, has become a part of my body. I normally fall asleep right away; but sometimes I cannot sleep, even if I am dead tired. At such times, I choose a theme and think about it. Under the damp bedding I invent and write. I have also composed poems. But as soon as I fall asleep, all these achievements evaporate into the stagnant air that floods my room.

When I wake up, I find I am a bundle of nerves, like a pillow stuffed with cotton rags or buckwheat husks.

I loathe bedbugs. Even in winter I find a few in my room. If I have any problem in the world, it is my hatred of bedbugs. I scratch the bitten spots till blood oozes.

In the midst of a contemplative life in bed, I seldom thought about anything positive. There was no need for me to. If I had, I would have had to consult with my wife, and she would always scold me. Not that I feared her scolding, but it bothered me. Trying to do something as a social being or being scolded by my wife—no, idling like the laziest animal suited me. If possible, I sometimes wished to tear off my mask, this meaningless human mask.

To me, human society was awkward. Life itself was irksome. All things were awkward to me.

My wife washes her face twice a day.
I don't wash at all.
At three or four in the morning, I go to the lavatory across the yard. On moonlit nights I used to stand in the yard for a while before returning to the room. Although I have never met any one of the eighteen families, yet I remember the faces of almost all the young women in the compound. All of them fall short of my wife's beauty.

My wife's first washing at eleven in the morning is simple. Her second washing at seven in the evening is more complicated, and she puts on far cleaner dresses at night than she does in the daytime. And she goes out day and night.

Does my wife have a job? Perhaps, but I don't know what it is. If, like me, she has no job, there is no need for her to go out, but she does. And she has a lot of visitors. When she has many visitors, I have to stay in my room all day long, covered with a quilt.

On such days I cannot play at making flames, or smell her cosmetics. And I am aware of being gloomy. Then my wife gives me some money, maybe a fifty-chŏn silver coin. I like that. But not knowing how to spend them, I put them beside my pillow and they accumulate. Seeing the pile, she bought me a piggy bank that looked like a safe. I fed the coins into it one by one, and then my wife took away the key.

I recall putting silver coins into a box thereafter, but I was too lazy to count them. Sometime thereafter I spied a hairpin in the shape of a beehive in her chignon; does this mean that my safe-shaped piggy bank has become lighter? However, in the end, I never again touched that piggy bank beside the pillow. My idleness did not call my attention to such an object.

On days she has visitors I find it hard to fall asleep, as I do on rainy days. On such days, I used to investigate why my wife has money all the time, and why she has a lot of money.

It seems that the visitors are unaware of my presence behind the sliding doors. Men tell jokes so easily to my wife, ones that I would hesitate to tell her. Some visitors, however, seem comparatively more gentlemanly than others, leaving at midnight, while others stay on the whole night, eating. In general, things went smoothly, however.

I began to study the nature of my wife's job, but found it difficult to fathom because of my narrow mental vision and insufficient knowledge. I'm afraid I may never find it out.

My wife always wears new stockings. She cooks meals too, though I've never seen her cooking. She brings me three meals a day in my room without fail. There are just the two of us, so it is certain that she herself has prepared the meals.

I eat my meals alone and sleep alone. The food has no taste, and there are too few side dishes. Like a rooster or a puppy, I take the feed with no complaints. But deep within me I sometimes feel her unkindness. I became skinny, my face grew paler, my energy visibly weakened day by day. Because of malnutrition, my bones began to stick out. I have to turn my body dozens of times a night, unable to remain for long on one side.

Meanwhile I kept on investigating the provenance

of her money and what kind of food she shares with her guests. I could not fall asleep easily.

I perceived the truth at last. I realized that the money she uses must be given her for doubtful reasons by the visitors who appeared to me nothing less than frivolous.

But why should they leave money and why should she accept it? I could never understand the notion of such etiquette.

Well, is the transaction merely for etiquette's sake? Would not the money be a kind of payment or honorarium? Or did my wife seem to them one who deserved sympathy?

Whenever I indulge in such probing, my head swims. The conclusion I had reached before I fell asleep was that the subject was unpleasant. But I have not asked her about it, not only because it would be a nuisance but also because, after a sound sleep, I used to forget everything.

Whenever visitors go away or when she returns from outside, she changes into her negligee and pays me a visit. Lifting my quilt, she tries to console me with strange words I cannot understand. Then with a smile that is neither sneering, nor sardonic, nor hostile, I watch her beautiful face. She gives me a gentle smile. But I do not fail to notice a hint of sadness in her smile.

I know she notices that I am hungry. But she never gives me the leftovers in her room. It must be that she respects me. I like her respect, which is reassuring even when I am hungry. When she leaves me alone, not a word she has spoken remains with me. I see only the silver coin she has left behind, shining brightly in the electric light.

I've no idea how full the piggy bank is now. I never

pick it up to feel its weight. I keep on feeding the coins through a slit, like a buttonhole, with no volition, no supplication.

Why she should leave me a coin is as difficult to solve as why her visitors leave money with her. I do not dislike the coin she gives me, but the feel of it in my fingers from the moment I pick it up till it disappears through the slit of the piggy bank gives me a brief pleasure. That's all there is to it.

One day I dumped the piggy bank into the latrine. I did not know how much money was in it. How unreliable everything seemed to me when I realized that I was living on an earth revolving fast like lightning through endless space. I wished I could quickly get off the speedy earth that makes me dizzy. Having pondered thus inside my quilt, putting the silver coins into the piggy bank became bothersome. I had hoped my wife would carry the piggy bank away. In fact, the piggy bank and money are useful to her, but they were meaningless to me from the start. I hoped she would take it away, but she didn't. I thought of putting it in her room myself but I had no chance because of her numerous guests. Having no alternative, I dumped it into the latrine.

With a heavy heart I awaited my wife's scolding. But no. She kept on leaving a coin in my room. Without my knowing it, the coins began to pile up in a corner of the room.

I resumed my probing—the reason for my wife's giving me coins and her guests' leaving her money. It dawned upon me at last that it had no other reason than a sort of pleasure. Pleasure, pleasure . . . unexpectedly I began to acquire interest in the subject. I wanted to experience the existence of pleasure.

Taking advantage of my wife's absence, I went out to the streets. I brought along all my coins and changed them into paper notes—five wŏn.[2] Pocketing them, I walked and walked, heedless of direction, in order only to forget the reason for my walk. The streets that came to view after a long time stimulated my nerves. I began to feel tired in no time, but I persisted. Until late at night I kept walking, heedless of direction and oblivious of my original purpose. Of course I did not spend a penny; I could not conceive the idea of spending money. I've completely lost the ability to spend.

I could not stand the fatigue any longer. I staggered home. To reach my room, I had to pass through my wife's. Thinking she might have a visitor, I stopped before the door and clumsily cleared my throat. To my consternation, the door slid open, and my wife and a man behind her glared at me. The onrush of bright light blinded me, and I fidgeted.

Not that I didn't see my wife's angry eyes, but I had to pretend I didn't, because I had to pass through her room to get to mine.

My legs gave out, and I could not stand. I covered myself with my quilt. My heart throbbed, and I was on the verge of fainting. I was out of breath, though I had not been aware of it on the streets. Cold perspiration broke out on my back. I regretted my adventure. I wanted to sleep in order to forget the fatigue. I wanted a sound sleep.

After a rest, lying on my belly, my heart's wild beating subsided. I thought I was living again. Turning to lie on my back, I stretched my legs.

However, my heart again began to beat fast. I listened through the sliding doors to my wife and her man whispering. In order to sharpen my auditory sense, I opened my eyes and held my breath. But by that time I heard my wife and the man getting up, the man putting on his coat and hat, then the noise of the door opening, the loud thuds of the man's leather shoes on the ground, followed by my wife's rubber shoes softly treading, and their steps finally receding toward the gate.

I've never seen my wife acting this way before. She had never whispered to a man. Lying in my room, I used to miss the men's talk when they were drunk, but I always caught every word my wife spoke in an even clear voice, not too loud nor too low. Even when she said something that was against my grain, I felt relieved at her composed tone.

But there had to be some reason for her present attitude, I thought, and I felt displeased. But I made up my mind not to probe anything that night and tried to sleep. Sleep did not come for a long while, and my wife did not return until late. I must have been sleeping at last. My dream roamed amid the incoherent street scenes I had been witnessing.

Someone shook me violently. It was my wife after she had sent off her guest. I opened my eyes and stared at her. There was no smile on her face. After rubbing my eyes, I looked at her more attentively. Her eyes were filled with anger, and her lips trembled convulsively. It seemed her anger would not go away easily. So I closed my eyes. I awaited her tirade. But presently I heard her rise, breathe gently, swish her skirt, and then there was the opening and closing of the sliding doors. Lying still like a frog, I repented my sortie more than my hunger.

Inside the bedding, I begged her pardon. I told her it was a misunderstanding. I had returned home thinking it was past midnight—indeed not before midnight, as she had said. I was too tired. I had walked too far and too long, and that was my fault, if fault there must be. I wanted to give five wŏn to someone in order to feel the pleasure of giving away money. That was all there was to it. If you think that sort of wish is wrong, it's all right with me. I concede I was wrong. Don't you see I am repenting?

If I could have spent five wŏn, I would not have returned before midnight. But I could not. Because the streets were too complex, swarming with people. Indeed I could not figure out to whom I should give five wŏn. And in the midst of it all, I ended by staggering with exhaustion.

The first thing I wanted was rest. I wanted to lie down. Hence I returned home. I'm sorry I miscalculated— I thought it was past midnight. I am sorry. I'm willing to apologize a hundred times. But if I failed to dispel her misunderstanding, what good is my apology? What a disheartening thing!

For an hour I had to fret like this. I put aside the quilt, rose, slid open the door, and staggered into my wife's room. I almost lost consciousness. I remember throwing myself down on her quilt, producing five wŏn from my trouser pocket, and shoving it at her.

The following morning when I woke up, I found myself inside her bedding. It was the first time I had slept in my wife's room since we moved to compound number thirty-three.

The sun's rays were filtering through the window, but my wife was already out. Well, she might have gone out last night when I lost consciousness. I did not want to investigate. I was out of sorts, had no strength left to move my fingers. A sunny spot the size of a wrapping cloth dazzled my eyes. In the bright sunbeam countless particles of dust danced wildly. I felt my nostrils blocked.

I closed my eyes, covered myself with the quilt, and tried to take a nap. But her body odor was provocative. I twisted and turned, and in the midst of recalling all the cosmetic bottles lined up on her dressing table and the perfume that wafted up the moment I uncorked them, I could not fall asleep, however desperately I tried.

Unable to calm down, I kicked the quilt to one side, got up with a jerk and returned to my room. I found a tray of food neatly arranged, already cold. She had gone out, leaving my feed behind. At first, I was hungry. But the moment I scooped up a spoonful of rice, I felt a sensation akin to putting cold ashes into my mouth. I threw the spoon down and crept into the quilt. The bedding that had missed me the previous whole night welcomed me. Covered with my quilt, this time I slept a deep sleep for a long while.

It was only after the sunlight came in that I awoke. My wife seemed not yet home. Or she might have returned but gone out again. But what was the use of examining the matter carefully?

I felt refreshed. I began to recall what had happened the night before. I cannot adequately tell of the pleasure I had felt when I thrust five wŏn into her hand. I think I've discovered the guests' psychology when they leave money for my wife, and my wife's state of mind when she leaves coins for me. I was delighted beyond measure. I smiled to myself. How ludicrous I've been not to know such a state of mind. My shoulders began to dance.

Therefore I want to go out again tonight. But I've no money. I regretted having given my wife five wŏn all at once. I regretted having thrown the piggy bank into the lavatory. Disappointed, but out of habit, I put my hand into the trouser pocket that had once contained five wŏn and searched. Unexpectedly my hand caught something.

Only two wŏn. It doesn't have to be much money. I mean, any amount will do; I was grateful.

Oblivious of my only shabby suit and the assaulting hunger, I went out to the streets swinging my arms. Going out, I wished time would fly like an arrow so that it would soon be past midnight. Handing money to my wife and overnighting in her room are fine in every respect, but to return home mistakenly before midnight and to provoke her into looking daggers at me is terribly frightening. I kept watching the street clocks while roaming about, heedless of direction. I did not get tired easily this time. Only time's slow progress frustrated me.

After ascertaining by the Seoul railway station clock that it was past midnight, I turned toward home. That night I encountered my wife and her man standing at the gate talking. Assuming an unconcerned air, I brushed by them and went straight into my room. Presently my wife returned to hers. Then she began to sweep the floor, which she had hitherto never done. As soon as I heard her lying down, I slid open the door, went into her room, and thrust two wŏn into her hand. She stole a glance at me as if she thought it strange that I returned home again without spending the money. At last she allowed me to sleep in her room. I would not exchange that joy for anything in the world. I slept well.

When I woke up, my wife was already out again. I then went to my room and took a nap. When she aroused me by shaking me, light was already streaming in. My wife asked me to come to her room, the first time she had ever bestowed such a favor. With an unending smile, she dragged me by the arms. I was apprehensive, lest a terrible conspiracy lurk behind her changed attitude.

Leaving everything to her, I let her drag me into her room. There was a neat supper table. Come to think of it, I had gone two days without food. Forgetting that I was starved, I equivocated.

I began to think. I would not regret it even if she raised hell soon after this last supper. In fact, I have been bored to death by the world of man. With my mind at ease and in peace, I ate the strange supper with my wife. We two seldom exchange a word, so after supper I returned to my room. She did not detain me. I sat leaning against the wall, and lit a cigaret. And waited for a thunderbolt. Let it strike me if it must.

Five minutes, ten minutes . . .

But no thunderbolt. Gradually tension loosened. I thought of going out again tonight and wished I had money.

Of course I had none. What pleasure would there have been had I gone out? I felt giddy. Incensed, I covered myself with a quilt and tossed and turned. My supper seemed to rise up in my throat. I felt nausea.

Why does not paper money—even a small amount— rain down from heaven? Sadness overtook me. I knew no means of obtaining money. I must have wept in the bed, asking why I didn't have money.

My wife came into the room once more. Startled, I crouched like a toad and held my breath, anticipating her thunderbolt. But the words she spoke were tender and friendly. She said she knew why I wept. I wept because of the lack of money, she said. I was taken aback. How does she read others' minds? I was a trifle frightened, but hoped that she might from the way she talked intend to give me money—if so, how happy I would be. Wrapped in the quilt, I did not raise my head, and waited for her next move. "There," followed by the sound of something falling beside the pillow. Judging from its light sound, it must be paper notes. Then she whispered into my ear that she would not mind if I returned a bit later than last night. That wouldn't be too difficult; what made me happy and grateful in the first place was the money.

At any rate, I went out. Since I am night-blind, I decided to walk around the brightly lit streets. Then I dropped in at the coffee shop next to the first- and second-class passengers' waiting room at Seoul station. That shop was a great discovery.

First, no acquaintances of mine patronize the place. Even if they came in, they left right away. I made up my mind: henceforth I would while away my time there.

Also, the shop's clock, more than any other in the city, must tell the correct time. If I tactlessly trusted incorrect clocks and returned home ahead of time, I would faint again.

Occupying a whole booth, I drank a cup of hot coffee. Travelers seemed to be enjoying their coffee in the midst of rushing. They drank it quickly, gazing at the walls as if they were meditating, and then went out. I felt sad. But the sad mood here pleased me more than the cumbersome atmosphere of other tearooms in the city. Occasional shrill or thundering steam whistles were louder than the Mozart played in the shop. I read and reread, up and down, down and up, the menu with its list of few dishes. Their exotic names, like the names of my childhood playmates, came in and out of my vision.

I had no idea how long I had sat there, my mind meandering, when I noticed that the place was almost deserted, and the boys were tidying up the shop. It must be the time to close. A little after eleven. This is no haven after all! Where could I spend one more hour? Worrying, I left the coffee shop. It was raining. Heavy streaks of rain fell, intending to afflict me who was without a raincoat and an umbrella. Loitering in the waiting room with my weird appearance was out of the question. A bit of rain would not do me harm. I stepped out.

Soon I felt an unbearable chill. My suit began to drip, and in no time the rain soaked through to my skin. I tried to keep on wandering about the streets braving the rain, but I reached the point where I could no longer endure a chill. I shivered with cold, and my teeth chattered.

I quickened my gait and thought: probably my wife would have no visitor on a wet night like this. I decided to go home. If unfortunately there were guests, I would explain the unavoidable circumstances. They would understand my problem.

No sooner had I got home than I discovered my wife had a guest. I was cold and wet and, in the confusion, forgot to knock. I witnessed a scene that my wife would have liked me not to. With drenched feet I strode across her room and reached mine. Casting off my dripping garments, I covered myself with a quilt. I kept on shivering; the cold became intense. I felt as if the floor under me were sinking. I lost consciousness.

The following day when I opened my eyes, my wife was sitting beside my pillow, looking concerned. I had caught cold. The chill and headache persisted, and my mouth was full of bitter water.

Pressing her palm on my forehead, she told me to take some medicine. Judging from the coolness of her palm, I must have fever. She reappeared with four white pills and a glass of lukewarm water. "Take them and have a good sleep. You'll be all right," she said. I gulped them down and covered myself with the quilt; I fell asleep at a stroke, like a dead man.

I was laid up for several days with a running nose, during which time I kept on taking pills. I got over the cold, but a bitter taste like sumac lingered in my mouth.

I began wishing to stir out again. But my wife advised me not to. She told me to keep on taking the pills every day and rest. "You got a cold by roaming about to no purpose, causing me trouble," she said. She had a point. So I vowed not to go out, and planned to swallow the pills just to build up my health.

I kept on sleeping day and night. Strangely, I felt sleepy day and night and could not stand the feeling. I believed it to be a sure sign of regained strength on my part.

Thus I must have spent almost a month sleeping. My overgrown hair and moustache were uncomfortable, so I went to my wife's room while she was away and sat before her dressing table. I decided to have my hair cut and to smell her bottles of cosmetics at random. In the midst of the various odors I detected her body fragrance, which made me feel entangled. I called her name to myself, "Yŏnsim!"

Once again after a long while I played with her glasses. And I played with her hand mirror. The sun filtering through the window was very warm. It was May, come to think of it.

I took a good stretch, laid myself down on her pillow, and wished to boast to the gods of my comfortable and joyful existence. I've no traffic with the community of man. The gods probably could neither punish nor praise me.

But the next moment I caught sight of a strange thing: a box of adalin—sleeping pills. I discovered the box under her dressing table, and thought they looked much like aspirin. I lifted the lid and found four tablets missing.

I remember taking four pills this morning. I slept yesterday, the day before yesterday, the day before that . . . I was unable to withstand sleep. My cold was over, but she kept on feeding me aspirin. Once, fire had broken out in the neighborhood while I was sleeping, but I slept through the fire. I slept that soundly. I must have been taking adalin for a month, thinking it was aspirin. This was too much!

All of a sudden I felt giddy, and I almost fainted. Pocketing the adalin box, I left home. I climbed up a hill. I loathed seeing all the things in the world of man. Walking, I resolved not to think about anything related to my wife. I thought about flat rocks, about azaleas I've never seen before, about larks, and about the rocks laying eggs to hatch. Fortunately I did not faint on the way.

I found a bench. I sat in meditation, thinking about aspirin and adalin. My head was too confused to think coherently. In five minutes, I got frustrated and became cross. Producing the adalin case from my pocket, I chewed all six tablets. What a funny taste! I then laid myself down on the bench. Why did I do such a thing? I do not understand. I just wanted to. I fell asleep right there. In my sleep, I heard the faint gurgling of a brook among the rocks.

When I woke up, it was broad daylight. I had slept one day and one night. The scene around me looked yellowish. Even in such a state, a thought flashed through my mind: aspirin, adalin.

Aspirin, adalin, aspirin, adalin, Marx, Malthus, Madras, aspirin, adalin.

My wife had cheated me into taking adalin for a month. Judging from the adalin box I had discovered in her room, the evidence was indisputable.

For what purpose did she put me to sleep day and night? After putting me to sleep, what did she do day and night?

Did she intend to kill me bit by bit?

On the other hand, it might very well be possible that what I took for a month was aspirin. She might have taken it herself in order to sleep away something that troubled her. If so, I am the one to be sorry. I was sorry to have harbored such a great suspicion.

I hurriedly climbed down the hill. My legs gave in, my head was dizzy, and I barely made my way home. It was shortly before eight.

I intended to apologize about my perverse thought. I was in such a hurry the words failed me.

Oh what a disaster! I witnessed something I should absolutely never have laid my eyes on. In confusion, I closed the door and stood leaning against the post, head lowered and eyes closed, trying to allay my dizziness. In a second, the door opened, and out came my wife, her clothes still in disarray. My head swam, and I fell head over heels. Astride me, she began to bite me all over. Pain almost killed me. Having neither intention nor energy enough to protest, I remained prostrate, awaiting what would come next. A man came and lifted my wife in his arms and carried her into the room. I loathed her for so docilely submitting to his arms. I loathed him.

"Are you spending the night prowling or whoring around?" she reviled me. I was mortified. Dumbfounded, words failed me.

I wanted to shout back at her. Didn't you try to kill me? My allegation might prove to be groundless, which would bring a disaster. I'd rather keep silent in spite of my undeserved treatment. I stood up, dusted, and emptied my trouser pocket—God knows what made me do it—

and stealthily pushed a few paper notes and coins under her doorsill. Then I ran out.

Narrowly escaping a few collisions with passing cars, I managed to find Seoul station. Sitting in an empty booth, I wanted to remove the bitter taste in my mouth.

Oh for a cup of hot coffee! As soon as I stepped into the station hall, I realized that I had forgotten the fact that I was penniless. Dazed, I loitered helplessly, heedless of direction, not knowing what to do. Like a half-wit, I wandered here and there . . .

I could not recall where I'd been. The moment I realized that I was on the top floor of the Mitsukoshi department store, it was almost noon.

I sat down at the first place I spied and recalled the twenty-six years of my life. In dim recollection nothing emerged clearly.

I asked myself: What desire have I had in life? I did not want to answer yes or no. I disliked such a question. It was hard for me to recognize even my own existence.

Bending over, I looked at some goldfish in a bowl. How handsome they were! The little ones, the big ones— all of them looked fresh and wonderful. They cast their shadows in the bowl under the May sun. The movement of their fins imitated people waving handkerchiefs. Trying to count the number of fins, I stayed bent over. My back was warm.

I looked down on the merry streets. The tired pedestrians, like the goldfish fins, jostled wearily. Entangled by a slimy rope, they could not free themselves. Dragging along my body crumbling from fatigue and hunger, I too must be swept away into the merry streets.

Coming out, a thought flashed through my mind: Where would my steps lead me?

We're misunderstanding each other. Could my wife

feed me adalin in place of aspirin? I could not believe it.
There is no reason for her to do so. Then, did I steal
and whore around? Certainly not!

As a couple we are destined to go lame. There is no
need to see logic in my and my wife's behavior. No need
to defend ourselves either. Let fact be fact, misunderstanding be misunderstanding. Limping through life endlessly.
Isn't that so?

However, whether or not I should return to my wife
was a trifle difficult to decide. Should I go? Where shall
I go?

At the moment, a shrill noon siren sounded. People
were flapping their limbs like chickens; the moment when
all sorts of glass, steel, marble, paper currency, and ink
seemed to be boiling up, bubbling—the noon with extreme
splendor.

All of a sudden my armpits began to itch. Ah, these
are traces of where my man-made wings had once grown.
The wings I don't possess today. Torn shreds of hope and
ambition shuffled like dictionary pages in my mind.

I halted, wanting to shout:

Wings, grow again!

Let me fly, fly, fly, let me fly once more.

Let me try them once again.

The Author

*Kim Haegyŏng or "Yi Sang," born in Seoul on September
20, 1910, was graduated in architecture from the College
of Engineering in 1929 and worked as a civil engineer in
the Bureau of the Interior of the governor-general's ad-*

ministration. Something of a maverick, he was talented and restless and tried painting, design, management of a tearoom and a cafe, and editing of a journal. In order to reverse the family's financial decline, he first unsuccessfully ran a tearoom, the Swallow (1933–1935), and then a cafe, the Crane (1935). Making his literary debut in 1931 with the publication of a group of enigmatic verses reminiscent of e e cummings in the mechanics of style, he remained a controversial writer. He went to Tokyo in 1936, and until his death from consumption, on April 17, 1937, he produced some dozen stories. "Wings" first appeared in the journal Chogwang *in September 1936. A collection of his works was published by Korea University in 1958–1959 (3 volumes).*

Built on two contrasting human types, the narrator and his wife, the negative and the positive, the inward-directed and the outward-directed, "Wings" is a relentless analysis of the flabby intellectual's struggles to combat a sense of futility and boredom, and to impose order on man's chaotic subconscious life. In order to liberate himself from defeat and despair, impotence and emptiness, his self puts on a mask of resignation, and finally demands freedom so that he can soar above the fetters of tradition and the pangs of self-awareness.

by Kim Tongni

Portrait of a Shaman

he *Portrait of a Shaman* was a sort of darkish india ink picture scroll representing a scene like this: a mountain crouching in back; a dark, wide river flowing in the foreground; pale stars hanging in the sky as if to shower down on the mountain ridge, on the fields, and on the dark river; it is the witching hour. On the riverside sands a huge tent has been pitched, and in its shade are village women, sitting in thick clouds, all bewitched by a sorceress' incantation. Each of their faces is touched with a pathetic excitement and a fatigue that never betrays itself until the last hours of a vigil, toward daybreak. Gasping out her suppliant chant, the sorceress now turns round and round, gently waving the skirt of her robe as if she had been transmuted into a fleshless, boneless spirit.

It was in the very year of my father's wedding, they say, that this scene was painted—a time long before I was born. I am of a family of old standing. My family won

Translated by Kim Yongch'ŏl

fame not only by its wealth and power but also as a busy salon for learned men. It was widely known across the country, especially for its rare collections of paintings, writings, and antiques. A dilettantish taste for them was part of the family tradition that was handed down, along with the family estate, from generation to generation.

It was during my father's generation that the fortunes of the family went to ruin, but even then my grandfather could afford, as of old, to entertain roving guests in the visitors' quarters, as poets and artists were always dropping in to stay with us.

It is said that on one of those good old days—just at dusk on a spring day when the wind, mixed with sandy dust, kept blowing all day long, and the apricot blossoms burst forth in the front yard—some odd-looking wayfarers came along and knocked at the front gate. A man of small build, looking about fifty, wearing a jacket and a mourner's bamboo hat, whose top was fastened round with a silk cloth, stood there holding a donkey by the reins; mounted on the donkey was a girl of about seventeen with a terribly pale complexion. The pair seemed to be a manservant with his master's daughter.

But the next day the man said, "This lass is my daughter. They say that she is a good hand at drawing, and that is why we have paid a visit to my lord's mansion."

The girl was dressed in white, and in her face, which was whiter than the white of the dress, there was visible a touch of deep sadness.

"What is your name, young lady?"

She made no answer.

"How old are you?"

Still no answer.

The host had addressed himself to the girl, but she merely cast a glance with her big eyes and never opened her mouth.

"My daughter's name," her father at last offering to speak for her, "is Nangi. She is seventeen years old." Then he went on in a lower voice, "She inclines to hardness of hearing."

The host nodded assent. Then turning to the man, he said that he and his daughter could stay at his house as long as they wished, and that he hoped to see the girl's good hand at drawing. It is said that the father and daughter stayed at our home for more than a month; they enjoyed their stay, sometimes drawing pictures, sometimes telling stories of old times in a movingly sad tone.

On the day they left, it is said, my grandfather provided the wretched father and daughter with valuable silks and sufficient traveling expenses. The poor girl mounted on the donkey, however, kept in her face the same note of deep sadness that had been perceived since her arrival.

The girl left the picture behind—my grandfather named it the *Portrait of a Shaman*—and from him I heard a story connected with it which runs as follows.

On the outskirts of Kyŏngju, more than four miles away from the town walls, there was a small village known as Yŏmin or Chapsŏng.

In a corner of this hamlet there lived a sorceress named Mohwa—so called because she had moved in from a place of that name. She lived in an antiquated, tile-roofed house with one of its upper corners already crushed out of shape. On the roof tiles mushrooms sprouted dark green, yielding a sickening smell of decay. A thin stone wall, crumbled here and there, meandered around the household like an ancient city wall. In the spacious yard surrounded by this stone wall, the rainwater stood stagnant, as the drain was clogged; the pool of water was covered all year round with dark green moss, and above it, standing entangled, was a mass of bulrushes, goosefoots, foxtails, and many other weeds, all taller than a man of average stature. Underneath this growth long serpentine earthworms wriggled, and aged frogs, as loathsome as toads, budged once in a while, awaiting the approach of night. The house was like a haunted den, long deserted by human inhabitants—deserted perhaps over scores of years.

In this old, crumbling house lived Mohwa the sorceress and her daughter Nangi. Nangi's father peddled seafood at a street corner in a town on the east coast, about twenty-five miles away from Kyŏngju. He was so fond of Nangi, as rumor had it, that he would appear every spring and autumn to bring her delicacies such as well-dried kelp and tidily bundled seaweed. Except for Ugi, Nangi's half-brother, who made a surprise visit to this house sometime later, the only persons calling upon the two female inhabitants of this ghostly den were those who came to ask Mohwa to perform an exorcism for them, and Nangi's father, who paid a routine visit to his daughter twice a year. Indeed, mother and daughter lead a desolate life, with little contact with the outside world.

Such being the case, anyone coming to ask Mohwa for an exorcism would meet nobody even after he found himself in front of the door and had called out several times, "Hello, are you at home, Mohwa? Hello, Mohwa!" Suspecting that the house was vacant, the visitor would then take the liberty of trying to open the door. Only then would a girl take the lead in opening the door from within, and would peep out without a word. The girl, of course, was none other than Nangi. Every time this kind of thing happened, she, who was usually drawing by herself, would become terrified at the intrusion and fling down her paint brush, trembling all over, her face turning deadly pale.

Mohwa too led a strange life. Not a day did she keep house as a good wife should. At dawn every day she walked to the town wall, but never returned home till sundown. Half tipsy, she would come waltzing along with handkerchief-wrapped peaches in hand, and chant a plaintive note as she entered the edge of the village.

Dear girl, dear girl, dear girl of the Kims,
Flower of the Region of Water, my dear girl Nangi.
I entered the Dragon Palace and found
The twelve gates all locked tight.
Open the gates, open the gates,
Please open the twelve gates.

Often she was greeted on the way by her neighbors, who said, "You've had a wet time again today, Mohwa!"

"Yes, yes. I've been to market," she answered, twisting her shoulders as if she were shy, and making a low bow to the speaker.

Mohwa was so fond of drinking, except when she was out for an exorcism, that she spent most of her day at wineshops. On the other hand, Nangi was partial to peaches, and so her mother, however tipsy, never returned home, at least during the summer season, without bringing some. Even when she was about to enter her house, Mohwa kept up a ritualistic tone, chanting, "Dear girl, dear girl, dear girl mine!"

Then Nangi would devour her mother's peaches, just as she had, when a child, habitually dashed in and nursed at the breast of her mother who was just returning home from an outing.

According to the sorceress, Nangi was the incarnation of the dragon god's twelfth daughter, Flower, for Mohwa gave birth to Nangi seven days after she had a dream in which she met the dragon god of the Realm of Water and was treated with a peach. The dragon god had twelve daughters, Mohwa said. The oldest was Moon, the second oldest Water, the third Cloud, and so on to Flower, the twelfth. It had been agreed that the twelve of them would be wedded to the twelve sons of the mountain god—that is, Moon to Sun, Water to Tree, Cloud to Wind, and the like. As they were being matched in the order of their ages, Flower, the youngest daughter, who was impatient by nature, could not wait for her turn, and intrigued with Bird, who was to be mated with Fruit, her eleventh sister. Fruit and Butterfly, now left with no proper spouses, wept in grief, and asked aid of the dragon and the mountain gods. The dragon god became furious; as retribution for Flower's offense he not only deprived her of her hearing but expelled her from the Realm of Water. Flower, now transformed into a peach blossom, indeed blooms pink in the springtime, along the riverside or at the foot of the mountain, but the legend goes that she remains even now helplessly deaf to the earnest calling of Bird from the bough.

At the wineshop, Mohwa would often scamper suddenly away from her glass of spirits or her elated dancing with shamans, as if beside herself. If asked what caused her to act so, she would say that Nangi, daughter of the dragon god, had been entrusted to her care only for a brief time. If she did not serve the girl well enough, she feared, she might incur the wrath of the dragon god.

Mohwa conceived not only of Nangi but also of any other being she met as the incarnation of a spirit, thus calling one a tree spirit and another a stone spirit. She often asked any acquaintance of hers to pray to the Great Bear or the Dragon King.

Every time she passed a human, Mohwa twisted her shoulders as if she were shy, and made a low bow to the passerby. Even on meeting a mere child, she stood in awe of the youngster, trembling all over. Often she played the coquette with a dog or a pig.

In her eyes, she said, every creature seemed like a spirit. Not only humans, but also pigs, cats, frogs, earthworms, fish, butterflies, persimmon trees, apricot trees, pokers, jars, stone steps, straw sandals, spines on jujube trees, swallows, clouds, winds, fire, bowls of rice, kites, gourd dippers, pouches, iron pots, spoons, oil lamps . . . all these she thought of as no different from her human neighbors, with whom she could exchange glances, calls, talk, and such feelings as hatred, jealousy, and anger. So she addressed them all with the designation of "dear."

Then one day, after an absence of ten years, Ugi returned home to stay. Since he had returned, the ghostly den had taken on signs of human habitation. Nangi, who had so disliked working in the kitchen, now often cooked meals for her brother. And at night, a glimmering paper lantern hung quietly from the eaves of this crumbling house, where in former days profound darkness under the starlight had been its constant nocturnal aspect.

Ugi was illegitimate, born to Mohwa while she was still living in Mohwa hamlet, and still free from the spell of a demon. As a child, Ugi proved so bright that his neighbors called him an infant prodigy; but the fact that he was of low origin denied him a chance to receive a normal education. At nine he was sent, through the good offices of a friend of his mother's, to a Buddhist temple as a novice, and since then they had heard nothing of him until he suddenly came home. To Nangi he was a beloved brother.

When she was five or six—before she lost her hearing from an illness—Nangi was very fond of Ugi, to whom she spoke endearingly. Soon after Ugi left for the temple, Nangi fell ill with a sickness which forced her to remain in bed exactly three years. When she was at last out of bed, she could no longer hear. But no one had any idea to what degree she was deaf. Once or twice she had asked her mother, though stammeringly:

"Ugi, Ugi, where is he?"

"He's gone to a temple to study, dear."

"Where? To what temple?"

"To Chirim Temple—the great big temple."

But that was a lie, as Mohwa herself did not know to what temple Ugi had gone. She gave a random answer merely because she did not want to disclose her own ignorance.

Now, when Mohwa first caught sight of Ugi on her return home, a flash of terror suddenly crossed her pallid face. For a moment she jiggled up and down and twisted her shoulders as if to beat a hasty retreat. Then suddenly she thrust out her two long arms from her tall, thin body and rushed to hug Ugi, like a huge bird embracing her chick.

"Whoever are you? Oh, my! It's my boy!" Mohwa cried out. "My boy! My boy! You're home at last!" Though her face was drenched with tears, Mohwa was ecstatic.

"Mother! Mother!" Ugi called out, and then he too dissolved into prolonged weeping, his cheek pressed against his mother's shoulder. Like his mother, the nineteen-year-old youth was slender-waisted and slim of neck. He did not seem like a man who had lived a solitary life, wandering from one temple to another; he looked dignified and handsome.

Now even Nangi seemed to recognize the young man as none other than Ugi. At first, when this strange youth opened the door of her room and found her there alone, Nangi was stunned and startled beyond speech—speech perhaps in gesture. Then, crouching in a corner of the room, she shuddered. But when she saw her mother in tears hugging Ugi and calling out "My boy! My boy!" Nangi felt that she too was melting into tears. (After witnessing that even her mother had such feelings, Nangi was thrown into indescribable ecstasies.)

It was not many days after his return home, however, that Ugi began to seem unaccountably enigmatic to Mohwa and Nangi. For whether sitting down to table, going to bed, or arising, he never failed to make a certain incantation, with his eyes closed and his lips moving. Once in a while, from his bosom he took out a tiny book and read it. When Nangi cast a doubtful glance at the book, Ugi opened it and said with a smile on his handsome face, "You should read this book, too."

Nangi could just manage to read any work written in the vernacular, and had read over and over a book called *The Life of Sim Ch'ŏng*. As she took a closer look at the small book handed her by Ugi, she saw clearly inscribed on the front cover in large letters, *Sin Yak Chŏn Sŏ*.[1] It was a name she had never heard of. Again she gave a puzzled look, to which Ugi responded with another smile, saying, "Do you know who brought man into being?"

To words, of course, Nangi was deaf; what's more,

the question was too difficult for her to muse on, even if she had been able to make out Ugi's words from his gestures and facial expression.

"Then do you know what becomes of a man when he dies?"

She made no answer.

"This book is full of those kinds of questions, you know." So saying, Ugi repeatedly pointed his finger at heaven, but, after all that, Nangi succeeded in making out only one word—"God."

"It is God who created mankind," said Ugi. "He created men and all the other creatures in the universe. It is before God that we are all to be brought when we die."

Several days passed with conversations like this, and the concept of "God" as inspired by Ugi roused suspicion and revulsion in the mind of Mohwa. One morning he was about to pray at breakfast, when Mohwa demanded, "Was there such a thing in the Buddhist ways?"

Believing that Ugi had been in Buddhist temples over the past years, Mohwa was apparently convinced that whatever her son did had something to do with Buddhism.

"No, mother, I am not a Buddhist."

"If you repudiate the Buddhist creed, what other creed is there to follow?"

"I came to detest the Buddhist creed while at the temple, mother, and ran away."

"Detest the Buddhist creed, you say? Buddhism is a great doctrine, I know. Are you, then, a believer in Taoism?"

"No, mother. I am a believer in the Christian creed."

"The Christian creed?"

"Up in the northern provinces they call it Christianity. It is a newly introduced religion."

"Then you must be a Tonghak adherent!"[2]

"No, mother. I am not a Tonghak member. I am a Christian."

"Well, then, in that creed of Christianity or the belief of what's-its-name, are you supposed to chant a spell at every meal with your eyes closed?"

"You shouldn't call it a spell, mother. It is an act of prayer before God."

"Before God?" said Mohwa, opening her eyes in wonder.

"Yes, because it was God who created mankind."

"My dear, I am afraid you are possessed by a devil!" cried Mohwa, her face at once turning pale. Then no more did she care to ask him questions.

The next day Mohwa came home from a ceremony of "rice in water" to save a neighbor-client from evil spirits.

"Where have you been, mother?" Ugi asked.

"I have been at the Pak's to exorcise the devil there."

At this, Ugi seemed to give thought to something for a few moments, and then he said, "With your rites, was the devil talked into going away?"

"He surely was," said Mohwa in a tone that brushed aside such an absurd question. "The fact that the man came alive is proof enough, isn't it?"

All around Kyŏngju she had performed hundreds of exorcisms and healed thousands of people of their illnesses, yet in none of those rites had she ever doubted, or worried about, the response of her divinity. Furthermore she had regarded the driving away of someone's devil with the "rice in water" ceremony as natural and simple an act as offering a bowl of water to a thirsty man. It was not merely Mohwa herself who was convinced of this; those who asked her for exorcisms and who were possessed by devils also felt the same way. If they became ill, they would consult Mohwa first instead of going to a doctor—the exorcism by Mohwa was far more responsive, effective, and handy.

Ugi was now brooding over something, with his head bent down. Raising his head, he said, "Mother, that means you are sinning against God." He stared into her face. "Look here, mother—chapter 9, verse 32 in the Gospel of Matthew: 'As the men were leaving, some people brought to Jesus a man who could not talk because he had a demon. As soon as the demon was driven out, the man started talking.'"

By then, however, Mohwa had left her seat and sat down before the altar that was ordinarily in a corner of the room. She began:

"Divine spirit, divine spirit—
On the four corners, between Heaven and Earth,
Winged creatures are on the wings,
Crawlers are on all fours.
Their life short as hair's breadth,
Fleeting as the dew on the grass,
Thin as a fine thread,
They make their way fair and square,
They make their way fair and square,
Nestled in the bosom of divine spirit,
In the all-embracing bosom of divine spirit.
You spurn impure hands, accept decent hands,
God of the house gives us lots to live on,
God of the kitchen gives us food to live on,
God of the mountain gives us life to live with.
Seven Stars enfold us, Maitreya guards us.

Though our life is thin as a fine thread,
We make our way fair and square,
We make our way fair and square."

All this while, Mohwa's eyes sparkled like gems; her back vibrated as if she were seized with a violent fit, and she constantly rubbed her hands together. As soon as her necromancy was over, she held up the bowl of water from the altar. Sipping water from the bowl, she suddenly spouted the liquid over Ugi's face and body. Then she cried out:

"Away, demon, go away!
This is the loftiest peak, Piru of Yŏngju,
The steep and rocky cliff,
The blue water fifty fathoms deep.
Never is this a place for you.
Away, evil spirit, away at once,
With a sword in the right hand,
With a firebrand in the left,
Pshaw, pshaw!"

At first Ugi gazed bewilderedly at Mohwa; after a moment, he said a short prayer, bending his head down. Then he took to his feet and went away without saying a word. Even after Ugi left the room, Mohwa kept on with her necromancy for a while, spitting water into every corner of the room and chanting a spell.

Ugi was determined to call immediately on fellow Christians in the community. He was supposed to come home early that day, but he returned neither at sunset nor at midnight. Mohwa and Nangi squatted miserably in a corner of the room, expecting him at any moment.

"Don't you have there that book of the Jesus devil?" Mohwa said to Nangi after a period of waiting.

Nangi shook her head. But then, suddenly, even Nangi could not help regretting that she had not earlier cared to keep for her brother his *New Testament,* which Mohwa was wont to label the "book of the Jesus devil." Mohwa seemed to regard Ugi as a man possessed by some evil spirit, just as Ugi took it for granted that both Mohwa and Nangi were victims of a demon. He was convinced that an evil spirit had taken possession of both women and that Mohwa's demon had caused the girl to become deaf and dumb.

"Didn't Jesus himself cure many of the possessed dumb in the early days?" Ugi thought to himself.

He was then determined to heal his mother and sister himself or through the power of earnest prayer, as he read the appropriate words in the Bible: "And when Jesus saw that a crowd came running together, he rebuked the unclean spirit, saying to it, 'You dumb and deaf spirit, I command you, come out of him, and never enter him again.' And after crying out and convulsing him terribly, it came out, and the boy was like a corpse; so that most of them said, 'He is dead.' But Jesus took him by the hand and lifted him up, and he arose. And when he had entered the house, his disciples asked him privately, 'Why could we not cast it out?' And he said to them, 'This kind cannot be driven out by anything but prayer.'" (Mark 9:25–29)

Ugi came to the conclusion that he would be able to drive the evil spirits out of his mother and sister only if he could offer earnest prayers to God.

In the meantime, he wrote to P'yongyang, to the Reverend Hyŏn, sponsor of his education during recent years, and to Elder Lee in the same city. In his first letter he wrote:

Dear Reverend Hyŏn,

By the grace of God I have come back safe to my mother's. In this community where the gospel of our Lord has not yet reached, I find a considerable number of people possessed by devils and worshipping idols. Having seen all this, I feel that we ought to have a church built so that we may spread the Lord's gospel in this community as soon as possible.

To my great shame, I must confess to you, Reverend Hyŏn, that my mother is possessed by witchery and my sister is affected by a deaf and dumb spirit. Following the words of our Lord, Jesus Christ, in the Gospel of Mark (9:29), I offer fervent prayers to God to drive those devils away. Because there is no church available here, however, it is very difficult to find a place where I can pray in a devout mood.

Kindly pray for us to God, Reverend Hyŏn, so that we may have a new church in this community at the earliest opportunity.

The Reverend Hyŏn was an American missionary. It was entirely through his help and assistance that Ugi had been able to earn his subsistence and education. At fifteen Ugi had been in a Buddhist temple as an altar boy. In that summer he set out for Seoul on a visit, only to wander from one place to another until he went as far as P'yongyang in the fall of the following year. In P'yongyang he came to receive the Reverend Hyŏn's assistance, with good references from Elder Lee, in the winter of that year.

When Ugi had revealed in P'yongyang his plan to pay a visit to his mother, the Reverend Hyŏn called him in and said, "Within three years I plan to go back to my own country. If you wish to come with me at that time, I would be glad to take you with me."

"Thank you, sir," said Ugi. "To go to the United States with you is my constant wish."

"Then go at once and visit your mother."

Soon after his arrival, as we have seen however, Ugi discovered that his mother's home offered a world very different from that he had enjoyed in the homes of the Reverend Hyŏn and of Elder Lee. Having seen the desolate, crumbling stone wall, the ancient tile-roofed house with dark green mushrooms sprouting above its tiles, the frogs and earthworms wriggling among the tangled weeds, and the two females living in such surroundings— one possessed by a witching charm and the other by a deaf spirit—all this in contrast to the merry voices singing hymns, the church organ sounding great melodies, the voices reciting the Bible, the brethren saying prayers, the lively faces smiling over splendid meals—Ugi now could not help wondering whether he himself was trapped in a dreadful cavern haunted by a ghost.

Since his return from recent visits to fellow Christians in the community, a strange change had come over Nangi. Always slight of build, sheet white and glassy of complexion, with big, sparkling eyes, now she confined herself all day long in the corner of her room, saying not a word, smiling not at all, and merely gazing at Ugi's movements. But then, as night fell and the greyish paper lantern hanging from the eaves was lit, she walked out to the corner of the yard where bloodthirsty mosquitos sang angrily and flitted about in swarms. There she often hurled herself onto Ugi's shoulders or chest, her hands and lips as cold as ice. Ugi started with fright every time he felt the icy, abrupt touch of her hands and lips. But each time she appeared, shaking all over as if she were about to faint, he held her frantic hands and walked with her beneath the paper lantern.

As Nangi began to show these odd changes in behavior, so Ugi's complexion grew paler and paler. A fortnight elapsed in this strange way, until Ugi again left home without telling his destination.

On the second night after Ugi left, Mohwa sat up suddenly in bed and gave a long sigh. Shaking Nangi, who lay asleep, Mohwa said in a mournful tone: "How soon did Ugi say he would return?" Then seeing that her daughter would not give an answer, she said sullenly, "How come you haven't set dinner for him as I told you to?"

As days went by, Mohwa grew more and more impatient; night after night she kept lit the perilla-oil lamp in the kitchen and offered prayers before the dinner table set for Ugi by the fireplace.

"God of the house who is ours,
God of the Seven Stars who is ours,
God of the kitchen who is ours,
I implore you, divine spirits.
Stars are in heaven, pearls are in the sea.
My heir precious as gold and silver,
Scorpion glitters as a crown jewel—
By the decree of the god of the mountain,
By the ordinance of the Three Gods of Life,
By the blessing of the Seven Stars,
By the virtue of the Dragon King,
He is given food by the god of the kitchen,
He is given gifts by the god of the house—
Stars are in heaven, pearls are in the sea.
May the Three Gods and the god of the kitchen
Never decline to answer my summons.
Jesus devil, hungry fire devil of the Western Regions,
You are burning, fire devil is burning with flames,
In the ashes sits my star Scorpion
Like gold and silver,

Now it descends to seek the Three Gods,
Now it descends to seek the god of kitchen."

Mohwa fell on her knees, rubbing her palms together
in worship. As soon as she got up she danced, moving
about with all the airs and graces of a madwoman. Nangi
peeped through the opening in the window from her
room into the kitchen; for a long time she breathlessly
watched her mother's wild movements, until she suddenly
felt a chill creeping over her from head to foot. Then, in
spite of herself, her teeth were chattering. Frantically she
sprang to her feet and took off her blouse, then her skirt.
Thus, mother and daughter became a perfect pair, one
in the kitchen and the other in the bedroom, both dancing
as if tuned to one single rhythm and cadence.

Next day early in the morning Nangi came to herself
and discovered that she was lying naked on the floor.

Before long, Ugi showed up again before his mother
and sister, with a smile on his face. When he came in,
Mohwa was trying on new shoes for a trip to an exorcism.
Seeing Ugi, she threw out her long arms, bending forward from her slender waist. Then she started to cry,
hugging her son just like a huge mother bird would brood
her chick. This time she did not rave, but gave only a
whimpering cry, pressing her cheek against his for a long
time. Her face, though usually purplish, was now tinged
with a rosy color, and, judging from her natural gestures,
she did not seem like a woman possessed by an evil spirit.

"I think I will rest in the bedroom, mother," said
Ugi, as he broke loose from his mother's embrace and
rose to his feet. He went into the room and lay down.

Even after Ugi had gone, Mohwa kept sitting all

alone on the veranda. She looked terribly forlorn, her head dropping downward. But after a moment she stood up as if something had occurred to her and walked into the room, where she began to rummage among the many pictures done by Nangi.

That night, about midnight, Ugi awoke and groped, half asleep, for the Bible he habitually kept next to his chest, only to find the book missing. At that moment he heard a voice muttering an incantation. He sat up to search more closely in his bed for the Bible, but all in vain. But then he saw that his mother, who should have been lying between Nangi and himself, was gone. A shudder ran through his body, together with an ominous feeling that something disastrous was in the offing. At that instant he heard the voice, now more distinctly, that sounded as if it were coming from a ghost weeping underground. The next moment he pressed his eyes to the opening in the window looking into the kitchen.

Dressed in white and clad in her ceremonial robe, Mohwa was making all the erotic gestures, sometimes rubbing her hands together, sometimes kneeling down, sometimes dancing hilariously. Then she was heard crying:

"O hungry fire devil of the Western Regions,
A firebrand in one hand and a sword in the other,
Hither you flee only to face the god of the mountain,
Thither you flee only to face the Dragon King,
You run around the Seven Stars lying in ambush,
You plod along in the cloud,
You run about buried by the wind,
Here the cloud waits for you,
There the wind waits for you.
As you reach the Dragon Palace,
All twelve gates are locked tight.

You knock on the first gate;
Four Deva kings rush out
With glaring eyes and iron hammers brandishing.
You knock on the second gate;
Two pairs of Fire Dogs dash out.
The male dogs gulp down the blazing fire,
The female dogs swallow the kindling coal.
You knock on the third gate;
Two pairs of Water Dogs dash out,
The male dogs blow out the sparks,
The female dogs blow out the kindling coals . . . "

Above the kitchen fireplace the lamp of pirella oil was lit in a tidily arranged dish, and upon a tiny table, set beneath the lamp, there was only a bowl of cold water and a dish of salt. Beside the table lay the thick front cover of the *New Testament,* emitting a plume of blue smoke just after the last blaze had flickered out. The cover was now turning into a heap of pale ashes.

A wry smile came over Mohwa's lips as if she were about to bid defiance to something. She picked up some salt from its dish, and as she sprinkled it over the ashes that now turned smokeless and black, she cried:

"There goes Jesus devil of the Western Regions,
Having obtained travel money from the shrine,
Having obtained shoes from the temple,
With bells dangling from his ears,
Keeping pace with the tinkle of the bells,
Over the hills, across the waters.
He will never dare return again
Because of the sore in the foot.
He will never return in the spring;
No, because of the hunger, no."

The sounds thus uttered by Mohwa, now reeking with the scent of satanic wine, seemed to penetrate Ugi's body from head to foot. After gazing at the erotic look in her gemlike eyes and at the hand gestures she made in time with her flowing skirt, Ugi felt so depressed that his heart seemed to bleed. As if to awaken from a nightmare, he heaved a long, heavy sigh and jumped to his feet. Before he knew it he ran out of the room and into the kitchen, kicking the door open. There he tried to pick up the bowl of water from the tiny table, but before he could do so he saw a kitchen knife flashing in Mohwa's hand. She was waving the knife between Ugi and the bowl of water as she quietly danced and cried:

> "Away, devil, go away at once,
> Hungry mean devil of the Western Regions.
> This is the highest peak, Piru of Yŏngju,
> With its rocky cliff and thorny ash trees,
> With its blue water fifty fathoms deep,
> This is no place for you to come.
> With a sword in the right hand,
> With a firebrand in the left,
> Away, mean devil of the Western Regions,
> Go away at once!"

At this instant Mohwa made a stab at Ugi's face with the kitchen knife. As soon as he felt the blade graze his left ear, Ugi turned under her arm, picked up the bowl of water, and hurled it at his mother's face.

While this commotion went on, the lamp was pushed against the paper window which caught fire instantly. Ugi stamped on the fire to keep the blaze from spreading into the room. As the water fell about her ears, Mohwa became furious, and then she too jumped on the fire, waving the knife to and fro, and closing in on her son.

Ugi dropped into the spreading blaze in a desperate effort to check it; then he felt a tingling sensation somewhere in his back. As he was about to turn over sharply, he found he was bleeding, and fell into his mother's bosom. With her white teeth set hard, Mohwa's face was now set in a grin.

Ugi was injured in his head, neck, and back; but he was ailing of something more than just these three stabs. Day after day he grew more and more haggard so that his ribs visibly stuck out and his eyes sank deeper.

Mohwa worked with all her might looking after Ugi; day and night she rushed about in search of what he needed. Once in a while she sat him up in bed to hold him in her arms. She tried everything—medication, exorcism, and incantation. Yet none of them helped to cure Ugi's illness.

Soon after she became devoted to nursing Ugi, it was apparent that Mohwa was now disenchanted with her exorcising. If someone asked her to perform one, she declined in most cases on the pretext of her son's illness. Then more and more people concluded that Mohwa's exorcising rites or incantations no longer worked as effectively as before.

About this time a small church was erected in the community, and missionary work soon spread throughout the country like a fire in the wind. The church in Kyŏngju sent out gospel-preaching parties to every village in the county, and eventually reached Mohwa's village. The message was:

> Parents, brothers and sisters, we should give thanks to
> God for allowing us all to get together here. God created
> us all. He loves us dearly. We are all sinners. In our
> hearts there is nothing but wickedness; but for our own

sake Jesus Christ was crucified upon the cross. Thus by our faith in Jesus Christ shall we be saved. We shall praise Him with a very glad heart. We shall pray before God.

Some people said that it was more fun than watching apes to look at an American missionary with blue eyes and a razor-sharp nose.

"They charge you not a penny for the watching. Let's go and see," said villagers to one another, and gathered in crowds.

Mrs. Yang, wife of the assistant preacher, who came with the missionary and was a relative of Mr. Pang, the village elder, called upon every house in the village and said: "To believe in a sorceress or a blind soothsayer is to sin against our Father, the one and only God, who is holy. What in the world is a sorceress capable of? Behold, does not a sorceress pray and kneel down before a rotten ancient tree or a stone idol who can never see nor hear? What is a blind soothsayer capable of? Behold, with no power to see before his own steps, he walks over the ground groping with his stick; how could he possibly save men who can see? It is our Father, the one and only God, who created our life. Therefore our Father said, 'Never serve another god before me . . . '"

Preaching like this was followed by numerous stories: one that Jesus, God's only son, had healed a number of possessed people who were lepers, cripples, and deaf and dumb; and another, that Jesus was resurrected and ascended to heaven on the third day after his crucifixion.

"Such worthless devils!" said Mohwa, who responded to these stories with ridicule. But it was apparent that the Christian denunciations and curses were weighing heavily on her. For she often chanted, striking the brass tambour and the gong:

"Away, devil, get along with you.
You who lived begging from old days,
How could you be unaware of this Mohwa?
If you linger on here
Your heirs will be locked and starve
In the blue water fifty fathoms deep,
In the cliff with thorny ash trees,
In the grilling iron cauldron,
In the white horse's hide.
They shall not see the light of day.
Away at once, devil, get along with you.
Run away at thundering speed
To the Western Regions millions of miles away,
With sparks of fire on your tail,
With bells dangling from your ears,
Clinking, clanking, clinking, clanking."

Yet the "Jesus devils" refused to go away; on the contrary, they kept growing in number. What's more, even those who had once asked Mohwa for an exorcism or conjuration now came to be seized, one after another, with the "foul spirit" of Jesus.

In the meantime, a revivalist preacher from Seoul came to town for canvassing. Hearing that he was capable of curing the sick, the townspeople thronged around him. They said that if he offered a prayer saying, "This sinner is in great sorrow for his own sin," with his hand on the head of the sick person, in most cases a woman would be "purified" of such common disorders as menstrual irregularity or leukorrhea; or a blind man would recover his sight; or a cripple would walk again; or a deaf man would recover his hearing, or a dumb man would speak again; or even those who suffered from paralysis or epilepsy would be "purified"—as long as they were pious enough. From the pulpit it was announced daily that silver and gold rings were being contributed in growing numbers by the village women; donations poured in. Compared to these spectacles, watching an exorcism performed by Mohwa was as nothing, the villagers said.

"They're jugglers' troupes brought in by Western aliens," said Mohwa tauntingly of the Christian healers.

For it had been an extraordinary authority allowed solely to Mohwa by her divinity that she should drive evil spirits out of the human soul. And her divinity was no less than that of an ancient tree or of a stone Maitreya or of a mountain or water spirit. Yet every one of them was now despised and abhorred by the Christians.

"To believe in witchcraft and sorcery is to sin against our Father, the one and only almighty God who is holy and holy," announced the "Christian devils" to the accompaniment of trumpets and drums. Retorting to them all alone, Mohwa struck the brass tambour and the gong as she chanted:

> "Go away, devil,
> A hundred thousand leagues to the west,
> With sparks of fire on your tail,
> With bells dangling from your ears,
> Clinking, clanking, clinking, clanking."

Autumn of that year passed. Early in the winter Ugi's illness took a sharp turn for the worse.

"My dear, my dear, what is happening to you?" Mohwa often said to her son in a trembling, mournful voice, holding him by the hand and shedding tears. "After all the trouble of coming to me from afar, what misery have you fallen into?"

"Please never mind my condition, mother" said Ugi

calmly. "I shall be called before our Father in the world beyond."

Whenever Mohwa asked him if there was anything he wanted, he would quietly shake his head. But when his mother went out, leaving him at home with Nangi, Ugi often said, holding her by the hand, "I wish I had a Bible."

The next spring, just three days before he died, Ugi was visited by the Reverend Hyŏn whom the youth had missed so badly and had anxiously waited to see. When Hyŏn arrived, guided by assistant preacher Yang, he frowned at the devastated scene and the sickening smell of decay.

"Don't tell me," he said, turning to Yang, "that this miserable place is Ugi's home!"

As soon as he saw the Reverend Hyŏn walk in, Ugi, with his eyes brightening, called out "Minister! Minister!" Hyŏn came over and quietly held Ugi's wizened hands. Suddenly his face grew red all over, as if dyed, and innumerable wrinkles appeared on his brow and cheeks. He kept his eyes closed for a while, apparently trying to calm the emotion raging in him.

"It was the personal effort of this man," assistant preacher Yang said, as if to break the strained silence in the room, "that brought about the early opening of our church in Kyŏngju."

Ugi first made petition, he went on, to the Reverend Hyŏn in P'yongyang, who in turn solicited the Parish Council in Taegu for help. While the Christians in the Kyŏngju area worked together under the leadership of Ugi, they also kept in close touch with the Parish Council in Taegu. The result was, he said, that the church construction work made far more rapid progress than expected.

The Reverend Hyŏn said that he intended to make another visit, along with a physician, and as he rose to leave, Ugi said: "Would you buy me a Bible, sir?"

"You can keep this one for the time being," said Hyŏn, handing his own Bible to the youth. Ugi took the Bible and closed his eyes, holding the volume to his breast. Below his closed eyelids tears appeared.

In the garden in front of Mohwa's house weeds still grew, entangled with one another just as in previous years, and amid the rank growth there lay hidden a number of frogs and earthworms. Since her son's death, Mohwa had seldom been out to do exorcising. Instead, day after day, she kept chanting and striking the brass tambour and gong in her crumbling house, surrounded by weeds. People said that Mohwa was now completely out of her mind. From the kitchen ceiling she had hung multicolored strips of cloth and some flags made of Nangi's drawings. Being very erratic about her meals, her lips now turned a purplish black, and her eyes gradually took on a weird radiance.

Daily she repeated the same words of conjuration, accompanied by the brass tambour and gong all the while:

"There goes Jesus devil from the Western Regions,
With sparks of fire on his tail,
With bells dangling from his ears,
Clinking, clanking, clinking, clanking.
Away at once, devil, get along with you.
Linger where you are, and your heirs
Shall be locked to death
In the blue water fifty fathoms deep,
In the cliff thick with thorny ash trees,

In the grilling iron cauldron,
In the white horse's hide.
Away at once, foul devil!"

Every once in a while her neighbors would call on
her and offer wine to console her, saying, "Terribly sorry
you have lost your son, Mohwa."

"It was that Jesus devil who took my son away,"
Mohwa would reply, sighing.

The villagers, who now took Mohwa for insane, often
missed the spectacle of her incantations and said, "We
wish we could once again see Mohwa's exorcising."

Then a rumor arose that Mohwa would perform an
exorcism for the last time to save the departed soul of
Lady Kim, the daughter-in-law of a rich man in town.
Lady Kim had lately committed suicide by drowning herself in Yegi Pond. Some said that Mohwa had been talked
into performing after receiving two silk dresses as gifts.
Others said that she would attempt in the forthcoming
ceremony to drive the dumb spirit out of the body of
Nangi so that the latter might regain her speech. Or,
Mohwa was quoted as saying, "Humph! We shall see
which is the more veritable being, the Jesus devil or my
divinity." Thus, a lively feeling of expectancy and curiosity
arose among the people of the community; they flocked
to the ceremony site from beyond distant hills and rivers.

The exorcism was to be held on a tract of sand beside
a stream, which took a gentle bend, flowing down from
a pond that nursed in its dark blue body a deep secret and
a grudge. (In the pond, deep enough to conceal a huge,
colorful monster, so legend goes, a man or woman is
destined to drown each year.)

Onto the sands scores of people had thronged, full of
commotion—taffy vendors, rice-cake vendors, wineshops,

and eating houses, had all set up shop. In the midst of the tumultuous crowd there stood a huge tent, and inside it, the exorcism was in progress. There, gauze lanterns of five different colors—blue, red, green, white, and yellow— were hanging, beautiful as flowers. Beneath the lanterns were set in a row: the table for the house gods, heaped with steamed ricecakes, a jar of wine, and a whole boiled pig; the table for the Buddhist tutelary god,[3] provided with a bowl of raw rice, a coil of thread, a skewer of cured persimmons, and a cake of bean curd; the table for Maitreya, laden with fruit of three different colors, steamed snow-white ricecake, cooked vegetables, vegetable soup, salted fish, and honey candy; the table for the god of the mountain, spread with cooked mountain vegetables of twelve different kinds; the table for the god of dragons, holding seafood of twelve kinds; the table for the alley spirits, provided with plates of every kind of delicacy; the table for Mohwa, set with only a bowl of water; and, many other offering tables, large and small.

Mohwa wore a look of unusual modesty and composure; she had been grieving over the recent loss of her son and, in addition, she had suffered the accusations and abuses of the Christian newcomers. Despite all this, however, she looked incredibly aloof and composed. Tonight she was neither ingratiating nor given to talk in public as she used to do. Nor did she seem to be content, even after looking over the sumptuous food on the offering tables. On the contrary, she pouted as if in derision.

"Scurvy bitches! How pitiable to think that a gorgeous offering is everything," she said bluntly.

Before long, some of the spectators began to whisper that a new spirit might possess Mohwa tonight.

"It's the spirit of the late Lady Kim that is with her!" cried a woman in the crowd suddenly.

"It's Lady Kim that she is possessed by all right," other women nearby concurred. "Look at her face that appears even ominously modest and shy. And was Mohwa ever as fair as she is now? She is the very picture of Lady Kim indeed."

Then, a report sprang from villagers in one corner that tonight's exorcism might help Nangi regain her speech, while people in another corner spread a rumor that Mohwa was with child by an unknown man. The women spectators felt vaguely that all the questions raised by their common talk should be answered by the close of tonight's exorcism.

Mohwa began with a lengthy description of the deceased Lady Kim, relating the circumstances of her life from the time of her birth to her death by drowning. Her recitation over, Mohwa danced jubilantly to the tune of the flutes, pipes, and strings played by the ritual band. Her voice now sounded more plaintive than ever, and her body undulated as if it were transmuted into a fleshless, boneless spirit swinging in rhythmic cadences. The women spectators watched as if in ecstasy; their breathing rose and fell closely with the movement of Mohwa's robe. The train of her robe in turn seemed to wave after Mohwa's own breathing. And her breath seemed to have swallowed up even the stars in the sky, moving momentarily in time with the water of the mysterious, gently winding stream from Yegi Pond, as she gasped out a plaintive chant under the influence of the grieving Lady Kim's spirit.

It was now the middle of the night. People said that all their attempts to save the departed soul had been to no purpose. A group of male shamans and young sorceresses attending Mohwa had tied bowls of cooked rice onto the ends of their "soul saver" lines, and had thrown them into the pond, one after another. Seeing no trace of the deceased woman's hair in the rice bowls raised from the water, they concluded that the late Lady Kim was apparently resisting their attempt to summon her spirit.

"It's a shame that the departed soul should be still down in the water unsaved, isn't it?" an attendant shaman whispered in Mohwa's ear with a look of agitation on her face.

Mohwa showed no sign of impatience, but walked down into the water with a soul saver rod in hand, apparently taking such delay for granted. A male shaman, who was assisting Mohwa by holding the soul saver line, shifted the rice bowl at the end to and fro in the water, following the movement of the rod.

Mohwa beat the pond water, using the soul saver rod, and summoned the departed soul in a voice choked with tears:

> "Rise, rise,
> Our Lady Kim of Wŏlsŏng, age thirty-three.
> You were born under the Scorpion,
> With offerings to the Seven Stars.
> You blossomed like a flower,
> You were reared like a gem.
> Leaving your parents still alive,
> Leaving your small child lying in bed,
> When you plunged into the dark water,
> Even the Dragon King grieved and sighed.
> Your skirt floating up,
> Did you land on the Lotus throne?
> Your locks flying about,
> Did you turn into a spirit of water?"

Step by step, Mohwa went into the deeper part of the pond, holding the soul saver rod out before her. As she walked deeper into the water, one of her skirts entwined round her body while another waved floating on the surface. Now rising as high as her waist, and now as high as her breast, the dark water kept swelling round her. Gradually her voice sounded more distant and her summons emitted greater flashes of fire:

"Let me go, let me go,
Sharing the white wine in dragon-shaped cups.
Call me, my sister, call me to you.
When peach blossoms bloom on this river bank,
Come and hear me, my daughter Nangi, clad in white;
Then ask the first bough of my health,
Ask the second bough . . . "

At that instant the pond water engulfed her entire body, and her chanting ceased.

For the first few moments, the skirt of her robe was seen drifting on the surface, but even that disappeared in a short while. The soul saver rod, now out of hand, whirled round and round on the water; then it too disappeared downstream.

About ten days later, a small-statured man, who was said to peddle seafood on a street corner in a town on the east coast, came riding on a donkey to see Nangi. With sunken eyes she was still convalescing in bed.

The man soon nursed her back to health. As soon as she recognized him, Nangi called out, "Father!" Her speech sounded unusually distinct and intelligible, perhaps because, as rumor had predicted, Mohwa's last exorcism took effect.

Another ten days went by.

"Get up here," said the man to his daughter, pointing to his donkey.

Without saying a word, Nangi did as her father directed.

After their departure no one ever called at Mohwa's house. Each night only mosquitos sang in swarms amidst the rank growth in the yard.

The Author

Kim Sijong or "Kim Tongni" was born in 1913 in Kyŏngju. He was largely self-educated, and read widely. Around 1936, with a group of stories in which he depicted traditional Korean characters, realities, and emotions, employing a refined style, he emerged as a promising writer. Drawing upon the myths and legends of the south, he handled them skillfully to give unity to his works. Winner of a number of prizes, including one (1958) from the Korean Academy of Art, of which he is a member, Kim has taught since 1953 at Sŏrabŏl College of Arts in Seoul. He has published several volumes of stories, novels, and critical essays; his selected works appeared in five volumes (1967).

The world of Kim's stories is a world of primitive mysticism in which mountain spirits, local tutelary deities, Taoist and Buddhist saints, and the Dragon King reign supreme. His characters are farmers and shamans who appeal to these gods for remedy, but cannot extricate themselves from their gloomy fates, as in the "Portrait of a Shaman" (1936). Kim's escape into a labyrinth of superstition, and his fatalistic and nihilistic belief that man is doomed by the forces of nature, have often been attributed to his lack of historical consciousness. Later, he attempted to portray social and moral issues of postwar Korea, but the results have not been successful.

by Yŏm Sangsŏp

The Last Moment

ou ought to show more devotion. You could at least have got some medicine if the doctor was not in town," said the patient, sitting on his bed, supported by his attendants. Although his hour of death was approaching, he was alert. He had difficulty in breathing, but his voice was clear. Since the previous day he had wanted to bring into the hospital a herb doctor whom he had earlier dismissed because of the inefficacy of the medicine he had prescribed. For this mission the patient had chosen his younger brother, Myŏngho who, he thought, was the only person likely to know his symptoms and persuade the doctor to appear. So he had sent Myŏngho twice, but on neither occasion had he been able to see the herb doctor who, it was said, had gone to the country. The strain on the patient was so great that one slight touch on a nerve might make him collapse. It was understandable, therefore, that he should make harsh remarks.

Translated by Peter H. Lee

It was warmer today. As the herb doctor's clinic was not far enough to warrant taking a streetcar, Myŏngho had walked, or almost run, both ways. Perspiring profusely, he took off his shirt to dry himself as he stood by his brother's bedside.

"Let's leave the hospital first. The herb doctor will be available in the evening." Myŏngho felt sorry for his brother, who would probably not survive the day, and did not want to be blamed for his apparent lack of devotion. However, it was more important for the patient to leave the hospital without delay than to get one or two bowls of herb medicine. Fearing that the patient might refuse, Myŏngho pleaded with him as if he were talking to a fretful child.

"What, you want me to leave the hospital? Leave it without medicine—I'll probably die on the spot!"

The patient was resentful and angry because the people around him seemed to be thinking more of their own convenience than of the unbearable pain he was suffering. His anger seemed to increase his gasping, and his latest words were indistinguishable mutterings. The patient seemed to be unhappy over the lack of sympathy and concern of his attendants. His pain was so severe that he forgot that sympathy was beautiful but could be humiliating. As the pain mounted to an intolerable pitch, he complained more and more about the lack of devotion of everyone, who seemed to be malevolently against him.

The question of leaving the hospital had been discussed ever since the doctor had said, "The crisis is over, but recovery will require a long time." The patient, however, never wavered in his desire to remain. Taking advantage of the patient's craving for herbal medicine however, Myŏngho succeeded in persuading his brother to agree to leave the hospital. When his senses were clear, the patient would worry about the rapidly accumulating hospital fees or the cost of his funeral. As his condition got worse and his physical pain more intolerable, he became more and more obstinate, and insisted on remaining in the hospital. He himself knew that lying in a hospital bed was not the solution, but he liked the injections that relieved his pain.

Once, when he had been on the verge of apoplexy, he had obtained relief from high blood pressure by doses of herb medicine. However, when he had been hospitalized a month before, his blood pressure had been very high and some blood had had to be drawn off on two occasions. He was also given several injections of an American medicine, procured at an exorbitant price. Such was the condition of his brain and heart; besides, he had kidney trouble, with swellings on his body, but these symptoms had disappeared a few days before, for no apparent reason. His appetite had improved, everybody felt relieved. Just as the light of a lantern is kept burning by continually raising the wick, so the patient's life was prolonged by dose after dose of medicine and morphine.

"The war is over now, I won't die of the shortage of medicine. What is lacking is money." The patient uttered these words in a choked voice. He knew that the repeated injections had nothing to do with the crux of his illness, but he wanted to stay in the hospital because he thought he would immediately die of pain without the injections.

The interval between the shots was reduced from four hours to three, and then to two. Even at midnight, when he had an unbearably stifling pain in his chest, he could not help asking for a shot. He was then relieved of the pain and could relax. This feeling of relief and relaxation gave him unsurpassed comfort. "Now I can understand why opium addicts cannot stop the habit," he thought to himself. However, when he recovered his senses he suddenly realized the danger of an overdose of morphine and felt the need for herb medicine again as the last resort. Ideally, he wanted to arrange for a nurse with a supply of medicine to come home with him, so that he could have both shots and herb medicine. But he couldn't afford that. He wondered if there were any Chinese medicine that could bring about the same effect as the hospital medicine, and plaintively asked for such an anodyne.

"You don't have to worry," said his brother consolingly, "Dr. K promised to come twice a day to give you the shots."

It was, however, evident that the members of the family could not think of the patient's convenience alone. They wanted him back home, not because they did not want him to die away from home, but because dying at home would be less trouble for them. Some argued that dying in the hospital would cost less, but that the family would make too much fuss, and consequently, when the hospital was willing to release him, they all felt relieved. There was something in what the patient said, that the family was concerned only with its own convenience. His illness worsening, the relationship between him and his relatives had been growing less intimate, and they could not help it that their affection and devotion wore away layer by layer.

His wife tended him assiduously, never leaving his side for two months, the first month at home and the second, in the hospital; but she too was exhausted and wanted to go home. Even if he got out of danger, he would end up bedridden with apoplexy like other old people. Then, the monthly hospital fees alone would run twenty or thirty thousand hwan,[1] which they could hardly afford, and the drain would affect everyone. That was his wife's present worry. She had thought that the death of the head of the family would drive her children and herself out into the streets. Therefore, as long as he had hopes of recovery and as long as she could afford it, she had devoted herself to his care. The living must live on, starting tomorrow. Such a weighty concern blocked her path. But what about blood ties, obligations, and face? Were they not what kept her going? The patient was craving more and more love and sympathy and devotion from the healthy, and he became more and more irascible.

Neither the lack of devotion nor the priority given by his family to its own comfort was enough to convince the patient, thin and worn-out as he was, that he would pass away in a day or two.

"There's enough space to bury me beside father's large grave. We cannot afford the funeral expenses. The times are too out of joint. Simply cremate my body and bury the ashes there."

He used to make such suggestions when he was talking about his children's education, and about jobs which would arise upon his death. Once he had said it might not be a bad idea to pulverize his bones and scatter them into the thin air on top of a clean mountain. Those remarks surprised the family—although he was simply taking advantage of an occasion to express himself in case of death (which spares nobody); he did not intend that he would not recover.

In spite of his misgivings that his life was being prolonged by the action of the morphine, the relief he felt after each injection, and the recognition that he could control his body enough to sit up with minimum support, were enough to give him confidence and the hope of recovery. As a matter of fact, when, in the midst of a heated argument over his release from the hospital, a certain young man, Mr. C, had come to see him, he chatted with such cheerfulness that it appeared he might be able to leave the hospital in a day or two—much to the embarrassment of the family present.

"I didn't know that you were so ill. They are setting up a foundation, and many seem to be willing to make you vice-president. At least a director for sure. What a time to be in bed. I hope you'll get well soon."

C's inside story had been not so much to comfort the patient as to assure a cordial relationship with the future director. C seemed to have had difficulty locating the patient before he turned up at the hospital.

"Is that so? I shall get out of bed in a while. Please remember me to them. Your visit was unexpected, C. This might be a turning point in my life. Use your influence on my behalf, please," the patient implored, holding the young man's hand. The young visitor, after asking the name of the illness, seemed to scrutinize from time to time an ashen expression in the patient's face and his unintentional mumbles. Intent on making excuses to leave, his initial enthusiasm seemed to wane. He had arrived a talkative man, but left, a frightened mumbler.

The patient, pleased by the news, had asked his wife to go to Mr. P and find out the details. He also had told her to talk with Mr. A about the matter and request his recommendation to the organization. The family members, both astonished and relieved to see the change of condition, thought this might indicate a chance of recovery. How ridiculous now seemed their private whispers about getting him released or how to bury him!

Late in the afternoon came in the Dr. K whom the patient wanted so much to see every time he had a chest pain. The previous injection was still working, so the patient was not visibly suffering; yet he welcomed him as if the mere sight of the doctor were a relief.

"Now that you are here, why don't you give me another shot." Fearful of an imminent attack of pain, he wanted to have enough medication while the doctor was around.

"Surely!"

After a brief examination, the doctor went out to get the medicine. Myŏngho stole out of the room and followed the doctor.

"We're planning to get him out of the hospital this afternoon. But you weren't around. How is he now?"

"I foresee little change for a day or two. Why don't you take him home?" The doctor seemed to be delighted at the family's plan, as previously he had said that the illness would be prolonged. He seemed then to imply that he could do little for the sick man and would rather see him discharged. The family decided not to leave the hospital until the following day, partly because the patient would not do so without herbal medicine and partly because of the doctor's prediction of no sudden change.

Dr. K returned with a syringe and administered the injection with some difficulty. As he was leaving the room, he motioned Myŏngho to follow him out. Sensing an inauspicious omen, and shunning the alert eyes of the patient, Myŏngho furtively followed.

"You had better get him home this evening, if possible. As you noticed, his heart and arteries cannot circulate the medicine properly. The heart is beating only because of the medicine." Now the doctor was anxious to send the patient home, as the injection had been difficult. The doctor had had to pause several times, waiting for the medicine to be carried by the vein. However, raising the issue of leaving the hospital again was the last thing Myŏngho could now do. That would again dismay the patient, who had been pleased by the news that he might be the foundation's director, however unreliable the news might be.

The patient was anxious to find out the verdict from his brother, who had had two talks with the doctor. He immediately lost his peace of mind, and fell prey to fear and uneasiness. With an unnatural smile, he was going to speak, but the words he was about to utter seemed to have horrified him. Without opening his lips, he kept staring at Myŏngho. In days before, when Myŏngho had rushed to the hospital in the early morning or late evening, the patient had worn an expression of fear, aversion, and excitement that asked, "Why did you come?" The manner in which the patient stared at him with doubt- and fear-ridden eyes could be likened to trying timidly and stealthily to read the expression on the face of a guard of the devil's den in which he was illegally imprisoned. Myŏngho did not know where to look or what to say.

"The doctor says you are remarkably better. He advises us to get you out of the hospital tomorrow afternoon. He will give you plenty of medicine before your discharge." In order to buttress the statement, Myŏngho even forced a smile.

"Really," the patient answered, with faint hope, as if nerves stretched to the breaking point had suddenly snapped loose. "Can it be true?" Harboring suspicion in his look, he added doubtfully, "Why on earth didn't he break the news to me directly?"

But derision quickly gave way to inquisitiveness. He wanted to find out the details of the conversation between Myŏngho and the doctor. Concentrating on Myŏngho's face and lips, he asked, "How have I so suddenly improved?" As if Myŏngho's answer had the power to decide his fate, the patient implored him hopefully. Myŏngho felt depressed and distressed. Only a few minutes ago, this man had reason to hope for a better life. Myŏngho dared not tell the truth but had to find something to say, just to avoid the issue. "Probably he meant that, having a strong constitution, your recovery might be brought about by well-prescribed herbal medicine."

"Nonsense!"

The patient had been tense since the visit of C; hence, although from the movement of his lips he was trying to say more after the last exclamation, he did not seem to have enough strength. He was lying with his face up, his vacant eyes staring at the ceiling. When he said "Nonsense," he had expected some explanation or protest from Myŏngho, but seeing him light a cigaret without retort, despair engulfed the patient. "No reason whatever not to have broken such news directly to me." Even at the risk of his own exhaustion, the patient could not put such a thought from his head.

"This is worse than the fate of a condemned man. At least he knows what to expect. He will be informed of the time of his execution. The man who should know first is denied the knowledge of what is to come. The doctor and my family, with whispers and vacillations, behave as if my life belonged to them. Am I to live? Are they going to let me live?"

His eyes were closed, but his head became clearer, and he could follow his train of thought logically. He opened his eyes suddenly, feeling something radiant through his eyelids. He gave a quick look around, intending to roar at the first person he spied, but his voice choked as if he were in a nightmare. His sight grew dim and the face of his wife retreated farther away. His eyelids closing by themselves, he fell into a sleep. In a few moments he began to snore; awakened by his own snoring, he opened his eyes and scrutinized the surroundings. "I must have been sleeping." He was relieved to find that he had not died. Death might follow sleep and sleep was fearful to him.

"Well, then, I'll go get the herb medicine," Myŏngho said, seeing a young man coming upstairs after filling out the discharge papers. He put on his jacket. About to go out of the room, he spied his sister-in-law, who was waving to him not to leave. Myŏngho left nevertheless, pretending not to have understood the message. A renowned herb doctor had visited them a few days before the hospitalization, but went away after pointing out the futility of treatment. Thus they wasted the return taxi fare. The urgent desire of the patient notwithstanding, his sister-in-law was against calling in another doctor. Moreover, there might not be enough money for taxi fare home after payment of the hospital expenses. She, therefore, wished to forego herbal medicine which the patient might not even take. Myŏngho of course understood all this, but he was anxious to satisfy the patient's last wish so that there might be no regret on the part of the bereaved.

Myŏngho emerged from the office of the herb doctor, a nearby acquaintance, with three packets of medicine. Thinking that they might do the trick and that he might return for more, he asked for the prescription. He was asking for a miracle, but considering the patient's confident adherence to life and his mental and physical energy, he might be able to pull through. It would be a terrible blow to the family's economy and future if he were to die. But these considerations were, of course, made from the standpoint of the living. When the patient was free from the fear of death, his foremost concern was his family and children. But family affairs and the strong instinct to wade out of the terrible physical pain were two things.

"As a matter of fact, he won't have many years to live, even if he does recover." Myŏngho recalled a discussion held among his brothers at the beginning of the year to make preparation for the patient's sixtieth birthday celebration, and was struck with fear, for the remark seemed to imply some kind of reproach of the ailing brother. Everyone else might say the same thing, but he could not ridicule his brother, who was so anxious to retain his life, even for an hour or a day.

"Even in a span of one hundred years, a man has covered only half his destination, and dies without a sense of completion. Fulfillment of the self is out of the question—perhaps life means leaving behind what one has left unfinished. A dying man should not worry about his wife and children. It is the instinct of all living beings to put up a stout resistance to death to the last moment— a kind of self-assertion, as long as the biological condition permits; a fearful pitched battle to preserve one's existence. If self-fulfillment is out of the question, why consider death as surrender, rather than as taking the initiative to withdraw to make room for one's posterity? In short, it is a return, a quiet return. But how many can attain it?"

Pacing back to the hospital, Myŏngho was tracing these thoughts, fold upon fold, and felt gloomy and lonely.

"I'll be the next one to die."

Myŏngho thought he would not regret leaving a world full of hardships and unpleasantness, but the thought of the pain that he must endure before death, tantamount to the sum of all the suffering he had undergone in his life, dismayed him. It would be a happy

death, if one could die without being addicted to nar-
cotics, Myŏngho thought, giving an uncontrollable laugh.
His second cousin, a devout Buddhist, had been bedridden
for sometime, but he, tied to his brother, could not find
time to visit him. It would be a visit of inquiry, as
Myŏngho wished to know how a Buddhist faced illness,
and what his views on life and death were. Conscious of
his greying hair, he reflected that he must prepare for
death.

As he entered the sick room, Myŏngho showed the
herb medicine to the patient.

"Here is the prescription. If the medicine works, you
can ask me to get more, or you can have it fetched from
your nearby herb store."

The patient did not smile, but seemed to be content.

The bundles of herbs were put into the baggage,
which was almost ready.

While a taxi was being summoned and a stretcher
brought upstairs, several women entered and, after brief
whispering to the wife, began to pray around the bed.
The patient did not know them, but they were old friends
of his wife's who came to inquire after him. Finding out
the patient's condition, they were offering the last prayers.
On the previous day, Myŏngho heard from his sister-in-
law that some people from the Catholic church had come
while he was out and that they had baptized the patient.
"There is holy water," she remarked, pointing to a little
bottle on the table. Myŏngho had felt a shade strange, but
he kept silent, not wanting to fret about trifles.

Originally the patient had a liking for Buddhism,
and had called in Buddhist monks for his parents' funeral
services. This time, Myŏngho and his younger brother
had already discussed whether they should have a monk

officiate at their brother's funeral or forego such a ceremony on account of the expense. But a Catholic nurse
in the hospital was intent on obtaining his conversion;
the patient was finally won over and baptized. Myŏngho
had no objections, as long as the patient had consented
and nothing seemed to be wrong. But, upon witnessing
the prayers, Myŏngho felt strange and odd. Standing
behind the ladies by the stretcher, he, a man of tender
feelings, was moved to tears by the words of the prayers.
He stepped out into the hall.

It is said that a drowning man grabs at a straw. Not
that Myŏngho condoned a blind prayer to some spirit or
some Buddha for mercy, but he could not object to people's praying for the patient's recovery or for his soul,
according to their belief. It was, he thought, something
gratifying and beautiful. There was, however, no way of
ascertaining whether the patient was listening. He was
lying still, his face without expression, his eyes closed.

When the patient was carried to the stretcher, he
opened his eyes wide and looked around. As he was being
transferred to the taxi waiting in front of the hospital,
he remarked, "Tell the driver how to get home." Amazed,
the attendants looked at each other and smiled. As soon
as he was laid on the seat, his eyes looked glassy. Stealing
a glance at the patient, Myŏngho rushed back to the
ward and brought the nurse with him to administer
another injection of heart medicine. Watching the nurse
in her white attire, Myŏngho jumped into the front seat.

Myŏngho could not see how the patient was doing.
He felt relieved when he saw the attendants in back ex-
changing words in a cheerful manner.

Regardless of the patient's condition, Myŏngho hoped
that he would not die on the way. He had rushed inside
to fetch the nurse without reflecting on the efficacy of the

camphor injection. His main concern was not to carry home a dead body (traditionally considered bad luck). It was a matter of honor to avoid censure for having dragged a corpse into the house. But Myŏngho's efforts were in vain.

The room in which the body was to be laid out was heated and had already been cleared of everything but a folding screen. Indeed, the room had been provided before the party left the hospital. The widow from the next room unpacked the baggage. She was looking for something. The first thing that rolled out on the floor was the bundle of herb medicine for which Myŏngho had been rushing about all morning and for which the patient had so much wished during the past two days. The widow then produced a small bottle of holy water—obtained after the baptism—and sprinkled it around the body.

"What sort of rite do you have in mind? Are you going to do away with the Confucian ceremony?" asked Myŏngho, watching the widow's actions.

"No, we cannot go that far," replied the widow, adding that she was doing only what the church thought was good and had asked her to.

The first argument to be settled was the three-day versus the five-day rite.

"If the body is to be cremated, according to the deceased's wish, a three-day wake will do," proposed Myŏngho, mainly with finances in mind.

"In our state, it will of course have to be a three-day affair, but no cremation. Your brother once mentioned it, but changed his mind and wished to be buried near his father's grave."

On this matter, nobody was in a position to dissent. The widow might be thinking of her own future funeral

—she, who would in all likelihood be following the deceased, might have disliked the idea of cremation; it was
also understandable that, although the deceased had once
hinted at it, he was viewing the matter hypothetically as
belonging to a distant future; when it had turned out to
be an imminent reality to be squarely faced, he had
probably changed his mind. Some even go so far as to
specify the material of their shrouds or objects to be put in
their coffins. But, having chosen the site of burial, the fear
of not being buried there was not unnatural.

"It's easy to talk about a three-day wake. But this day
has gone and there remains only one day to work on the
grave," said the funeral manager. "A hearse, and at least
a bus, should be hired, all of which will cost at least forty
thousand hwan." The trip to Hongjewŏn Crematory
would cost only about six thousand. (Forty thousand was
an amount the family could not afford.)

"After death, what's the difference, cremation or
burial?" remarked some younger people casually. But
nobody said whether they were right or wrong.

Anyhow, both men and women had a busy day and
night, and the first services were held at the right time.
When they had finished the ceremony, the second cousin,
who had been ill, walked in, leaning on a long cane.

"I thought I should go before you. O calamity!"

After weeping over the coffin, and showing a deeper
grief than other mourners, he took a string of beads from
his pocket and began to pray. The prayer lasted long
enough to make the others fidget. Then he produced an
envelope wrapped in white paper and placed it under the
funeral banner bearing the name, title, and rank of the
deceased. The envelope appeared to contain some Buddhist scripture hand copied by the old man himself. When
they lowered the coffin, they did not forget to place the

envelope, together with other funeral gifts, beneath the covering of the grave.

Now, the soul of the deceased might be sleeping peacefully, cleansed by the holy water and blessed by the merciful Buddha. But, above all, the soul must have been pleased that each of the bereaved had done his best.

The Author

Yŏm Sangsŏp was born in 1897 in Seoul and attended a high school in Kyōto before proceeding to Keiō University, where he studied English literature (1918). In 1919, implicated in the Korean independence movement, he was imprisoned by the Japanese, but was released after a year and returned to Korea. He began his literary career with the publication in the journal Kaebyŏk *(August-October 1921) of a story, "The Green Frog in the Specimen Room." From 1936 he was editor in chief of a newspaper in southern Manchuria. After the liberation, he returned to Seoul, where he worked for a while for another daily. In his later years, he was honored by a series of prizes, including one from the Korean Academy of Art (1957). He died March 14, 1963.*

Yŏm was the first to introduce psychological analysis and scientific documentation into modern Korean prose. He also created his personal symbols, as in "The Green Frog," in which the hero's anxiety, fear, and anguish are compared to the feelings of a green frog about to be dissected in a zoology class. Throughout his long career, he portrayed with a camera eye the dark side of Korean society, without interpretive comment or moral judgment.

His zeal for fidelity often led to overdescription. The realism of his stories is heightened by the use of Seoul middle-class speech, for which he had fine ear. "The Last Moment," which first appeared in the journal Munye *in August 1949 and was republished in* Hyŏndae Munhak *in May 1963, transforms an otherwise dry and common subject into a story invested with subtlety and tension and with characters who are remarkably alive.*

by Hwang Sunwŏn

Cranes

he northern village at the border of the Thirty-eighth Parallel was snugly settled under the high, bright autumn sky.

One white gourd lay against another on the dirt floor of an empty farmhouse. The occasional village elders first put out their bamboo pipes before passing by, and the children too turned aside some distance off. Their faces were ridden with fear.

The village as a whole showed few traces of destruction from the war, but it did not seem like the same village Sŏngsam had known as a boy.

At the foot of a chestnut grove on the hill behind the village he stopped and climbed a chestnut tree. Somewhere far back in his mind he heard the old man with a wen shout, "You bad boy, you're climbing up my chestnut tree again!"

The old man must have passed away, for among the

Translated by Peter H. Lee

few village elders Sŏngsam had met, the old man was not
to be found. Holding the trunk of the tree, Sŏngsam
gazed at the blue sky for a while. Some chestnuts fell to
the ground as the dry clusters opened of their own accord.

In front of the farmhouse that had been turned into
a public peace-police office, a young man stood, tied up.
He seemed to be a stranger, so Sŏngsam approached him
to have a close look. He was taken aback; it was none
other than his boyhood playmate, Tŏkchae.

Sŏngsam asked the police officer who had come with
him from Ch'ŏnt'ae what it was all about. The prisoner
was vice-chairman of the Farmers Communist League
and had just been flushed out of his hideout in his own
house, Sŏngsam learned.

Sŏngsam sat down on the dirt floor and lit a cigaret.

Tŏkchae was to be escorted to Ch'ŏngdan by one of
the peace policemen.

After a time, Sŏngsam lit a new cigaret from the first
and stood up.

"I'll take the fellow with me."

Tŏkchae, his face averted, refused to look at Sŏngsam.
They left the village.

Sŏngsam kept on smoking, but the tobacco had no
taste. He just kept drawing in the smoke and blowing it
out. Then suddenly he thought that Tŏkchae too must
want a puff. He thought of the days when they used to
share dried gourd leaves behind walls, hidden from the
adults. But today, how could he offer a cigaret to a fellow
like this?

Once, when they were small, he went with Tŏkchae
to steal some chestnuts from the grandpa with the wen.
It was Sŏngsam's turn to go up the tree. Suddenly there
came shouts from the old man. He slipped and fell to the

ground. Sŏngsam got chestnut needles all over his bottom, but he kept on running. It was only when they reached a safe place where the old man could not overtake them that he turned his bottom to Tŏkchae. Plucking out those needles hurt so much that he could not keep tears from welling up in his eyes. Tŏkchae produced a fistful of chestnuts from his pocket and thrust them into Sŏngsam's . . . Sŏngsam threw away the cigaret he had just lit. Then he made up his mind not to light another while he was escorting Tŏkchae.

They reached the hill pass, the hill where he and Tŏkchae used to cut fodder for the cows until Sŏngsam had had to move near Ch'ŏnt'ae, south of the Thirty-eighth Parallel, two years before the liberation.

Sŏngsam felt a sudden surge of anger in spite of himself and shouted, "So how many have you killed?"

For the first time, Tŏkchae cast a quick glance at him and then turned away.

"How many did you kill, you?" he asked again.

Tŏkchae turned toward him once again and glared. The glare grew intense and his mouth twitched.

"So you managed to kill many, eh?" Sŏngsam felt his heart becoming clear from within, as if an obstruction had been removed. "If you were vice-chairman of the Communist League, why didn't you run? You must have been lying low with a secret mission."

Tŏkchae did not answer.

"Speak up, what was your mission?"

Tŏkchae kept walking. Tŏkchae is hiding something, Sŏngsam thought. He wanted to take a good look at him, but Tŏkchae would not turn his averted face.

Fingering the revolver at his side, Sŏngsam went on:

"No excuse is necessary. You are sure to be shot anyway. Why don't you tell the truth, here and now?"

"I'm not going to make any excuses. They made me vice-chairman of the league because I was one of the poorest and I was a hardworking farmer. If that constitutes a crime worthy of death, so be it. I am still what I used to be—the only thing I'm good at is digging in the soil." After a short pause, he added, "My old man is bedridden at home. He's been ill almost half a year." Tŏkchae's father was a widower, a hardworking poor farmer who lived only for his son. Seven years ago his back had given out and his skin had become diseased.

"You married?"

"Yes," replied Tŏkchae after a while.

"To whom?"

"Shorty."

"To Shorty?" How interesting! A woman so small and plump that she knew the earth's vastness but not the sky's altitude. Such a cold fish! He and Tŏkchae used to tease her and make her cry. And Tŏkchae had married that girl.

"How many kids?"

"The first is arriving this fall, she says."

Sŏngsam had difficulty swallowing a laugh about to explode in spite of himself. Although he had asked how many kids Tŏkchae had, he could not help wanting to burst into laughter at the image of her sitting down, with a large stomach, one span around. But he realized this was no time to laugh or joke over such matters.

"Anyway, it's strange you did not run away."

"I tried to escape. They said that once the South invaded, no man would be spared. So men between seventeen and forty were forcibly taken to the North. I thought of evacuating, even if I had to carry my father on my back. But father said no. How could the farmers leave the land behind when the crops were ready for harvest? He grew old on that farm depending on me as the prop and mainstay of the family. I wanted to be with him in his last moments so that I could close his eyes with my own hand. Besides, where can farmers like us go, who know only living on the land?"

Last June Sŏngsam had had to take refuge. At night he had broken the news privately to his father. But his father had said the same thing! Where can a farmer go, leaving all the chores behind? So Sŏngsam left alone. Roaming about the strange streets and villages in the South, Sŏngsam had been haunted by thoughts of his old parents and the young children, left with all the chores. Fortunately, his family was safe then, as now.

They crossed the ridge of a hill. This time Sŏngsam walked with his face averted. The autumn sun was hot on his forehead. This was an ideal day for the harvest, he thought.

When they reached the foot of the hill, Sŏngsam hesitatingly stopped. In the middle of a field he spied a group of cranes that looked like men in white clothes bending over. This used to be the neutralized zone along the Thirty-eighth Parallel. The cranes were still living here, as before, while the people were all gone.

Once, when Sŏngsam and Tŏkchae were about twelve, they had set a trap here, without the knowledge of the adults, and had caught a crane, a Tanjŏng crane. They had roped the crane, even its wings, and had paid daily visits, patting its neck and riding on its back. Then one day they overheard the neighbors whispering. Some-

one had come from Seoul with a permit from the governor-general's office to catch cranes as specimens or
something. Then and there the two boys dashed off to the
field. That they would be found out and punished was
no longer a weighty concern; all they worried about was
the fate of their crane. Without a moment's delay, still
out of breath from running, they untied the crane's feet
and wings. But the bird could hardly walk. It must have
been worn out from being bound.

The two held it up in the air. Then, all of a sudden,
a shot was fired. The crane fluttered its wings a couple
of times and came down again.

It was shot, they thought. But the next moment, as
another crane from a nearby bush fluttered its wings, the
boys' crane stretched its long neck with a whoop and
disappeared into the sky. For a long time the two boys
could not take their eyes away from the blue sky into
which their crane had soared.

"Hey, why don't we stop here for a crane hunt?"

Sŏngsam spoke up suddenly.

Tŏkchae was puzzled, struck dumb.

"I'll make a trap with this rope; you flush a crane
over here."

Having untied Tŏkchae's hands, Sŏngsam had already started crawling among the weeds.

Tŏkchae's face turned white. "You are sure to be shot
anyway"—these words flashed through his mind. Pretty
soon a bullet would fly from where Sŏngsam has gone,
he thought.

Some paces away, Sŏngsam quickly turned toward
him.

"Hey, how come you're standing there like you're
dumb? Go flush the crane!"

Only then did Tŏkchae catch on. He started crawling among the weeds.

A couple of Tanjŏng cranes soared high into the clear blue autumn sky, fluttering their huge wings.

The Author

Hwang Sunwŏn was born on March 26, 1915, in Taedong, South P'yŏngan, and was graduated in English literature from Waseda University in Tokyo in 1939. His literary career began with the publication of a collection of verse in 1934, but since 1940 he has written mainly short stories and novels. "Cranes" was published in 1953, and his short story "Cain's Descendants" (1954) won him the Free Literature Prize in 1955, and a novel, Trees Standing on the Mountain Slope *(1960), the Korean Academy of Art Prize in 1961. His short story "Shower" (1959) appears later in this collection. His collected works were published in 1964 and selected works in 1969, each in six volumes. A member of the Korean Academy of Art since 1957, Hwang is currently a professor at Kyŏnghŭi University in Seoul.*

A master of the modern Korean short story form, Hwang has attempted to capture the images of his people in lyrical prose and delicate natural scenery. His evocation of the inner mood of characters by private images and symbols, and his subtle insight into their psychology has often been praised. He has dealt with the people close to the soil, concentrating especially on children and older people—childhood for its innocent freedom, and old age for its spiritual loneliness. Drawing upon Korean myths and legends, his concern has been to perceive the Korean character with an intuitive faith. In his recent novels, Hwang has dealt with one's own and others' selves, and man's essential loneliness.

by Son Ch'angsŏp

The Rainy Season

henever it rained like this Wŏn'gu's heart became almost unbearably heavy. The steady pelting of rain always brought the dismal life of Tonguk and his sister back to his mind. Their somber room and the crumbling wooden shack loomed gloomily in his imagination beyond the screen of rain. Even on a fine day when he thought of them he heard the raindrops as they seeped into the corner of his heart. For Wŏn'gu, the image of Tonguk and Tongok was always filled with rain.

Wŏn'gu had met Tonguk on the street one day, and they had had supper together. But Tonguk wanted to drink, not eat. Wŏn'gu saw that Tonguk was very fond of drinking, for he didn't spare even the last drops that flowed down the outside of the glass. Remembering that Tonguk had been brought up in a Christian family and that he had led choirs at several churches in the past,

Translated by Peter H. Lee

Wŏn'gu asked him whether he still went to church. He smiled awkwardly and said he had been to church on and off, but that it aroused in him an almost suffocating desperation.

Tonguk was clad in a threadbare jacket with tattered sleeves and a pair of black-checkered grey trousers which, he said, had been given him from the church relief box. His shoes were black, and narrow at the middle, like an ant's waist, and big and round at the toe. They were more striking than anything else he had on. They were obviously meant for a Chaplin. While Wŏn'gu poured wine for Tonguk he could hardly keep his eyes away from the shoes.

Wŏn'gu asked him what he did for a living. Tonguk unwrapped the parcel he had with him and produced a scrapbook. As he turned the leaves, Wŏn'gu saw pasted on them portraits of Western women and children. Tonguk said that he went around American military barracks with the book and got orders for drawings from the soldiers. Then, with a slight grin, he added that his study of English literature at college had paid off after all. For a long time Wŏn'gu did not like his grinning. When Tonguk grinned he looked scornful of others and mocking of himself (but his expression had its own charm). His grin induced a kind of fateful pressure, and depressed Wŏn'gu. When Wŏn'gu asked who the painter was, Tonguk said he lived with his sister, Tongok, who had developed a talent for painting when she was very young and was good at portraiture.

Wŏn'gu remembered hearing about her. When he was in primary school he used to go to Tonguk's house, and he remembered how the little girl, then only five or six, followed him around annoying him. She used to sing a ditty popular among children, "Bonze, bonze, little bonze, where are you going with a knapsack?" However, after twenty years, he could hardly visualize her now. Tonguk had brought her with him at the time of the great retreat, but these days she was burdensome, and he often regretted having brought her. When Wŏn'gu asked whether or not her husband had come from the North with her, Tonguk said that she was still unmarried. Wŏn'gu was going to say she should have been married by then since she would have been old enough, but he said nothing. After all, he and Tonguk were also unmarried, and it wasn't a crime for a girl to remain single beyond the usual marriage age. By taking his own age and the years that had passed since their childhood, Wŏn'gu calculated that Tongok must be twenty-five or twenty-six.

Tonguk became quite drunk, and as he patted Wŏn'gu on the shoulder again and again, he said repeatedly that he felt sorry for Tongok with her talent and good looks. Then he gulped down another drink, shaking his head, and said it was her destiny and nothing could change it. Then he dropped his head and remarked reassuringly, as if to himself, that if he were Wŏn'gu, he would get married to her right then without hesitation. Without knowing what Tonguk was driving at, Wŏn'gu readily consented, shaking the other's hand.

When they left the chophouse and were about to part, Tonguk put his hands on Wŏn'gu's shoulders and said that he intended to become a minister. That was the only way for him to pursue a career. When the new semester started, he would enter a seminary. Looking at Tonguk's shabby back, with shoulders drooping forward, Wŏn'gu again thought of the other's past and of his family, and felt that he should value Tonguk who, for all his love of wine, still wanted to become a minister.

It was a day at the beginning of the long rainy season, which lasted for forty days, when Wŏn'gu paid his first visit to Tonguk. He got off the streetcar at Tongnae terminal and, following the map which Tonguk had drawn for him, slowly climbed the muddy slope. The rain was pouring down steadily. He had an umbrella, but his lower legs were soaked because of the strong wind and the mud splashing on the road.

The house in which Tonguk lived stood by itself quite apart from the others. It was a dilapidated old wooden house. The decaying structure was propped up with two poles at the side. Weeds were rank on the tiled roof. During the Japanese occupation, Wŏn'gu later learned, the house had been used as a sanitarium. Originally the front had been covered with glass panes, but now no glass was to be seen. Inside the right window hung a worn-out straw bag, which helped to keep the rain out.

The house looked deserted, and Wŏn'gu stood motionless, sheltered under his umbrella. Could anyone live in a place like this? It reminded him of a goblin's den in a storybook, with horned goblins rushing out at any moment, flourishing their clubs. Hardly believing that Tonguk and Tongok actually lived in that house, Wŏn'gu took out the map to double check for a mistake. But he had followed the map correctly, walking along the river and then crossing it at the hillside. And this was the only house to be found anywhere.

Taking a few steps forward, Wŏn'gu called out to see whether anyone might be in. No answer came. He called out again. Still there was no sound. Except for the pelting rain and the flowing river growing louder, the house lay in a silence deep as death. He called out louder this time, so loudly that he was frightened by his own voice. It burst out of his clogged throat and sounded like shrieking. At that moment, a corner of the straw bag hanging inside the window was lifted, and there emerged the face of a woman, with unusually fair skin and black eyebrows, like a portrait drawn in black on a piece of white paper. She just stared at Wŏn'gu. He thought that she must be Tongok. Asked whether Kim Tonguk lived there, she only nodded. Her way of reply seemed haughty. When asked if Tonguk had gone out, she gave the same response.

In her manner Wŏn'gu perceived a look of contempt and silent protest. Being afraid that she might have mistaken him for a suspicious person, he told her that his name was Chŏng Wŏn'gu, that he was a close friend of Tonguk's, that they were classmates from primary school all the way through college, and that as schoolboys they often met at each other's houses.

Still she did not change expression. In a very tender voice, he asked if she was Tongok, Tonguk's sister. She nodded for the third time, at last wearing a vaguely mocking smile. Asked if she knew where Tonguk had gone, she finally answered that she did not know.

She had a clear voice. He asked again whether she knew when he would return home; she again shook her head. Displeased with her rude manner, he regretted coming and, asking her to tell Tonguk of his visit, he turned and walked away, but Tongok did not say goodbye.

As he walked back along the railway track, which was covered with pumpkin vines, his mind was full of gloom, just as his shoes were full of muddy water. It seemed that his neck was too thin to hold up his head. He felt uncomfortable and uneasy.

Having walked for a while, he impulsively stopped

to look back. Beyond the rain and mist, the dilapidated house looked as if it would tumble down with a shriek at any moment. At the thought that it might fall the moment he turned his back, Wŏn'gu stood there in expectation of the imminent disaster. He perceived an image of the pale woman, framed like a picture on the straw bag in the window, and shivered with fright. It must have been Tongok's face. Why was she staring obstinately at him from behind the wet window?

As he began to walk away, he recalled a story he had heard in childhood about a fox that bewitched men. Then he saw someone covered by a torn paper umbrella coming through the rain. It was Tonguk. He had been to the market, he said, and was carrying a bag with vegetables and fish. He pulled at Wŏn'gu's hand, saying he would not let go the visitor who had come a long way in the teeth of such terrible weather. Like a man who had lost the strength even to speak, Wŏn'gu followed him.

Tongok's puzzling attitude from their meeting before hung heavily on Wŏn'gu's mind. As he entered the room, after being invited in by Tonguk, he saw Tongok glance protestingly. She did not budge from the spot where she was sitting. Since it was still raining, the window was covered with the straw bag, and the eight-mat room was like a cave. The floor was pasted with cement bag papers. From one corner of the ceiling rain dripped into a bucket placed below. The water splashed and spattered into the bucket. In the room, dark as a grave, only the sound of falling water relieved the gloom and desolation. Even the sound of the falling water, as it gradually filled the bucket, grew more melancholy.

Tonguk did not introduce Wŏn'gu to his sister. He hung up his wet clothes and walked into the kitchen in his trousers and T-shirt. He said he was going to prepare a meal for Wŏn'gu. Actually it was not really a kitchen, but just an ordinary empty room. The mats were set against the wall, and the floor was covered with papers. The ceiling was leaking; pots and pans were strewn carelessly about. Tonguk, warning that it would get smoky, closed the door between the two rooms and busied himself by starting a fire in the stove. Wŏn'gu's watch indicated a few minutes past ten and, through the crack of the door, he asked Tonguk whether it was breakfast or lunch. Tonguk grinned and said they made no distinction among the three meals. They ate when they felt hungry.

While Tonguk was bustling in the kitchen, Tongok did not budge from her spot. She thumbed through the leaves of old foreign picture magazines, yawning from time to time. Wŏn'gu did not know what to think and found it hard to remain seated. He would rather help Tonguk in the kitchen because his presence in the room was unbearable. But even a slight movement would be a dramatic change, requiring considerable courage on his part.

He suddenly became aware that the seat of his pants was getting wet. The bucket was overflowing, and water had trickled toward the spot where he sat. Fingering the wet spot, he stood up. Tongok noticed the overflowing bucket but did not make a move to do anything about it. She only turned toward the kitchen and reported that water was running out of the bucket. Tonguk opened the door a little and shouted back at her to empty it herself. Wŏn'gu decided that it was time for him to take action, and lifted the bucket. However, before he had taken even one step, the hook at one end of the bail slipped, and the bucket turned over, sending water all over the floor.

The room was flooded. Even Tongok, who had not

hitherto budged, quickly got up and moved to the side. At this moment, Wŏn'gu noticed that her movement was not normal; one leg was shorter and thinner than the other. When she stepped aside, her body inclined to one side, as if she would fall. The next moment, without moving her legs, she flopped down in the dry corner, her face now much paler. She glared bitterly at Wŏn'gu. Shivering as if he were floating in the middle of a great flood, he tried to escape from her glare by wading falteringly through the water.

Since then, Wŏn'gu called on them often when it rained, for he could not then set up his stall on the street. Although he was not fond of Tongok, whose character was as crippled as her body, he sought her out again and again, as if drawn toward her by a strange destiny. Was it because he wanted to hear these raindrops trickling down from the ceiling of that dark, gloomy room? Or was he infected by the bitter sadness of looking at that horribly thin, short leg of hers? Or had he been slowly awakened to a kind of outlandish charm in her changing manner, which became more normal at each visit?

Indeed, her manner grew softer each time he saw her. On the second visit, she blushed at the sight of him and dropped her eyes. On his third visit, she even smiled a gloomy smile. He was glad to see these changes in her. He was as happy as if he was witnessing the return from a coma of a patient who had shown no response at the first call, but at the second had opened his eyes a little, and at the third had looked around and asked for a drink of water.

On his second visit, Wŏn'gu did not see the bucket under the leak in the ceiling; instead there was a hole as big as two fists through the floor. The trickling water dropped down to the ground beneath the boards with a dull sound. And the roof seemed to leak in many spots, as there was a pitter-patter above the ceiling of thin boards. The leaking water flowed slantwise to one corner, falling through a knothole as big as a bull's eye.

That day Tongok was still aloof, as Wŏn'gu and Tonguk chatted. After the third visit, however, she laughed when they laughed, and joined in their conversation a few times. After an early supper with them, Wŏn'gu had decided to leave, but a heavy rain compelled him to remain. He had stood hesitantly by the window, umbrella in hand, looking out into the grey curtain of rain. Tonguk said he should not be obstinate and should stay overnight. Then he heard Tongok say that after such a heavy rain he would not be able to cross the swollen stream.

That night, for the first time, Wŏn'gu was able to speak to her with a light heart. When he asked her how long she had painted, she smiled gloomily and said she did not think of her portraits as painting. Wŏn'gu was careful in his choice of words; he did not want to hurt her feelings. When their talk drifted to their childhood days, he told her that whenever she doggedly tagged along after him he had been annoyed with her, and also that she went around proudly singing a song about the little bonze. Her eyes lit up for the first time. When Tonguk abruptly sang that song, she joined him in a soft voice. When they stopped singing, the sound of falling water became louder, filling the room. A strong wind caused the water to seep through the wall of boards and then into a corner of the inside wall.

There was one thing Wŏn'gu could not understand —Tonguk's attitude toward his sister. On trifling matters he shouted and swore at her. When she took the dishes in one hand, as he passed them from the kitchen, he glared at her, shouting that she should take them with both hands. When she failed to light the oil lamp with the first match, he would again shout at her, saying she was not good even at lighting the lamp. On such occasions, she would glare back without word.

Tongok did the washing and sewing, and Tonguk the cooking. When she left the room for the toilet, Wŏn'gu asked him why he treated her so badly instead of comforting her. Tonguk replied that a cripple was never amiable and that she had never been good-natured. Until recently, the income from the portraits had been equally divided, but lately she had become distrustful of her brother, and unless he paid in advance for her work, according to the size of the picture, she would not start drawing. He also added that they shared their living expenses. But she insisted that, being a cripple, her parents were the only ones likely to look after her, that her brother would one day desert her, and that she had to make provisions against having to live in utter misery. When he was not with her, Tonguk pitied her for her wretched thoughts, but when with her he became irascible in spite of himself.

Tongok could not sleep with the light off, for loneliness; Tonguk could sleep only with the light out, darkness being his only privacy. During the daytime, try as he might, he could not relieve himself of accumulated fatigue; he felt like a soaked rag. Tonguk became angry when he saw Tongok turn down the wick, and shouted at her to put the light out. She stretched out her hand to turn the wick farther down, and grumbled that she would have been happier had she been left with her mother. At this, Tonguk suddenly sat up and shouted angrily that if she ever said another such word he would break her neck. He had never wanted to bring her along, and would not have done so were it not for their mother's appeal. Tongok silently turned away.

The lamp was dim, but the heaviness of darkness weighed Wŏn'gu down unbearably, and he could not fall asleep. Tonguk too was awake. Tongok was also not sleeping, but keeping very still. As he heard the raindrops slash against the window frames, Wŏn'gu thought of Noah's Ark.

As time passed, he became sleepier. Then he heard Tonguk asking if he had enough courage to marry Tongok, out of pity. It seemed like a nightmare. Wŏn'gu opened his eyes and stared at the ceiling without moving, waiting for Tonguk to continue. However, he did not utter another word; there was only the sound of falling water in the darkness.

When Wŏn'gu began to fall asleep again, he heard a strange sound, like gritting teeth near the wall at his feet. He listened carefully. It sounded like a frog being swallowed by a snake, and it came from beyond the wall. He quickly sat up. At this moment, Tonguk also opened his eyes. To Wŏn'gu's inquiry, he answered that it was the sound of a girl in the next room gnashing her teeth in her sleep. When Wŏn'gu asked if people lived in the room, Tonguk replied that an old woman over sixty lived there with a granddaughter of twelve. According to him, the old woman was the owner of the house and eked out a meager living by selling cigarets, matches, fruit, and candy at the streetcar terminal. The girl, it seemed, always gnashed her teeth in her sleep. He said that he was annoyed with it at the beginning, but was now accustomed to it. Thinking that anyone would be driven to neurosis living in a room with rain leaks and the sound of gnashing teeth, Wŏn'gu brooded over what Tonguk had said a while before.

Four or five days passed. One evening when the rain cleared up and the skies were somewhat brighter, Wŏn'gu was standing behind his cart with various goods spread out on it when someone tapped him on the shoulder. It was Tonguk. He was still clad in the same threadbare jacket and checkered grey trousers. These were his only clothes, wrinkled all over from constant wearing. His shoes with the big, round toes, worn in place of rubber boots or overshoes, were caked with mud. Wŏn'gu felt a strange affection toward Tonguk's appearance.

He left the cart with the man who rented it to him and took Tonguk to dinner. Tonguk said he would rather have drinks than a meal, so they went into a chophouse where they could have both. After several rounds, Tonguk was getting quite drunk and said that he had quit taking orders for portaits. Recently the American soldiers had become shrewd; they did not pay his fees and often cheated him. Moreover, the guards at the gate barred the entrance of those without passes. Recently he had sneaked into a compound to collect money due him and, having been caught by an orderly officer, spent a night in jail.

In addition, he had lost his military service card and could not go around easily without being caught by the police. Wŏn'gu asked why he did not get another card. Tonguk said he had applied several times at the ward office and the police station, but the clerks had just harassed him with trifles. He decided to resign himself to these facts. However, he thought about entering military service, since he had heard that they were recruiting interpreter officers. He went to get application forms.

When Wŏn'gu asked to see them, he grinned and replied that the procedures were so complicated that he had given that up too.

Tonguk silently licked his glass for a while and then asked Wŏn'gu to come and comfort his sister. Assuming that everyone in the world laughed at her, Tongok stayed in the house like a toad, even on fine days, and harbored ill feelings toward everyone. She thought that only Wŏn'gu did not despise her and was kind toward her, so she longed to see him. Since the portrait business broke up, she had become increasingly lonely. Tonguk added that he couldn't bear to look at her. Then, as he had said that previous night, if he were Wŏn'gu, he would surely marry her, and he nodded reassuringly.

Out of the chophouse, Tonguk again took Wŏn'gu's hand and declared that he would become a minister, the only way for Tongok and himself to get rid of the overwhelming burden they had lived under for so long.

Soon after, Wŏn'gu stopped at Tonguk's home on his way to some business. The rainy season still persisted. When he got to the veranda and stood folding his umbrella, Tonguk came out to receive him, but there was no sign of Tongok. As he entered the room, he found her lying with the blanket drawn over her head like a corpse. Tonguk said she had been in bed for two days.

She had loaned twenty thousand wŏn[1] to the old woman in the next room, without his knowledge, but the woman had disappeared, disposing of the house. They had discovered it the day before, when the new owner had moved in and had begun harassing them to vacate the room at once.

On finishing his explanation, he shouted at Tongok how stupid she was to lend the old woman money for that crumbling old shack, and then he kicked her in the side. He continued that twenty thousand wŏn was a fortune corresponding to two hundred thousand hwan in the old currency. Why should he bother with her when she had lost her own money? Why, she could not even live without him. Surely, a cripple could never live alone for a month. He could hardly suppress his resentment, it seemed. Tonguk wanted to prepare vinegared rice for Wŏn'gu, and busied himself in the kitchen, but Wŏn'gu could not bear to sit in the room. He felt uneasy and wondered if she had swallowed sleeping pills and was already dead, especially since Tonguk said that she had been lying there for two days. While Wŏn'gu was there, she didn't move once.

He could not stand the situation any longer. Standing up to go, he said to Tonguk that he would find a room for them, if they had to move out immediately. Tonguk said he had no choice but to try to find a place least frequented, for Tongok never liked to live among other people.

Wŏn'gu too began to feel threatened. He had not run his business for nearly a month because of the rain, and his meager investments were dwindling. In his rented room, his clothes and bedding were damp and musty. He felt that even his mind was becoming musty. To stay in a musty room on such a day was unbearable, and he could not shake off his gloomy thoughts of Tonguk and Tongok.

About lunch time, he left his room in the teeth of rain. He wanted to relieve his mind and heart about Tonguk and comfort the unhappy Tongok, so he bought a few cans of food and a bottle of wine.

The dilapidated house was still standing in the rain, ready to fall down any minute. Behind the window, the

straw bag still hung as before. When he called out for
Tonguk, a man crept like a bear out of the room; it was
not Tonguk. To Wŏn'gu's question about where the young
man and his sister had gone, the man, about forty, who was
rough in appearance but looked not unkind, asked
whether he was Chŏng Wŏn'gu. The man said he was
the new owner of the house and that Tonguk had not
returned one day. After that, Tongok had also left the
house, but he did not know where they had gone. It had
been nearly ten days since Tonguk's departure; Tongok
had been gone for only two or three days.

Wŏn'gu stood there in silence for a while, a bundle
in one hand and an open umbrella in the other, and
stared vacantly at the man. He turned and walked away
a few steps, but came back to the man, unwrapped the
things and gave them to him. Expressing his gratitude
with a broad smile, the man said that his wife and children had gone out peddling and although he could not
offer lunch, Wŏn'gu should come in and have a chat.

When Wŏn'gu told him that he didn't feel like staying, the man called him back and with an apology said
that Tongok had left a note for him, but that he had mis-
placed it. Later he learned that his children had torn it
to pieces. Wŏn'gu stood there unable to speak, staring at
the man blankly. The man became more apologetic, and
said that Tonguk had probably been whisked into the
army, and as for Tongok, she was crying and calling for
her mother like a lost child, but he had scolded her, and
she had left the house the next evening. As Wŏn'gu
turned around, asking himself whether she was dead or
had committed suicide, or perhaps even had died of star-
vation, the man said to his back that she had taken her
belongings with her, so that she would not have had any
thought of killing herself. Although she was a cripple,

she could make her own living, since she was pretty, he added.

Hearing that she was pretty and could make her own living, Wŏn'gu turned around at once. He almost exploded at the man, shouting in his mind that he had sold her out. However, he was unable to hold up his head, which had suddenly become very heavy, so he just walked on without saying another word. The next moment, he felt as if he heard a distant voice shouting at him that he himself had sold out Tongok; he shivered. He staggered in the rain like a convalescent, along the bank overgrown with pumpkin vines.

The Author

Son Ch'angsŏp was born in P'yongyang in 1922 and left Nihon University in 1946 without earning a degree. He moved to South Korea in 1948. "The Rainy Season," first published in the journal Munye *in November 1953, was one of his earliest works. In 1959 he was awarded the fourth Tongin Prize for another story. His selected works appeared in five volumes (1970).*

A relentless researcher into the conscience of the lost generation, Son's characters are mostly the handicapped— a cripple, a consumptive, an epileptic—who view others as selfish, hypocritical enemies, and who indulge in sardonic self-mockery and cynical self-abandonment. The mentally and physically disabled, crouching in a dark room (or cave) on a rainy day, devoid of will power to order their lives, are powerless against the tragic solitude that devours them. Son often reproaches these men, but still tries to sympathize with their anguish. In an age where success means money and conscience is foolishness, a symbol of authority—as one character was made to say—is a rubber doll and a beautiful woman, a lump of fat. Their lives are caricatures, as titles of some of his other stories suggest—"Chalk Mark Tribes" and "Human Zoo." The spiritual ruin brought about by the disintegration of values and the dehumanization of society has been his major concern.

by An Sugil

A Third Kind of Man

t was Saturday afternoon.

Even the children who had been bustling about with brooms and with buckets of water for the weekly cleaning session had gone home. From the first-year classroom, which was set apart from the others, came the sound of the high-school choir at practice, their voices blending pleasantly with the tune of the harmonium. Apart from five or six boys sweating in their shirtsleeves at basketball practice on the playground, the classrooms and yards, where fifteen hundred or more children had been packed in like sardines wriggling in a net, were now deserted. It was not so much like a summer resort out of season, as like the empty feeling after a great banquet is over: the languor of the mind relaxing in grateful tiredness. That was Sŏk's state of mind as he slouched in his chair in the staff room, gazing out the window.

Fortunately his chair was set in a place where he

Translated by Richard Rutt

could sit and look out at the sea. If he looked up, he could see beyond the breakwater, between the jutting cliff where the school stood and Yŏngdo Island lying out over the mirrorlike sea through which the sleek passenger boat from Yŏsu would plow as it traveled back and forth. On a very clear day he could see Tsushima in a mauve mist on the horizon far to the south. With the seagulls skimming the surface of the waves in playful groups, and the dark brown of a sailing boat gliding slowly in front of the low hills of the island, the scene made a beautiful picture.

But that Saturday afternoon the view through the window was dull. He could see no elegant passenger ferry nor romantic sailing junk, not even the mauve blur of a foreign land on the horizon. Only an old motor boat, chugging away like an asthmatic old man, slowly crossed the roadstead between the cliff and the island. When the boat had passed out of sight there was nothing to be seen but the smooth outline of the island and the depressing sight of the honeycombed shacks gleaming in the fading sunshine of a late winter afternoon on the island called Second Songdo. This was the everlastingly unchanging view from the staff-room window: a miserable sketch of an empty stage, with nothing but a backdrop.

However, this motionless picture was peculiarly in accord with Sŏk's feelings of satisfaction after school was over on this particular day. The week's work done, he felt as if he had laid down a heavy burden. Tomorrow would be Sunday, and his contentment was increased by the promise of a day of complete freedom. Sŏk lazily began to fill the empty stage with plans of what he would do with his Sunday.

Maybe he would sleep late and then in the afternoon go out to see R at Haeundae. R traded in souvenirs for the American troops and probably had other, less mentionable, interests, for he seemed to have money. He had asked Sŏk to visit him. "I'm so busy, I have no chance to rest even if I want to, but if you come I shall have a good excuse to forget everything for a day." Quite apart from R's invitation, Sŏk was inclined to go because after three years in Pusan he had still not yet seen Haeundae.

But when he thought of the tiring journey on the packed bus, his laziness overcame him, and he just didn't feel like going. "If you invite a friend, you ought to fetch him or at least send a hired car." As he was kidding himself with this impertinence, an expensive car purred onto the empty stage and stopped in front of the staff room. The door opened and a good-looking man got out. Sŏk saw him walking toward the staff room and rose from his chair.

Sŏk met the visitor at the door and grasped his hand.

"What cloud have you come from, to appear suddenly like this?"

"Some wind must have blown it this way."

"I'm glad I lived long enough to see it happen."

"There's no choice. Life is grim, but one has to hang on."

"I sometimes wondered whether you were dead."

"You should have held a memorial service."

Sŏk led him to his desk and sat him down in an empty chair beside it. Most of the teachers had gone home for the weekend and the staff room, which could be as noisy as a marketplace when all fifty-odd people were there, was now quiet. The few who still had desk work to do looked up from their papers at Sŏk and his noisy friend Choun. Their eyes were full of curiosity, but this was not because of the expensive car, nor because of the way the two friends were talking loudly together as though there were nobody else in the room. What struck them was that the two men seemed to be on the most intimate terms, though one was exceedingly rich and the other extremely shabby. The difference in their appearances matched so ill with their behavior as to suggest that they were animated characters from a comic strip. The other teachers were intrigued.

Sŏk himself was astonished at the change in the appearance of his writer friend Choun; a change that was too great for him to register all at once. He had unthinkingly begun the conversation with the sort of banter that had been normal between them in earlier days, but he was soon brought up sharply by the contrast with his own shabbiness and felt a bit intimidated.

"How do you come to look so well? That good suit and expensive hat and the big car you came in. The world must have changed a bit."

"Looks like a miracle, doesn't it?"

Indeed, it did look like a miracle. Choun had been a writer who dealt with specialized philosophical questions in an obstinately obscure style. He was respected among literary men for his loyalty to his ideals, and many girls admired him. Maybe it was their curiosity about the obscurity of his work and his image, and maybe they were just girls who did not care for ordinary everyday things. On the other hand he was also a man with many literary enemies and, because of his turgid style, he had comparatively few readers.

"I have no room for a man who does not earn his success," was his criterion for humanity and literature. Forever cogitating, and accepting as truth only what he himself had arrived at by mental effort, he produced little and was always poor. Thanks to his forceful wife, his children did not starve, but he was as careless of them as he was of his appearance. He never appeared in public. Weddings and funerals were a headache to him. He gave no thought to greetings and farewells.

Seeing what had become of this Choun, one had to grant a miracle.

"I am glad you call it a miracle."

Choun did not reply to this. He changed the subject.

"I'd thought you'd be gone by this time on a Saturday. I'm glad I caught you."

"Seems I must have been waiting for you. I was just on the point of leaving. But what have you come for?"

Sŏk was often visited by friends seeking to transfer children to the school. The school had a rigid rule that forbade the acceptance of late entries, and he had more than once been embarrassed by having to refuse his friends. Such people frequently came to the school by car because it was far out of town, and he wondered whether this was the purpose of Choun's visit.

But Choun said, "Is it all right for you to leave now? Let's go out together."

"After all this time I want to have a good chat with you, but . . . what is your errand? Is it to transfer some child?"

The vice-principal of the school had not yet left, and if this impossible matter were to come up, Sŏk would take it straight to the man responsible.

"No, nothing like that. Transfer a child?" And shaking his head, he repeated, "No."

"Then let's go."

Sŏk did not think of going with Choun, but intended to take him to a little chophouse nearby where he ate on credit and paid up every payday. But when they went out, Choun opened the car door and said:

"Get in."

It was clearly an order. Sŏk protested, but was practically thrown onto the car cushions and stood little chance of resisting. The car glided forward. As they passed through the school gate, the driver turned around and said, "Where do you want to go?"

"Where we went yesterday."

The car gathered speed. Neither of the two men spoke before the car came out in the square at Ch'ungmu Street. Choun sat proud and plump with his arms folded, sunk into the cushions with his eyes closed, apparently thinking something over. The puzzled Sŏk stole sidelong glances at the complicated expression that was drawn on his fine, healthy face.

He had last seen him the day after the invasion, on the fourth floor of the K newspaper building. Sŏk was working there then, and Choun had listened to a news broadcast with a lowering expression on his dark face. It was impossible to distinguish fact from fancy in the broadcasts, news agency reports, and army reports at that time. Sŏk could not recall what the news item they heard had been about, but he remembered Choun looking worried, grimacing, and going out. During the ninety dark days that followed, they did not meet again, nor did Choun appear when Seoul was recaptured. He did not reappear, that is, in their old world of writers and tearooms.

At first there were many guesses as to what had become of him. He had defected to the North, he had been captured and kidnapped, he had been killed in a bombardment; but when Sŏk got to Pusan after the January retreat it was reported in the papers that Choun had been one of the first of the refugees to arrive, held an important post in a motor business, and had made plenty of money.

Sŏk was not the only one to be astonished by this news. No one could help being surprised that Choun, with his martyr's devotion to literature, had turned out like this. At that time his friends, who had fled to Pusan in the clothes they stood up in, were congregating in the corners of tearooms, facing a black future, not knowing where their family would sleep that night, nor where their next meal was coming from. Choun's unexpected good fortune sent ripples through them.

"He's done well. Farewell to the life of a writer and poverty."

They had done nothing but get their names into print, had faced more misery and poverty than most but had nearly overcome these, and now just as they were getting back on their feet, their future was again threatened. In the impotent leisure of literary life they envied Choun.

An inimical group sought cynically for the reason why he had defected from literature; other "friends" hurried to sponge off him.

But he was not in Pusan. He had been there for a while soon after the retreat, but now he had covered his tracks completely. "He's off with one of those girls that trailed him." "So? A neat escape. That's the way to live a refugee life!"

Such rumors circulated, but Choun eventually passed out of mind. Three years passed. During that time, he did not let even Sŏk, who had been his best friend in his literary days, know where he was living. What had he been doing? It was not just a matter of looking well, being well dressed, and going about in a fine car. His spirit had improved with his exterior circumstances. Perhaps he had spent a happy three years with one of those admiring girls. But that could not be all. His detractors would like to have seen him buried.

He had never written to attract his readers, but only to exercise them in self-awareness. It was unlikely that he had really completely cut himself off from writing. During the three years of idleness he could have perfected his style. Maybe he had produced some masterpiece and now had it stowed in the car and had appeared suddenly like this to get a reaction to it.

Sitting there on the cushions with his arms folded and his mouth shut, he looked to Sŏk like a man of importance. He seemed to have forgotten Sŏk's existence, and every now and then nodded his head in secret delight over something that he was thinking about. When Sŏk recalled the man who used to sit in the corner of a tearoom unashamedly chain-smoking, not good foreign cigarets, but those wretched "Peacocks," he felt overcome.

But this was not entirely due to Choun. Sŏk was always liable to blame himself, and his present unhappy feelings may have been partly due to excessive self-reproach on seeing the happy condition of his friend. He was rather like some wretched coward of a soldier who takes fright and runs at the sight and sound of the enemy.

Sŏk had gone into school work at the time when the political upheaval had been at its height. For two months he had tasted the bitterness of unemployment and needed some means for filling his stomach. He had only one kind of ability and experience and would have to work at something cultural. But in that field things were at their worst. The printed word, drawings, songs: all had been turned to propaganda purposes. People's ideas rubbed off on each other like sparks from friction.

Sŏk had no taste for politics and did not wish to

plunge himself into that storm. But his children were whining for their rice, and his wife complained continually. The old people sighed. For the sake of these wasting, hungry, ill-clothed people, suffering through no fault of their own, maybe he would have to take up some uncongenial work. If he just took whatever came along, they would be able to eat.

Clutching his empty stomach, he had to walk fast through the crowded streets, a lost man. To Sŏk in this state, the school was like a paradise. When, with the help of a friend, he first went into the school compound he felt his nerves come to rest as he saw the boys brightly and bravely learning and playing, out of reach of the political storms. In his free time, he would stand at ease on the rocks at the end of the playground, listening to the sound of the waves as they cast their snowlike spume at his feet; and as he looked at the dust that hung over Dragon's Head Hill and the weather observatory, he felt as though all the grime were being washed from him.

A producer friend of his met him in the street. "What are you doing these days?"

"I'm teaching in a school."

"What school?"

"Y School."

"Ah, that's good."

"Why?"

"I teach in a college now—it's like taking a bath."

"A bath?"

"After I've chattered to the students for a couple of hours of a morning, I feel like I've just come out of the bath . . ."

A bath! Thinking of it like that, Sŏk found it good that he had landed in a school. His monthly pay too was regular and reliable. Now he would be able to arrange his life better, and would not be forced to sell silly pieces of writing that he was not really interested in. He would have time to write what he liked. Gazing at the islands around Yŏngdo, which sometimes looked like kettles and sometimes like lumbering tanks, he spread his chest and drank in the clean air.

But the summer and winter vacations had passed; in a few weeks the school year would end, and he had written nothing; he had not even sold an odd article for ready cash. The teaching life was not all that good. It was a constant succession of trivial jobs. The demands of the students meant that, even though he taught for only three hours a day, he had to strain his nerves for twenty-four hours to do justice to each one of the boys.

It took an hour and a half to walk home, and it was not easy to use a bus or tram to get there. The streets were dreary, with never so much as a blossom showing over the wooden fences, and on wet days, they were ankle-deep in mud. In the morning, he walked along rubbing his eyes; and in the evening, he came home so tired that he dropped off to sleep and slept like a log till morning. The idea of leisure for writing flowed away from him like the strength that drained away when he sat down at his desk, flogging his tired body and confused brain, to write in the little red squares of the manuscript paper. Power would ebb from the pen in his hand and, as his eyelids involuntarily closed, he would surrender and lie back on the floor muttering, "Teaching is a worthwhile job. Better become a good educator."

But Sŏk was still unproved at teaching; he was nothing more than an extra on the set. When he thought of the ideal he had cultivated faithfully for twenty years, and how one morning he had simply taken to chalk in place of the pen, he felt that he was a traitor to himself.

Yet if he tried to return to his loyalty and foresake school, he would only be abandoning his livelihood. For more than ten months now he had been daily toting his heavy briefcase, loaded with his lunch box and his manuscript paper, back and forth through the dreary streets, neither faithful to his avocation nor able to extricate himself from it. His discontent was mounting.

He could escape only into enjoyment of the seascape around the school, a lazy man looking forward to Sunday once every seven days. That was the reason why he was overwhelmed by Choun.

As the car turned at the Ch'ungmu circle, a boy crossing the road recognized Sŏk in the car and saluted him. Sŏk nodded to him.

Choun turned and spoke with a chuckle as he saw the greeting between teacher and pupil. "You've got the teacher's manner properly." Sŏk blushed a little, as though he had been caught in the wrong. Choun spoke again, "Have you been teaching for a year yet?"

"In three or four months' time it will be a year . . . but how did you know that I was teaching?"

"I knew all about it. Not just about you. I know all about the literary world."

There was nothing extraordinary in knowing what was in the papers, but Sŏk thought that if Choun, who was assumed to have rejected the world of letters, had been keeping an eye on it from his hideout, then for sure he was intending to surprise the lesser fry with a masterpiece.

"Then where were you so that we heard nothing of you?"

"In Chŏlla today, in Kangwŏn tomorrow, flashing from east to west."

"So you weren't in Pusan?"

"I came back to Pusan less than a fortnight ago."

"Is it true you are working in a motor business?"

"Of course."

"So this is your own car?"

"I bought it to let it out for hire."

"Then the rumors were true."

"There must have been all kinds of stories . . ."

"At first they said you had been killed by a bomb, or defected and gone north."

"They said I had gone north?"

"That you had a good job in a motor business, that you were among the first to flee, that you had made a pile . . . "

Choun grunted. Sŏk hesitated before he spoke again, with a light laugh: "Didn't you expect them to say that you were living with one of your literary females?"

Choun did not answer this, but his face set again. Silence returned to the car.

When Sŏk was going to and from school he cursed people with cars every time he crossed the street; but now, although it was only his friend's car, he leaned back on the cushions and stared through the windows at the people crossing the road, watching their various movements with the fascination of a child. Thinking of nothing else, he took no notice of Choun's expression.

"I wonder where he is taking me? Are we just driving round the suburbs?"

Sŏk suddenly remembered a story a friend of his had written before the war. It told how the friend had hired a car for a day and told the driver to take him around and about, wherever he liked, all day long. It had cost ten thousand wŏn in the old money, and the story had regretted the waste of money. It would be one way to relax a worried mind or a weary spirit, though not particularly pleasant or interesting, but Sŏk was now in much the same state of mind as the narrator and he laughed to think that he was living out his friend's story.

Supposing that by some miracle ten thousand wŏn should come into his hands today, and he could use it just as he liked, he doubted that he or even that friend would now want to hire a car for a whole day. His mind came back to harsh realities but, in spite of the thought, a smile was playing on his lips when the car turned into an alley in Pumin-dong and came to a stop in front of a Chinese restaurant, the Kwanhae Pavilion.

"Have you got any decent Chinese corn spirits?"

"Yes, we have."

The waiter brought towels, and while Choun was wiping his face and ordering the food, Sŏk asked him, "Are you going to have a drink?"

"Of course. Have you decided just to eat without drinking, then?"

Even if Choun had not spoken, Sŏk would have felt a fool for asking such a silly question.

"Well, no, but . . . "

Choun interrupted him suddenly: "You're trying to avoid drinking!"

Sŏk was not actually a teetotaler but he thought he ought to be chary of drinking. He had been taught to drink by his father, and had acquired good habits. When he drank a little he was a witty conversationalist and sang well, so that people enjoyed his presence in drinking company. Indeed, after he became a teacher he was very popular with his fellows at their parties. After work, when his spirits were low, he would allow himself to be persuaded by his more congenial friends to go drinking in a chophouse, sharing the cost of Korean rice wine with them.

Lightened by wine, his imagination would begin to flourish, and he would start talking. His conversation was all right when he was actually drinking, but by the time he got home he would just be rambling on and would keep the family from sleeping, so that first thing in the morning he would have to face his wife's reproaches.

His talking was quite proper in itself, neither malicious nor liable to offend his family. "When 'The Narrow Gate' is published, five thousand copies at six thousand wŏn each means, at ten percent royalty, three million wŏn—that's what we shall get. We'll buy two bags of rice and store them in the cupboard, and let mother and father visit a temple, and what's the price of velvet now? If we're going to buy, we must buy the best. I'll buy you the very best velvet for a new skirt. I don't care if they do say those horrible trousers are good for working, we'll get rid of them, working clothes or not . . . "

When he carried on like this, his little daughter, who had crept under his quilt, would wake up and ask, "Buy something for me too, daddy!"

"Of course! I'll buy something for you too. What do you want?"

"A satchel for my school books."

"So that's it. Of course we'll buy one. Is that all? A smart coat, new shoes . . . "

Then his little boy, who was in the last year at primary school, would speak up with, "I need a hundred and fifty thousand wŏn for graduation."

"A hundred and fifty thousand? All right. Is that all? I haven't once been to see your teacher. We must take him out sometime and make a present to the school."

The little lad, who was always ashamed that he could

not pay up his debts at school, was delighted to hear this sort of thing.

"I don't know about velvet and all that, but there are a lot of back payments to be made at the school, and rice to buy to fill the children's stomachs in the long summer days," was his wife's reaction.

His mother was more interested in buying a supply of tonics than in improving their appearance, and his father told him not to wear himself out teaching school, but to stay at home and write for a living.

"Just hold on for a while. The book will soon be out, and then the royalties will start coming in. I'll get better and my face will fill out . . . "

All the family was then happy, but days, weeks, and months passed, and the royalties from the book did not appear, nor did a fee for an article churned out in his spare time. The family was deceived a few times, and then grew tired of his boasting. Not only that, but because of his loud voice his wife could no longer borrow rice from the neighbors. The people living in the rooms on either side, separated from them only by paper walls, heard all his wine-fed hopes, and made it trying for his wife when she went borrowing.

"No rice in your house? You always sound all right."

"Who cries when they've no need?"

"Doesn't your husband teach at school? And won't that book bring in three or four million wŏn?"

After being crushed by remarks like these, she would go for him.

"You with your silly drunken fancies. They do nothing but make people laugh at your wife."

"Isn't that better than saying, 'I give up, let's starve to death?'"

"If we are poor, better to admit it. Your stupid talk makes the neighbors think we are not."

"Isn't it better than saying we've nothing?"

"You want to pick your teeth after a drink of water?"

"You've got to pick your teeth sometimes."

"I can't borrow a grain of rice, but little you care!"

"If they won't lend it, stop bothering them."

After that the effects of Sŏk's drinking changed. Wine now made him cry. He was coming home as usual after drinking in the chophouse with his friends. It was a moonlit night. He was carrying his heavy briefcase in one hand, with the other stuck in his coat pocket, and as he turned by the city hall he bumped into a businessman friend of his.

"Is that you?"

They wrung one another's hands, and suddenly Sŏk burst into pointless, uncontrolled weeping. This friend was an affectionate person, but he was embarrassed to be seen in the street with his wailing friend.

"Sŏk, wherever did you get so drunk? You could hurt yourself!"

He put his hand on Sŏk's shoulder and hailed a passing taxi. He put Sŏk into it and then got in himself. As the car started off, Sŏk buried his face in his friend's thick overcoat and wailed, "Poor Sŏk! I have no luck! No luck at all."

"Things will change. The sun will shine again."

His friend patted Sŏk's shoulders as he tried to comfort him, but after he had left him at his home, Sŏk lay on the floor crying his heart out. His wife and the old people were miserable. His father puffed at his pipe and said, "You have to take the rough with the smooth. Things will get better. No need to carry on like that."

His mother blew her nose piously and said, "When your health is good, what's a little difficulty like this? The children are growing up fine . . . "

His wife came and put a pillow under his head and stroked him and straightened the quilt, "Stop crying and go to sleep. It will all turn out all right."

That night he fell asleep quickly, but as he got into the habit of coming home drunk and weepy, the family soon stopped comforting him and shook their heads in despair.

"Crying like a baby . . . " was his father's angry reaction. And in the morning his wife scolded him.

"Is this just a modern comedy? Even good news is boring after hearing it the third time, but this everlasting wailing . . . "

"And who complained that good news made the neighbors so that they would not lend a handful of rice?"

"Didn't I tell you to stop drinking?"

"If I can't even enjoy a drink, I might as well give up."

"Oh, you're impossible!"

Ten days later, Sŏk was out with his friends again and drank too much on an empty stomach. On his way home that night, he got his face bloodied. The family was astonished. After the doctor had attended to the cuts, Sŏk could remember nothing except that he had been drinking. Until then the family had been considerate of his only pleasure, but now all of them had to be harder with him.

"Look. You may get killed when you're drunk. You need your wits about you in busy traffic."

Sŏk saw the idiocy of it and said, "I must stop drinking."

But you do not stop smoking and drinking simply by

vowing to. Drinkers cut their fingers off to seal a vow of abstinence, and then have a drink to their lips again before the wounds are healed. It is not a matter of will but of biology. Sŏk was not a smoker, and he was not incapable of giving up wine, but he did not want to do so entirely. He did not want to become the sort of man who turns his glass over at a party or leaves early. The point was to be restrained about drinking. When he had been happy with his work there had been no problem. A miser refuses drink not simply to save money, but to be faithful to his aim of hoarding useless money, and priests who drink don't get drunk. When Sŏk came round he did not drink for a month.

Choun spoke as though he was able to drink a good deal. "What's your limit if you drink and then stop?"

"Not enough to talk of giving it up, but I think I shall have to," Sŏk grinned.

"You seem ten years older. Have you suffered a lot? I wouldn't have known you at the schoolroom door. How did you become so much the teacher?"

"If you think I'm a typical teacher after only a year, I'm sorry. But I wouldn't have known you either. A lean nose and sunken eyes were your trademark, and if they had changed I would hardly have recognized you."

Choun did not answer, so Sŏk spoke again. "I would like to know what happened during those three years. Didn't we last see each other in the newspaper office at the invasion?"

"Never mind. My story comes later. Tell me about yourself."

The food came in.

"Let's eat."

The fragrance of warm wine rose from the china cups. They both drank a little. Choun picked up a piece of sea cucumber in his chopsticks. Sŏk recalled that they are said to be full of hormones and smiled to himself. Choun took another big piece and, as he was chewing it, said, "I was a renegade for three years."

"A renegade? I thought you looked as if things had been going very well with you."

Choun's expression was complex. He drained a cup of wine, then handed the empty cup to Sŏk. The cup went back and forth; Sŏk's face grew hot. It was his first drink in a month, and he was enjoying it along with the good food. He felt like talking.

"I have been in dire straits and pretty wretched, but you've been pretty comfortable, haven't you? I am sure you've been writing and produced something good."

"Writing?"

"Yes."

Choun bowed his head for a moment, then suddenly got up and took something out of the inside pocket of his coat, which he had hung nearby.

"Look at this."

Sŏk unwrapped the paper from the packet and stared at it with amazement.

"What is it?"

It was a white envelope on top of a new black necktie. The envelope was formally and simply addressed to Choun in what was unmistakably a woman's handwriting. Choun took out the letter and handed it to Sŏk.

"Read it."

"May I?"

"Yes. Go on."

It was a short and simple note.

Sir: You have been extremely kind to me, but I have made up my mind about the future. Without telling you, I have applied to take the nursing officer's examination. The exam is not till Monday at Taegu, but I am leaving now to get ready for it.

Your necktie disappeared that time at the house. This is to replace it. A black tie seems to suit you best.

Yours, Miyi

"Miyi?" queried Sŏk, "Is it *that* Miyi?" He was slightly surprised.

"Yes."

Miyi was a girl who had admired Choun. Sŏk also had known her. Had Choun run off with Miyi, then, as rumor said, and spent three years with her? He remembered Choun's silence in the car when he had chaffed him about running away. So his much admired Choun had become just a buyer and seller! He did not care for the vision of Choun living by the turning of motor wheels. His heart suddenly felt full. He spoke fiercely.

"Then you did run off and live with Miyi, just as they said?"

"No, I did not. Nothing of the sort."

Choun said no more. He closed his eyes for a moment and then opened them. He drank some wine and appeared to have made up his mind to talk.

You remember that Miyi was one of the literary girls who ran after me. She was always saying that she would write a novel. She was quite different from me, bright and gay and frivolous. You remember how she used to flit about a tearoom, chattering about this poet and that writer. Far from writing a novel, she looked as though she could not write even a line in a diary. I had no great opinion of her, but one day she brought me a hundred or so pages of manuscript, and I was very much surprised. It was limpid writing, like Katherine Mansfield's. She portrayed a character recalling witty Bertha Young in "Happiness." Of course it was all very immature, but I thought that with training something could be made of her. I became interested in her, and after that I thought her sprightliness was a sign of her intelligence. I could recognize a new sensibility in her twittering. Her comments on people in tearooms were devastating. I discovered that she was the daughter of an executive. She had left college in the middle of a medical course in order to write. Her only brother, older than she, worked in a bank.

Of course her sensibility was due to her coming from a good family. I tried to encourage her not to bury herself in some magazine or newspaper office. Then one day she introduced her brother to me. He was quite unlike her, rather solemn. He greeted me politely and said that as Miyi seemed to have a literary bent they were considering letting her follow it, and asked me to advise them. I demurred, but after that Miyi was always hanging around me, wherever I went.

One day she pointed to my necktie.

"Why do you always wear a black tie?"

"Is it black?"

I became conscious of my old black tie and fingered it with a smile.

It doesn't mean anything. It's the only one I have."

"Isn't it a sign of mourning for humanity?"

"Mourning? If you fret over things like that, you'll wear yourself out with worrying about your clothes."

"Every time I see you, you have a black tie, so I thought you must be in mourning."

"You can think that if you like."

"Do you know Chekhov's *Seagull*? I was reading it last night. The captain's daughter, Masha, always wears black clothes. When the young man asks her why she wears black all the time, that's what she answers. Mourning for humanity."

"So she does. But there's nothing symbolic about my necktie."

"But a black tie suits your attitude."

"What do you mean?"

"Standing aloof from the world—frowning at it. But I don't see the world as it is in the *Seagull*."

"You mean you're not pessimistic?"

"Of course not."

"That's a good idea."

"Isn't it? I think that it's too wonderful just to have been born."

"What?"

"Before I was born my mother had a miscarriage. She was only four months gone. And then two months later I was conceived. I don't know whether it was a brother or a sister, but had it been born in the ordinary way, I would never have seen the world, would I?"

"Of course not."

"When I think of that, it's marvelous to have been born."

"That's why you're so cheerful."

"Why shouldn't I be cheerful?"

Then she suddenly stopped laughing.

"Why don't you take a more cheerful view of life? Be a bit smarter, take the creases out of your forehead. But first of all, throw that tie away. Here, come with me."

She grabbed my arm and pulled me off to the Tonghwa department store.

"Now just wait. I'll choose one for you."

She chose one with a red dahlia on a dark blue background and tied it around my neck there and then, tucking the old black one away in her handbag.

A few days later, the war came. For three months I was off with my family hiding in my wife's people's place in a village near Suwŏn. I heard all about the doings of the Communists and got a clearer view of the worst side of humanity. They came again and again. Families that had lived there for generations, worked, married, and died there, were entirely destroyed. Men were killed like flies. I grew weak in my hiding place under my wife's uncle's house. Though I was in constant fear of the enemy, it was not their ferocity that was sapping my will to live. I was taking a lower view of life. Yet I began to think more sympathetically of humanity, and determined that if I lived through the war I would try to get the frown off my face. When I thought of what Miyi had said when she bought the necktie, I smiled to myself. Miyi was glad to think that she had been conceived as a result of her mother's miscarriage, but isn't anybody's conception due to fantastic luck among a myriad of spermatozoa? Thinking of the astronomical number of unborn brothers and sisters, who can fail to be thankful for his own birth? Of course it's a silly speculation, and you may laugh at it, but I tell you it's the way I was thinking at that time.

When Seoul was retaken in September, I admit it was not really that way of thinking that made me do it, but I joined up with my wife's uncle in a garage business. He was a smart man, and after the recapture of Seoul there was a great deal of transporting to be done. He added two more trucks to the one he already had, and practically ran them to pieces. He was still doing so when the January retreat happened. That made another opportunity; the money rolled in. I had never been so well off. Somehow or other I got settled in Kwangju, until I moved to Pusan to try a bus and taxi business.

Making money was new to me, and I did not notice how I was slipping into a new way of thinking. I began to despise my old life, frowning at the world, chain-smoking fifty or more cheap cigarets a day, cooped up in a tiny room, getting mad with the children, scribbling on manuscript paper. I scarcely realized how much better my face was looking, my forehead smoothed out, my mind freer. I slept well and ate well, and the color came back to my cheeks. My old life seemed nonsense. I had hoped to be another Flaubert, another Gide! But I had produced nothing worthwhile; only got my name in the papers so that the Communists were after me. So I dropped my pen name of Choun and returned to my ordinary name, Ch'oe Ch'unt'aek. You know the Chinese phrase: "In spring there's water everywhere." Business was good, I drank like a fish, and went after women as I felt like it.

On the afternoon of the day after I arrived in Pusan, I bought this car and was just going to the repair shop to see about some spare parts, when I saw Miyi crossing the road in front of the railway station. The car was going slowly, and I easily recognized her as she hesitated on the curb, deciding whether to cross the road or not. I stopped the car, opened the door, and leaned out and called her name. But she did not know who I was.

"Ch'oe Ch'unt'aek—I mean Choun!" I called out.

She recognized me.

"Choun," she said.

I got out of the car, told the driver to take it to the repair shop alone, and took Miyi to a nearby tearoom.

"How you have changed!" she said.

"Didn't you tell me to smooth out my forehead and take a happier view of the world?"

She did not answer.

"It seems that I did what you told me, and now you don't know me," I laughed. I expected her to laugh with me, but there was no reaction. Even in the street, before we went in the tearoom, I had noticed that she seemed to have grown soberer. In the old days in Seoul, she would have offered to order the tea and fetch a newspaper, and laughed and chatted, but now she just sat still and barely answered my questions.

"I've changed, but you've changed too. It's opposite to what it was in Seoul. I have become cheerful, and you've become gloomy. How have you grown so modest?"

She covered her mouth with her hand in an embarrassed giggle. "I was just thinking the same. The war seems to have changed our characters."

"Did you suffer much? Are your parents well? And your brother?"

"My brother is missing. Father is half paralyzed. The house was destroyed."

"Oh dear!"

I was about to say something kind and ask more details when she raised her head again and started talking.

The house was destroyed at the end of July, and nothing was saved from the wreckage. It was a wonder that they all survived. They moved from Yongsan to Anam-dong where they lived in one room of a relative's house. Miyi and her mother started trading in rice and kept themselves alive on gruel. Her brother had managed to hide, but ten days before Seoul was retaken he went out to learn what the news was and never came back. The parents were heartbroken when he did not reappear after the retaking of the city. They had not gotten over this before they had to join the retreat of January 4, and finally came to rest as refugees in Kimhae. To crown all their woes, her father had a cerebral hemorrhage and became partly paralyzed.

Her father's firm started up again in Pusan, but business was poor, and he was unable to do anything from his bed. He sold his shares for a song, and they lived off what they had left, but money ran out like dried persimmons off a stick, and a couple of months ago they themselves moved to Pusan where they got a shack, and her mother started selling bits and pieces of goods off a packing case outside the door. Miyi was looking for a job for herself.

I felt very upset to see the tears glistening in her eyes as she told her story. Her changed attitude was pitiful to behold. Could I restore her happy mood? Could I make her regain her sensibility? I was singleminded about helping her.

She finished her story and fell silent for a moment.

Suddenly she said, "Are you glad to be alive?" It was almost as though she were reproaching me.

I felt ashamed. Forcing myself to sound cheerful, I replied, "That question is most unlike you. The war has changed your view of life. You seem to have swung through 180 degrees and taken up pessimism."

"It's not pessimism."

"Not pessimism? That's all right, then. If it's not pessimism, it must be some kind of optimism."

"It's neither pessimism nor optimism."

"Is that so? Then it must be in between. There's no neutral position."

She smiled. "Where did you learn wit?"

It looked as though her gloom might clear, so I tried to recall the things she had liked to talk about in Seoul.

"It's nothing. Supposing one had not been born. You never know whether it was a brother or a sister who made way for you . . . "

"Your memory is good; you haven't forgotten that story. But I don't think about that. I am glad I was born. I'm grateful for it."

"If you say that, I feel better. In fact, your ideas haven't changed. Cheer up and be happy as you were in Seoul."

"Maybe my thinking has really changed."

"How? In what way?"

"People aren't born into this hard world for nothing. They must have a purpose."

"You mean we each have a mission?"

"Yes, that's it. A mission with a purpose."

I was a bit surprised, but Miyi continued.

"But I think that some people find their mission, and others go through life like beggars and end by achieving nothing."

"And what's your mission?"

She bent her head down and said very quietly, "I have to go out and look for it."

I was busy in Pusan, but I saw Miyi once a day and visited her parents in the shack. It was pitiful—her wasted sick father and her poor mother, unused to hardship, selling stuff off a wooden box. I was more than ever determined to rescue them all. But I must confess that my original good intentions were changing. I was used to wine and women, and I began to have designs on Miyi. I must have shown it in my outward behavior, and she guessed the truth.

I eventually decided to set her up in a tearoom. I

thought I could easily raise the capital, and it would restore her happiness and wit, and there would be no
question about the eventual income. I spoke to her about
it, and although at first her face lit up, and she seemed
keen, the next day she asked for five days to think it
over. The hesitation was strange, but I agreed to it and
nevertheless went ahead with arrangements for getting a
tearoom next to the Tong'a cinema. The five days were
up today, and when I went to the tearoom where we had
arranged to meet, the girl there gave me this package. I
was amazed when I opened it. I don't think she chose
to be a nursing officer simply to earn a living; but what
affected me most was the black tie. When she had been
talking about "mission," was that what she had meant?
I felt thoroughly ashamed. Holding the black tie in my
hand, I thought of the three years of faithlessness to my
ideals, and it stung me to the quick. Because of the war,
I had lost my way in searching for the mission she had
been talking about. I was a fool to have deluded myself
into believing that I had understood anything right. I
thought Miyi was frivolous and feckless, but the war has
made her strong. I was falling through bottomless space,
with nothing to cling to. I needed a friend. So I came to
find you . . .

When Sŏk had heard Choun's long story, all the
curiosity he had felt about him melted away. Even his
own troubles seemed to evaporate. He was overcome by
the thought of the strong-minded Miyi. He could not help
being affected by her even more than Choun was. It was
not just because the food was good that the strong
spirits could not make him drunk tonight, but because,
owing to Miyi, his mind was clear and alert.

He went home in Choun's car, but he did not carry
on or cry when he got into the house. He went to bed

quietly and did not disturb the family. He looked so serious they could not complain that he had been drinking.

As he lay down he thought, "According to Choun, because of the war he renounced his mission; but because of that same war, Miyi was changed to meet the situation with courage." Blinking his eyes, he said to himself, "I have neither renounced my mission nor been loyal to it. I am just wasting away. Am I a type created by the war too?"

The Author

An Sugil was born on March 2, 1911, in Hamhŭng, South Hamgyŏng, and spent his earlier years in Yongjŏng (Lungching) in southern Manchuria. His first published story dates from 1935. In 1948 he moved to Seoul, where he served as a cultural editor for a daily newspaper. "A Third Kind of Man," originally published in 1953 in the journal Chayu Segye, *won him the Free Literature Prize in 1955. His five-part novel* North Kando *(1959–1967), a sweeping portrayal of the struggles of Korean settlers in Chientao in southern Manchuria from 1870 to 1945, is his major work. A record of the ordeals of four generations of the Yi family—first as immigrant farmers (I–III) and finally as soldiers in the Independence Army (IV–V)— illuminated by real episodes and brilliant analyses of complex motives and relationships, has resulted in a great* roman fleuve *in which the real hero is Chientao itself, the stronghold of Korean resistance before 1945.*

"A Third Kind of Man" reflects the author's experi-

ence as a high school teacher in Pusan, Korea's temporary capital during the war. The three characters are sharply drawn individuals, all students of literature in one way or another, and all victims of the war. The human cost of the war was immense, and the gulf between the demands and needs of the self and society has been a persistent theme in postwar Korean fiction. Choun has become a successful entrepreneur—in fact, a victim of success, a fraud of time; Miyi has resolved to find a sense of mission in the career of a military nurse. Sŏk, who has weeded ambition and tilled conscience, has he misdirected his talent? Is there room for his kind in a meretricious society? Will a society in transition still acknowledge the power of literature as a civilizing force?

by Ch'oe Sanggyu

Point

hat morning he received his draft notice. His sleep was shattered by an incoherent noise—his wife came in, holding a piece of paper in her kitchen-stained hand. There was a look of extraordinary agitation on her face, so he asked her what the matter was, shouting as though still talking in his sleep. He picked up the paper that his wife had wordlessly let fall, looked at it, and saw what it was.

"It's a draft notice!"

When one expects the worst, its arrival is no surprise. He sat up indignantly. A cold wind brushed chillingly against his spine; as if to shake water off his body, he got up with a start, and began to dress.

"Why are you just standing there like a gunnysack?"

Actually there wasn't a thing to tell her to do. Outside the door it was winter. Winter for sure. There was pure white snow. He thought about crying out, then

Translated and abridged by Charles Rosenberg *and* Peter H. Lee stifled himself with a hard swallow. The footprints made in the yard just a moment before were already being buried with elaborate care by the snow.

Winter, snow, a draft notice, his wife—he wished he were a poet at such a time. The misty white city was far off. The church was always visible. Why can't these things establish some bond with me?

The landlord's wife came out of the main kitchen. Her careworn face was truly about to burst out crying.

How could I not somehow applaud her humanity!

"So now what are you going to do?" she asked.

"So now, did you say? That's a question one hardly need ask."

"Uuhhh . . . not sure . . . " he coughed up a foolish answer, went out and gazed at Seoul. Misty . . . white. It is aswarm with streetcar noises there. It seems like the sky has come down to sit gently there. Why was it so oppressive, then? But the snow in the yard was an even more terrible white. The members of the household had still not come down to the yard; all their footgear was serving as a memorial to yesterday. But somehow it was ludicrous to think that he alone had to experience today.

"Please come inside. There's no point in agonizing over it . . . that's the way things go."

"Oh, on the contrary, uh, even so . . . "

The landlord's wife was not totally without retentive powers. Still, she was benign even though unable to communicate. I am immensely grateful to you, Ch'ungch'ŏng Province auntie. He stepped down into the yard and made his own footprints over the footprints of a short time before, then turned back. The bubbling stewpot was steadily boiling, and the odor of raw radish slices floated up his nose. He bent over and peered into the kitchen; this was possible because the kitchen was a sort of base-

ment, about a half-story below the main floor. In what
passed for a household there were three or four jars, three
bundles of firewood, the mouth of the charcoal sack gap-
ing open, breakfast still awaiting cooking on the stove.
The washed rice neatly filled up the inside of its pot, and
the two rice bowls were stuck together inside the cramped
cooking area. In the brazier, the blue flame shot up and
he put out a hand, but it seemed either too hot or not hot
enough; he once again stuck his two hands into his
pockets and wandered out. Aaaauuhhnh . . . summoning
up a sound which was neither a stretching noise nor a
sigh, he went into the room.

"Hurry up with the food."

My wife's back shakes. My wife cries. I do not cry;
my wife cries. If I were ordered to laugh, perhaps I would
do that. He embraced his wife's back protectively and
nudged her cheek with his own.

"Are you cold?" he asked.

His wife cut her tears short and sat up. It was easy
for her to cry and easy for her to stop crying. His wife's
tousled hair was somehow charming. Her pure brow
showed every sign of genius.

"Are you cold?"

Wordlessly, she started to get up. He sat her down
again and wrapped her in the bedding, but she drooped
her head dejectedly. There was only one quilt. Again she
tried to get up.

"So what if the damn stew is boiling—I'll take care
of it and be right back."

"I'm going out."

"No, forget it, today is a day for me alone."

"But I have to fix the meal."

"I already said to forget it."

He went outside. It was winter, layer upon layer. He

took the piece of paper out of his pocket. He peered at
the paper and gnawed at his lower lip. He went to fuss
with the stewpot as if he were a man looking for grief.
He took the pot from the fire and it stopped boiling. A
slender thread of steam rose up, a challenge flung at
winter. He smiled softly. A weakling, a weakling. He
took out the firewood. From the three bundles he ex-
tracted one; that left two. If you take one more, there is
only one left. Take one more of the frigging things and
there would be none. So it is—there is no design to it.
He learned his arithmetic. So he went over it again: three
minus one equals two, two minus one equals one, one
minus one equals zero. And he always had compassion
for zero. He curried favor with three.

He unbound and laid out one bundle. There is no
kindling. He turns his pocket inside out and takes the
paper. He lights it. It burns. Uh-oh! He regrets his great
blunder. His name burns. His place of register, too, burns.
His birthday also burns. So if he were to put the fire out
now, what good would it do? He just gives up, defeated.
And he eagerly takes out the paper and lights it. He
places the paper below the firewood. Just seated there,
squatting down, clasping his knees, he is an audience of
one. He sets fire to the firewood. It crackles and drives out
winter. He feeds in another bundle. There's only one way;
I give up.

Seoul is misty . . . white. Somehow he had thoughts
of the Chinese bakery in Myŏngdong. Somehow he
smelled the odor of the waiting room at the Seoul station. He longed for Seoul. He wanted to go back inside
the city gates. He went into the room; his wife was no
different. Nor was he. He hugged his wife tightly.

"Aw, it's night—guess I'll turn in," he said, mimicking going to bed. His wife rolled her head distractedly on her breast and choked with sobs.

"I'm not crying, so why are you crying, huh?" His wife cried with no letup.

Well, I am just the same as yesterday, he thought. I have received no wounds, suffered no indignities. My fortunes have neither increased nor declined, just like yesterday, eh? So why are you crying, huh? If I am the same as yesterday and you who are exactly the same as yesterday were not crying yesterday, what do you mean crying today, huh? Upon his moving the quilt slightly, his wife raised her head.

"Yes?"

"Ah, I haven't said anything, up till now, but . . . oh, never mind. It's nothing." Why do I try to aggravate my wife's unhappiness? "I," the same as yesterday. Yet I think that the "I" of today is not the "I" of yesterday. For what reason is that? What is the evidence? An unexpected calamity has befallen the piece of paper, my sole evidence. Now surely there is no evidence. Show me the evidence. I mean show evidence to prove that "I" have changed as of today. No pickpocket victimized me. Nor did my wife die. Nor was the pot upset. Nor did strange omens manifest themselves. I woke up in the outskirts of Seoul, exactly like yesterday. And exactly like yesterday I looked at Seoul. I did not go blind. I can even feel the cold. I go so far as to think of the Chinese bakery in Myŏngdong. What is different, huh? What is different? Yet I think that the "I" of today has become a different "I" as of today. Who says so? Come forth, show your evidence.

The landlord's wife stopped outside the door to the room.

"The food has to be prepared."

"Yes, yes."

"Well, it's snowed; Lord knows why it's so cold. Shall I put the ricepot on for you?"

"No, don't. I'm coming."

"No, you both should stay here inside. I'll take care of it. You've already washed the rice, so it's all the same to me."

In such circumstances his wife felt compelled to get up. Furthermore, even he couldn't just sit, clinging stubbornly to his wife; she went out. He didn't know the reason he let her leave. Isn't it reasonable for her to go make breakfast when it is time for breakfast to be made?

He followed her. But then he left her and came in again. He stared quietly at a pile of books. Then he began to scatter them around. Books on the bare floor. He picked out a book. More and more he picked out just books with a high market value. They were large and small and weighty, black and red, but they were not nervous. They looked the same as ever. In the instant just past, as he hunkered down, their fates were diverted. They received a grand decree. According to its dictates, they must take part in a great transformation. But they were composed. You dummies, you are sacrificial offerings. Yeah, you. In wild haste, he wrapped them up in a bundle and shoved them beneath the desk. He looked at his watch. Eight o'clock; he makes up his mind to give the watch to his wife. His wife is clattering around in the kitchen. She certainly seemed to be botching it up. It seems as if she is surely making rice. How is it we have to eat or even try to eat. Oh yeah, it's because of Ch'ung-ch'ŏng Province auntie. Something to be grateful for. A product of human nature at its zenith.

Winter is below the freezing point. So I wouldn't be

surprised if someone confronted me with below zero affection. And as for heat, doesn't it invariably grow cold? My wife is surely making a botch of it. Now she's botching it up. Setting it straight is out of the question. He lay down jerkily. With another jerk he sat up. He began to smoke a cigaret; it was very flavorful. While so doing he was waiting for an opportunity. He was biding his time with a view to going out and selling off the wage slaves inside the bundle. He sucked incessantly on the cigaret; the smoke was quite repellent. His wife kept botching things in the kitchen. He tried to fathom his wife's heart. He felt he would burst out crying. Today what should I do? It was already determined. If the fateful day were imminent, what then? How would he pass the time until that day? Enough, enough, stop!

The paper screens cried in the wind. It seems that winter is continually angry. The room is dark as before. The wall—is blue. The corner—is dusty. His mind groped about inside the room. The corners were just that, four bare angles. His thoughts made their way into the drawers in the corner. His wife must be cold. How cold? How cold is my little sweetheart? Even so, his wife was an adult. My wife earns money, but I can't earn money. My wife buys things for me, but I can't buy a thing for her. So my wife is the grown-up. My wife's mother held her dear in times past, but now it is different. She detests her.

It is because of him who has become the husband of the daughter of his wife's mother. That and because he is poor. Because he cannot grow up. And because his wife is beautiful. My wife's mother is envious of this no-goodnik who has assumed the role of son-in-law. Because he keeps her beloved daughter all to himself. But if I were to disappear, she would probably give my wife a scolding and once again cherish her. She would not abandon her to die in this hole in the wall. If that were to happen, then wouldn't everything be just dandy? He is at peace with his immaturity.

At last his wife came out of the kitchen; it appeared she was going to the toilet. He picked up the bundle of books and went out furtively and put on his shoes. Then he plowed through the winter like a shot arrow, fleeing away.

There was winter, spread out limitlessly. It seemed to be infinite. Even if he were to run until he dropped, there seemed to be nothing one could call a cul-de-sac. Why of all times is it winter now? He entertained this question. Even if it were summer, what matter? Even if it were fall, what matter? And so what if it were spring, what then? Why should I bear this winter today? Why is it winter in the first instance! This is dotage. This is groundless absurdity.

His feet slid around. The soles of his shoes are thin and his feet cramped with cold. He shuffled his feet incessantly. The city was stirring from sleep. There are billboards, void of language; they only stare at the street. He decided not to look at these billboards. A hot-chestnut vendor started to make his fire. From there on he saw his father of thirty years before, his father who was a hot-chestnut vendor. His father read while plying his wares, and he alone had inherited those books. For wasn't he an only son, who had never known his mother? He knew only poorly the history of his own upbringing. I know my history only from the day I became aware that I was getting fed at someone else's house, he thought. Carrying a few items of his inheritance, he went along the street. The hot-chestnut vendor was right next to him. The smoke was blue; he smelled the odor. It seemed to be the odor of his father. He lowered his head. The ignorant chestnut vendor was bewildered. The vendor's gaze followed him down the street. His breath was all frozen over at the end of his whiskers. The charcoal fire sputtered in the chestnut pot. The vendor turned back around and stared into the fire.

As for him, he walked. Plowing through winter is really fun. It is the sensation of having become a man of courage. His two cheeks tingle. They come to tingle incessantly. And then they leave off tingling. And when that happens, it is his ears he becomes aware of. Now he runs, runs for life. He now walks, conscious only of his two ears. Finally even his ears give up resisting the cold. He went into a bookshop. There is a charcoal fire here as well. On top of a tidy table, one ink pot, one pen, and a brazier. The charcoal fire is reddish. It's a refreshingly pleasant bookstore; he lays the books down on the table. And he slowly wriggles his stiffened fingers.

"Would you like to buy these?"

The old man looked at him curiously.

"Let's have a look at them."

The old man's fingers were exceedingly sensitive to the cold. It wasn't easy for him to untie the bundle. He put himself out and untied it for him. He wasn't sure whether to be grateful for his father's legacy or resentful of it. Ignorance isn't a disease. However, it is more than a vice. He held his hands over the fire. The old man rummaged through the books.

My wife is probably waiting, is probably concerned. But since I didn't show any signs of dying, she probably wouldn't be all that concerned. But I guess she is waiting anxiously. She may even have come out looking for me. But there is nowhere to come out to look for me, so she probably went right back in. But I wonder if she is standing outside the gate. It is so cold; I wonder if she is standing just outside the gate with her hands tucked underneath her apron. But if Ch'ungch'ŏng Province auntie is there, my wife probably won't freeze to death.

At any rate, why are this man's hands so slow? It seems his eyes are slow. Ah—my wife is probably waiting. This old granddaddy is robbing time from me. And he is stealing so many precious minutes of me from my wife, whom he has never seen in all his life. Old man, you'll never get to heaven acting this way. Hurry it up. He rubbed his hands. He shuffled his feet. The burning charcoal sputtered. Charcoal is oak wood. Isn't this charcoal chestnut? Or isn't it mixed together? He thought of the time that his wife had fainted dead away. While she was lighting a chestnut-charcoal fire, she inhaled some of that goddamn carbon monoxide or whatever it is, went pale, and collapsed. So he got some pickled turnip broth from Ch'ungch'ŏng Province auntie, fed it to his wife, and she revived. Wasn't he worried sick that time? He was almost ready to cry over her death. Just then she revived. At that time, he patted his wife's back and was pleased, and then his wife, still not knowing quite what she was doing, clung to him, eyes blurred with tears.

"How much will you take for them?"

Well whata ya know, the old man is asking me for a price after all. Wouldn't I be too embarrassed to take ten thousand hwan from him? And how about one hundred thousand hwan? The old man is foolish. No, it's me that seems the greater fool.

"Gee, I dunno. I . . . "

The old man browses over them again. And he spoke as if he were just amusing himself.

"You really have to tell me what price you'll take."

He is confused. Doesn't know what to do. I certainly didn't think this far ahead. I'd like to just throw them down and leave. But the old man and I are looking at each other, so . . . ah, what should I do?

"I really don't know. How much do you think I can get for them?"

He tries to simply avoid the question. The old man peers at the books again. He thumbs through them. He actually turns the pages nonsensically, fingers trembling. Is this a beauty contest? He is utterly exhausted. My wife must be waiting, surely. She is standing just outside the gate. He really must go. Damn it all, he is temporizing in the face of all these "musts." He'd like to slap the old man on the cheek. Ten hwan is fine. One hundred hwan is fine. Give it here.

"I'll offer you three thousand hwan."

He was shocked. Hey, it can't be that cheap. Should be a bit more perhaps. Well, say, old granddaddy. His feelings were hurt. I'm sure my wife is waiting. God-dammit, who cares?

"Please give it here."

The old man momentarily made a disgruntled face. It looked like he wished he weren't paying out so much. Come on, granddaddy, let me have the money. The old man pulled out the money and began counting it. Our granddaddy here doesn't seem to have been to a bank in all his life. He's not in the least envious of speedy money counters. How can he be so sluggish? He wants to seize the old man and collar him. At long last the old man hands the money over. He took it and stuffed it away. And went out carrying his empty bundle.

He had sold the books. He was intentionally con-scious of it. He sold the books. It was so simple. What did I sell those books for, anyway? So I could use the money. There's nothing strange about that. Not one thing. We are always poor. So we want to have money. So, I sold. It's something you could do yesterday or tomorrow. There's nothing in the least bit strange about it. There's nothing unnatural about it. And that's that. Dammit, he came up with three thousand hwan today. He is a much wealthier man than yesterday. So he is going to be happy with that fact alone.

A bus passed by, jammed with people. There are so many it seems the bus may explode. Where to? Fine. You are all going. I too went yesterday. Where was it to? My wife went too. I mean along with me. She was such delightful company. But today we are not going out. It's a different thing from yesterday. Another bus goes by, packed with people. Even though we are missing, the bus doesn't blink an eye. The people are all so handsome, and the women are beautiful. Any way you look at it, my wife could be squeezed in there. But my wife is certainly not among those people. This is a simple matter, the question of my wife and me being squeezed in there. The fact that we are not squeezed in there, that's a simple matter, too. But the fact of today is not simple. It seems that it is a million miles away. For today and yesterday are different.

Another one is coming. Even more people. Yesterday my wife was among them. Every day she goes to an entrancing department store to work as a salesgirl. So my wife can't be un-beautiful. If she didn't wear lovely clothes, I suppose they would tell her to get out. Even omitting this factor from consideration, I am envious of my wife's beauty alone. It seems I am a child who doesn't understand dishonor. My wife must be waiting. Why is it today, of all things? Why must it be winter?

The owner of a little hole-in-the-wall store recognized him.

"How are you?" I greet him nicely.

"Is something the matter, that you're up and about so early today?"

"Yes!" I retort like some kind of an idiot. The shop-keeper starts dusting his shop. He is like someone else. Perhaps he is filled with solicitude for his old granny's illness.

"It's different from yesterday, somehow or other," he wanted to answer further. Good uncle, you are nothing but self-effacing; day after day it is the same. You are not the least concerned whether it's the nineteenth or twentieth century. It's all his fault that his wife is a department store salesgirl. Why can't he support the two of them? Ah, but he writes, distilling his illustrious works like precious gems. And his wife reads them for him. And they are pleased with one another. When he found occasion to fault himself for not getting someone else to read them, his wife usually defended him. If he couldn't write something that was suited to live, how could one call it literature? Finally, his wife told him to put off finding a job. First he must become a better artist—that was the main thing. He deliberately gave in to her blandishments.

His wife, when it was winter, would earn money and buy a turtleneck sweater for him. And then he would put it on and write stories. Even in this action his wife was revealed as the grown-up. The wife read only the writings of her husband, and he had only his wife as readership. In the long run, what could be better? So it was that his wife became a salesgirl to earn money. His wife said earlier that she would suppress her talent for his sake. So from time to time, just for him, she would unearth the talented woman buried within. He was regretful, but his wife was the adult, so it was best to submit. But today he had in mind to be deeply, passionately, in love with his wife. He arrived outside the gate, stamped his feet clean, and went inside. Snow was stuck like cake powder to his shoes. The landlord was there; he was at the point of standing up, having just tied his shoelaces.

"Ah, I've heard all about it. You've gotten a draft notice, is that right?"

"Yes. Are you going to work now?"

"Congratulations. Of course, I'm sorry for you, too. But then you are so young—I'm sure you'll fight splendidly. When do you report for induction?"

"Well . . . " His mind went blank. "Oh, something around a week or so." Good-bye, good-bye. Just go, that's all. You old fart. His wife came out of the room, a grieved expression on her face. I thought it would be like this.

"Where have you been?"

"Uh, you must be busy, why don't you be on your way? Since I can expect to see you again this evening . . ."

"Yes, sorry to be a bother. Perhaps in the evening we can share a drink."

"Thank you so much." It seems our landlord will really be late at the office; my wife came out to the kitchen. He went into their room.

"Well, sorry to have bothered you." The landlord again. Bother, what do you mean by bother?

"Sure, so long now."

The room was all tidied up. The floor was warm. He thought of the old chestnut vendor. He even thought once of his mother, whom he had never seen. Ah, now for the three thousand hwan. His wife, in an opportune move, went out to the kitchen. He took out the money. He started counting. Dammit. I'll count faster than an old miser. 1,2,3,4, . . . 29? Hey I blew it, counting so fast. No good that way. Once again, 1,2,3,4, . . . slowly . . . 6,7 . . . 29 again! Swindled. Son of a bitch . . . I

must have lost track when he was counting. But even if
I had known I got only twenty-nine, what could I have
done? Anyway, count fast, count slow, what's the use. Ah,
food. The wife was setting the table. He sat, legs folded,
over the warm spot on the floor. Simply clasping his two
hands on his lap. His wife set down the portable table.
He accepted it with dignity, pushing away the myriad
thoughts that assaulted him. His humble wife sat at a cold
spot. He held his spoon in readiness. She uncovered the
stewpot. Instantly steam billowed up. His wife's face was
misty . . . white. He looked at her and commanded her
to laugh. She did not try to laugh. It is not spring, it is
winter. He began to eat. His wife sat very still.

"Where did you go?"

"Hold your peace. I'll tell you."

He put food into his mouth. He chewed and swallowed. It was tasteless. So he just sat back. His wife didn't
even look at the food. The two brass rice bowls are full.
What a pity. You bowls, too, are completely different
from yesterday, it seems. Good-bye; his wife pushed the
table aside. Then she moved closer to him, and his gaze
alighted on the corner of the room.

He thought of times past, when they had been in
love. Then they had been two college students. One a
male student, one a female student, one shabby, one chic.
Even then they would be seated nicely like this. And even
then she would buy him things. Granted, it was only
something like an apple or a cake. His wife's mother was
a rich widow. A plump matron. And she loved her only
daughter very much. And she considered one of her duties
the selection of a splendid son-in-law. They usually met
in his room. While eating things that his wife bought on
the way, they talked. However, his room was not very
warm. So ordinarily they covered up with the bedding,

lay down and whiled away the hours. They played as
though they were still little kids. And then they went out
onto the street. When they did that, his wife usually
suggested they go to the Myŏngdong Chinese bakery.
They ate honeyed Chinese pastries. They were a little hot.
The tea was hot too. Afterwards they saw a motion picture. They did such things and waited for spring. The
fact is that they are even now waiting for spring.

"How will I live?" said his wife, and she began crying again.

"How will *I* live?" he thought, but didn't say it,
lest his wife be embarrassed. He just silently hugged
her.

"I will die," she said, sniffling, with a choked voice.

"You? Die? Don't be silly. Why should you die?
You'll live just as you are now, the same." Liar! You're
not going to die, and I have nothing to say about it. That
being the case, then I suppose I will die a hundred times,
how about that.

"Why don't you go back home?"

"That's idiotic nonsense."

"Not at all. However much she likes her new bridegroom, do you really think she would drive you away,
her own flesh and blood? Besides, if I should disappear
. . . what could she do but take you back?" He really
did steal his wife away from her mother. His wife had
abandoned her mother, who had couched the choice in
terms of "ma" versus "that shiftless bum," and come
running to him dowryless. Even ma, however heartless
she may be, had cause to love her daughter more than
she despised him, after all. So later on she had written
her daughter a few times. Telling her to come back,
since they were not married legally, or telling her to
remarry for the sake of her future. Is there anything better

than mother's love? So why is it that she rejects her affection? She was an impious young daughter. There was no doubt about it. And so even a mother abandoning her daughter is probably not unnatural. But even now if his wife would just go to her, she would once more become "honored daughter." But the point is that a mother isn't good just because she's called "mother." Rather, she's a good mother if she feeds and cossets and nurtures her daughter. Why do you try not to have a mother if you already have a mother—this was his most constructive favorite argument to date. Even though mistaken in its grammar, that is what he said. He looked at his wife and told her to go. She said ugh. It was an amusing gag. It's such a droll thing to toss about a moral principle like a toy.

It is not that way today, however. It was likely that his wife actually must assume the daughter's role. If you think about it, it's clear-cut. There's no other way. I mean, what well-fed son of a bitch coined such terms as "treachery" and "dishonor"? But if I told my wife to go and she went immediately, she would probably regret it. Therefore, I'll have to keep pestering her to go.

Thinking along these lines, he began to pester his wife. She stared at him. He kept telling her to go, but she said nothing. Only her face became more and more serious. There was even a point when she looked downright nasty. But he pestered incessantly. Finally she was enraged. Her face angry, she began to punch him with angry fists. She battered him mercilessly on the nose and the mouth, on the cheeks and the forehead. He was startled, astonished. But this was such an interesting phenomenon. He threw his wife down on her back, laid her out flat, and sat on her. And then he quickly grabbed her hands and pinned them to her sides.

"Now, how can you possibly beat me? Here, you, this is better," he exclaimed, and quickly kissed her on the lips.

She laughed dumbfoundedly. At last she is laughing. He helped her to her feet.

"There, now that we've had enough of that, shall I tell you about my going out a while ago?"

His wife is speechless. She is lovely listening. He holds out his hand. The right hand. The palm. The index finger quivers. It is the finger of a man of genius. It is indeed the finger of a man of the world.

"Look here, look at this finger. My hand. Before long, it will be a trigger-pulling finger—isn't that splendid?" His face was agonized. But as for his wife, hers is not a tearful face. It is a hateful face.

"What nonsense . . . even your emotions are expedient!" That is what she said. He laughed and laughed.

"I can't seem to grow up for some reason," he roared, laughing. Winter is gratifyingly sluggish. It is sluggishly content. And there isn't a single loophole anywhere. So this couple can't seize the opportunity to escape. That's why we're awaiting spring!

He thought that it was heartbreaking. But that's not it. He tries to think it is fascinating. Nor is that it. That's like a lie. We say "today" so that it's a lie. Such being the case, why must I believe this lie? But they say truth is not a lie. They call it truth. They call it reality. On the other hand, today reigns over me ever so majestically. Couldn't it realize itself for me with a little more intimacy? At any rate, I cannot help but believe in today. I have to submit myself to this monarch called "today." Dammit, last night . . . if it was going to be this way . . . why did I dream? I mean a dream neither good nor bad. Why couldn't it foretell today, give just some small

indication of whether it would be promising or ill-fated?
My wife is truly serious. She wasn't playing a bit. That's
because she is an adult. Even if I too were an adult by
now . . . but there's not a particle of my wife that pretends to be an adult. And so she seems to be a genuine,
true-life grown-up. But there is one aspect of my wife
which is not adult. She has not yet been able to become
a mother. Well, a woman has to become a mother to be
a grown-up. Said to dignify her for sure. But for all that,
it seems that she is more adult than I.

"Where did you go?" Hey! I am contrite!

"To make some money. Say, look. Today, let's say
the two of us forget everything else for once and live for
love. Let's try once to love with all our might."

"Love?" She seemed to be really caught off guard.

"Yes, of course I mean love. But don't think I'm saying this because it's today. It's something we do today,
since I thought it all the way through today, before tomorrow came, that's all."

"How . . . my God, what on earth are you saying?"

"Now you're asking senseless questions. Listen to me.
For there to be love, you have to have a man and a woman, and beyond that, affection is either present or absent
or equally shared, but better present than absent, and
next there has to be money, and next you may buy a day's
worth of food, or perhaps you can't buy that much, but
as long as you're about it, it's still better to buy three or
four days' food, and . . . isn't it love, doing that? Well,
what else do you need to know."

His wife sat back down, sniffling.

What the hell . . . I'm the one who's going, and
she's crying! Girls, yes, women are more realistic. No,
no, if I keep this up, our love will fail.

"Well, let's see now . . . " Let's just pretend to ignore

her crying—"I mean, today, let's just try to live life to the fullest. To our heart's content. We have everything we need. The only thing left to do is love, that's all. If we are to make it happen, then we must have as our goal living several years today. Come on, let's. Change your clothes, hurry."

He isn't at all sad or gloomy. But a little bit later he thinks he may feel gloomy when his wife is not crying. He stood up and got ready to go out. His wife moaned and then cried. He looked at her. Why is it all so very sad?

That's the way it is. That's the way it is. All at once he started to cheer up. I too have become an adult, he thought. The realization dawned on him. Why it was that he has become so dignified, why it was that he has become so magnanimous—it is precisely because I have become grown-up. It is because I too am an adult.

He has finally separated yesterday from today. It is because he believed that he was not a grown-up yesterday, but that he became a grown-up today. Yet he is strangely ecstatic. So he pulled his crying wife up to a sitting position and slapped her cheeks a few times, thinking neither to intimidate her nor to cajole her, and began to change her clothes. She pretended to ignore him and just sat there limply. But there's no need for him to be at all concerned. Go out quickly, go out quickly. Loving, love. Loving among adults. He is busy. Constantly fighting and wrestling with his wife. But when he looked at his wife, still half-dressed, trembling and crying, when he heard the choral voices of the neighborhood school children reverberate in his ear, he simply lost his willpower. All he could do was tenderly embrace his wife, who was prostrate on the floor, still choking back her tears.

However, after a while, summoning up their strength,

they dressed and went out the front door. They set out toward faraway Seoul. It may be that they were headed for the Myŏngdong Chinese bakery, in particular. Winter stretched out limitlessly before them. It seemed there was no end to it, no matter how long or hard they pushed their way through it. So it was they went, and so it was that the "today" of that day started increasingly, bit by bit, to clarify itself for them.

The Author

Ch'oe Sanggyu was born in 1934 in Poryŏng, South Ch'ungch'ŏng, and was graduated in English literature from Yonsei University (1957). In the same year, he entered the air force; he was discharged in 1963. "Point," first published in the journal Munhak Yesul *in May 1956, is his maiden work. Since 1966 he has taught at Kongju Teachers' College.*

His earlier works were characterized by self-mockery, and his nimble style, marked by ellipses in the dialogue and the stream-of-consciousness technique, verged on paradox; but since 1960 he has tried to explore a new dimension, as, for example, in such stories as "Green Well" and "Great Vigil," both published in 1964. "Point," which uses two contrasting modes of narration, the first and third persons, deals with the protagonist's passage into adulthood, the birth of a new life.

by Sŏnu Hwi

Flowers of Fire

ountains, mountains, and more
mountains. A continuous range
of mountains and meandering
valleys. Eternal stillness.

From a distance, this valley, flowing from north to
south, appears like a carpet of soft green hues. Screened
by the shrubs which veil the valley, the precipitous cliffs
look like giant, prostrate beasts. Flowing along the bottom is a stream, cold enough to sever a hand.

Looking westward across this valley, toward Owl
Mountain Ridge, there is a cave; Ko Hyŏn sat with his
back to the cave. As the sun began to sink behind the
mountain ridge, the shade of this side of the valley
gradually dyed the opposite side. In the dense pine grove
was the grave of Ko Hyŏn's great-grandfather; to the
north was the site of the invisible blade of disgrace[1] that
severed the timeless mountain range. But now only the
effects of the blade remained. A day of roaring artillery

Translated and abridged by Peter H. Lee

and oozing blood spreading southward. Disgrace. Disgrace on the land and its people.

Ko Hyŏn felt his chin; the long hours of hiding like a hunted beast told on his chin and back. His unkempt beard was as coarse as a straw sack. His skin was torn by brambles and thorns.

It was two hours since he had climbed to the cave; now he had finished cleaning his rifle. For more than two months the rifle had lain, wrapped in tattered rags, on a rock shelf in the cave with a twig packed in the barrel—the rest of the rifle had become a rusty red. CCCP —a Russian-make A-type rifle. And three rusted bullets. And cold from the floor seeped through his body.

Ko Hyŏn quietly fingered the shoulder strap of the rifle on his lap. Click! The metal ring on the strap hit the barrel, shattering the deathlike stillness.

A breeze rose, rustling the vine leaves on the rock, and he could hear the insects among the shrubs. Suddenly he was overcome by loneliness. He clasped his arms across his chest as if he could suppress the feeling. He heard a drop of water falling from the cave's roof. Quietly he turned his head and looked into the dark interior.

Thirty years ago in this cave, his father had died in his twenty-fourth year.

Early March 1919, on a weekday afternoon—P. town, thirty-five miles from Seoul. In a small church, a group of some thirty Christian men and women held a quiet meeting. When an old man stood up with hands tightly clasped and head bowed, the others remained sitting with their eyes closed. The sound of the old man's prayer rose to the ceiling while an occasional "Amen" flowed out from the congregation.

When the prayer ended, the old man unwrapped a

package and handed each member a small, neatly folded cotton cloth. No one said a word, but quietly spread and examined the cloth. Each was a three-colored Korean flag. A young man quietly brought a sheaf of sticks; everyone attached the small flags to the sticks. One person calmly waved his flag, while a young woman clutched hers in an embrace. Then the congregation quietly went outside. Suddenly a tense expression floated over the pious faces of the believers. Once on the street, the tall youth who had handed out the sticks took the lead. With a determined face, he suddenly raised his arms and shouted "Manse!" The group following echoed his shout of "Long live Korean Independence!" The steps of the congregation became faster; their shouts rose louder and louder. As the shouting of "Manse!" died down, there followed "Onward Christian Soldiers."

At the unexpected sound of "Manse," doors opened and peering eyes looked at the group in amazement. Some were surprised, and hastily slammed their doors; others unconsciously raced outdoors and, following behind like the possessed, joined in the shouting. Pale faces, taut lips, trembling legs, and glowing eyes—eyes full of fear and pride.

By the time the milling crowd arrived in front of a small rice shop near the police station, the earsplitting shouts of "Manse!" sounded like sobs. Waiting for the crowd on the walls around the police station were the cold barrels of rifles.

From inside the rice shop, the owner, with a wen on his neck, suddenly recognized the tall young man at the head of the group and instantly let out a shrill scream. The wen on his neck shook with convulsive spasms, and his legs and arms trembled. Then, a black curtain seemed to descend upon him.

"My son, my son . . . "

But the sounds remained stifled in his throat. It seemed as though a heavy weight had been thrust upon him. "O heaven," he said and collapsed on the spot. The percussive rifle shots rang out, mingled with the shrieking sound of "Manse."

"Our family is ruined," screamed the shop owner, tearing at his chest, grasping the torn string from his coat with trembling hand. Like the popping of roasting beans, the rifle shots came again. The sounds of "Manse" were replaced by the rumbling, running sounds of many shoes.

The shop owner saw the bloody, wounded crowd, pursued by the firing rifles, running into alleys and shops on the opposite side of the street. Suddenly recovering his senses, he got up and, in his stocking feet, raced to the door of the shop and began furiously ripping the wooden shutters off, throwing them into the street. Throwing out the last shutter, he raced toward the back room of the shop where, just as he reached the inner door, some of the crowd ran into his shop, pursued by the flying bullets.

His eyes wide with astonishment, the owner picked up a rice measure as a weapon and sprang at the intruders like a beast.

"Get out, get out of here quickly!" he shouted hoarsely. At his display of nerve, the crowd again ran outside. One of them, as he leaped across the threshold of the shop, was driven into the cesspool by a flying bullet. Then quickly the owner rolled up his trousers and, hastily sitting cross-legged on the floor in the middle of the shop, drew out his pipe and began calmly smoking. With eyes closed, he sucked on his pipe. The police, arriving at the front of the shop, chasing and shooting the fleeing crowd, peered inside with fiercely distorted faces, and then left.

Every time this happened, the owner slowly opened his eyes and heaved a long sigh.

After an hour, the remainder of the crowd, tied together, was led away like dogs along the road strewn with blood-spattered bodies. The police beat the limping wounded with their rifle butts.

Fear and death hung heavily over this town for several days. Eight people were killed and more than twenty were wounded. More than eighty were imprisoned in every available place, including stables. Throughout the night dull moans came from these places.

The young man who had led the congregation had been shot and, as he could hardly drag his wounded leg, two of his friends supported him and hid him some fifteen miles away, in a cave on the ridge of Owl Mountain. He bled excessively, and his leg became inflamed. The face of the youth, who with fading spirit had endured great pain, darkened with the color of death. He passed the night in agony; at dawn he drank water brought by his friend from the icy stream of the valley, and died.

The next day it rained. The two surviving youths were captured by the police, whose search had extended to the cave, and the body of the youth was turned over to his father, the shop owner. The father shed not a single tear, and buried the body in the public cemetery. He did not pity the dead youth, but despised him.

"This is not my son," he said, and not for fear of the police. A son who dies and leaves his father behind is not a son, but a monster, he reasoned.

Upon hearing the news, the daughter-in-law, who happened to be in her own home at the time, fainted several times. Although she could barely move, she rushed out and spent the night by her husband's grave. The next morning other people went to the grave and found her unconscious and covered with mud.

The daughter-in-law, a widow at the age of twenty, returned to her own home, where in a few months she gave birth to a son. This son was called Ko Hyŏn.

A month later, cuddling the child in her arms, she returned to her husband's home, where she had to bow humbly to the young wife of the old man, who had married again three months earlier.

One day the shop owner, accompanying his daughter-in-law, was returning from the cemetery when, upon entering the shop gate, he began to vomit blood, and fell like one dead; he had to be carried in by the daughter-in-law.

In three days the old man recovered and told his daughter-in-law that she should leave the boy with him, return to her own home, and seek remarriage. Determined to remain in her husband's home, she calmly and clearly refused her father-in-law's command. A life of some thirty years of tears and sweat began for Hyŏn's mother.

In the year following his son's death, deep wrinkles etched the old man's face, and his hair and beard became grey. People began to call him "old man Ko."

While it may have seemed that old man Ko acted coolly to Hyŏn's mother, he actually loved the boy. After all, Hyŏn was his grandson, not a granddaughter. While the old man saw traces of his own blood in the boy, he sometimes thought he saw a dark shadow hovering.

This year the old man exhumed the bones of his father from a site some seventy miles away from P. town and reburied them on a sunny slope on the opposite side of Owl Mountain. An old geomancer had told him that the orography of his father's grave site had influenced his son's misfortune. Now, with the change of site, the old man lived in greater confidence.

The next winter, old man Ko became the father of a boy, Yŏngsŏn; and a year later he moved the bones of his first son to the foot of the mountain, where the ancestral mound was located. The dead son was reburied because he transmitted the ancestral bloodline to Hyŏn, in whom the old man had seen a bud of hope. But he was still severe with his daughter-in-law. In the first place, the death of his son was predetermined by the daughter-in-law's destiny, and, second, he could not trust a young, widowed daughter-in-law whose future was uncertain. The old man had never given a pennyworth of value to womanhood.

Old man Ko gave Hyŏn several paddies and fields across the river; working in them made Hyŏn's mother's hands like the twisted ends of a rake. Hyŏn's mother had to do the work by herself while Hyŏn, tied with a piece of cord, played under a tree. When they arrived at their own two-room grass hut, after groping their way down the dark road after sunset, the penetrating loneliness intensified the pain in the mother's legs. Lying down after supper, she would groan, and her groans often changed into weeping.

The old man tended his rice shop as usual, and occasionally crossed the river to see Hyŏn. Hyŏn quickly grew to the age when he began to appreciate the smell of the copper coins his grandfather would tie to his coat strings.

The enjoyment of watching her son grow and of listening to the gospels read at church on Sunday were the only rewards in the harsh life of Hyŏn's mother.

In the church, she could sense the presence and warmth of her husband. Not in paradise, but inside the church, she came face to face with her husband. In the hymns, she sensed her husband's voice; in the prayers, she could picture him. Though it was an illusion, it was the dearest thing she possessed. It lightened her burden and made her forget the pains in her hands and legs. Thus, once every week, Hyŏn's mother met and spoke with her husband.

"I'm so distressed . . . "

"You must have suffered a lot!"

"Look how Hyŏn is growing well . . . "

"It's all owing to your hard work."

"When can I come to your side?"

"Through Hyŏn I am always at your side."

"Help me! There are times I cannot bear anymore."

"The Lord will help you, for all is known unto Him."

Love of Hyŏn, admiration of her husband—there was the grace of God.

In the fall of the year when Hyŏn became four years old, old man Ko informed Hyŏn's mother that if she persisted in dragging Hyŏn to church, she could no longer take care of him. From that time on, Hyŏn played in his grandfather's rice shop every Sunday. To young Hyŏn the concept of his father was very dim. His mother said that his father was waiting in the kingdom of heaven—somewhere beyond the blue sky, floating clouds, and the Milky Way.

Consequently, for Hyŏn, ridicule of his grandfather was more unbearable than being called "fatherless," an irreparable insult. One Sunday when a group of urchins ridiculed his grandfather's appearance Hyŏn fought bitterly against them, receiving a bleeding face and torn clothing.

Boastful of the struggle he put up for his grandfather's honor, Hyŏn related all the facts to his grandfather and quietly waited for assent and praise, but what came was an unexpected reprimand:

"What, making fun of my wen? Really! Look at your appearance! With whom? What? You fought with Kim Chusa's[2] son? How could you? Why did you cause such trouble? Really, just like your father . . . "

Watching his agitated grandfather, Hyŏn felt an unexpected sense of anxiety. His feelings were comparable to those of the dog that attacks his master's assailants and, in return, is beaten with his master's club. Thereafter, on similar occasions, Hyŏn simply walked away. At first these situations were difficult to endure, but afterwards Hyŏn felt a kind of relief.

From the time Hyŏn was ten years old he often asked about his dead father. His mother, her gaze wandering, would praise her husband in a quivering voice.

"He was truly a splendid person. He was mindful of others' welfare and stood firmly for the right cause. He established a night school and taught the children. He never sent a destitute person away empty-handed. In this village there was no one as dignified and kind as your father." Then she would attentively read Hyŏn's face, and observe her dead husband's features in Hyŏn's eyes and lips.

"If you wish to see your father, look in the mirror," she would gently pat him on the head with her fingers. "My pitiful, charming son, my only life."

The old man's merciless criticism of her husband was a heavy burden for her.

Summer of Hyŏn's seventeenth year, on a sunny day.

At some distance from his son's grave, the old man ordered Hyŏn to bow after the sacrificial food and wine had been spread. After Hyŏn had bowed, the old man drank a cup of wine and then ordered Hyŏn to drink.

Hyŏn's mother saw this and turned her face away. Seeing Hyŏn hesitating, old man Ko said, "You're old enough to drink," and pressed Hyŏn on with a wave of his hand. Hyŏn took the cup, hesitated, then quickly swallowed the contents, and began to cough.

"Young people should learn to drink from their elders; their drinking habits will then be refined. Lately the young do not know how to behave. Those who have studied new learning are ill-mannered. They are talking about the new learning, or some such thing, but the ability to write one's own name is enough; as for manners and morals, a collection of maxims³ will do."

"Certainly, grandfather, but please tell me about my deceased father."

"Mmmmmm, your father was a bright man; because he was so outstanding I had great hopes for him as my successor, but he would not listen to me and from the time he espoused Christianity things began to go wrong." The old man knit his brow and looked at the church in the sunlight on the other side of the valley. Hyŏn's mother lowered her head.

"From that time on, your father went to the ancestral tombs but he would not partake of sacrificial food; when he bowed, I did not know to whom he was paying his respects. Because he stubbornly turned against the beautiful customs of ancestor worship, he ended as he did. I don't know where it came from, the so-called Christ demon, the cause of his downfall."

Hyŏn stole a glance at his mother, who was weeding silently, and with a boldness from wine spoke again:

"But, even my teacher told me that my father did fine things before he died."

The old man got angry and shouted at Hyŏn, his greying beard quivering.

"Who would say that? Fine things? Leaving his father behind—is that what a devoted son would do? And making a widow of your mother—is this a fine thing?"

"But wasn't that because he tried to restore our country?"

Hyŏn's mother pulled at his sleeve, cautioning him with her eyes.

"Restore our country? What kind of a country was our country? Officials just sat boastfully on the common people, drawing off everything from them. Those who couldn't give were flogged. Who would miss a country run by such extortionists? What's there to restore? The sellers of the country were the same ones who bled the people. Even if it were not so, why should your father alone take the lead in trying to restore it?"

"But, grandfather . . ."

"Of course, we live better now than we did at that time, and people are awakened. The death of your father pains my heart, but he did a foolish thing. To throw one-self empty-handed against guns and swords. He went crazy only to get killed."

Hyŏn was silent.

"If your father were alive, your mother wouldn't have to bear these hardships. Every time I look at your mother I resent your father." The old man's voice gradually became choked up.

"If your father were alive, how comfortable your grandfather would be. Because of rheumatism I cannot move these days."

For a moment the old man was quiet, wiping the

sweat from his forehead. Then he shouted again angrily.

"You say your father did splendid things for people. What about those people who live shamelessly today and whisper these worthless things in your ear? Look at the village people. Where will you find one who offered any help after your father was killed? Such is the world! And the man who killed your father—he was not a Japanese policeman but a Korean assistant. And isn't all of this the very reason why you have had to go to a Korean private high school instead of a public one?"

From behind Hyŏn's back came the sobbing of his mother, unable to endure the ordeal.

"Man must accord with reason. The seizure of our country was not right, but from the beginning the ones charged with responsibility did not perform their duty worthily. And when did our country feed all its people well? People should manage their affairs with naked fists according to the situation of the time. Who else can they rely on? Why should one lift a finger for others? Why should one expect even one bit of help from others? We should manage our lives with our share."

He stopped and looked across at Hyŏn's mother.

"I may have talked too much, but what I want to say amounts to that."

The old man filled and lit his pipe. After several dignified coughs he said, "Now let's go home," and, without looking behind, strode down the hill.

Upon returning home, Hyŏn's mother cried her eyes out, and she implored Hyŏn never again to drag out the business of his father in front of grandfather.

However, Hyŏn did not think that the stories of his grandfather were as cruel as all that. Of course, he could not think of his father's death as his grandfather did.

What was it in his father's mind that made him do

what he did? What was it that had caused his father to snuff out his own life, bravely confronting death empty-handed?

In high school, Hyŏn became a swimmer. Not because he had any special interest in sports, but because swimming rather than team sports agreed with his character.

One day Hyŏn was placed on the school's championship team. Paying money for a swimming champion put old man Ko in a bad humor.

"When I send you to school, I want you to study. What is this business of pouring money into swimming? You do not even know our proverb, 'A good swimmer can also drown!'"

Hyŏn soon began to feel disgusted with swimming—and not because of his grandfather, but because of the regimented life and competitive consciousness in which every second counted. What once had been pleasurable exercise now became unbearable corporal punishment. Within a year he begged to be let free, and thus came to the end of his life as a champion.

Hyŏn next got interested in botany. He felt a special pleasure in collecting various kinds of flowers and plants as he wandered over the mountains and valleys. Accompanied by his stooped botany teacher, he roamed the mountains for half a day; usually they did not exchange a word. When they became tired and lay down, the streaming clouds in the high blue sky made their eyes squint; and they could hear the sounds of life flowing from the flowers and grasses.

One day early in summer, when Hyŏn was a fifth-year student, teacher M, who had just finished his class and left the room, was immediately taken by the Japanese secret police. On the following day two students in the same class were arrested; and five students, including R, who was a native of P. town, were missing.

Young and vigorous, teacher M had often told allusive stories in his classes, always with a sneering tone. It was rumored that M, together with several students, had established an ostensible reading club, in which they plotted revolutionary activities. Hyŏn now recalled having received an invitation from R to the club, but he had refused because of heavy homework and approaching examinations.

Teacher M became an idol of the students. Moreover, the rumor that he was sending notes to the students from inside the prison caused a flurry of excitement at the school.

Several days later, Hyŏn heard that R's father had died of a stroke, anxious about his only son and pressed by a police search. For some reason Hyŏn was hesitant to immerse himself in the excitement. What were they planning? Was it something so great that M could not carry it out by himself?

In the spring of the next year, Hyŏn graduated from high school. While his friends were preparing for professional school or college, Hyŏn thought only of returning home. Even Hyŏn's adviser, who knew him well, was greatly surprised at his indifference.

"This is enough schooling for me—I don't attempt the impossible. I wish to return home and live peacefully with my mother."

"But don't you have any purpose or ambitions?"

"No. I don't want to trouble others. I just want to live as I wish; this is all I want."

Returning home on the train, Hyŏn was deep in thought as he caught glimpses of the familiar countryside flashing by. Is the way I wish to live my life the same as my grandfather's? No, I think differently than my grandfather. But suppose my thoughts are the same? Purpose of life? Ambition? Aspiration?

These were fleeting vague words to Hyŏn.

Regardless of others, why should I be involved?

The wet rice fields were spread out before him at the foot of Owl Mountain, and through the open window came a breeze carrying the smell of the earth; an exhilaration akin to pain flickered through Hyŏn's chest, and an electric excitement flowed through his veins.

My cherished soil, he thought—to him this was the only thing that was real.

Hyŏn took great pleasure in relieving his mother's hardships. Together they would complete their breakfast, till and plant the fields; or while Hyŏn cleaned the ditch with a shovel, his mother would help by pulling on the rope attached to the shovel. At dusk she would return to the house first to prepare the evening meal, and, while waiting for her son, would sing hymns to the tunes of folksongs. The seasonal vegetables—their only side dishes —were sweet and succulent. During this time Hyŏn's mother never once missed the Sunday church services.

Every time she passed through the brushwood door, dressed in white, Bible in hand, Hyŏn would watch and picture to himself traces of her youth. Removing the shadows of hardships and trials, he could find yet traces of beauty and could revive her young face. When his thoughts reached his mother's youth, which had been sacrificed only for him for these many years, Hyŏn felt sad.

His mother would occasionally groan and rub and stroke her thigh. When Hyŏn showed signs of anxiety, she flushed for no apparent reason. Once she was unconscious with a high fever, and Hyŏn called a village doctor. Whatever the reason, Hyŏn's mother, in her dim consciousness, pressed her two hands to her thigh and rejected the examination. Hyŏn suddenly jerked the hands away and examined the spot his mother had covered. A spot near her knee was festered, and a long red line extended upward. To the right and left of this line were innumerable scars, scars of wounds inflicted with a sharp object. It took Hyŏn five years to understand the true nature of these wounds.

One year passed; came the day of the Harvest Moon Festival. Upon returning from the cemetery, Hyŏn was tending the flowers in the yard. His flowerbed was the most beautiful of those in his own village as well as in P. town. From early spring to late fall, some ten kinds of flowers continually adorned the yard.

Sitting on the edge of the veranda and looking at Hyŏn's broad shoulders, his mother spoke as if to herself.

"Yŏngsŏn is going to college next year, I understand."

"Yes, I guess so." Hyŏn found no interest in the topic.

"Do you intend just to stay home and farm?"

"Yes." Hyŏn quickly turned his head toward his mother, whose gaze fell to the ground. Brushing his hands together, he got up and sat down beside her. "It's all right with me to pass my days like this with you."

Hyŏn's mother gazed at Owl Mountain for a while and then said, "By hiring a little help I can manage the farm, so why don't you talk with your grandfather and plan to go to college?"

For a few moments, struck dumb, Hyŏn could not speak. He realized that helping his mother for the last year had been nothing but an illusion of self-consolation. Looking at the white cosmos and red dahlias swaying in the breeze, he was momentarily sunk in sorrow.

This last year had been wasted, as the love and un-wavering resolve springing from his mother's benevolent bosom had reminded him.

But his mother's destiny, accompanied by the shadows of predetermined loneliness and trials—these thoughts caused the uneasiness that clouded Hyŏn's mind.

Old man Ko did not apply his philosophy that the ability to write one's own name is enough to his own son, Yŏngsŏn. Ever since the son of Kim Chusa, the old man's rival since youth, had been appointed a magistrate old man Ko had borne in mind a similar hope for Yŏngsŏn. The fact that Hyŏn obtained a high school education was probably a by-product of the old man's educational zeal for Yŏngsŏn. Hyŏn hoped that his grandfather would stubbornly reject the proposal, but he consented to Hyŏn's wish, though extending only minimal support.

So in the spring of the next year Hyŏn, carrying a tattered old suitcase, went to Japan. He thought it beautiful and the people much kinder and gentler than he had anticipated. But somehow they were too clever and not as open as the villagers back home.

Finally, three years of preparatory school were over and, on the day he entered university, the grey-haired president, in dignified tones, told the class that one of the great benefits of university life was making friends. Hyŏn became close to a Japanese student, Aoyagi, if he could be called a friend. A native of Nagasaki, Aoyagi's father had died in the so-called Manchurian incident, and he had been raised as the only son by his mother, who managed a general store. His face was pale, and in his tall clogs he reached only to the bottom of Hyŏn's ears. Possibly their similar backgrounds brought the two together. Aoyagi loved to recite Takuboku: "On a white strip of sand/ On a tiny island/ in the eastern sea/ drowned in tears/ I play with a crab."[4] Sometimes he sang it to one tune or another.

The knowledge Hyŏn acquired in university life came from books rather than lectures. Texts on the philosophical idealism of the Oxford School, which influenced his contemporaries, fascinated Hyŏn. This philosophy contained a deep concern for individuals and a humble, burning passion for ideals.

Some students sneered at this philosophy and called it the final convulsion of capitalism; they also evinced a great concern for Marxism, which was not fully out of fashion in some quarters. Marxism's attempt to interpret history according to a schematized ideology and to coerce the individual into rigid obedience by the power of the masses seemed to Hyŏn perilously to approach brutal coldheartedness. It was like the gradual trend to totalitarianism seeping into the Japanese students, and Hyŏn felt an instinctive aversion to such beliefs.

Hyŏn could choose a philosophy most suitable to his temperament; for he felt no pressing conditions or urgent problems that called for his consent to Japan's current national needs. For all its attractiveness, however, a philosophy was but a dream on paper, having no true power to change Hyŏn. The only reality that still captivated his mind was P. town, of which he dreamed often—the blooming azaleas of Owl Mountain, the green valley below, the summer berries in the groves, the cold water from the valley stream, the grass on the ancestral graves, the people of the village, his grandfather tending the rice shop, and his lonely mother.

"We did it, at last, we did it!"

One cold, gloomy winter day, Aoyagi burst into Hyŏn's room waving a newspaper extra. Pearl Harbor Attacked! Other headlines followed: Fall of Singapore. Landing in the Philippines. Victory Celebration March. Everywhere lunatic excitement, and khaki, the wartime color, overflowed; yet Hyŏn received the impression that this play, ignoring the scenario, was rushing toward a terrible last scene, unexpected by players and spectators alike.

One day Professor Takada, who lectured on Eastern ethics, suddenly assumed a solemn expression and began to stress the decline and despair of Western civilization and the universal significance of Eastern culture. On that day Takada spoke with great fervor as if he were addressing the two billion people of Asia.

"Each will be placed in his ordained position—this is the eternal truth. With the individual as the absolute unit, the goals of the West's social order have been baseless equality and unlimited freedom. Thus the West fostered extreme confusion, and its civilization is on the verge of decline, as Nietzsche and Spengler candidly prophesied. Dialectical materialism, an inevitable monstrosity born of the conflicts of Western thought, has provoked the class struggle, and the West's machine civilization is now on the verge of collapse. Indeed, now is the time the light will shine in the East, the time for 'God's chosen people' to rouse themselves to action—an embodiment of the principle of harmony of existence and a paean to the humble value of the human spirit."

Up to now, Hyŏn thought, I can follow.

"The great historical mission, the eight corners of the world under one roof; how solemn a proclamation! The Greater East Asia Co-prosperity Sphere will effectuate it. Liberate the yellow races from the suppression of America and England, and recover a New Order in Asia. Japan has the mission of being its leader—how heroic and magnificent is that mission!"

And?

"Accordingly, we must hold fast to our lofty pride and spread our glorious spirit to save the peoples of Asia; we must gladly annihilate ourselves and contribute to this great cause. This is our destiny, our great glory! Even cows and pigs gladly submit to death for the greater benefit of man."

Gladly?

"For the races of Asia to live in their rightful position, we must annihilate ourselves in order to live for justice. The sad and beautiful principle of humanity."

Disgusting!

This was the coercive philosophy that justified the actions of the Japanese police in pouring bullets into the peacefully demonstrating crowd, in making a victim of his own father, the coercion that demanded submission—morally wrong submission like that of his own grandfather. God's chosen people of Japan and the peoples of Asia! Men and beasts! A fraternity of cats and mice!

What disgusted Hyŏn was the teacher's lofty expressions and the cheap sentimentality that inflicted pain upon others. And his self-deception. Hyŏn found his own hand raised in the air. The teacher, engrossed in his own lecture, ceased talking and wore a displeased look.

"I have a question. I understand your point that it is necessary to destroy our ego and to sacrifice for the great cause. However, you also said that cows and pigs would gladly sacrifice their own lives for men—of course, men will inevitably eat them—but, when I was young I once went to a slaughter house. A cow being dragged into the shop resisted violently and refused to enter. Pigs especially made quite a fuss by screaming before they were slaughtered. It did not seem to me that they 'gladly' gave up their lives. Would you please elucidate the point."

The teacher smiled sardonically, and the students laughed loudly. However, when the smiles died away even the students who had unthinkingly laughed seemed to feel that their doubt could not be relieved.

By the time Hyŏn sat down he already regretted his action. Not that he had aroused the displeasure of the teacher, but that he received a shock and had stood up all of a sudden—his unpremeditated behavior displeased him. As if he had received a request from the two billion people of Asia to register a protest—that was disgusting. So what?

"Comparison can err at times. But in this case, the intuition of Asian peoples . . . "

Hyŏn did not hear the teacher's jabbering, but only sank more deeply into his own self-hatred. He was like a conch that, after exposing its naked body, draws farther and farther into its shell.

Assistant professor of the history of philosophy Hidaka was different from Takada. He had a good mind and delicate sensibility. And when Hyŏn went to visit Hidaka, who had been called away to war, the latter said:

"Their minds are twisted and distorted. Japan has lately jumped into the tide of world history, and everything she has done has gone wrong. Her seventy years of racing has overstrained her. A combination of the Victorian dream and totalitarianism; a groping after a deer on the plains of China![5] But such a time is over. We cannot even pacify the Chinese people, you know. No wonder we have a rigid battlefield code. We may win on the battlefield, but ultimate victory is difficult. We lack the backing of a strong civilization. Emancipation of the Asian people! How beautiful! If we mean what we say, then self-government for Korea should have been established first. Yet, all that happened was the change of Korean names to Japanese—what do you accomplish by changing names?[6] Disgusting nonsense. I am going off to war—my only sin is that I was born Japanese—to harvest the seeds sown by this country."

Hidaka left for Central China where, within a year, he was killed in action.

Another year went by.

The war situation grew worse. The military authorities, feeling the lack of lower echelon officers, devised a plan to give students a shorter period of training before sending them to the front lines.

Aoyagi, returning from a big demonstration of student recruits, dropped in to see Hyŏn and, with an agitated face, talked only of death.

"Everyone probably does not die on the battlefield. No! The determination to die will guide us to a bright mirrorlike state of mind."

Hyŏn realized that Aoyagi was attempting desperately to collect his scattered thoughts.

"Now I have no lingering attachment," his face became gloomy. "I worry only about my mother, but people back home will somehow help her."

Hyŏn only listened.

"I will give you my books on Thomas H. Green and the Student Library series. It will be enough for me to keep *Hagakure* and the *Manyōshū*.[7] To tell the truth, I do agonize somewhat, but to me the moral duty of liberating the Asian peoples relieves all my agony."

Hyŏn could not suppress his feeling of sympathy for Aoyagi even though he considered him a gear that did not mesh. The willful attempt to rescue others who do not want it is a thankless interference.

As the pattering of Aoyagi's clogs faded in the distance Hyŏn's thoughts turned toward home. Free from the whirlwind that had swept the Japanese students, Hyŏn found himself extremely lonely.

He wrote a long, yearning letter to his mother. In her answer she told him that everyone was fine and that Yŏngsŏn, owing to poor health, had returned and was working in the local government office. At first his grandfather had been dissatisfied, but now he was content to have his own son home in a safe place. At the end of the letter, she did not fail to pray for Hyŏn.

Very soon Hyŏn found himself in the same situation as Aoyagi. The only difference was that Hyŏn could not stomach such slogans as "Emancipate the Peoples of Asia" or nationalistic literature like *Hagakure* or the *Manyōshū*. He could see no meaning in his participation in the war.

Hyŏn returned to Korea with a little money his mother had given him, then escaped to Haeju, where his maternal grandfather was the head of the local fishing guild. However, after a few days, Hyŏn's thoughts began to be dominated by a sense of guilt.

What is this growing anxiety? I'm hedged in! I'm in an enclosure. In an enclosure turned into a gigantic prison, where the prison's taboo soaks into the bones. I feel the uneasiness of a criminal who violates the taboo. The impending whip of the guard. A prison within the prison. There was still one way. But this fence was too high for Hyŏn to get over. He simply had to flee like a criminal.

After two weeks Hyŏn received the visit of a keen-eyed detective and was forced to put his name to an overdue "volunteer application."

Uneasiness dispelled, a slave's relief, a criminal's submission.

One evening, while passing through Haeju, he stopped in at a tavern and drank to his heart's content. Then he slept with the tavern woman. A passion triggered by anger—this was his first experience with a woman. The next day he left with dizziness and a continuous queasy feeling.

Upon returning home, he learned that his capture was not because of the efficient Japanese police net. His grandfather had been afraid of the repercussions Hyŏn's escape from the internment camp would have on his second son's admittance to middle school the next year. Hyŏn did not resent his grandfather's action; he did not want to cause any disaster to his younger uncle. He was even rather relieved.

On the day before his departure, he calmly passed the day with his friends from P. town and with his mother. His mother begged him to forgive her for encouraging him to go to a university. Inasmuch as Hyŏn's age was exactly the same as her husband's at the time of his death, she sensed some ill omen and trembled. Hyŏn tried hard to comfort her, but she could not sleep and, turning her head to the wall, she offered prayers.

"O Lord, holy Father, forgive this sinner and bestow mercy upon her. This is the only wish of this sinner . . . "

Hyŏn's mother, seized by great agony at not being able to extricate herself from sin and obsessed with misfortune, implored Him to exclude her son from the punishment that would be heaped upon herself.

"This sinner has been able to understand from her

love for her son her deeper love of his father, whom You have called. Through her love for her only son she is, though her faith is weak, able to understand Your goodness. Father! Forgive my sin and give my son his life."

Hyŏn shook, as blind anger surged through him.

I myself have not believed, but I have admitted the existence of God, because it gave my mother peace of mind in her life of hardship. But now, for no reason, mother calls herself a great sinner and trembles in front of God. All human beings may be sinners, but my mother cannot be. A jailerlike God! Groundless original sin. Mother! How can you feel responsible for things that happened before you were born?

The next day, at the farewell ceremony in front of the station, the county magistrate gave a pep talk, and the chief of police led the people in the shouting of "Manse." B, a fellow recruit, was drunk and sarcastically and loudly raised a clamor, but Hyŏn, feeling that this was only adding meaninglessness to meaninglessness, did what he was told without expression.

In the midst of the raucous march Hyŏn saw his grandfather receiving the greetings of the magistrate and police chief. Grandfather turned around to Hyŏn's mother, who was covering her eyes with a handkerchief, and consoled her now and then.

Grandfather would probably feel that my departure to face death is nothing but my own unavoidable destiny, caused by the orography of the ancestral grave site. My uncle Yŏngsŏn's weak health, his dropping out of school, and his job as a subcounty clerk were also caused by orography. He would probably be figuring out which calamity was caused by which grave site, marshaling his knowledge of geomancy. Chaos in a distant era, high-temperature gas, flowing lava rocks, erosion of wind and rain, bones in the graves. His face is saved by sending me to war and, because of Yŏngsŏn, taxes will be reduced in the family; how satisfied he must be! But, please do not think that my mother's weeping behind you is unlucky.

Watching the ever-receding dark green peaks of Owl Mountain, Hyŏn continued to think in the train. If destiny were so, it would be cruel; I by no means wish to die.

Hyŏn's name, now changed into Japanese style, became Takayama ("high mountain"), and he was sent to the Nagoya Army Corps. He was in the transportation section and had to scoop up horse manure with his hands. One moonlit night while groveling around under the horses, Hyŏn turned his head toward the unusually bright moon. The moon's bright rays shining on a long cylinder hanging from the horse's underside transformed it into a large brass rice paddle with a black handle. Hyŏn laughed in spite of himself; the sound of his laughter echoing through the vacant stable gave him a strange sensation. Suddenly, he felt insulted or mocked by the horse. By this thing! And in a fit of anger, Hyŏn swung the shovel and whacked it with all his force. The startled animal jumped smartly, and Hyŏn fell backwards.

One Sunday, accompanying his Japanese friends, he went to dinner and gorged himself. He ate so much it was difficult to breathe and impossible to move freely. All night he was busy going to the toilet.

The next morning he learned that some government property was missing. The fist of the squad leader exploded in Hyŏn's face.

"Stupid, now that you have lost it, don't just stand there. Go out and steal from some other group."

The next day Hyŏn got some burnt rice from the mess hall and ate it in the same latrine where he had sat the night before. While chewing the burnt rice he thought about Thomas H. Green's "On the Different Senses of Freedom as Applied to Will and to the Moral Progress of Man."[8]

Most painful to Hyŏn was the drill which required the men to stand in two columns facing each other and to strike the man opposite. To inflict bodily pain on someone against whom he had not the slightest grievance was hard to bear. When struck, strike; strike, be struck, and repeat—then gradually a groundless hatred boiled up. How transitory and sad a thing it could be!

Next spring Hyŏn, together with some old soldiers, was sent to northern China. Upon setting foot on that vast and desolate land, Hyŏn was determined to escape at the first opportunity.

Assault, abuse, brutality, arrogance, baseness, and falsehood. The army was not a place for a human being. If there were any justification, I would persevere. But there is not the slightest justification. Why must I kill Chinese people?

The frozen ground began to thaw, but when night fell the coldness still soaked into one's bones. On a dim moonlit night, while Hyŏn was on sentry duty, his chance arrived.

Hyŏn's vague plan was that he would simply run to the west and be safe. With two bags of dried bread, one can of food, and two pieces of candy, Hyŏn walked all night through the waist-deep dried grass. Several times he fell, and his hands and face were scratched. He felt alone, flung into a gloomy space outside the earth. It was like walking toward the gates of hell.

By the time the east was faintly lighted, Hyŏn's rifle was lost. The sky began to be dyed red and a great crimson mass was rising. There on the great earth, Hyŏn, like a driven nail, stood without stirring, and gazed at the magnificent spectacle. Ah! This vast universe, and in front of it, this miserable vestige! Suddenly, he let out a cry like a beast, and the sun seemed to infuse a new life into him as his awakened voice burst the stagnant filth inside him.

The next day, as soon as he reached a hill overlooking a small village, Hyŏn, weak from cold and hunger, fear and exhaustion, collapsed into a deep sleep. The sun was overhead when he opened his eyes. In the village several people were visible. A narrow road extended to the village from the bottom of the hill on which Hyŏn stood.

He was not sure how he would explain his situation when he finally met the Chinese. He must go to the village, but it was difficult for him to move and he thought he would like to stay forever where he was. Vacantly, he leaned against a crag and chewed on the remaining pieces of bread, while looking at the village. At the entrance to it he saw a short person moving in his direction. Walking slowly and coming close on the road at the bottom of the hill was a young Chinese girl with bobbed hair. When she passed along the road close to the crag, Hyŏn could distinctly see the black pupils of her eyes and her moist red lips. Hyŏn gazed steadily at her breast and the stimulating curve flowing from her waist down her thigh. Hyŏn swallowed hard in spite of himself. The bottom half of his body seemed intoxicated. The fear of the previous two nights was gone. Hyŏn stared unseeingly at his surroundings. Numbness spread over his body. The peculiar sensation he had experienced with the tavern woman revived with a rush. He forgot the queasiness he had felt; only the warmth of the woman's body remained.

His throat was burning, and his swallowing made a strange gurgling sound. He could not stop his reason from becoming muddy. He rose with a jerk and grabbed the bayonet from his waist. His shadow caught his eyes. Motionless, he looked down at his wretched outline. A Tarzan he had seen in the movies, a Tarzan aiming at a savage beast. The wild beast and the girl. Tarzan and the wild beast and the girl and I. His head swam, but suddenly he regained his composure as he felt something twist in his chest. He sank to the ground.

Already the girl was some distance away. For a moment Hyŏn felt like a half-wit in a daze; he wiped the sweat from his forehead as he tried to sheathe his bayonet. The feelings of intoxication in the lower part of his body still persisted. This lump of flesh! He plunged the sharp end of his bayonet into his thigh. Swish—red blood oozed from his army trousers. His longing for the girl died instantly. Tearing his underwear, he wrapped the wounded leg, pulled himself into a crevice of the rock, and looked at the oozing blood. In an instant an incident out of the past flashed into his mind like lightning. What kind of scars were those incised on my mother's thigh? Those many, many scars?

He felt an uncontrollable anxious yearning for his mother, and her image appeared in his mind. The sublimely melancholy beautiful face of a young woman who had resisted life's unbearable conditions. He heard a melody hanging over the earth, floating in space over his head, his mother's hymn! The sorrow and pain of human existence swirled like a whirlwind in Hyŏn, who was throbbing with hunger and cold, and he shed some tears.

In the evening Hyŏn went down to the village and, by writing Chinese characters, convinced the villagers of his situation. While he ate warm millet porridge, the apprehensive and youthful eyes of a young girl gazing at him gave Hyŏn unending joy and relief. He was in a district of active guerilla warfare carried on by the Eighth Route Army and he was directed at once to Yenan.

Once in Yenan he was amazed at living conditions. People were living in caves and their diet was poor. What impressed him was their conviction that they would soon live freely.

Hyŏn was astonished by a shabby old man named Kim who predicted that emancipation would come soon and who awaited a good opportunity to avenge himself. The Communist argument was not different from the prophecy in the *Chŏng Kamnok*,[9] with the possible exception that the former was a prophecy pretending to be science. By Communist theory Kim pictured to himself a future bonanza of great value, compensating for the lost half of his poor life. But if this did not come about, then he at least hoped to have his shabby picture framed and hung, or his name listed in one of the illustrious pages of the party history. Those who attached absolute meaning to the equation of emancipation were "contractors" without clients.[10]

Why are these people spending day and night worrying about others? The urgent thing for them should be their own emancipation from the lice infesting their cotton clothing. Probably when their liberation comes they will demand a hundredfold reward for their misery and agony.

Within a month Hyŏn was able to escape and lie low in southern Manchuria in July 1945. Manchuria was occupied by the Russian army, and he witnessed that men could become baser than dogs—plunder, rape, destruction, murder. Hyŏn could not concur with the opinion that blamed war; there must be something basic in men who commit such actions—worse than dogs. The only difference is that men fabricate some pretext.

The Russian contractors who replaced the Japanese in the role of emancipators were from the beginning awe-inspiring. Indeed, contractors are bound to profit. Beset by disappointment and disillusionment in man, Hyŏn repeated these thoughts to himself with a bitter smile.

Hyŏn returned home to P. town in mid-September 1945. When he entered the familiar brushwood door in rags, his mother, who was idly sitting on the veranda, was momentarily stunned at the sight of him. Then she rushed to him, embraced him, and cried. When the villagers crowded into the yard, Hyŏn's mother, kneeling on the veranda, lifted her voice in prayer. She had felt no great excitement over the liberation of August 15, 1945, but now her heart seemed to be bursting with the feeling of liberation. A fatalistic hope like a deeply rooted primitive belief was now erupting like an active volcano. And in the void at the end of the explosion she felt God's grace pouring down like a shower.

For old man Ko, August fifteenth meant liberation from delivery of a quota of rice. He had received benefits from Yŏngsŏn's position, but the passive Yŏngsŏn's ability was nothing special. At the end of the war the old man heaped abuses upon the conduct of the Japanese authorities. "Why shouldn't they be destroyed? They have always plotted and schemed," he shouted.

P. town was just south of the Thirty-eighth Parallel and was soon flooded by American luxury goods. Everything was worthy of the old man's envy, and he firmly advised his second son to study English. The fact that Yŏngsŏn was safe and that Hyŏn had escaped death was caused by the reburial of his father and confirmed his belief in geomancy.

Hyŏn felt that the tangled web of political factions,

crooked and taut, deviated from the main point of the current situation.

Liberation had been obtained effortlessly; why should people yell and shout? And no one was qualified to throw stones at others. What they needed was a strong sense of disgrace and a quiet humble tone. Despite this, stonethrowing and ear-splitting shouts!

The liberation was rightful—some would argue— what should have been ours long ago. Now, to whom should we bow reverently, and whom should we flatter? "Thank you, Red army!" or say childishly, "Wonderful C rations?"

What would be the outcome of all this? Gloomy disappointment spread through Hyŏn's mind, and he felt he was treading on vacant air. Thus, once again frustrated, he withdrew into his shell.

On the anniversary of the independence movement, both Hyŏn and his mother, as bereaved family members of patriots, were seated at a special place—even grandfather sat respectably beside them. The national anthem was unevenly sung, fervent speeches were made resembling the exclamations of patriotism, and Manse, vibrating sounds of Manse rent the air.

Returning home with a commemorative brass table, Hyŏn suddenly saw something glisten in his grandfather's eye—tears beneath the wrinkled inelastic eyelids. For Hyŏn this was a new discovery. For all his evil speaking, he might have been as sorrowful as others about my father. Father's death, mother's trials, grandfather's agony, a poor society, the special seats, and now the commemorative table.

The next year Hyŏn, at the earnest request of the principal, became a teacher in the district girls' school.

The confusion of the society became accentuated, and

the opposition more acute, but inside the school's hedge it was comparatively quiet; however, the school was not to remain so for long.

The condition of the society was beginning to be reflected in the students, and some teachers set fire to the situation. Students who scattered leaflets were dragged to the police station like martyrs. Hyŏn felt compassion for young students caught up by the giddy excitement. What is the reason for this excitement? For whose sake this martyrdom?

For excited teachers, oblivious of their duty, to agitate young students by irresponsible speeches was tantamount to crime. If the teachers were self-confident, they should sally forth and take some kind of direct action, keeping in mind the difference between a teacher's platform and an agitator's rostrum. Not a finger should be placed on the students—but this idea was Hyŏn's alone and found no application.

In the midst of all this turmoil, the number of refugees from the North to the South was endless and increasing. The footsteps of those who spent a day or two in P. town were heavy; they were people who had refused the bids of awe-inspiring contractors! Hyŏn thought of old man Kim, in Yenan, now reported to be occupying a high position in North Korea. He must be bathing several times a day and enjoying dazzling white rice.

What was the price that compelled the refugees to abandon their ancestral lands? To Hyŏn these people were a motion picture that passed before his eyes. He was content just to watch the procession with the same sympathy felt by onlookers at a tragedy in a theater.

Hyŏn's true interest lay in his flower garden, which had been enlarged in the two years; he felt relaxed by the flowers that adorned it from spring to fall.

Hyŏn stretched his legs, tired from the day's work, and smelled the delicious odor of the food from the kitchen. If he pressed his mother to hurry, she would scold him, saying he was still a child. The resplendent flower bed—the songs of the cicadas and the birds—this was life. A small area of life that could be enjoyed by any human being!

During this time Hyŏn rejected several marriage proposals, for he thought it improper to think about marriage in the confusion of society.

People spilling out from the North, with eyes full of sorrow and indignation in wearied and tired faces. Were these the kind of lukewarm eyes that meant a peaceful life, if there were a place to settle? The newly arisen awe-inspiring contractors who instilled a flame of indignation: when they ended a project, could they become disciplined and stop there? Stubborn pursuit of profits, abuses heaped upon the established groups—that was what they inherited from the old days. Hyŏn thought that one should refrain from such a foolish act as building a new home when a typhoon was approaching. It was impossible for him to drag another into the uncertain future. Now that he had lost confidence in himself, how could he have confidence in others?

At such a time, Hyŏn tried to picture the last half of his mother's life, the life that pierced him to the bone—thirty years spent in that dreary thatched house! Loneliness and trials!

His own marriage might produce another mother like his own. After several attempts, the old man gave up, and Hyŏn's mother no longer attempted to advise—much less command—him, even though she wanted to feel a grandson in her arms.

Forsaking this kind of anxiety, Hyŏn wanted to try

to be faithful to his own responsibility. He adhered strictly to his class schedule and was therefore not a popular teacher.

Fall arrived and an unfortunate problem arose about the extension of the school buildings, involving construction funds and the principal. Several aggressive teachers caused trouble, and the atmosphere was charged with threats of impeachment of the principal. Hyŏn felt that the matter was not worth consideration when the whole situation was so unclear. However, the teachers who had raised a row brought the issue out into the open and attempted to avenge the humiliation the principal had previously inflicted on them because of their ideology.

When a student faction created a political disturbance and brought out a slogan calling for banishment of the principal, the latter shifted the blame for the affair to the troublesome teachers, and three faculty members were hauled to the police station for interrogation.

Everybody felt it unjust that the teachers should be blamed for the disturbance. However, in front of the cunning eyes of the principal, the other faculty members could not open their mouths and oppose him.

At the faculty meeting the principal expressed regret in a dignified tone, and called the detention of the three teachers unfortunate. Hyŏn was astounded. He looked into the principal's face, which reflected his cunning and baseness, and suddenly rose to his feet.

"Sir, shouldn't you consider a counterplan?"

The principal was surprised at Hyŏn, who was usually moderate but was now looking at him with a tense expression.

"You speak of a counterplan, but there is no way to devise one."

"You say no? You yourself know that these teachers

had no connection whatsoever with this disturbance this time."

"Mr. Ko, how would I know such a thing?"

"Mr. Pae was not here at that time, as he had gone to attend his father's funeral, and the two Kims did not return from the week-long school excursion until then, did they?"

"I don't know about that. Their absence does not exonerate them."

"Well, we can clearly understand that from the circumstances and common sense."

"Mr. Ko, why do you defend these people in this way?"

"I am not defending them. Despite what has happened in the past, if we leave the teachers where they are now, that will not be impartial treatment of them."

"Well, they will receive impartial treatment from the police, won't they?"

Seeing the principal feigning ignorance, Hyŏn felt his blood boil.

"Sir, if you take such a cool attitude toward our situation, how can we properly teach the students without anxiety?"

Suddenly, the principal said in a louder voice:

"No, Mr. Ko, what are you saying? What do you expect me to do when the police say that these teachers are seditious?"

"If you talk like that, sir, you are sure to be accused of deliberately driving the three to prison because of the financial deal over the school extension."

The principal changed color.

"Mr. Ko, be careful of what you are saying. What are you talking about? Do you mean to implicate me in that deal?"

Should I advance one more step? Should I make a decisive attack? But . . .

"That's not my point. Others are apt to see it that way. That's all."

To decide the issue would be tantamount to denying the principal a fair deliberation, and that thought made Hyŏn stop talking. A sad affair. The old principal from the North had a tendency to link everything difficult or unpleasant to ideology.

Yet another unpleasantness. Every time there was a small rumor, these teachers would, before ascertaining its validity, make a fuss. It was they who brandished their up-to-date tendencies before the young students.

Whatever the case, it was disgraceful.

As Hyŏn went out the school gate with heavy steps, he heard someone coming behind him. It was Miss Cho, who had dropped out of a women's university. She had on a well-pressed white blouse and a black skirt.

"Mr. Ko! How courageous you were today. You not only defeated the principal, but *completely* defeated him."

Hyŏn gave a bitter smile and, walking silently, felt his stiffened mind begin to untangle. When Miss Cho is near me I have a warm feeling. Something draws me toward her, and yet, it is not passion.

There could be no competing with Miss Cho, who had studied in a Korean language department, while he had, with some difficulty, only glanced at Korean orthography. It was Miss Cho who quietly instructed him every time he mispronounced certain Sino-Korean idioms.

In spite of her tender appearance, Miss Cho had a strong character. Once, when the men and women faculty members were walking together, they saw an American soldier walking with a Korean girl. A male teacher sneered at the couple and reproached them.

"That woman without any sense of shame, she calls herself a human—carrying her chin high and walking around—the dirty thing!"

Miss Cho stopped him and asked, "Why do you place the blame on that unfortunate girl?"

"Unfortunate! It's her own choice to bring disgrace on herself."

"You shouldn't argue that way. Who has had a choice? Isn't it the society ruled by men that has placed women in this circumstance?"

"How have men made this kind of society?"

"Well, even you must come to some sense! How sad the men of this country who are unable to protect even one weak woman."

A similar discussion happened another time when Miss Cho asked Hyŏn, who would never take part in a discussion or express his view:

"Mr. Ko, you never show any interest in anything, do you?"

"I beg your pardon?"

"Why do you never express yourself in a situation?"

"Well, there are people who take such things upon themselves, but I am not in a position to interfere with others' business."

"You're passive, aren't you?"

"Well, it may be so, but I have no interest in other people's affairs. And I have no thought of encroaching into others' domain."

"How could you be like that?"

"Trying to stop a quarrel may at times lead to a bigger quarrel. When I cannot manage my own affairs, how can I think of meddling?"

"Is it all right whatever happens around you?"

"What can I do about the world around me?"

"Mr. Ko, you do not look like such a person."

"I have seen many times what kind of trouble an intervention brings to all concerned. What one thought would be a benefit to others turned out to be a disaster."

"But doesn't it turn out differently sometimes?"

"Of course it does, but only when it involves one who, like a sage, has penetrating wisdom and a moral nature."

"Mr. Ko! Don't you think that you are outstanding?"

"Why, not at all. I know myself well. I am just mediocre without any outstanding characteristics. That's why I try to preserve only myself."

"But in a situation like mine where a certain life-style was forced on me—even then could you live just preserving yourself?" (In the fall of 1946, Miss Cho, with her family, had fled to the South.)

"Well, I can't guess until I am faced with the situation."

"I *was*. And my father had a bitter experience."

"What kind of damage did he suffer?"

"Not physical injury. At first, people held him in esteem. My father, when young, was active in the socialist movement and suffered many hardships, I am told. He had retired to care for his orchard, but with the liberation, he was called out to serve as head of the people's committee. With the entrance of the Soviet troops, my father became very sad and, when he was forced to make compulsory rice delivery, he resigned his awkward position. He became very melancholy and said, 'What I wanted to do in my youth was not this kind of work.' After this, people began to bother him on one pretext or another, and at one time they took him to the security police on some dubious charge. After two weeks, he returned home but did not say a word; then, suddenly, he told us to move south. In that situation, it was impossible to preserve oneself."

"Of course, I would have to change my thinking, if I had to forfeit the time to cultivate my flower garden or lie on the veranda looking up at the sky."

"That was not all. What if you had to join a group, never miss a meeting, hate someone, expel someone, kill someone, clap your hands for a speech, clench your fists and wave them high?"

"In that case, even I would do something."

"What would you do?"

"Well, I would do the same as your father did." Then Hyŏn burst out laughing at his own story, and Miss Cho followed.

"You are passive to the end."

When they were close to a forked road, Hyŏn awakened from his recollections and spoke.

"Actually, I have regretted my speech to the principal a great deal."

"Why?"

"It was senseless. What remained was only displeasure."

"But . . . "

"I could never be a 'contractor.' "

"What?"

"Nothing."

Soon afterwards, the three teachers returned from the police cell and immediately resigned from the school.

Hyŏn was depressed; having to attend the school was uncomfortable, and seeing the principal was painful. Before another month had passed, he tendered his resignation. When Hyŏn visited Miss Cho's room, she gazed at him as if to drill a hole in his face.

"What's up? Something bothering you?"

"Everything is bothersome." Hyŏn avoided her piercing gaze.

"Well, I don't think so. Is it that you are too embarrassed to look at the principal?"

"That also may be right."

"Again, your mind is weak. No doubt you are completely defeated." After a long silence, Hyŏn opened his mouth.

"This has nothing to do with defeat. Whatever you may think, I have come here only to say goodbye."

Because Hyŏn immediately turned around and left the classroom, he did not see her tears.

Hyŏn's mother was quiet. Grandfather only clucked his tongue.

"You have no luck with officials. This too is part of your own destiny."

In the winter of that year, Hyŏn visited a nearby district where he heard the story about the uprisings in Yŏsu and Sunch'ŏn.[11] For what reason do people wish to kill each other?

Hyŏn began to raise a calf. Cutting the fodder, cleaning out the shed, and changing the straw bedding kept him busy. Right in front of his eyes the animal seemed to inflate like a balloon when he mixed beans with the bean and rice straw. This was quite different from the Japanese army days when he had had care for the horses. No constraint now; and Hyŏn considered his calf as another member of the family.

When the harness used in plowing irritated the animal's back and drew blood, Hyŏn pitied the more the expressionless animal. And at such times he thought of his old teacher, Takada, who had said that animals gladly offered man even their last piece of bone! Well, if he were still alive, what would he be doing? If he is doing what he wishes, he is sticking chopticks into a pot of sukiyaki, pulling out pieces of beef and, unable to destroy his own ego, he must be eating them contentedly. He must be old by now.

It was a plain that stretched away endlessly. Hyŏn looked anxiously for his lost rifle. His legs were stuck fast in the ground and he couldn't move them. His and enemy soldiers were shouting, running pell-mell. And there he saw Aoyagi and Hidaka. Both the Chinese and Japanese armies looked like enemies. Shells exploded. My rifle! It's not here! Rifle? Here it is! Bayonet and bullets are not here. Down came a flood of enemy troops, the heavy sound of cannon, screams.

Hyŏn awoke from his sleep. The sounds of cannon. Throughout that whole day he heard the roar of guns and trains loaded with wounded jerking their way past P. town to the South. The following morning there passed through the town the roar of the tanks and the People's Army. The dead were spread out and red flags displayed.

What on earth is this? Well, let them act who will. Anyway, I don't care; I have no connection whatsoever with it. You are you, and I am myself! Everything looked grey, the sky, the mountains, the fields, even the flowers.

A few days later, Yŏnho, who was said to have gone north, entered P. town, wearing long, dangling hair, and the first thing he did was to look up Hyŏn.

"Well, you've gone through many hardships, haven't you?"

"Not really."

"You must have suffered a lot. Well, now that the gangsters have retreated . . . "

Hyŏn said nothing.

"But what are you doing, Hyŏn?"

"What?"

"You must dash out and do something."

"Do what?"

"My God, haven't you been waiting all this time, lying low for this moment?"

"Waiting for what moment?" Hyŏn wore a suspicious expression.

"Of course, we did not expect this. However, there is no reason to be stunned."

"Quite frankly, this thing came as a shock, but I am nothing but a common person."

"Do you plan to remain as you are now?"

"Well, I am satisfied the way I am."

"Then you intend to eat cake while watching the ceremony?"

"I have no interest in either the cake or the ceremony!"

"Why do you act this way?" Yŏnho's expression seemed to say it was unexpected.

"Why do I behave this way? Haven't I always been this kind of person? Please leave me quietly alone the way I am, I beg you."

"Leave you alone! But aren't you the kind of person who should zealously be doing something?"

"There are enough people capable of doing something. There is no need for me to plunge into action. To me all things are troublesome. Before you came, I had just gone out to the field, where I saw the body of a youth with long eyelashes and long black hair. He had a young face—at least ten years younger than mine. Who knows but that within the last few days he sent a letter to his family and was yearning for the girl who lived next door? And when I think about that, I come to the question of why that youth should have given up his life here by the roadside? A man, who should have lived, died by human hands. Why? Whose fault is it?"

"Of course, to die is not a pleasant thing. However, without shedding blood, how can we hope to achieve revolution?"

"Whose blood? Whose blood is suppose to flow?"

"The blood of the enemy that blocks the revolution and the noble blood of the people's fighters who offer themselves to the revolution. However, more enemy blood is demanded."

"Have you ever considered the circumstances of the dying? The deaths of people who are trying to live? The agony and fear! In that moment of dying, man loses his whole self, no, the whole world!"

"However, the new hope, the proletariat, must advance over dead bodies."

"Advance? In what direction? That sounds like a convincing story at first. But that emotion is a problem."

"Everything is a process of the inevitable revolution."

"What is the objective of that revolution which must cross over dead bodies?"

"The establishment of a classless society without extortion."

What a childish question, Yŏnho's face seemed to say.

"I also fervently wait for such a society. However, the process of arriving at this objective—what kind of process and how lengthy is it? For people must live during that process, and isn't living a continuous process? The whole objective of life is living. There cannot exist only an ultimate goal. There must be middle goals somewhere along the way."

"Then you absolutely refuse to acknowledge this revolution?"

"What has been obtained by the revolution cannot be as precious as human life."

"Then you negate history itself."

"This word *revolution* is fascinating. Even the historians—half of them—consider it an important opportunity and one necessary for historical change."

"Then you do not negate history."

"Not at all. Only that revolution is a subject that historians love to discuss. Those who hold the fortunes of a good life can repeat, on their sofas, the ill-fated stories of others: 'sacrifice a few lives and the like!' Revolutions in the past did not improve our society."

"I'm surprised at you."

"Well, I do not have the courage to sacrifice my life or cast hating looks at others for the sake of an unclear objective!"

"You look at the people's struggles in this way?"

"Struggles? Why do you wish to fight that way? Why don't you organize a club of fighters and play a game? But in reality those who are not interested are also drafted to fight. These are the ones who shed blood for no reason. Look at the case of Iksu!"

"Iksu! He is an amazing fighter!"

"Do you think he now has the right frame of mind? I can understand why a person like Iksu has to escape poverty and live like man. But today's Iksu is . . . "

"Well, what about Iksu now?"

"Look at his eyes! Enthusiasm is fine, but now his eyes are full of poison. Now only bloodthirstiness and hatred fill those eyes that were once affectionate and good. When I look at him, I have to ask myself, why must a man have such eyes? And I feel sympathy for him. I am sure now you feel sympathy for a man like me."

"Do you know what the current situation is?" Yŏnho seemed to be frustrated.

"The time when groundless hatred is boiling."

"Groundless hatred?"

"For whom have you come to harbor such ineffaceable grievance? Who in the world do you curse and how do you hate?" Hyŏn stared straight at Yŏnho with clear eyes.

"You raise such a question now?"

"Capitalists, landowners, pro-Japanese, reactionaries— these are what you hate?"

"And opportunists," Yŏnho's voice rose suddenly.

"I'm not an opportunist. The object of hatred is not someone you can point to. This so-called hatred is a hatred that does nothing but produce a vicious circle of hatred."

"So?"

"The object of hatred is the absurd human condition. The poison that lurks in your breast and mine. The barbarity which oppresses others. Arrogance that pretends to have excelled others. Self-promoting, cheap, heroistic meddling. Impudence that arrogates the right to kill or let live."

"Since when did you become a preacher?"

"I am not even a believer, but nearly two thousand years ago, it was taught that one must love his neighbor and that if one cheek is struck, he must turn the other. But look at men in their wretched state. You, of course, would not strike my cheek, and I would not have the magnanimity to turn the other cheek if you did . . ."

"Then?"

"I abhor fighting; I would flee before presenting my other cheek. I have come to think that to be born a human being is disgraceful. I am tired of myself and all of mankind. But it's not a despair that would compel me to end my own life, so I will try to live as long as my life lasts."

Yŏnho looked at Hyŏn with a mixture of derision and pity. The retrogression of the confused petit bourgeois grasping at a straw in muddy capitalist society! He tried to give Hyŏn an understanding of the heroic suffering and sacrifice of the revolutionary.

"Try to think of the self-sacrifices of the people's fighter."

"Why is that self-sacrifice? Who requested it? It is compensation for self-intoxication and vanity. The only fact is that the cost is too high. Rather, the miserable plight of the masses is really something to see, subjected to unexpected calamities and incomparable insults."

"Insults?"

"Of course! Where will you find greater insults? If the masses received something, they deserved it; but who stopped this bestowal but the unsolicited contractors!"

"Contractors?"

"The contractors who, from self-intoxication, get excited and indignant; sometimes they smile, sometimes they shed tears. And in the midst of all this, innocent people are sacrificed! What kind of respect and applause do these contractors expect? Every person is born with his individual life, however miserable it is, and each has his own world. This is inviolable. People are never extras, mobilized for a play by the contractors. This is the way I feel—those who are quick to jump in for their share, anticipating a great future—they are nothing but shrewd merchants who win a bid on disposing of waste material under the pretext that only they can sell it at a cheap price and rescue society. In fact, they are worse than merchants. Normally the merchants lust only after profits, but these demand even respect and adoration. Unsolicited contractors bring torment to the people."

"Do you believe your opinion will hold?"

"I gave you my view on the subject since it was brought up. Until the time that the Japanese dragged me into the army I lived my own life, and even after the liberation I have lived the way I wanted. From this time on, I also want to live as I wish. One may make a fuss, but life is life. I only wish to live quietly as I see fit."

"That may be difficult. The revolution does not tolerate an idler. We must awaken the people from their paralyzed sleep and instill consciousness."

After Yŏnho left, Hyŏn sat on the veranda, sunk in sorrow. He felt no regret. He had to talk; something compelled him to.

Vacantly, he looked at the flower garden. He felt the flowers' individual characters, which he had not been able to do in the past few days. Man attaches various meanings to flowers—passion, anxiety, sorrow, purity, sin, anger, vagueness, gentleness, wild elation—but flowers are only beautiful. When the time comes, they bloom; when the time goes, they silently fall. But man attaches meanings as he wishes. Moreover, men separate themselves by color, form factions, and point the sword at each others' chests.

Up until now, Hyŏn had somewhat inverted the Golden Rule in his own way, to "don't do unto others as you would not have them do unto you." This was Hyŏn's credo. However, now Hyŏn began to feel a rapidly approaching threat.

The current contractors are not the same as those of the past, but are able and cruel workers who do not rest until not one is spared. These persistent and subtle calculators dig and lay open every corner. And Hyŏn, crouched in his shell, seems unable to escape their sharp stare.

Walking away, Yŏnho clucked his tongue, "What kind of a fellow is this?"

Yŏnho had been sent as a contractor to his hometown to repay his own sufferings over the last three years. He felt satisfaction in the manner in which the villagers looked at him: with respect and admiration, dread or envy of the victor, or the thorny look of anger and hatred. Whatever it was, there was always some kind of reaction. Yet, not from Hyŏn; his eyes lacked any sense of reaction. Far from dread, wasn't there indifference and fatigue and aversion, mixed with compassion and sympathy?

How dare Hyŏn so lightly underestimate the structure built with much labor in the midst of fear and a rigid system. In addition, the logic of the false story which Yŏnho could not grasp. You call us contractors?

With the generosity and magnanimity of the victor he dismissed Hyŏn's talk, but his gesture was foolish rather than commendable. In one corner of his mind lurked a great void, and Yŏnho filled it with flames of hatred.

Ten days later, the contractors sponsored a "party" on the hot ground which seemed to broil under the Seventh Month sky. The burning sun blazing down on this gruesome "party" was too strong an illumination. By means of a living sacrifice before the still vacillating people, the contractors, smeared with human blood, had to plant the seeds of fear and hatred in their breasts. Sins must be partitioned among all!

The people's trial opened in the town square. Yŏnho summoned Hyŏn. He would point out the blood and watch for Hyŏn's reaction. When the prearranged denunciation and the crowd's clamor rose to a fury, Yŏnho steadily gazed at Hyŏn, who was quietly standing by.

Certainly, there must be some change now. Surely, you who stand aloof above all others, as long as you are not a stone, will feel fear, confusion, shock, supplication. Then you will come easily into my hand. That will be surrender; your heresy is nothing but a play of ideas.

The first sacrifice—the chairman of the local chapter of the National Patriotic Society. When the sentence was delivered, to the unexplainable screams of the crowd, the huge clubs of the executioners pounded the man's greying head, his face the color of earth. There was the cracking sound of bones, the dull sound of tearing flesh.

"How's that?" Yŏnho threw a sharp glance at Hyŏn, as if to bore a hole. But he could not find a trace of fear in Hyŏn's face; from the stiffened face of Hyŏn only sweat flowed.

"Look at that fellow . . . "

However, Yŏnho miscalculated; the sweat on Hyŏn's face was not from the heat, but from the flames of wrath in his breast; and when the second sacrifice was dragged out, what flowed was not sweat but blood, oozing from every pore.

The second offering was none other than Miss Cho's father, the helpless old man who had rejected an unsuitable mode of life and fled to the South. The image of Miss Cho suddenly flashed in Hyŏn's brain.

Hyŏn turned his sweating face and looked at Yŏnho. Unexplainable smile in his strange eyes and lips—is this the face of my childhood friend, the face of a human being?

A scream parted Hyŏn's lips as the face in front of him seemed to become magnified: "Murderer!"

Sunk in reminiscence, Hyŏn opened his eyes wide

and looked up at the stars studding the dark sky. From the cave's floor came the sound of a drop of falling water. The wind died down, as did the rustlings of the insects.

He could not clearly recall what happened after that scream—a discontinuous line of events. His own fist suddenly springing up and felling Yŏnho, his grabbing the carbine of the security officer and running into an opening in the crowd. The square turned into pandemonium—the shouts of the executioners and the screams of the crowd, the sounds of rifles, a yellow veil spreading before his eyes and, through this veil, he ran on the ground which leaped up to his eyes. And where and how he ran—at the end of the chase, he jumped into the lower reaches of X river. And now he found the carbine still clutched in his hand.

An impulse of the instant—what was the mind's impulse so that he could but act the way he did? Witnessing murder was tacit approval. As part of the crowd, he could not just stand by sluggishly. He felt excruciating pain. The pain inflicted upon the head and shoulders and waist of the victim was pain suffered by Hyŏn's own head, shoulders, and waist. Why? In all of the crowd, there was no connection between it and him, but still he felt pain from which he wanted to escape. Which he finally did. Hyŏn traced his impulses of resistance in the past.

Revolt against the Japanese teacher; hatred of myself leading to a retreat into myself. Protest against the principal; defeat completed by my own resignation. Desertion from the Japanese Army. And again, escape from Yenan. A succession of escapes!

Have I ever fought face to face? Once only, when I was very young. Because of the wen on grandfather's neck, my face bled and my clothes were torn to shreds.

Unexpectedly, grandfather got angry. My habit of turning my back to every strained situation, when did it begin? Finally, by escaping, I have settled the accounts of thirty years of shrinking into my shell.

Then, for what reason do I return to P. town, dragging myself there? Isn't it because I cannot extend this escape to the ends of the earth? Was it the rifle I left in the cave? If not these reasons, then, because of loneliness? Indeed, I have been lonely, and even now, unspeakably lonely. Overcome with loneliness in the darkness of bushes and valleys, how many days have I longed for my mother like a child? I abandoned my mother, who bore thirty years' trials, and escaped.

Loneliness, but not a loneliness coming from isolation from others. Rather the loneliness which comes from the recognition that I have never been with them. Even though I was living among others, an impenetrable wall cut me off from them. It had completely cut me off from everyone.

Unbearable loneliness and the thirsty yearning that accompanies it. Why am I so afraid of men and yet also yearn for them? In this surging loneliness only one face vividly emerges therefrom.

Before climbing to the cave, Hyŏn had passed through S. village. By a stream he had met Miss Cho, dressed in tattered hempen clothes and worn straw sandals, dusty hair tied behind carelessly, with a sunburned face, and eyes filled with astonishment.

There Hyŏn saw the disgrace of a human being. Dull eyes mixed with despair and sorrow—should a living human being have such eyes? Then, the light of joy surged up suddenly, bursting into tumbling tears, nay, blood.

When the dawn comes, Miss Cho will search for the cave. Even here there is a thread of light. Now, waiting for that moment, Hyŏn must take a nap.

He gathered scattered grass into a mat. He loaded his carbine and used it as a pillow. The smell of the rusted iron came to him. He lifted his eyes and saw that the stars were beautiful. They were pulling against each other, but they were always in their proper places—how strange!

Suddenly, he felt an uneasiness, remembering the glance of the youth who had stared at him from the flour mill when he was leaving Miss Cho and passing the entrance to the village.

Soon, that momentary uneasiness was dissolved in his fatigue, and Hyŏn closed his eyes and slept.

The blood red sun rose, clearing the fog that was covering the valley and hanging over the cave. From the woods in the chilly valley two shadows emerged, wrapped in fog, and started to walk toward the cave—old man Ko, with drooping head, followed by Yŏnho. Across Yŏnho's waist was the Russian carbine.

BOOM! From far to the south came the rumbling of cannon.

The rumble stretched Yŏnho's nerves taut. A stretch of crags loomed ahead. Yŏnho walked impatiently. At the people's trial, when Hyŏn had knocked him to the ground, Yŏnho was able to get up quickly; but in that instant, the structure he had laboriously built crumbled into pieces. Now it was not a question of fighting Hyŏn psychologically.

Afterwards, Yŏnho had received instructions to arrest and hand over Hyŏn to the Party's central committee because of his escape from Yenan, so that he took pains to hunt Hyŏn both from duty and for personal revenge. Got as far as Yenan, eh? In spite of his laborious career, Hyŏn betrayed the revolution and pulled down the structure I had built with my own blood and sweat.

Receiving an intelligence report of Hyŏn's whereabouts the evening before, he had dragged old man Ko along as bait. Rather than walking normally, old Ko did no more than barely move his weakened legs; the old man had never in his eighty years felt such despair as when the People's Army had shown up in P. town—his cards were on the table and he had no play. Yŏngsŏn, who had worked for the national patriotic society, had fled, and his second son had been dragged into the People's Volunteer Army. He had faint hope for Hyŏn, who now drew an endless curtain of despair in front of the old man's eyes. There had been a ray of light which barely penetrated that curtain. Now, looking for that ray, he struggled along a rocky, thorny path.

When, through an opening in the fog, the old man spotted the rock in front of the dark blue cave, he stopped.

"Move!"

From behind him came Yŏnho's chilly voice, along with the click of cocking his gun.

Old man Ko moved toward the cave, and opened his heavy lips:

"Hyŏn!"

The tone of the husky shout, fraught with long years of ups and downs, created a sorrowful echo.

"Hyŏn!"

A head with unkempt hair and two bright, sharp eyes appeared above the rocks.

An unspeakable yearning swelled up in the old man's chest, a yearning like an incomparable pain.

"Tell him quickly," said Yŏnho.

Old man Ko slowly spoke.

"Hyŏn, listen to my words. Only if you will come down—all of the gentlemen—everybody will forgive you. Why don't you come down?"

Old Ko finished and waited for Hyŏn's reply. A moment of agonizing silence. Then Hyŏn, without a response, withdrew behind the rocks.

The old man advanced one step. "Hyŏn!" And another step. "Hyon!" Without knowing it, he called Hyŏn's name and drew closer to the cave. "Hyŏn! Hyŏn! Even your mother . . . "

Suddenly the old man thought of Hyŏn's mother, whom he had seen on his way to the cave. Without even glancing up at the old man and Yŏnho, she called out, "My son, my son," and recited a story from her Bible. "God tested Abraham, and said to him, 'Take your son, your only son Isaac, whom you love, and go to the land of Moriah and offer him there as a burnt offering upon one of the mountains of which I shall tell you.'" That anxious tone of her voice, full of inviolable dignity, still rang in the old man's ears.

"Stand there!" From behind came the cruel voice of Yŏnho. Old man Ko stopped on the spot. He felt that his life had already come to an end, as certainly as that of an unripe chestnut in his palm.

Boom. Again came the distant sound of cannon—coming closer and then fading away, and then returning. If the sound only grazed him and never returned, the old man would have struggled to hustle in the midst of cruelty. Even when his second son had been dragged into the People's Army, in spite of the pain penetrating to the very marrow of his bones, he still found a small piece of ground to stand on. And that sound which was returning might be the signal that his first son was returning.

The old man's mind was torn and twisted. He turned his head and looked out over the tomb of his father; and he softly closed his eyes as if to overcome the pain. In that moment, the old man caught a glimpse of his eighty years of life. A long weary life—how many times has the world changed? How much pain and humiliation just to try to continue his own lineage, that of his father and grandfather, the generations of ancestors spread far into the past.

At this moment the threat of Yŏnho had no impact on the old man. He felt only pity for himself, who had had to tremble at threats all through his long existence. It occurred to him that he had tried to live his life of eighty given years unyieldingly.

Again, the rumbling sound of cannon came. Were it not for that sound, the old man might have tried once again to entice Hyŏn out. However, that was a sound of life and death, a sound which urged the selection of one or the other.

Old man Ko again looked up at the cave, where his own son had died and where now his grandson faced death. And at this moment of crisis, he himself was again about to witness death. This fatal coincidence of misfortune. Once again he directed his gaze at the ancestral grave sites. Had he not buried the bones of his ancestors so as not to be tangled in the chains of merciless destiny? Then before this calamity—war—the past's principles are all worthless? The loss of the norm of lineage. Soaked to the marrow in the belief of geomancy he had moved the ancestral bones around—wasted efforts of the past.

In the collapsing mind of the old man a new feeling

began to flow. A feeling of liberation from predestination, and a realization that no one could calculate the very next moment of destiny. And from this new feeling, the old man, for the first time in his eighty years, uninhibitedly decided by his own pure will.

My praiseworthy eighty years of life have been borne admirably, he thought. I have lived eighty years with my own empty fists and naked body, not due to the graves or this symbol of luck which hangs on my neck. This is sufficient; now I should go, and Hyŏn, you must live.

Deep emotion flooded through the old man's body. The hairs of his head and his beard glittered silver in the sun. The old man breathed deeply.

"Hyŏn! You must live! Listen to the sound of that cannon! You must escape from here somehow . . . "

Instantly, the old man felt a lump of fire pierce his back. As he was falling to the grass, he heard Hyŏn's shout in the echo of the noise of the gun. Lovely sound!

"Grandfather!"

Click! As Hyŏn pulled out his misfired first round and pushed the next round in, his rifle and Yŏnho's pistol fired at the same time.

Instantly, as Hyŏn felt the penetration of a hot rake in his left shoulder, he saw Yŏnho slowly twist to the left and fall, rolling among the bushes.

As he was trying to jump across the rock down the slope, Hyŏn suddenly felt dizzy and collapsed. Blood oozed from between his fingers as he clutched his shoulder. The pain and his weakened consciousness were dragging him to the ground. Thirty years of life, and now I'm going to die here. I must collect my thoughts before the end of my life. Is this the life of one human being? Thirty years! How have I lived? Avoidance, escape, regardless of day and night, escape and avoidance and flight. Aside from this, what have I done? I can think of nothing. Thirty years of life is a misfire like my first round! Zero! A living corpse! Then I have not lived.

With the next round I pierced Yŏnho's chest. I have killed a man. Pitiful Yŏnho. Yŏnho and I had no grievance toward each other. Is this the reason man is called a sinner? Unavoidable murder that man sometimes commits. Man's destiny that connotes sin. The Original Sin.

Inside the hedge of my luxuriant flower garden I lulled my supposedly innocent self to sleep, while on the outside raged black clouds and violent storms, as well as the dying screams of human beings.

It might be a scream that I should have made first. I should have taken the place of that young soldier lying on the roadside. A man like me still lives, and people who should live are dying. Is it possible these kinds of things are allowed to take place? Father died in this cave. His life, intensely and liberally lived, was burned out in a minute. He died for the people and instilled a sense of significance in their lives.

Grandfather lying in the bushes—he is not a corpse but the proof of life. With his naked body he defied all absurdity, and insisted on absurd life in the midst of absurdity. The bloody history of one human, death reminiscent of the death of a giant.

Mother. With the body of a weak woman, she has borne so much. Her love of me transcended her pain, the love of her dead husband, and her love of God, in whom she trusted everything.

You, when and what kind of pain did you endure? Inside a shell, baseness and cowardice that rejected all pain. A worthless fellow who has deceived himself through masturbation in fear of the warmth of a woman's body. Self-deceiving cowardice exculpating fear of your responsibilities.

Pulling yourself into your shell, you shunned the sun like a mole. You have not lived but existed. Like a rock, you have not experienced life. And if you did not live, you cannot possibly die. To die without experiencing life, frustration of not being allowed to die whirled through Hyŏn's mind. And he tried to resist this fear, revitalizing his failing life.

I must live. I must die after showing proof of my life!

And in the depths of desperate resistance he felt an unexpected new strength bursting forth. Bit by bit, his mind felt a new weight and a new satisfaction of mind and body. He then heard the sounds of his own hard shell cracking. A bursting shell scattering pieces, and with it, a sudden shower of sparks! Sparks promising a leap into a new dimension. Countless flowers of fire, dazzling glitter, burning urge for life, a flood of life whirling through his guts, an intense feeling of liberation!

Hyŏn felt an exhilaration opening into the endless blue sky. One bullet remained. My life, like this bullet, remains; what, then, will be the result? Nobody knows. First, I must choose, and next? Again, nobody knows.

One thing is certain—there will be no turning away or escaping. I will not turn away, but I will confront, confront the impending impasse where there is no escape. At last a moment has come for me to confront it face to face.

Already, the era of the flower garden is over.

I will live, and first of all I will resist the contractors. I must teach them that their noisy arguments will only intensify the futility of life. (I will carve this into their bones.) I must deny them, fighting with my naked body,

not by avoiding and ridiculing them. There are number-
less people in my situation, nay, in worse than mine!

Men careful in their ears and eyes toward their
neighbors, endeavoring not to bother others even in
words. Old or young, youthful faces of men and women.
Aren't those the faces that I yearn for? I cannot be lonely.
From now on I must search for my lost self among them.
We will isolate the contractors, and we will build a new
village on our inherited land. To that I will dedicate my
extra life. And to the meek who bore hardships and considered the contractors' haughtiness and cruelty as their
own disgrace! We must banish the insane contractors and
wait for a new world belonging to the meek.

A world for the meek.

Hyŏn could not control something warm blossoming
in his chest. The pain returning in his shoulder, and the
earth covered with a hundredfold pain. He must gladly
suffer this much pain and overcome it easily. And he must
live to tell his friends his own past story.

Hyŏn heard a voice calling him away from his own
cloudy consciousness: a shout that was closer than the
approaching boom of cannon.

"Listen! That sound. That approaching sound I
yearn for."

That shouting akin to crying came closer to the cave,
and the echoes resounded from mountain to mountain,
and valley to valley.

Mountain upon mountain, an endless range of mountains, and meandering valleys. The eternal stillness was
broken where a new life began to grow and move its
wings.

The Author

Sŏnu Hwi was born on January 3, 1922, in Chŏngju, North P'yŏngan; was graduated from Seoul Teacher's College in 1943, and taught for a while in a middle school. Upon the outbreak of the Korean War, he enlisted in the army as a second lieutenant and retired as a reserve officer with the rank of colonel (1958). "Flowers of Fire" was published in the journal Munhak Yesul *in July 1957, winning the Tongin Prize, and "The Ducks and the Insignia" appeared in the* Chisŏng, *autumn 1958. Since 1959 he has worked first as an editorial writer for the* Han'guk Daily *and then as editor in chief of the* Chosŏn Daily, *both in Seoul. His novels include* Myth of Clover Village (1962).

Sŏnu Hwi is often credited with having given expression to historical and cultural consciousness hitherto dormant in postwar Korean fiction. "Flowers of Fire" encompasses three generations, from 1919 to 1950. Ko Hyŏn's grandfather, the archetype of premodern Korea, believes in geomancy and accepts the forces of fate. Set against him is Ko Hyŏn's father, a leader of resistance, a patriot who gave his life for the Korean independence movement. Poised between the two is Ko Hyŏn himself, who vacillates between revolt and resignation, and toys with eremitic ideas. Old Korea's calm resignation to fate and habit of detached observation were the evils which brought about the loss of the country and the humiliation of servitude. The fall of the Yi dynasty, the Japanese seizure, the Second World War, the liberation, the Thirty-eighth Parallel, the Korean War—can Ko Hyŏn turn away from such a historic panorama? Can he save himself by escaping from history, which destroys man? Ko Hyŏn finally resolves to become a witness, destroying false ethical values and illusory images of man, and repudiating the irrational terror imposed in the name of ideology.

Whatever the promise, one must battle against the suppression of the powerless and the degradation of humanity. History, for all its ambiguity and betrayal, demands action, an impassioned involvement in the shaping of the destiny of a nation and a people. One must shatter the shell of sterile egocentrism and devote one's life to the establishment of an authentic relationship with the world. "Flowers of Fire" stands for the awakening of the conscience of Ko Hyŏn and his people, a moment of genuine awareness for every Korean in a war-torn and divided country. The style at times is a captive of its subject, and the translation has omitted some verbose passages.

In "The Ducks and the Insignia," Sŏnu Hwi has created authentic characters and dialogue. Teacher Kim and Ch'unbong talk in a northern dialect that is difficult to capture in translation. The former Communist and the diehard terrorist have turned recluses, and they design a new life in the country. But even in such a simple economic arrangement, they need the help of the insignia of their friend, Colonel Sŏng. A nostalgia for power, their pride and consolation in the colonel's badge—these are the realities in Korea, which the author has succeeded in portraying with fierce honesty and lyrical sadness.

by Sŏnu Hwi

The Ducks and
the Insignia

The colonel got into the jeep and turned around. "Sorry, brother, I've taken the comfortable front seat."

"Not at all," said Ch'unbong. "It's your jeep after all."

"It's not mine any more than it's yours."

"What's the difference? It's yours as long as you ride in it."

The engine started, and the vehicle glided off with an explosive muffler sound.

"This jeep is pretty much of a wreck."

"Yes, I should have the muffler fixed."

"Other jeeps look so slick. How come yours is like this?"

A group of children was playing in the middle of the road ahead of the car. The driver blew the horn.

"Yeow, what a sound," said Ch'unbong.

Translated and abridged by Peter H. Lee

"It's the same horn we've always had, brother."

"But other cars have two-tone horns which sound a lot better."

"But they're against regulations."

The jeep went rattling along the bumpy road, on the broad sides of which barley fields stretched to the foot of the distant mountains.

"Brother, can we make it in two hours?"

"We can do it in an hour and a half."

I wonder with this jeep, though, the colonel said to himself, thinking of the worn-out tire.

"Well, you've done pretty well. A full colonel!"

"A full colonel does not mean much."

"For a Korean to be a full colonel under the Japanese occupation was a rare thing," said Ch'unbong. "Even a second lieutenant was awe-inspiring. Look at me, I haven't done too well."

The colonel started to turn around, but something caught his eye. A tumble-down thatched hut by the roadside. A boy in ragged clothes lifted his arm.

The colonel returned the boy's salute. "Poor kid." He folded his arms with a sigh, remembering. Ten years ago, his home town in the North, the familiar hills and waters and the peaceful village. "Do you remember the first anniversary of Independence Day after the liberation?"

"It seems as though it took place in a fairy tale. You defected to the South immediately after that, didn't you?" asked Ch'unbong.

"Yes, it was tough going in the North. The Communists defiled the spirit of the March First Movement, even mobilizing primary school kids to drum up enthusiasm for their cause. I can still vividly recall the scene: the girls whom I led bowled over in the crush, with their skirts pulled up around their necks."

"You remember that part of it, for you were then a bachelor."

"Oh, cut it out," said the colonel.

"Remember, Mr. Kim who pumped out propaganda as a party representative?"

"Yes, it really made me sad."

"Wasn't he your first-grade teacher?"

"Yes, when we were a lot of sniveling kids," said the colonel.

"Kim really seemed to go nuts after the Communists' takeover. We were ashamed of him."

"Wasn't it in May of that year that you escaped from the North after raiding the Party headquarters?"

"Yes, I think so," said Ch'unbong.

"I believe I first met you near Kwanghwa Gate in Seoul, soon after your arrival."

"Wasn't it in front of the headquarters of the Northwest Youth Corps?"

"That's right," said the colonel.

"You were working on a newspaper then?"

"Yes, my office was near the corps headquarters, where I used to go see friends and look for news items."

"Were you a member of the corps?" asked Ch'unbong.

"No, I wasn't. Now that it's a closed book, I can tell you, I was rather scared of what you were doing then."

"You were right to be. We were a bunch of silly fools."

The colonel remembered the bloody terrorism, rabble-rousing, handbills, messages, battle cries, intrigues, scandals, invectives. . . . Was it yesterday that he was roaming around in this chaos, equipped with a press card, not knowing what to do?

"I once went to cover an incident where the police were trying to crack down on besieged workers. In the midst of confusion I found myself giving first aid to a blood-soaked striker who had suffered a head injury. Then a policeman came up to me and ordered me to let him alone. It made me wonder—instantly I recalled similar scenes I had witnessed in the North, and I felt more and more confused and baffled."

"Yes, it was a time of confusion," said Ch'unbong.

"I felt so alienated that I soon abandoned the newspaper and tried various things, stevedoring, farming."

"You're a queer bird."

"But I found I was not up to that sort of job. So I found myself teaching in a middle school."

"You're not exactly a military type either."

"Well, to be frank, I didn't go into the army out of high-flown patriotism or racial consciousness. I simply volunteered to keep myself alive."

"Never heard of a man going into army to keep himself alive."

"I did. Do you remember, brother Ch'unbong, the military revolt at Yŏsu when I was teaching school there? Every morning the teachers scrambled for a newspaper— 'Oh, this is really serious,' 'Oh, they've got as far as here!' in a seemingly worried tone. But I could read their minds: they were inwardly cheering and welcoming the advance of the rebels. Watching them cheering like onlookers from a safe distance at the sight of people being butchered—I was dumbfounded. I had serious thinking to do. I said to myself: I would have been killed if I had been there or if the fighting had broken out here in our midst. This reasoning prompted me to make a decision about which side I was on, so that at least I would not suffer or die for nothing. That's how I came to enter the army."

A bus approached, stirring up a cloud of dust. It passed them with a roar.

"You were a captain when the war broke out?" asked Ch'unbong.

"Yes, it was like a bad dream. From the moment I crossed the Han River Bridge, I considered myself a dead man and felt that each day I was living on borrowed time. I volunteered for the Special Forces, preferring to end my own life rather than be pushed down to the water's edge, in the port of Pusan, to drown."

"Don't talk about the Special Forces."

"You landed on Changsa, right?"

"Yes, it was sheer hell."

"It was too much for us."

"But you didn't go through the worst of it."

"Still, nobody knows what would have happened if the Inch'ŏn landing had been delayed."

"You were lucky to have gotten as far as P'yongyang," said Ch'unbong.

"We didn't see much, though, except for looters," the colonel said.

"Considering the fact that it was a war to kill, you never knew what really took place."

An ox cart lurched aside hurriedly on the top of a slope as the jeep made a sudden curve.

"Mr. Kim was captured in Yŏngdong, I understand?" asked the colonel.

"Were it not for Sŏngho, he would have been killed."

"He was lucky to meet Sŏngho, who was a chief of the Thought Control Section there."

"Yes," said Ch'unbong. "He guaranteed Mr. Kim's parole and later arranged for his marriage."

"What is she like?" asked the colonel.

"A former guerrilla, a country girl."

"Mr. Kim must have changed a lot since then."

"Beyond recognition, I would say," said Ch'unbong.

"We've all changed, haven't we?"

"Indeed, thanks to the war."

Bang! The colonel was taken by surprise. The car came to an abrupt stop. Ch'unbong's head bumped against the back of the colonel's.

"Hell," shouted Ch'unbong.

"A flat tire," said the driver. He clicked his tongue and glared at the rear wheel as he climbed out of the car.

The colonel and Ch'unbong got out. The colonel gave an awkward grin at Ch'unbong and felt the back of his head.

"Why don't you change the tire?" said Ch'unbong to the driver.

The two men sat on the grass at the edge of the road.

"I'm afraid we won't get back home before sunset."

"It'll only take a minute," said Ch'unbong.

The colonel produced a pack of Paegyang cigarets from his pocket and offered one to Ch'unbong. "Does Mr. Kim know I'm coming?"

"Yes, he's anxiously waiting for you."

"I think we'd better buy him something."

"There's a market on the way," said Ch'unbong. He inhaled the cigaret luxuriously. "You know, they're still rolling their own with newspaper."

"How's the food situation there?"

"They get a bag of barley, but their side dishes are mostly wild vegetables."

"The same goes for Mr. Kim, I suppose," said the colonel.

"Yes, everyone gets the same. Come to think of it, he has a hard life. Had he stayed in the North, he would have ended at least as a bureau chief."

"He must have changed a lot since then."

"Yes, he's quite a different man. I was making the rounds of all my friends when I learned of his whereabouts. He received me warmly; the previous quarrels we had had in the North were forgotten on the spot. Mr. Kim had fallen on bad times, and I had become pretty much of a rolling stone. We're more or less in the same shoes. Kim had only one wish: to live in a quiet village and bring up his kids."

"How many kids?" asked the colonel.

"A girl five and a boy three. He has his own ideas of making a living. He's a graduate of an agricultural school. He says that by raising chickens and ducks during the winter he will have enough eggs to buy a couple of milk goats in the spring. The two will yield two thousand wŏns' worth of milk every day, he says."

"He's counting his chickens before they're hatched."

"No, really, he's got it all worked out. Let him explain it to you. So I've decided to join forces with him. The time for demonstrations and fistfights is over. Anyhow I've had enough. I also have kids—and his offer came at the right moment, when I was thinking of settling down somewhere. That's why I brought my wife and kids up here."

"You've done the right thing," said the colonel.

"I still have to make it work, though."

The driver finished changing the tire and honked the horn. The two got into the car; soon they were at the marketplace.

"What're you going to buy?" asked Ch'unbong.

"What about a bottle of wine and a pound of beef?"

"Beef is expensive. Pork will do. Give me the money. I'll get them for you."

"No, let me do it."

"It doesn't look right for a colonel to do his own shopping."

Some time passed before Ch'unbong returned with a bottle of wine and a pound of pork.

The jeep crept laboriously up the winding road and crossed several hills. At the last hill came a plain, dotted with farmhouses.

"You see the tile-roofed building over there. That's the police station."

As the car approached the station, Ch'unbong asked the driver to stop. "Shall we drop in at the station for a minute?"

"Why?" asked the colonel.

"You'll find out."

The colonel followed Ch'unbong into the station. A police sergeant and two policemen looked up at the two unexpected visitors. Ch'unbong, with his arm resting round the colonel's shoulders, introduced him to the sergeant.

"Sergeant, this is Colonel Sŏng of the X Division."

The colonel and the sergeant exchanged salutes almost at the same time. He then introduced his friend to the policemen. Now the colonel realized what his friend was up to.

"Ch'unbong was like an elder brother to me back in our hometown. I'd appreciate anything you can do for him."

They came out of the station and got back into the jeep.

"There's no harm in knowing the right people," said Ch'unbong. "I think you're the first colonel they've ever seen." Ch'unbong seemed extraordinarily pleased with himself. "If I'd kept out of politics and joined the police force, I'd be a police captain by now."

"Sure, you would. How far is it now?"

"Er . . . just over the hill."

By the time the jeep entered the village it was pitch dark.

"Here we are, here we are," said Ch'unbong.

The colonel looked in the direction Ch'unbong was pointing and saw flickering lights like fireflies glowing at the distance.

"Blow the horn."

"No need to wake up the whole village," said the colonel.

"Please blow the horn."

The driver blew the horn.

"Keep on blowing," Ch'unbong insisted. The driver sounded the horn once again.

Something dawned on the colonel—it was to announce his arrival to the whole village.

"Here we are," said Ch'unbong.

The car came to a halt. Ch'unbong got out and was running toward his house, calling for his son.

The colonel stood there for a while, then slowly followed him. He was excited and yet nervous at the thought of meeting Mr. Kim after more than ten years. He was afraid of seeing the features of his former teacher changed beyond recognition. His heart pounded. When he had crossed the small stream, the colonel heard Ch'unbong calling.

"This way please!" In the light of the lamp, a wall, a wooden floor, and a stepping stone emerged like a stage. The lamp was hung on the center post, beside which the colonel could barely discern a shadow. Ch'unbong grabbed him by the hand and pulled him toward the shadow.

"Here's Teacher Kim!"

The colonel took off his cap and felt his way through the dark toward the teacher.

"How do you do, Mr. Kim?"

"Oh, Mr. Sŏng."

"It's been such a long time."

Teacher Kim grasped the colonel's outstretched hand.

"You must have had a hard time, teacher."

There was no reply. Mr. Kim just squeezed the colonel's hand more tightly than before.

The colonel felt that Mr. Kim's hands were getting hot as a ball of molten iron. The teacher's bowed head was trembling. Apparently he had clenched his teeth to hold back his emotion. Two lines of wrinkles carved deep furrows about his mouth. The colonel thought it fortunate that the light was dim.

"Teacher!" A hot drop fell on the colonel's hand.

"Teacher Kim!"

Ch'unbong dropped his eyes at the sadness in the colonel's voice. Teacher Kim led the colonel by the hand to the veranda. The colonel saw the teacher's eyes in the dim light, and could find no cheerfulness in them. There was no luster to be found in those vacant eyes.

"You've come a long, rugged road," said Mr. Kim.

"Not at all, teacher. I apologize for having taken so long to come and see you."

"It's very kind of you to come."

"Teacher," the colonel raised his voice as if to reprove him. "Please stop deferring to me."

Mr. Kim gave an embarrassed smile. "I hope your family are all well?"

"Yes, they are. Thank you," the colonel said.

"Your mother is still alive?"

Again he is addressing me in the same honorific form, the colonel said to himself. "Yes, she is in Seoul."

"How many children do you have?"

"Two."

At this moment, Ch'unbong came into the room, accompanied by two women, almost pushing them forward to the colonel.

"This is my wife," said Mr. Kim. "This is Colonel Sŏng."

At the teacher's introduction, the fortyish woman respectfully bowed her head. The colonel instinctively jumped to his feet.

"It's really nice to meet you, Mrs. Kim. I should have called on you long before."

Ch'unbong interrupted him: "And this is my wife."

The woman in a one-piece dress, around thirty, bowed slightly with a faint smile.

"How do you do? I should have called on you earlier, I heard some time ago that you were living here."

The introductions over, the three men went into the house. Ch'unbong looked out the window and called, "Ladies, make us a little snack!"

The colonel studied the teacher's face. Incredible changes wrought by the passage of a decade astonished him. Mr. Kim's hair was grey, and innumerable wrinkles carved his forehead.

"You haven't changed very much, Mr. Sŏng."

"Yes, I have. Only the dim light hides it!"

"I mean, you look better than before."

"Teacher Kim," interrupted the colonel, irritated by his insistence on using honorific forms. "Please stop deferring to me."

"Oh, I've got in the habit of speaking that way." Mr. Kim's voice faded with embarrassment.

The colonel felt a lump in his throat. He longed to see the face and hear the voice with which Teacher Kim had captivated large audiences ten years before.

Ch'unbong opened his mouth. "You know what? Teacher has been doing some writing."

"Oh, Ch'unbong, what are you talking about?"

Ch'unbong went on with animated gestures. "Didn't you know Teacher Kim was famous for his mighty pen even during the Japanese occupation?"

"Ch'unbong exaggerates," Teacher Kim raised his head as if to stop him.

"I've decided to follow Teacher Kim's advice in everything. As I've said before, I can't go wrong if I do what the teacher has planned for us." Ch'unbong picked up momentum as he went on. "First, we'll raise ducklings and collect their eggs. You'll see tomorrow morning. We've already bought thirty ducklings. But the trouble is, the owner of the plot, a real country bumpkin, says he'd rather die than part with ten p'yŏng of land,[1] when we've already prepared the fencing for a duckling coop. But he won't let us go on with it."

"Such a small lot is hardly worth the argument, is it?" said the colonel.

"You don't know what a crank he is," said Ch'unbong. "To begin with, it exasperated him to see the contrast between his house and ours, which the teacher designed and built. So how could he bear to see us collecting eggs and getting richer day by day?"

Mrs. Kim brought in a table set with wine and side dishes—roast pork with cabbage, fresh wild vegetables, crown daisy, roots of bellflowers, garlic, and scallions.

"We've raised all these here," said Ch'unbong. "See the fresh crown daisy the teacher has grown."

The wine cups were all of different sizes. The colonel picked up the largest one and put it in front of the teacher.

"Oh, it's too big for me," said Mr. Kim.

"No, it isn't. It's your day."

The colonel put the next largest one in front of Ch'unbong. "You were a great toper, at least you were once."

"No, the little one will do. I'll drink several cups to your one." The northern dialect was gradually creeping into the colonel's speech.

The three raised their cups.

"Well," the colonel hesitated—no words appropriate to the occasion came to his mind.

"Well," the teacher said as if to himself. He looked into his cup.

"Thank you," Ch'unbong grinned, looking at the colonel across the table.

"Well, this is nothing special, I am rather . . ."

The colonel emptied his cup in one gulp and handed it over to the teacher who, putting down his half-emptied cup, took it saying, "Oh dear." He emptied the remainder and handed his own to the colonel.

The colonel gulped it down and handed his to Ch'unbong, who grabbed it as if he were waiting for it, gulped it down, and handed it back to the colonel.

After the first few rounds, they began to relax. The teacher, his face aflame, said to the colonel nostalgically: "Mr. Sŏng, I'm very lucky to have such good friends."

"Teacher Kim, no more flattery, please. Let's just drink."

The colonel had several more drinks to loosen the

reserve in his mind. He instinctively brought his hand up
to unbutton his jacket.

"Oh, you should have taken it off long ago."

"No, just a second," Ch'unbong interrupted him.
"Just a second."

"Why?"

"You'll see."

Ch'unbong jumped up and bolted out of the room.
He soon returned with a villager of about forty. The
colonel tried to make room for the newcomer to his left,
but Ch'unbong forcibly seated the guest at his right.

"Well, introduce yourselves to each other." The
colonel and the villager introduced themselves.

"Colonel Sŏng of X HQ," Ch'unbong introduced his
friend again to the villager in his high-pitched voice.
The villager introduced himself as a Kim, stealing a
glance at the colonel's insignia.

The colonel felt the villager's eyes glued on his insignia and suddenly awoke to the meaning of Ch'unbong's "Just a second." "Now, let's take off our coats,"
Ch'unbong said.

A few more rounds were passed. The colonel repeatedly offered his cup to the teacher.

"You have gone through a lot, Teacher Kim. Wearing a uniform, I've no apology to offer."

"Mr. Sŏng, you know how badly I've behaved."

"What do you mean? Don't we all behave badly some
way or other?" The colonel went on as if his tongue was
numb. "And do stop deferring to me. After all, I'm your
former student."

"Still, we are growing old together."

"Yes, but you're still my teacher, and I'm still your
student. I've heard a lot about you from Ch'unbong. That
you have been dragged in three times by the police and

gone through severe interrogation each time. I am sorry, but war is war."

"The last time I was in the police station, I made up my mind to die. When the interrogator left the room on the second floor, I opened the window to jump out. Then I saw my poor wife walking into the station gate with a bundle of clothing and food. Moreover, she was then pregnant with that five-year-old girl sleeping over there. Seeing her made me change my mind. Then and there I decided to live on."

His wife interrupted him from outside and announced the arrival of a new guest.

"Who is it?" Teacher Kim asked, starting to get up.

"Oh, it's the policeman we met a little while ago," said Ch'unbong and went out to meet him.

The teacher and the villager nodded to the newcomer as if they knew him. Then, Ch'unbong introduced himself to the policeman. "Kim Ch'unbong is my name. Please forgive the rude way I barged in on you at the station."

The policeman introduced himself to Ch'unbong and shook hands with him.

The colonel was taken aback. Hadn't Ch'unbong dragged him into the police station and introduced him to him there? He had taken it for granted that Ch'unbong knew the policemen. Now it dawned on him that Ch'unbong had taken him into the station in order to impress them. As he worked it out in his mind, the colonel was astonished at Ch'unbong's impudence.

After a few more rounds of drinks, Ch'unbong became bolder. "Thank you for coming. I hope you won't mind if I bring my problems to you sometime."

"You're welcome, sir," the policeman said.

"Lots of my friends are in the police. Some are lieutenants; some are captains. I have a lot of influential friends who help me. Today, the colonel honored me with a visit bringing along wine . . ."

The colonel glanced across at Ch'unbong for a moment and then turned to the policeman.

"As I have said, please take good care of my brother. Mr. Kim is our former teacher who taught and looked after us when we were sniveling kids."

The teacher sat with a complacent expression on his flushed face.

Ch'unbong suddenly growled at the villager. "At least you don't look down on me, do you? I may appear to be nobody now, but I was once a pretty important figure, doing things ordinary people wouldn't dare."

"Yes," the colonel chimed in. "He is a man worthy of support by our government. He was a die-hard anti . . . " The colonel swallowed the word "Communist."

"Mr. Kim," continued Ch'unbong. "Tell Mr. Chu that nothing will come of his stubbornness. Why is he so selfish about that bit of useless land on which we want to build a duckling pen? Do I have to bow to him because of that little plot?"

The villager nodded without a word. The colonel pleaded with Ch'unbong. "No more fuss about the land. Let's just drink!"

"Colonel Sŏng," Ch'unbong said, "please be quiet. It's outrageous. When we're pleading with him to lease that useless bit of land, he's got no right to be so stubborn. Don't you agree, colonel? Compared with what we had in the North, that piece of land is simply nothing."

The colonel emptied his cup and handed it over to Ch'unbong. A few more rounds were exchanged, while Ch'unbong kept mumbling. When he stopped and there was a momentary silence, the policeman and the villager stood up and asked to be excused.

"Why?" asked Ch'unbong. "Because I lost my temper over the wine? No, this Ch'unbong is still a man to be reckoned with."

The colonel half rose in a gesture of farewell, while Teacher Kim saw them off to the door.

The three had a few more rounds. The teacher grabbed hold of the colonel's hand and wouldn't let it go, while the colonel said, "I am sorry," over and over again as if in a delirium. The colonel picked up the wine jar only to find it empty.

"Hey, brother," the colonel said to Ch'unbong, taking some money out of his pocket, "Won't you send out for one more jug?"

"Why not?"

"Haven't we had enough?" the teacher interjected.

After more wine was brought, they had a few more drinks. Ch'unbong said, "Colonel Sŏng, Colonel Sŏng," then "Teacher Kim, Teacher Kim, let's start all over again." He went on mumbling something and then with a jerk called to the colonel.

"Colonel Sŏng, let's sing."

"Yes, why not?" the colonel agreed. "Why don't you sing first?"

"All right. What shall I sing?"

Ch'unbong closed his eyes for a moment. He was pondering. At this moment, something occurred to the colonel, who knew Ch'unbong liked to sing the anti-Communist song of the Northwest Youth Corps when he got drunk. To sing such a song in front of the teacher would have embarrassed them all. But the colonel could not do anything about it. It was Ch'unbong's business, after all, and he was drunk.

Finally, Ch'unbong began.

"Oh, my god," thought the colonel at the first words of the song:

In the blue sky of the Milky Way . . .

The colonel was completely taken aback by Ch'unbong's astute choice.

With no mast and no sail . . .

The colonel looked across at the teacher, who was listening with his eyes closed.

The moon sails smoothly.
Far away glitters a lighthouse,
So sail home, moon, it's a morning star.

Ch'unbong finished; the three clapped.

"Now it's your turn," said Ch'unbong.

The colonel hesitated, stealing a glance at Mr. Kim.

"Teacher Kim, it's a song I learned from you when I was a first grader." He drew a deep breath and began:

Come, the bright moon has risen.
So full and round like a ball,
So full and round in the front garden
and on back hill.

The song finished, he looked at the teacher, who sat motionless with his eyes closed and mouth trembling. The teacher grasped the colonel's hand once again full force.

"Yes, there was such a song," said Mr. Kim with sudden enthusiasm.

"We used to dance to the tune," said the colonel. "You stood at the center of a circle of students. First, we raised our hands and drew a circle in the air with both hands; then we drew a circle with one hand and with the other, and then a smaller one with the thumb and the pinky. And . . ." The colonel stopped talking and called to the teacher, who had dropped his head.

"Sŏng," Mr. Kim said with a quiver in his voice. "Yes, we did! How long ago was it? Almost thirty years?"

"Teacher Kim!"

With his head buried on his chest, the teacher's shoulders twitched.

"Teacher Kim," said the colonel in a cheerful voice. "Now, it's your turn."

After a while, the teacher raised his face streaked with tears. He began to sing:

Arirang, arirang, arariyo,
He's going over Arirang Pass.

Unable to face the teacher, the colonel lowered his eyes. Suddenly Ch'unbong began to sing with the teacher. He was more shouting than singing.

If you go along without me,
Your feet will pain you before you walk one mile.

The colonel too joined them. They sang it over and over again, knitting their brows as they sang at the top of their voices.

A rustle came from the veranda; it seemed that the women were eavesdropping on their men.

As he listened to the teacher's choked voice, the colonel felt something in his throat and then in his eyes. He wanted to cry, but he suppressed a surge of emotion that was about to drown him. A feeling of indignation welled up from the bottom of his heart.

The colonel abruptly stopped singing. Instead he began to give military commands at the top of his voice.

"Stop singing. Attention! Forward! March!"

Overwhelmed by alcohol, the colonel suddenly fell heavily flat on the floor, thinking that he was listening to a chorus of a sonorous march.

Next morning when the colonel woke up, neither the teacher nor Ch'unbong was in the room.

He got out of bed and walked outside, rubbing his eyes. The morning sun dazzled his eyes. The mountain in front of the village, which he had not seen the night before, was a brilliant green in the sun. The clear blue sky and the brilliant green mountain made beautiful harmony.

He saw a stream below him and some twenty grass roofs beyond it.

Teacher Kim, who was hoeing the garlic field, straightened up and greeted him with a smile.

"Did you sleep well?"

"I slept well. I'm the last to be up."

The colonel walked into the garlic field.

"Where is Ch'unbong?"

"He's gone to hunt frogs to feed the ducklings."

"He's changed a lot."

"With his perseverance there is nothing he can't do."

"I am a bit vague about last evening, but didn't you say you were having trouble with building a duckling pen?"

"Yes, it's a stretch of stony field near the house, unfit for grain, but the owner has adamantly refused to lease it to us."

"What kind of a man is he? Why is he so mean?"

"Well, he's not the only one. Since I came here, I have learned something new. At one time I worked for laborers and farmers. But there is something about them which can't be lumped together in such abstract terms. Partly because we all have had a hard time of it. But I can't make myself clear."

"Well, all the same, I think he goes too far."

Then someone called "Colonel Sŏng" from the distance. It was Ch'unbong walking over the furrows with a string of frogs. He had rolled his trousers up to the knee and his sleeves to the elbow. He looked healthy and sturdy.

There was a noise of hooting. A mob of village urchins was sitting in the jeep eating candy and raising a rumpus.

"Any of your children over there?" the colonel asked.

"Yes, the two on the back seat—my son and daughter. The boy in the front is Ch'unbong's. I guess it's the first time in their lives they've sat in a jeep."

The colonel shouted to the driver: "Hey, give them a ride as far as the pass over there."

After a few minutes the jeep started with an ear-splitting noise. The children shouted ever more uproariously.

"It's really isolated here," the teacher said. "When I went over that mountain for the first time to gather bellflowers, the village elders told me they had never laid eyes on a motorcar, even though they had seen a lot of airplanes."

"Oh, yes, I know what you mean," said the colonel. But still he was amazed. (A cultured nation which boasts a history of five millennia . . .) He felt embarrassed when he remembered that one of his speeches began with those words.

Ch'unbong, who was still making his way toward them, called to someone in the distance and changed direction. He was saying something to a young man.

"That's the owner of the land who has refused to lease the lot to us," said the teacher.

"Oh, is he? Let me talk to him."

The colonel and the teacher joined Ch'unbong and his companion, who cast a suspicious glance at the colonel. Ch'unbong introduced them. The colonel made a bow.

"This is my elder brother. I'd appreciate anything you can do for him. And Mr. Kim is our former teacher."

The young man remained unimpressed.

"It won't do you any harm," said Ch'unbong, "to lease the lot to us till next spring."

"I've already told you I can't."

"Why in the world?"

"Just because I don't want to, that's why. Duck dung is said to be poisonous to pear trees."

"No dung is harmful to a pear tree. Besides, the trees are a long distance from the lot. Don't be so stubborn."

"You're the one who is badgering me."

The colonel took a step forward and said, "I think you should be a little more considerate and settle the issue amicably. It's a small lot, anyway."

"No," snapped the young man, averting his face.

The colonel felt hurt. "You've no right to be so rude," he said. "This is a time for helping each other."

"But I can't."

"Why?"

"There is no why. I live by the law. That's all."

"By the law?" asked the colonel brusquely.

"Why, can you live without it?"

"What are you talking about?" The colonel felt a big hot lump of rage. A yearning for violence swept his body like a tide. In an instant, he pictured a scene: one mighty blow will be enough to send him bloody-nosed to the ground! Instead of raising his fist, he closed his eyes and suppressed a surge of emotion which felt like an eternity. He opened his eyes. The young man stood there unmoved.

"You don't have the right to talk that way," said Ch'unbong angrily. "Simply say no, if you must."

The colonel calmed himself and said, "No, brother, it's I who am to blame. Hey, young man, don't misunderstand me. I didn't say that because I'm in uniform."

The colonel's conciliatory tone seemed to settle the young man a little. His expression changed.

"I am sorry," the colonel added.

"Um, I was in the army too," the man said.

"Oh, were you? Which outfit?"

"The Fifth Infantry Division."

"When?"

"During the battle of Bloody Peak."

"In which regiment, may I ask?"

"The Y regiment."

"When Colonel A was its commanding officer?"

"Yes."

The faces of the teacher and Ch'unbong gradually brightened as they listened to the conversation between the colonel and the young man.

After a breakfast of wild vegetable soup and a bowl of barley, the teacher and Ch'unbong went out and began to unwind a roll of fencing to set it up.

The lot was a pebbly field of less than ten p'yŏng, beside the stream. The fence in, they herded the ducklings into the pen—the whole twenty-seven.

"Three have died," Ch'unbong said sadly. "All young things are cute. Even piglets."

"You mean all adults are ugly?" the colonel retorted.

Everyone laughed—the teacher laughed, Ch'unbong laughed, even the ladies. The reluctant landowner grinned. The kids chirped delightedly, munching their cookies.

The colonel looked hard into the pen for a while.

The pebbly lot of less than ten p'yŏng—it looked like a vast estate. Maybe his help was needed to acquire this estate. He unconsciously fingered the insignia on the right side of his collar.

"O my fatherland, my race, my friends . . ." All of a sudden, the colonel uttered these words to himself.

A sudden wave of love for his country and his people rushed through him.

As he drove away, the uproarious explosion of the jeep's muffler startled the villagers out of their homes. They silently watched the jeep depart.

Teacher Kim and Ch'unbong came as far as the top of the hill to see him off. They parted there. They kept insisting that the colonel return for the Autumn Moon Festival, and he promised he would.

On the way downhill, the colonel looked back. The two were still on the hill waving, silhouetted against the blue sky.

The colonel turned around and, sitting up straight, looked ahead. The barley fields stretching as far as the foot of the mountain rippled like breakers. The colonel thought he must have the jeep repaired when he returned to the camp. He still felt the hangover from the night before, but the fresh scent of the plants borne on the cool breeze refreshed him.

Colonel Sŏng had no special worry to speak of except for a report he had to prepare once he got back to headquarters.

He felt lonely.

by Yi Pŏmsŏn

A Stray Bullet

ix o'clock had come and gone, but Song Ch'ŏrho, a clerk in a public accountant's office, was still sitting at his desk in the corner. There was no unfinished work to do—he had long since closed the account books. All the others had waited, their eyes pushing the minute hand, and then scurried away at five o'clock. Ch'ŏrho, who had gone without lunch, was hungry and had no place to go.

"Aren't you going, sir?"

The tone in the office boy's voice was saying: 'How about leaving now so I can clean up.' Ch'ŏrho pulled both hands out of the threadbare navy fatigue jacket.

"I suppose I must."

His reply was like a yawn as he put his hands heavily on the table top.

The office boy began to sweep in from the far corner. The dust came billowing heartlessly into Ch'ŏrho's face.

Ch'ŏrho dragged himself to his feet. He went over to

Translated by Marshall R. Pihl

the corner window near his desk and poured a bucket of water into the wash basin. He slipped his hands slowly down into the water. It was still early spring and the water was cold on his fingertips. Ch'ŏrho stared down fixedly at the two hands as they soaked in the water. A bean-sized callous had grown on the first joint of the right middle finger where he always steadied his pen. From this callous, a strand of something like blue silk was softly unraveling into the water. Ink. It slipped along the bottom of the basin, then floated up easily and blossomed into a faint fog that spread in all directions. As it left the fingertip, its color grew thinner and lighter. When it had carried its clear autumn blue to the very edge of the basin the silky thing doubled back toward the fingertip to trace a halo in darker blue.

Blood! This is surely blood!

Ch'ŏrho cautiously removed his hands from the water. He saw the face of a man at the bottom of the basin. The face stared straight up into Ch'ŏrho's eyes with a strange, listless twitching as it laughed through puckered lips.

Hair scattered long on the forehead. Underneath, two hollow sunken eyes. Gaunt cheeks, a bony chin. The sallow face of a corpse. This was a primitive man of the remote past, a man who carries a club fitted with a sharp stone. A man who wanders barefoot in the forest all day to feed the family left behind in a cave.

A bear? No, I haven't the courage.

A boar? I'm too weak.

A roebuck? It's too agile.

A pheasant? No, it flies away.

A rabbit? Yes, something like that would be all right. But even rabbits are hard to find lately. There are too many other hunters—more of them than rabbits.

But one has to bring back something, no matter what it is.

The man kneels on a rock and washes his hands in a stream. The blue water is dyed by red twilight. Congealed blood melts from his hands into the water with a red even deeper than the twilight.

He seems to have caught something. A bear? A boar? A roebuck? Pheasant? Rabbit?

But what he lifts out of the water is none of these. Intestines, disgusting just to look at. The man himself does not know from what animal they came. He has seen neither the head nor the tail of the animal. He has simply scavenged something that someone else had dragged into the forest and abandoned.

Ch'ŏrho picked up the soap which lay beside the basin and scrubbed his hands vigorously. An incomprehensible resentment boiled up within him.

Burdened not even by an empty lunch box as he dragged himself up the slope at Liberation Village, his hands felt light and free, but his stomach was hollow.

The village was a collection of wooden shacks, flung at random one against the other into gouges in the hillside. Ch'ŏrho turned into a blind alley. It was so narrow that the eaves covered with salvaged ration boxes nearly grazed his shoulders. The path was slippery with slop water tossed carelessly from the kitchens, and burnt out coal briquets were scattered here and there like scabs on an open sore. At the end of the alley was the door to Ch'ŏrho's house, a patchwork of yellow cement-bag paper tied to the frame with white string. Ch'ŏrho pulled the latch, its rag leatherlike with grime. Though hung loosely enough to admit a man's fingers in the cracks, the door was stuck and would not open easily. It hung tight to its sill, while the sound of his mother's voice leaked out through the cracks.

"Let's go! Let's go!"

It seems that a voice changes with insanity. This was no longer his mother's soft, quiet voice; it was harsh and crafty, the voice of someone else.

When Ch'ŏrho opened the door and stepped inside he was faced with an odor like rotten rags. He stood inside the doorway, staring down blankly toward the warm corner of the hot-floored room.

He had seen a mummy at the museum once during his middle school days. Here was another one, wrapped in its cotton tatters. Not one strand of the white hair was in its proper place—it twisted like the matted gourd fiber used for scouring. His mother just lay there, face to the wall, crying "let's go . . . let's go," with the insistent regularity of hiccups. It was strange to him that such a jarring sound could come out of this skeleton.

Ch'ŏrho went into the next room and sat down with his back against the wall. He closed his eyes tight and swallowed hard.

As recently as two months ago, Ch'ŏrho had been greeting his mother every evening with, "Mother, I'm home," whether she could comprehend or not. But lately he had given up even that. Now he would just look down at her for a while and then go on into the next room.

Ch'ŏrho's wife rose silently from her gloomy corner. Her pants of old blankets were patched at the knees, one in black and the other in grey. She was nine months pregnant, with a stomach like an overturned gourd ladle. She passed Ch'ŏrho like a sleepwalker and went out to the kitchen. His wife was not a mute—there was just nothing to say.

"Daddy!"

Ch'ŏrho started as if someone had struck him smartly over the head. Right beside him staring up with her eyes widely opened sat his five-year-old daughter. Ch'ŏrho turned his head toward the child. The smile he attempted faltered to a grimace.

"You know what? Uncle Yŏngho said he's going to buy me a nylon dress!"

"Mmm."

"And he's going to buy me some shoes, too."

"Mmm."

"Then mother and I'll go to see the Hwashin Department Store."

Ch'ŏrho looked into his daughter's sallow face. For a dress the child was wearing one of his old shirts with the tails cut off and a draw string sewn into the waist. Her unmatched socks were held up by thin strips of rubber scavenged from somewhere.

"Let's go! Let's go!"

Again, like a curse, from the other room came the sound of his mother's voice. He had listened to it for seven years now, but it was still the voice of a complete stranger.

Ch'ŏrho tightly closed his eyes once more. He ground his teeth with the desire to beat on something, anything, with his two fists.

Even though it was chilly, Ch'ŏrho preferred the boulder's rounded hump to the room in his shack. Every evening after supper he would sit out in back, his two knees cradled in his arms, and wait out the evening watching the lights of the city. Down there, in a street he couldn't quite identify, a neon sign advertising wine would spin round dizzily and then suddenly go black, only to flash on again and spin once more to sudden blackness.

Ch'ŏrho would keep endless watch over that neon sign.

The rock face cooled bit by bit. It finally went completely cold, leaving warmth only in the spot where Ch'ŏrho was sitting. A moment later and his perch would grow cold also. Then he would have no choice but to get up.

Finally Ch'ŏrho did stand up. His legs had gone numb from being in one position so long. He thrust his hands deep into the pockets of his fatigue jacket and then took a long look at the night sky. The stars flickered in even greater brilliance than the night lights he had been watching below. Ch'ŏrho tried to single out Polaris among the many stars. His head tilted to the sky, he turned round and round in place. It was easy to find the Big Dipper, which looked like a water ladle hung upside down. The star in front of the Dipper, a little bigger and brighter than the others: that was the North Star. Ch'ŏrho drew a straight line deep into the night sky, linking his spot on earth to the North Star and then north as far as his gaze would reach. He stood thus, for some time, facing north. Before his eyes he saw his home village. Its narrow streets, even the very stones on those streets, stood out sharply.

His body trembled. A chill like electricity crackled up from his toes and shot out through his nostrils. Ch'ŏrho sneezed loudly. He shivered again and climbed down from the rock.

Slowly he entered the alley.

"Let's go!"

Ch'ŏrho stopped in his tracks. During the day, he had never realized that his mother's voice would carry so far, but he could hear it now even from the mouth of the alley.

"Let's go!"

But Ch'ŏrho could not stand there all night. He took another step, a heavy step, indeed. And not simply because his legs were numb.

"Let's go!"

For every step Ch'ŏrho took toward his house, the voice grew that much louder.

Let's go. Let's go back. Let's go back home. Let's go back to the old days again. Even before she lost her senses, his mother was always saying things like that.

The Thirty-eighth Parallel. No matter how carefully Ch'ŏrho explained this to the old woman, it was no use.

"I don't understand it. I never will. Thirty-eighth Parallel. Are you trying to tell me they built a wall there that goes right up to the sky? Who on earth do you think would stop me from going home?"

Ch'ŏrho's mother so wanted to end her days back north that she would have died in the attempt to return.

"You call this a life? If it were only for a day or two . . ."

Then she would give a sigh, slap her thighs, and sit down heavily. And each time Ch'ŏrho would explain.

"But South Korea's a free country, mother, don't you see that?"

He would try to reason with her, saying what a precious thing freedom was and how in the South they could at least live and endure life but that to return home would mean immediate death. But if it was difficult to make his old mother understand the Thirty-eighth Parallel, it was many times harder to make her understand this word "freedom." No, he decided, it was nearly impossible. In the end, Ch'ŏrho gave up trying to explain. And his mother came to think him spiteful and pigheaded for not trying to escape their hardships. Her son she saw as bent only on trapping her in this wretched existence.

Even so, Ch'ŏrho could understand something of his mother's feelings.

She had led a peaceful and abundant life with her family in the North. They were not rich, but they had had their own land and were masters of the village. And though she knew little of the world, she still could not believe that this Liberation Village—its cratelike shacks tacked one upon the other, perched in cavities that had been scraped out of the mountainside—was really liberation.

"I cried for joy too when we got our country back. Oh, how I cried! I even put on my red wedding dress and danced that day. But is this what has come of it all? I can't stand it. I will never understand. Something surely went wrong. The whole world's gone wrong, that's what."

It was all beyond her. How was it that someone could win back his country and yet lose his home? It didn't make any sense.

After she had fled south, there was not one day she didn't say something about going back home.

That day when the war began, June 25, 1950, right before their eyes they saw the bombs turn the whole of Yongsan into a gutted inferno. When that day was over, Ch'ŏrho had lost his mother forever.

"Son. Now. Let's really go now. Look there. See, the wall has fallen down. That Thirty-eighth Parallel wall has gone away."

From that day on, the old woman was hopelessly out of her wits. She was no longer Ch'ŏrho's mother—where on earth was there a mother who did not know her own son and daughter? She had lost everything but that one shrill phrase.

"Let's go! Let's go!"

It was only a faint light that leaked through the holes in the paper-covered door. Ch'ŏrho opened the door to the inner room. On the sill between the two rooms the oil lamp was flickering. His daughter lay stretched out sound asleep over the warm spot in the heated floor. Her straight little body, wrapped round in a blanket, looked like a corpse. Beside her knelt Ch'ŏrho's wife, her weight back on her heels. On the grey and black patched knees of her pants of blanketing rested a pair of little sneakers made of red oilcloth. As soon as Ch'ŏrho came into the room, she held them up on the palm of her hand for him to see.

"Uncle Yŏngho bought them for her."

The unusually long-lashed eyes smiled thinly. It had really been a long time since he had seen his wife smile. It was the smile of a woman who had long since forgotten that she had once been beautiful—a smiling face Ch'ŏrho had not seen for so long that he, too, had nearly forgotten.

Ch'ŏrho sat down near the lamp and took the red shoes from his wife's hand to look them over closely, top and bottom.

"Did you go out for a walk?"

Beyond the lamp's light sat his younger brother Yŏngho. He smiled as he looked at Ch'ŏrho.

"When did you come home?"

"Just now."

Yŏngho had not even loosened his necktie yet.

"Ch'ŏrho."

At his brother's insistent tone, Ch'ŏrho handed the

shoes back to his wife and looked into Yŏngho's face with level gaze.

"Why don't we try living like other people do for a change? Damn it, everyone else enjoys life, why do we have to go on like this? Let's get ourselves a really first-class house and hang up a nameplate big as a chess board. We'll put your name on it—hell, we'll make the letters so big even a blind man could read them. And then we can really live."

Yŏngho had been out of the army for more than two years now without a job and started talking like this whenever he was drunk.

"Let's buy ourselves a twenty million hwan sedan. We'll load it with dung and ride around town all day long blowing the horn at all those bastards, whether we've got work or not. Shit!"

Slouched against the wall, Yŏngho blew cigaret smoke through a face red with wine.

"You've been drinking again!"

Yŏngho had joined the army after three difficult years of college as a self-supporting student. He had no particular skill and now, through no fault of his own, was unable to find work. Ch'ŏrho understood this, but what he disapproved of was Yŏngho's coming home drunk like this every night. Also, it was not at all clear where he did his drinking and with whose money.

"Yes, I did have a few. My friends and I."

Ch'ŏrho did not have to listen—it was the same answer every night. And he knew it was not a lie.

"You should cut out drinking so much."

"But when we get together, it's only natural to have a drink or two."

"Yes, I know. But what I'm saying is you shouldn't get together with them in the first place."

"Oh, I couldn't do that."

"But what do you think is the point of getting together for a drink all the time?"

"Point? We get together because we feel low. So we have a drink and talk about things, that's all."

"But I still say it'll lead to no good."

"Come on now. What's wrong with having a few friends, even like them? They're not so great but still, lots of times I wonder how I could get along without them—whatever you think. I mean it. So they're ignorant —this one without an arm, that one crippled. Not worth much, I guess. Real leftovers. But Ch'ŏrho, they're really good at heart. They're comrades, buddies."

Yŏngho tossed his head back and blew cigaret smoke toward the ceiling. Ch'ŏrho said nothing but just stared blankly at the figure of his younger brother. As Yŏngho watched the rising smoke, he pulled on his necktie with his free hand and slipped the knot halfway down.

"Let's go!"

Yŏngho quietly turned his head toward the sound coming from the next room. He blinked his eyes in silence as he gazed for a while in that direction.

Ch'ŏrho took a long breath. The flame of the lamp danced and flickered in front of them. He drew a pack of Bluebird cigarets from the pocket of his jacket and pulled one of them out. Almost half the loose, dry tobacco crumbled out each end of the cigaret. He twisted up the ends of the paper. What he then put into his mouth looked just like a piece of paper-wrapped taffy.

"Try one of these, brother."

Yŏngho picked up the pack of cigarets lying in front of him and offered them to Ch'ŏrho. It was a red package of American cigarets. Ch'ŏrho glanced obliquely for a moment at the unusually long cigarets and then, without

a word, brought the Bluebird between his lips over to
the lamp. Yŏngho casually watched his brother's shoulders
as they bent over the flame. There was a sizzling sound.
The hair falling on Ch'ŏrho's forehead suddenly frizzled
at the ends. Ch'ŏrho lifted his face and removed the
cigaret—after only one puff it was already a butt, burning
the tips of his fingers. As he slowly exhaled, three vertical
wrinkles deepened between his eyebrows. Yŏngho put his
own pack of cigarets back on the floor and quietly lowered
his gaze to the lamp. A smile slowly touched the corners
of his mouth: a strange smile, a pitying one—no, as if in
scorn. And then it passed.

Neither said a word.

"Let's go!"

From the next room, their mother spoke in her sleep.
It seemed even in her dreams she had now lost touch with
reality. The very low sound, like a sigh, slowly flowed
through the two rooms, filled them, and vanished.

Still no one spoke. Ch'ŏrho watched the flickering
lamp, the cigaret butt pinched in his gathered fingertips;
still slouched against the wall, Yŏngho gazed at the butt
burning between Ch'ŏrho's fingers. Ch'ŏrho's wife was
busy with the red shoes, arranging them this way and that
at the head of her sleeping daughter.

"Let's go!"

Again that voice, sounding as though it had leaked
out from someplace within the ground.

"You don't like my smoking American cigarets, do
you?" Yŏngho held up the half-burnt cigaret and looked
into its red ash.

"It's just not in keeping."

Ch'ŏrho kept gazing into the lamp as he spoke.

"I know, but which do you like better—Bluebirds or the American ones?"

"Well, of course the American cigarets are better. So?"

The look he slapped across Yŏngho's face said, here you can't even afford to eat barley, but you show off with American cigarets.

"So that's why I smoke American cigarets."

"What?"

"You don't understand, brother. What money do I have for American cigarets? But sometimes my friends buy them for me—so I smoke them. And you don't approve of my drinking every night, do you, and always coming home by minibus? I know. Sometimes you have to plod almost three miles from Chongno because you don't have even twenty-five hwan for the streetcar. But is that any reason why I should turn down friends who insist on seeing me home? Maybe it isn't real friendship, but just a foolish kindness that flows with the wine. They're strange guys, you know—they treat me to cigarets and wine, even pay my bus fare, but never give me money."

Yŏngho looked at his glowing cigaret, rolling it over and over between his fingertips.

"All the same, it's about time you sobered up. Do you realize it's already two years now since you got out of the army?"

"I know, I've got to get moving. Anyway, whatever happens I'm going to settle the whole thing sometime this month."

"You've got to get a job somehow."

"A job? Like you? What, you want me to balance someone else's household accounts, and for a salary that doesn't even pay the carfare?"

"You've got some other ideas?"

"Yes, I do. All I need is guts, like other people."

Ch'ŏrho stared dumbly into his brother's face. His fingertip stung. He ground out his cigaret in the beer can that served as an ashtray.

"Guts?"

"Yes, guts."

"What do you mean, guts?"

"The guts even a crow has. A crow doesn't need to be smart—brains don't have anything to do with it. He isn't scared by a scarecrow. Since he hasn't the wits of a sparrow to start with, a scarecrow means nothing to him."

Once more a smile skirted the corners of Yŏngho's mouth. The same strange smile he had a moment before when Ch'ŏrho was lighting his cigaret butt.

Tensing, Ch'ŏrho searched Yŏngho's face and swallowed hard. "You are not up to something wild, are you?"

"Wild? Oh, no. Nothing wild about it. We just want to get rid of all that baggage and travel light, like everyone else does, that's all."

"Get rid of what baggage?"

"You know, all this stuff about conscience, ethics, customs, laws, and all." Yŏngho's big eyes took on a curious gleam as they bore straight into Ch'ŏrho's.

"Conscience, ethics? You . . . you want to what?"

Yŏngho gave no answer, but just kept staring straight at his brother. "If I wanted to go live like that, I would be sitting pretty by now, you know."

"You would abandon conscience, ignore ethics and customs, defy the law . . . ?" Ch'ŏrho's voice was trembling.

At his brother's loud, excited voice, Yŏngho dropped

his eyes from Ch'ŏrho's face to his own feet stretched out in front of him.

"I do respect you, brother. All the hardship you've gone through and the way you've held up. But still, you're a weak man—no guts. You're a slave to conscience. Maybe the weaker a man is, the tougher the thorn of conscience . . . maybe that's what it is."

"Thorn of conscience?"

"Yes, thorn. A thorn in your fingertip, that's what conscience is. If you just pull it out, there's nothing to it. But if for no good reason you leave it stuck there, it startles you every time you touch it. And then there's ethics. Ethics? That's like a pair of nylon undershorts. Wear them or not, it doesn't matter—your parts show through all the same. Customs? That's like the ribbon in a girl's hair. It becomes her, but leave it off and nothing's changed. As for law, that's like a scarecrow—a scarecrow with a half-ripened gourd for a head on which they've drawn in eyes, a nose, and a very large beard. So there it stands, dressed in rags, with its arms sticking out at the sides. For the sparrows, I guess, it's a pretty good threat. But it doesn't work for something bigger, like a crow. They perch right on its head and wipe off the rotten soil from their dirty beaks. Nothing happens at all." Yŏngho gave a snort. He drew a fresh cigaret from his pack by the door sill; putting it in his mouth, he lit it from the butt he had just finished.

"Let's go!"

Mother's voice again. She was asleep but she still shrilled her "Let's go, Let's go!" Probably it was now a physiological function for her, like breathing.

Ch'ŏrho glared at Yŏngho who, slouched on his side,

was gazing glassy eyed at the ends of the two feet still stretched out before him. After a while, Ch'ŏrho turned his eyes away. He leaned back against the partition which divided the two rooms, then turned and settled on his side.

The little face of his sleeping daughter looked plaintive in the faint lamp light. Beside the child sat Ch'ŏrho's wife. One knee was drawn up, her hand resting on it to prop her chin. She had been sitting there all the while, listening quietly to Ch'ŏrho and Yŏngho as they talked—just thinking her thoughts while her free hand stroked and stroked the child's red shoes, arranged on the floor beside her.

Ch'ŏrho dropped his head, burying his chin in his chest. Yŏngho took three or four drags, one after the other, on his freshly lit cigaret. He went on speaking.

"Don't get me wrong, brother, I really do understand your view of life—no matter how poor we are, at least we'll live a clean life. Sure, it's good to live a clean life. But do we have to make such sacrifices just for you to keep clean? Dressed in rags, starving. You do it even to yourself. You have a bad tooth that throbs day and night, but you don't do anything about it. When someone has a toothache, he should see a dentist and get the tooth fixed or pulled. But you just put up with the pain. I suppose there isn't much choice since you don't have the money to pay the dentist. That's the trouble. What I mean is, you've got to get that money somehow. Your teeth are aching, so what do you do? You would say that putting up with a toothache is the same as making money—that not spending the money for the dental fee amounts to earning it. That may be true. But you can't say it's earning money when you've got none to spend in the first place, don't you see that? It seems there are three levels of people in this world. First are those who earn more than they need, just for the sake of collecting it. Then there are those who earn what they need because they need it. Finally, there are those who can't earn even what they really need, and so cut down on their standard of living. You probably belong in that lowest category— living as if you were fitting your foot to the shoe, rather than the shoe to the foot. You'd say you have no choice in the matter since you intend to lead a clean life. It's clean all right, but that's all it is. There you'll be, cupping your aching, swollen cheek, forever on the verge of tears. Isn't that right? If life were only a ten-hwan peep show set up in some alley for runny-nosed kids to watch, you could just look into that hole, see your ten-hwan's worth, and be done with it. But do you really think life's a peep show, where you can live as far as your pocket allows and then, if you like, be done with it? Do you? Like some obliging gullet that lets you eat only what you can afford and asks no more? The problem is that we've got to live whether we like it or not. Life isn't worth killing your- self over either. And that is a fact. To stay alive, you need money. And when you need money you've got to find it. Why shouldn't we give ourselves a little more elbow room? Who's to stop us from pushing the limits of the law? Why do we alone have to suffocate inside this cramped cell of conscience when other people have chucked all the niceties and gone beyond the law? What is the law, after all—isn't it just a line we agreed on among ourselves?"

Yŏngho threw his head back, undid his half-loosened necktie, and gave it a toss into the corner of the room.

Ch'ŏrho sat silently, his chin buried deep in his chest. He was looking down at his two big toes, which poked

boldly out of his worn socks. He had heard that a pair
of nylon socks could easily last half a year without wearing through. But he would still buy 100-hwan cotton
socks every time. With his salary he could not possibly
lay out 700 hwan all at once.

"Let's go!"
The mother turned over again.
"You're talking nonsense, Yŏngho."
Ch'ŏrho slowly lifted his head. The squatting shadow
of his wife loomed large on the newspaper-covered wall
across from him. Ch'ŏrho closed his eyes and leaned his
head against the wall.

Before him appeared his wife as she had been some
ten years before. Dressed in a white blouse and a black
skirt, she was the more beautiful standing up there on the
stage. It was the graduation recital at E. women's university and, when she finished her song, the applause went
on without end. How fresh was her beauty as they strolled
together around the streets that evening. But the one who
was squatting before Ch'ŏrho now was not the wife of
those days. She was more like some dull-witted animal.
She had even given up hoping. Ch'ŏrho slowly opened
his eyes. Only her eyelashes were the same—long and
black as they once had been.

"Let's go!"
Ch'ŏrho woke with a start from his reveries.
"Nonsense? Maybe, maybe so."
Yŏngho, who had been sitting with his eyes on the
flickering lamp, spoke listlessly.
"But according to what you say, Yŏngho, everyone
who has money is bad. What else could you mean?"
"Oh, no. When did I divide people into good and

bad? Who's bad? And for what reason? Or do you mean
bad for living well? Good or bad is no basis for drawing
lines, you know."

"But you just said that if you want to live well,
you've got to forget all about conscience and ethics. That's
what you said, isn't it?"

"Not at all; you don't understand. This is what I
mean: I admit you can live a model life and still be well
off. But that's very rare. On the other hand, if you just
forget about all the little niceties, you can be sure to live
well."

"That's just the kind of nonsense I was talking about.
You're wrong. You've got things twisted up in some part
of your mind."

"Twisted, you say? For all I know that may be true.
Twisted—no doubt about it. Only I should have been
twisted a long time ago. Before mother got the way she
is. Before the Han River Bridge was blown up, I mean.
Or before our little sister Myŏngsuk turned whore for
the Americans. Before we came back to Seoul when the
war ended. Then we could at least find an empty stall in
the East Gate Market. Or before I got this hunk of shrap-
nel blown into my belly—sitting there like part of my
guts. No, even before that. Back before I volunteered for
the army, like some kind of patriot swearing to pay back
mother's enemies—while all the others were dodging
the draft—even before that, way before that. It might have
been better had I been born twisted."

Yŏngho dropped his head heavily. He gave a long
sigh. Ch'ŏrho said nothing for a long time. His wife, as
in idle play, rubbed teardrops into the floor with her
fingertips. Yŏngho, too, was snuffing liquidly.

"But that's not what life is about. You still haven't the
vaguest idea of how a man must live."

"You're right. I really don't know how a man ought to live. But if we're going to keep alive, just survive right now when men are at each other's throats, I think I know how to take care of myself."

Yŏngho glanced toward the ceiling and with tear-filled eyes laughed as if in scorn for himself.

"Let's go!"

It was mother again. Yŏngho turned his eyes toward the next room. Ch'ŏrho heaved a long sigh. The lamp light fluttered abruptly. All the shadows around the room moved; it seemed as if the whole house moved. Just that, in the late night silence.

From somewhere out in the alley came the sharp sound of footfalls. They came slowly closer and stopped right in front of the door to the next room. Yŏngho turned his face. The warped door opened after a creak or two and their younger sister, Myŏngsuk, stepped inside. In her black two-piece suit, she looked just like any fresh, young office girl.

"You're late."

Yŏngho sat as he had been, legs stretched straight out, with only his head toward Myŏngsuk. She turned without an answer to remove her black shoes and put them in a corner of the next room. Then she gave her handbag a toss into another corner. She had just hung up her blouse and skirt when she flopped out on the floor and pulled a blanket up over her head.

Ch'ŏrho kept his silent gaze on the lamp light.

He was thinking of Myŏngsuk as he had seen her once outside the streetcar window on his way home from work. His streetcar stopped for the traffic signals at the Ŭlchiro intersection. Hanging onto an overhead strap, Ch'ŏrho was gazing aimlessly out the window when an American army jeep pulled up beside the streetcar. A

Korean girl in sunglasses was sitting next to the American soldier at the wheel. The girl was Myŏngsuk. There, just below where Ch'ŏrho was standing. One hand draped over the steering wheel, the American casually held Myŏngsuk close with his free arm. He was talking with his head toward her. Myŏngsuk sat, legs crossed, nodding as she looked ahead. On the other side of their jeep, a taxi drew up and the driver's young helper sniggered as he eyed Myŏngsuk and the soldier. It was the same inside the streetcar: the young men standing next to Ch'ŏrho were muttering to each other.

"She knows how to dress, though."

"Dress? Oh, the sunglasses, you mean."

"Not a bad business. No capital to worry about."

"Wonder if that kind ever gets married."

"Mmm."

Ch'ŏrho dropped his strap. He crossed over to the middle door on the opposite side of the car and turned away. He wasn't just sick at heart. Something beyond words, like burning charcoal, had thrust itself hard into his throat. His senses seemed dazed. Like after a yawn, his nose tingled and tears brimmed in his eyes. He gritted his teeth with a sudden urge to drive his head right through the large glass window in front of him. The bell sounded and the car lurched into motion. Moving forward, Ch'ŏrho leaned his shoulder against the door and closed his eyes.

Since that day Ch'ŏrho had said not one word to his sister. And she, for her part, had taken no notice of him.

"Why don't we try and get some sleep too?"

Yŏngho stretched himself up to an erect sitting position.

The lamp was put out, and between the rooms the sliding door was closed.

Ch'ŏrho was exhausted, yet he couldn't manage to get to sleep. The night was still—so quiet that time seemed to have stopped. His wife moaned, apparently in her sleep. Ch'ŏrho closed his eyes. He felt himself somewhere remote, distant. He was falling asleep.

"Let's go!"

The mother's voice was strangely loud in the sleeping night. Ch'ŏrho opened his eyes with a start and slowly adjusted them to the darkness. What day is it, he wondered. The moonlight slipped in through a crack in the door and drew a straight, blue line from the head to the feet of his sleeping daughter. Ch'ŏrho closed his eyes again. He sighed heavily and turned toward the wall.

"Let's go!"

Again that shrill voice. Ch'ŏrho did not stir again. Even he had fallen fast asleep.

But this time Myŏngsuk, in the next room, opened her eyes. Lying between her mother and Yŏngho, she quietly reached out into the darkness and groped for her mother's hand. Flesh just barely wrapped the bones. There was no warmth in the hand, only a slippery dampness. Myŏngsuk turned over and lay facing her mother. She reached out again and took the skeletal hand between her palms.

"Let's go!"

The mother gave no response to the daughter's touch, but cried out again into the void.

"Mama!"

Myŏngsuk's voice was low. She gently shook the bony hand.

"Let's go!"

"Mama!"

Myŏngsuk began to sob. She took her mother's hand and covered her own mouth with it.

"Mama!"

Her breath stifled, Myŏngsuk's weeping slowed to sighs and she began to nibble on her mother's fingers.

"You've nothing to be afraid of."

Beside her, Yŏngho spoke in his sleep.

"Let's go!"

The mother pulled her hand out of Myŏngsuk's and turned away.

Myŏngsuk yanked her blanket up over her head again. She lay sobbing underneath.

"Mama."

In Ch'ŏrho's room this time, the child called out for her mother.

Distantly, from within his sleep, Ch'ŏrho heard the sound but did not wake up.

"Mama."

The child called to her mother again.

"Uh, uh. What? Mama's right here."

The voice of the half-roused wife. She seemed to be taking the child in her arms. While he listened to the voices in the distance, Ch'ŏrho slipped wearily back into sleep.

"Wee-wee."

"You want to wee-wee? Up we go. That's a good girl."

Ch'ŏrho's wife sat up and lifted the child to her feet. Then she pulled a tin can from the corner and held it in place for her.

"Oh, look! Uncle Yŏngho bought you your shoes. Want to see how pretty they are?"

While she had her daughter propped on the tin can,

she reached over with her free hand and picked up the shoes lying by the child's pillow. Only their outline showed up in the faint moonlight, the color was lost in the dark.

"Are they mine, Mama?"

"Yes, dear. They're all yours."

"Pretty?"

"Very pretty, they're red."

"Mmm . . . "

The child's voice was full of sleep. She took the shoes in her hands and hugged them to her chest.

"Now, let's put them down and get back to sleep."

"Umm. Can I wear them tomorrow?"

"Of course, dear."

The child wriggled down into the blankets.

"Mama. Can I wear them tomorrow?"

"Of course."

She had always been told to take special care of anything good and so asked once more, just to be sure.

The wife carefully tucked in the edges of the child's blanket and lay down beside her.

They were all asleep again. For a while the moonlight shone across the breadth of Ch'ŏrho's chest.

The child gently lifted her head. She turned over on her stomach and stretched her small hands across the pillow to fondle the shoes there. Reassured, she lay back down, head on the pillow, and was quiet as though in slumber. But after a while the child stirred again. She pulled the shoes close to her and poked with her tiny fingers at their toes. This time she sat up in the bed and put the shoes on her knees. She held them up and examined them in the moonlight, turning them over to see the soles. One shoe in each hand, she matched the rubber soles against each other. Then she stuck her feet out and gingerly put the shoes on. From her sitting position she tried making steps on the floor.

"Let's go!"

The child was startled. She quickly took off the shoes and put them back where they had been. After one more look, she lay down stealthily and wriggled into the blanket.

When you go without lunch, the hardest part of the day is the hour from two to three. Ch'ŏrho laid his pen down on the account book. He looked over toward the office boy who sat with his back turned in the far corner. What he wanted was another cup of barley tea. It was all right, he thought, to ask the boy twice to bring him tea, but a third time would be an imposition. Ch'ŏrho pushed back his chair and got up. He picked up the tea cup sitting on the corner of his desk and went out the main door. In the hallway a large kettle was boiling on the burner. He poured himself a cup of the tea, the warm aroma wafting upwards. Ch'ŏrho balanced the hot cup between his fingers and carefully carried it back to his seat. He lifted the cup to his lips, blew on it, and was just having a sip.

"Mr. Song. Telephone for you, sir."

The office boy had come over to his desk to tell him. Ch'ŏrho quickly put the tea cup down and went over to the section chief's desk to pick up the receiver.

"Hello, Song Ch'ŏrho speaking. What? Police station? Yes, I'm Song Ch'ŏrho. What? Song Yŏngho? Yes, he's my younger brother. What was that? Yes . . . yes. Song Yŏngho was what? My brother? Yes, I'll come down immediately. Yes, sir."

Ch'ŏrho hung up and stood there, staring blankly at

the receiver in its cradle. The eyes of the whole office were on him.

"What's wrong? Was your brother in a traffic accident?"

The section chief looked up from his papers.

"Yes? Oh, yes, sir. It'll only take a moment. I'll be right back, sir."

Ch'ŏrho left the barley tea on his desk and went out the door. The other office workers exchanged wondering glances.

This was not the first time Ch'ŏrho had been called to the police station. Several times he had had to go identify his sister Myŏngsuk when she was picked up for soliciting American soldiers. Each time he would sit before the judge, head bowed, until Myŏngsuk was led in by a policeman. Without a word, he would then take her out the back door. And each time he cried. The only sister he had, but really he resented her. Without once looking at her, Ch'ŏrho would walk ahead along the streetcar line toward his office; and Myŏngsuk would at some point drop away into another street, as if she were a total stranger.

But this time it was not his sister, it was his brother Yŏngho. Ch'ŏrho recalled for a moment Yŏngho's drunken chatter of a few nights before. It made him feel uneasy. Impossible, he assured himself as he went through the station door.

Armed robbery. Listening to the details of his brother's case, Ch'ŏrho could only gape blankly at the detective. The color drained from his face and he felt it harden into an expressionless mask.

A fifteen-million hwan company payroll had been

drawn out of the bank and loaded into a waiting jeep. Just as the jeep was about to pull away, two strange looking men with sunglasses and low-brimmed hats had climbed in with drawn pistols.

"You've nothing to be afraid of! Just drive straight to Uidong!"

The driver and the company employee drove toward Uidong, the cold muzzles of the pistols at their backs. They were made to stop the jeep deep inside a remote, wooded area where they were ordered out. The car left them and headed back toward the city at full speed. It was stopped by the police before getting as far as Miari but only one of the men was inside.

The detective asked Ch'ŏrho if he wanted to see his brother, but he still sat there stupefied, his hands resting lifelessly on his knees.

After a moment the rear door of the detective's office opened and there stood Yŏngho.

"Come over here!"

Yŏngho, his hands cuffed in front, walked slowly up to the detective's desk. He nodded slightly toward Ch'ŏrho, who was rising from his chair. Ch'ŏrho's eyes bore into his brother's face, his bony cheeks pulsed. It was his habit to grind his teeth when distressed.

The detective motioned Yŏngho toward his brother. Yŏngho turned and stood facing him.

"I'm sorry, Ch'ŏrho. The law was no trouble, I got tripped up by human feelings—we should have shot them."

Yŏngho grinned into his brother's face. Then he glanced down toward his cuffed right hand, cocked his thumb back, and fired an imaginary pistol.

Ch'ŏrho stared without blinking at Yŏngho's forehead and the hair that fell over it.

"Why don't you go on home, brother?" Yŏngho spoke quietly. He seemed sorry for his brother, who stood there like a simpleton.

The detective turned toward the guard standing in the doorway. "Take him back."

Yŏngho moved toward the guard. As he was led out, he stopped for a moment and looked back.

"Ch'ŏrho. Take the child to see the Hwashin Department Store, will you? I promised."

The door slammed shut. Ch'ŏrho stood there, staring at it. His eyes clouded and dimmed. He couldn't see.

"Looks like he didn't intend to use his rights from the beginning."

The detective was murmuring to himself as he pushed the report to one side. Ch'ŏrho dumbly sat down.

"You wouldn't happen to know who the other young man was, would you?"

The detective's voice sounded very distant in Ch'ŏrho's ears. "He keeps insisting he did it all alone. But we've got witnesses and I think he'll be confessing everything pretty soon."

Ch'ŏrho was still silent.

Ch'ŏrho had no idea where he had gone nor how he had gotten there after leaving the police station. He was now climbing the hill to his house on legs that staggered as if he were drunk. He entered the mouth of the alley.

"Let's go!"

Ch'ŏrho stopped there. He tossed his head back. Not to look at the sky. He was crying with heavy sighs; the tears ran into his nose and trickled saltily down his throat.

"Let's go. Let's go. Where do you think you can go? Where in God's name can we go?"

Ch'ŏrho screamed out. Children playing house under the eaves got up and stared at him. But Ch'ŏrho passed them by, oblivious.

"Where've you been all this time, brother?"

Myŏngsuk, sounding upset, spoke just as Ch'ŏrho entered the front door. She was in a corner of the far room rummaging through an open wicker hamper; beside her was a pile of worn and patched clothing. His daughter was crouching by the basket, looking over the tatters as if they were treasures. Ch'ŏrho meant to ask where his wife had gone but instead just flopped down on the warm spot.

"You'd better get right over to the hospital."

Myŏngsuk spoke without turning as she poked through the wicker hamper.

"The hospital?"

"Yes."

"Why the hospital?"

"Your wife's in bad condition. The baby got stuck."

"What?" Ch'ŏrho felt dizzy.

Ch'ŏrho's wife had gone into labor about lunchtime, but the baby wouldn't come out. She strained so hard she nearly killed herself, but what finally appeared was not the baby's head, but a leg. So then they took her to the hospital. They called Ch'ŏrho's office but he was out.

"Maybe the baby's born by now. Either that, or . . . "

Myŏngsuk was folding up small white pieces of cloth. Probably for diapers. Something was odd. His dizziness was gone now, and all the strength had seeped out of his body. Ch'ŏrho felt his head finally clearing. It had been a long time, like the day you start recovering from malaria. He had no strength at all but his head was extraordinarily clear. What's there to be alarmed over, he thought in his new calm. He felt the way he did at

the office when given a new pile of work. He pulled a
cigaret out of this pocket and put it in his mouth. It was
a habit of his before starting a new piece of work. Ch'ŏrho
got up and opened the door.

"Where are you going?" Mŏngsuk turned toward
him.

"The hospital."

"But you don't even know which hospital."

Oh, so I don't, thought Ch'ŏrho.

"It's S. hospital."

Ch'ŏrho quietly placed one foot outside the door.

"You'll need some money, you know."

"Money."

Ch'ŏrho stepped back inside. He stood looking helplessly down at his toes. Myŏngsuk got up and went into
the next room. She took her handbag down from its hook
on the wall.

"Here you are."

A bundle of hundred-hwan notes landed on the floor
in front of Ch'ŏrho. Myŏngsuk had turned away again
and was busy straightening out her bag. Ch'ŏrho's eyes
stopped at Myŏngsuk's heels. There was a hole in her
nylons the size of an egg. He felt a kind of cleanness
about that threadbare heel. For the first time in a long
time, a really long time, Ch'ŏrho felt the love of an older
brother for Myŏngsuk.

"Let's go!"

Ch'ŏrho dropped his eyes to the money at his feet.
He bent over. His eyes burnt as if full of smoke.

"Are you going to the hospital, Daddy? Did Mama
have a baby?"

"Yes, dear."

Ch'ŏrho jammed the money into his jacket pocket
and stepped out the door.

"Let's go!" The sound of his screaming mother trailed him down the alley.

His wife was already dead.

"Oh, really?"

Ch'ŏrho looked even more matter-of-fact than the nurse. He walked back down the long hospital corridor out into the wide lobby. He didn't even ask where the body was. He felt as though some very burdensome task were now over with. No, it was also the heavy feeling that now there were all sorts of things to be done. But he hadn't the least idea of what it was he had to do. Ch'ŏrho stood vacantly in the hospital lobby, with only the thought that there was no longer any reason to hurry.

After a time, he went out the main gate and started walking slowly along the streetcar tracks. A bicycle whipped by and grazed his elbow. He stopped. He found he was unconsciously walking toward his office. It was long after six o'clock. There was no need to go to the office at this hour. He crossed over the streetcar tracks. Again he walked on, then he stopped again—this time finding himself in front of the police station. He turned around and walked once more. He had no thought of returning home, but his feet were mechanically leading him in the direction of South Gate. Stationery store, radio shop, photo studio, pastry shop: he turned and peered into each of the windows as he walked along without seeing what was there.

Ch'ŏrho pulled up short. He was staring at a sign the size of a chess board hanging right in front of his eyes. On a white background was lettered Dental Office in crimson paint. Ch'ŏrho suddenly felt the aching in his mouth. The decayed teeth which had been throbbing since morning—no, for much longer—suddenly began to pain him again. His molars on both sides, uppers and lowers. Actually, he could not even tell which were the teeth that really harbored the ache. He put his hand into his pocket and felt the ten thousand hwan there.

Ch'ŏrho took the stairs under the sign and went up to the second floor.

He sat in the dentist's chair, head back and mouth open wide. The dentist picked and poked around inside his mouth with all sorts of metal tools. Sleep came warmly over Ch'ŏrho and he sat, eyes closed, without a thought in his head.

"That hurt a bit, didn't it? The roots were crooked."

The dentist held up the black, decayed tooth in his pliers for Ch'ŏrho to see. Dark red shreds of flesh clung to the malformed roots. Biting on the cotton wad, Ch'ŏrho shook his head. Actually, it did not hurt at all— he couldn't feel anything.

"That does it. You can remove the cotton in about half an hour but it might bleed a bit."

"Would you please pull the one on this side, too?"

Ch'ŏrho spat blood into the basin beside him and pressed at his other cheek.

"No, I can't do that. There would be too much bleeding if I took out two molars at once."

"That's all right with me."

"It's not all right. We can pull it tomorrow."

"No, take them out right now. All of them, the whole works."

"Impossible. You've got to get them one at a time, repairing and extracting as you go."

"Repairing? I don't have time for that. They're killing me."

"I know, but I really can't do it. You'd be in real trouble if you developed anemia."

He had no choice. Ch'ŏrho left the dentist's and walked again. His gums ached dully but he also felt a kind of relief. He rubbed his hand over his cheek.

Soon he came upon another dental office sign. This one, too, was on the second floor.

And this dentist didn't like the idea of extracting a second molar either. That's all right, Ch'ŏrho persisted. The dentist ended by pulling the other molar for him. When Ch'ŏrho left he now had two wads of cotton to bite on, one in each cheek the size of a chestnut. It tasted salty inside his mouth. Now and then he would stop at the side of the street to spit. Each time he spat, what came out was a deep red, liverish glob of fresh-clotted blood.

Ch'ŏrho turned right after South Gate and headed toward Seoul station; a chill ran through his body and his head felt light and empty. The street lights flashed on— everything suddenly flared bright around him. But a moment later, the streets went even darker than they had been before. Ch'ŏrho closed his eyes tightly and then opened them again. It was just the same. He suddenly realized that he had eaten neither lunch nor supper. I'd better get something to eat, he thought. Saliva filled his mouth at the idea of stewed beef and rice. He squatted beneath a telephone pole and spat. But it was not saliva, it was thick blood. As he got up his whole body tingled with another chill. His legs seemed to be shaking. I'd better find a restaurant, he thought as he dragged on toward Seoul station.

"Stewed rice."

He pronounced it like the name of some medicine and fell forward onto the table. But his mouth filled again with the salty liquid. Ch'ŏrho raised his head and looked once around the eating house. His head was swimming. He stood up, then walked quickly out the door. Along the alley next to the restaurant he found an open sewer, where he squatted and spat out what was in his mouth. But it was dark out, and this time he couldn't see whether it was blood or saliva. He got up wiping his lips with the sleeve of his jacket. Pain jabbed deep at the empty sockets in his mouth; as if in sympathy, his temples gave a sudden jolt. Something's very wrong, he thought. I've got to get home to bed. He came out onto the main street. Finally a taxi came by and he raised his hand.

Ch'ŏrho collapsed into the taxi as if he had been thrown.

"Where to, sir?"

They were already moving.

"Liberation Village."

The car slowed down—to get to Liberation Village they would have to turn around. The driver looked for an opening in the rushing traffic. There was a sudden break in the stream of cars and he spun the wheel hard.

"No. Take me to S. hospital."

It was just as the driver was leaning into his turn that Ch'ŏrho cried out from the back seat.

He had suddenly thought of his wife's death. The driver whipped the wheel back the other way. The young helper sitting up front turned to look at Ch'ŏrho, who was wedged into a corner with neck thrown back and eyes closed. The car rounded the traffic circle in front of the Bank of Korea.

"No. Take me to X. police station."

She's already dead anyway, Ch'ŏrho was thinking. He didn't open his eyes.

This time the car did not have to change direction, but could just keep going.

"Here you are, sir."

Ch'ŏrho opened his eyes. He jerked upright in the seat but then slumped back again.

"No, no. Go on."

"But this is X. police station, sir."

The helper had turned to speak.

"Let's go."

Ch'ŏrho's eyes were still closed.

"But where are you going?"

"I don't know, just go."

"Oh no, a troublemaker."

"Is he drunk?"

The driver cocked his head toward the helper.

"Looks like it."

"Just my luck to pick up one of these stray bullets. Doesn't even know where he's headed."

The driver put the car in gear. Ch'ŏrho could hear the driver's distant grumbling as he slipped into what seemed a deep, murky sleep. In his heart, he was talking to himself.

"I've too many roles to fulfill. As a son, a husband, father, older brother, a clerk in an accountant's office. It's all too much. Yes, maybe you're right—a stray bullet, let loose by the creator. It's true, I don't know where I'm headed. But I know I must go, now, somewhere."

Ch'ŏrho got more and more drowsy. Sensation slowly slipped away, like a leg falling asleep.

"Let's go!"

As he slumped heavily on his side Ch'ŏrho could hear his mother's voice once more.

The car reached an intersection. The traffic signal went red, and the car stopped.

The helper looked back once more.

"Where are you going?"

But there was no answer from Ch'ŏrho, whose head had dropped forward.

The traffic bell clanged and the long line of cars began to move. Knowing no destination but caught in the moving stream, the car carrying Ch'ŏrho, too, had no choice but to move. As it passed under the green traffic signal and moved across the intersection, fresh blood flowing from Ch'ŏrho's mouth began a stain unseen on the front of his white shirt.

The Author

Yi Pŏmsŏn was born on December 30, 1920, in Shinanju, South P'yŏngan, and made his literary debut in 1955. "A Stray Bullet," first published in the journal Hyŏndae Munhak *in October 1959, was subsequently nominated as an alternate story for the Tongin Prize (1961).*

Yi has experimented with lyrical, social, and denunciatory styles. His characters are the common people one might meet in a public bath, tenement housing, tearoom, or a small office, and what absorbs Yi as a writer is the process of transformation of the decent people into insolent, stubborn, vain, and stingy creatures. The betrayal of society and the loss of hope often result in unbelief and self-abandonment. But without a faith in life and a system of belief, such an unbelief does at best lead to a passive response or a total defeat. In "A Stray Bullet," a study of the defeat and disintegration of the good, the protagonist Song Ch'ŏrho, a staunch defender of conscience, is ineffective in curing the misery of his family. What is, then, the role of conscience, and how does one find the right path in a cruel, unhappy society? His mother's "Let's go," an insistent and insane demand to return to her home in the North, is fated by the forces of history to be an impossibility. Yet it is the cry of a homeless exile and an echo of Song's conscience urging him to find a solution in the chaotic, inhuman world. One critic has said that Yi Pŏmsŏn possesses the aesthetics of the commoner. His aesthetics has an appeal of a kind, but without a firmly enunciated view of life and of the world adequate to contain the current condition of man, it would lack a persuasive force.

by Hwang Sunwŏn

Shower

The boy stood by the stream, saw the girl, and placed her as old Yun's great-grand-daughter. She had both hands playfully in the running water, as if she had never seen such a clear stream in Seoul.

For several days now, she had been playing in the water on her way home from school, and until yesterday she had done her water-stirring by the bank. Today she was squatting on one of the stepping stones in midstream.

The boy decided to sit down on the bank to wait for her to step aside. Soon a farmer happened by, and she stood up to make way for him to cross the stream. The boy crossed over too.

The next day he came to the bank a little later, and there she was at the same rock, washing her face. She was wearing a pink sweater with both sleeves rolled up, and her wrists and the nape of her neck were a glistening white.

Translated by E. Sang Yu

Washing done, she looked intently into the running water, at her reflection, no doubt. She scooped up some water—oh, that must be a tiny fish she had spotted.

Perhaps she noticed him on the bank, perhaps not. She just went on scooping up the water, absorbed in her game, and apparently not budging unless someone came by.

Now she picked something out of the water: a white pebble. She jumped to her feet and started to hop across the stones to the other side. One step short of the bank, she turned back: "Oh, silly boy!" and the pebble came flying toward him.

He ran after her. Her bobbed hair flapping on the back of her head, she made a dash for the reed bushes. The reed tops swished silkily in the autumn sunlight.

She could come out only over there at the other end of the reed bushes. He waited quite a while, but there still was no sign of her. He tiptoed closer, then a wisp of reed tops stirred, and she was back in sight with an armful of reed tufts, walking away leisurely. The bright sun shone on the tassels that rose high over the girl's head, and it looked as if a tuft, not a girl, was slowly moving down the path.

He kept on standing there until the reed tuft was out of sight. Then he looked down and saw the pebble she had hurled at him. Now it was almost dry. He picked it up and put it in his pocket.

The next day he came to the bank much later. She was nowhere to be seen, and it was a relief. She was not there the next day, nor the next. As days went by without her showing up at the stream, a strange emptiness began to form deep inside the boy, and with it, a habit of fingering the pebble in his pocket.

One day he squatted on the stepping-stone where she used to play with the water. He dipped his hands in. He washed his face. He, too, looked into the water. The water's surface mirrored his dark tanned features. He disliked his image. He cupped his hands and tried to scoop the image up. Then he started to his feet. Wasn't she coming his way across the stream?

She must have been watching him, hiding. The boy started to run. One foot missed a stone, and there was a splash. He ran on, unmindful of the wet foot.

A quick look around, but there was nowhere to hide on this side, not even a small reed bush: only several buckwheat patches, too low. The smell of the flowers seemed to sting his nostrils. For a brief second he felt faint, then some lukewarm, salty liquid was on his tongue. His nose was bleeding.

He kept running. "Silly boy, silly boy!" seemed to follow closely behind him.

Saturday came.

When the boy reached the stream, there she was, again playing with the water. He negotiated the first stepping-stone, pretending she was not there. He watched his step across.

"Oh, you." He pretended not to hear and walked on to the other bank.

"Oh, boy, what is the name of this clam?"

He turned around in spite of himself. His eyes met hers, clear and dark brown, and he shifted his eyes to her palm.

"A silk clam."

"What a lovely name!"

The boy and the girl were now at the fork of the

path. She had about a mile to cover, he about three, along separate paths.

"Ever been on the other side of that mountain over there?" She pointed to the far end of the plain.

"Oh, no."

"Why not go there together? I've been bored to death ever since we came to the country. Nobody to play with."

"That's a long way, you know. Farther than you think it is."

"Maybe, but it can't be too far for me. When I was going to school in Seoul we used to go long distances on trips, farther than that."

"Silly boy!" seemed to be right in her eyes, ready to come out aloud.

The boy and girl started along a narrow path between the paddies, past farmers cutting rice plants, the kind that ripen early. In the center of the paddy stood a scarecrow. Several ropes reached from its supporting pole across the paddy to the stakes driven at intervals around the bank. The boy bent down, twitched one of the slack ropes, and a few sparrows flitted away. (Oh yes, I'd better get back early and chase the sparrows off the paddy near our house.)

"What fun!" She took hold of the rope herself, shook away, the scarecrow twitching at each pull. Dimples appeared in her left cheek. She saw another scarecrow in the next paddy and ran for it, and off he went after her (half deciding to drop the idea of sparrow-chasing or helping around the house).

The boy ran past and ahead of her. Grasshoppers kept bumping into his face, pricking his skin faintly. He felt the blue sky suddenly going in a whirl, dizzily; a blessed eagle circling round and round up there, that's what it was. The girl was busily jerking on a rope, shaking a scarecrow, which danced even better than the first one.

The paddies ended in a stream, where a dry field began, planted with soybeans all the way to the foot of the hills, farther ahead. The girl hopped over the stream, one step ahead of him. They walked by the bend of a bean patch, where bundles of threshed sorghum stalks stood in shocks.

"Oh, what is that over there?" She pointed to a thatched platform raised on four tall poles.

"A watchtower."

"How are the melons here? Are they very sweet?"

"Of course they are, but the watermelons are best."

"I wish I had one right now."

He pulled up two of the radishes planted in a row around the patch, pinching the green tops off the still slender roots, and gave one to her. As if to show her how, he bit off the top and worked his thumbnail around the edge, peeling off the white skin.

She copied him, chewed a mouthful, then tossed the radish away. "How foul!"

"I can't eat it either. It isn't sweet at all." He threw his radish even farther away.

They were much closer to the mountain now. The flaming reds of the maple leaves were dazzling to their eyes. With a joyful shout, she dashed toward the foothill. The boy stayed behind, picking flowers.

"This one's a chrysanthemum, this is a bush clover, and this one's a bellflower . . ."

"I had no idea the bellflower is so lovely. Oh, I love this lavender . . . and what do you call this yellow one, like a tiny umbrella?"

"Mat'ari."

She held it up as she would hold an umbrella, and the dimples flashed in her cheeks.

He picked another handful, sorted out the fresh ones, and handed them to the girl.

"But don't throw any away!" she ordered.

Down below the ridge, a few thatched roofs were clustered together. The two sat side by side on a rock. It seemed as if a quiet had descended all around. The autumn sun that still felt hot seemed to carry the smell of drying grass.

"What is the name of those flowers up there?" Her finger pointed to a small steep mound, coiled with arrowroot vines, a few tardy pinkish violet flowers peeping out from the clusters of pods.

"They're just like wisteria. There's wisteria in my schoolyard in Seoul, one of those trellised things. That flower reminds me of the girls I used to play with there."

Slowly she went over to the mound, stepped backward and crawled downhill and pulled at the vine with the most flower clusters. It didn't yield to her twisting, and she strained and slipped. Her hand snatched at a vine and held it.

The boy flew over, seized her outstretched hand, and pulled her up. He regretted that he hadn't offered to get the arrowroot flowers for her.

He saw a scratch oozing blood on her right kneecap. He suddenly put his lips to the spot, started to suck it, and then leapt up and ran away.

He came running back, out of breath: "Put this on the wound! It will help." And he rubbed on some pine resin.

"There is a calf over there. Let's go see it!"

It was a brown calf, so young it didn't have a nose ring on yet. He grabbed the rein close to its muzzle, scratched its back with the other hand, and leaped up, landing astride its back. The calf started trotting around the stake to which it was tethered. The white face of the girl, her pink sweater, her dark blue skirt and her spray of wild flowers and all, suddenly blurred into one shimmering circle of colors. He was dizzy, but forced himself to stay on because he was so proud of his feat.

"Here, what are you kids up to?" The head of an old farmer emerged from a clump of sword grass. The boy slid off the back of the calf. The farmer surely would scold him for riding on a calf while its back was still tender.

But the man with a long beard only said, "Hurry back home, both of you, before the shower catches you."

There was a huge column of a black raincloud approaching overhead. Things were stirring. A gust of wind scudded through the bushes, rustling, then everything turned into a garish violet color.

The first raindrops came pattering down on the broad oak leaves as the boy and the girl passed over the crest of the hill. As they went down the slope, a big drop or two of chilly rain fell on his neck; then it came pouring in sheets, blocking out the view. A watchtower loomed ahead through the rain, a dry place. But it was in bad shape, with gullies in the thatch, posts atilt, the rain coming through almost as freely inside as out. He managed to find a dry spot for her to stand. Her lips had turned purple; she was shivering visibly. He took off his cotton jacket and put it around her. She looked up at him once, rain water dripping over her eyes, then began to sort out faded or broken flowers.

The roof began to leak on her, and the place was of no use as a shelter. He ran out to a nearby rick of sorghum stalks. He ran his hand into it to see if it was dry inside and picked up bundles of tall stalks to set them up on the outside for extra protection. He beckoned the girl.

Inside the rick there was no leak, but it was dark and there was hardly room for both of them. He stood out in the rain, and a mist of steam rose from his bare back.

The girl, almost in a whisper, asked him to come inside. She insisted, and he started to edge in cautiously. His back crushed the flowers she was holding, but she didn't mind. The sudden smell of sweat from his wet body surprised her. But she didn't turn away. Her trembling eased somewhat from the warmth of his body.

The steady pattering on the sorghum stopped. It had grown lighter outside, and they stepped out of the gloom. Just ahead, on the plain, the sunlight was pouring down on a bright, glistening patch.

They walked up to the stream, but the turbid water was high and too wide for one jump.

He turned his back toward her, and without a word she allowed him to carry her over piggy-back. Water was coming halfway up to his thighs when she, with a shriek, tightened her hold around his neck. Before he made the other side of the stream, the sky was blue again without a lingering speck of cloud.

For days she had not been around. Every day he went out to the stream hoping to catch sight of her again, but she was nowhere to be seen.

He looked into the schoolyard at playtime. He once peeped into the fifth-grade classroom for girls, but she wasn't there either.

Then one day he walked toward the stream, his fingers busy with the white pebble, and there, there she was, squatting on the bank on this side of the stream.

"I've been ill." She looked pale and thinner.

"Because of that shower the other day?"

She nodded.

"Are you all right now?"

"Not quite yet."

"Why, then you ought to be in bed."

"But it's so boring staying home, and I came out.
. . . What fun it was that day, though . . . I don't know
where I got this. This spot doesn't seem to come off." She
looked down at the front hem of her pink sweater.

A dark brown smudge, turning greyish. She looked
up, and the flush was back on her cheeks. "Where do you
suppose I got this?"

He kept staring.

"Yes, I know now. Remember, you carried me across
the stream? This must've come from your back."

He felt the blood rushing to his face.

At the fork in the road, she held out a handful of
jujubes.

"This morning they picked some of these at home.
They're going to use them in the sacrifice on the Full
Moon Festival."

He hesitated.

"Come, have some! They're very sweet. They say my
great-great-grandfather planted the tree."

He held out his cupped hands. "My, these are really
big!"

"Have you heard? We're going to let our house after
the festival."

The boy had heard villagers talk about how the Yun
family's business had gone badly in Seoul and how they
had had to wind it up to come back here to their place
in the country. It now appeared the family had to let
out that house as well.

"I don't really know what it is all about, but I just hate moving. It's something the grown-ups do, and I can't help it."

A sad look came into her eyes, something he had not seen before.

As he walked back home alone after parting, he mulled over the news. Somehow he failed to taste the sweetness of the jujube in his mouth. That night he stole over to the walnut grove belonging to Grandfather Tŏk-soe and began to strike the trees with a pole until the nuts fell to the ground, sending a chill to his heart. On his way home, he tenderly stepped on the shadow cast by the twelfth-day moon, savoring for the first time the warmth of the shade. Fingering his bulging pockets, he brushed aside a warning that cracking nuts with bare hands will infect them with scabies. His only wish was to have the girl taste the best nuts in the whole village. Then he suddenly remembered. He had forgotten to tell her to come out again to the stream before she left and as soon as she was well again. Silly boy! Silly boy!

When he returned from school, on the eve of the Full Moon Festival, he saw his father, dressed to go out, with a chicken in his hand.

"I wonder if this one is big enough?"

Mother handed him a mesh bag. "She's been cackling for days now, looking for a place to set. She may not be very big yet, but she's fat all right."

The boy turned to his mother and asked where his father was going.

"He's going over to the Yuns', and that chicken is for the offering at tomorrow's festival."

"Then why not take that big speckled rooster?"

"Son, this one is still substantial," his father said, laughing.

Flustered, the boy threw down his bundle of books, went out to the barn, and spanked the rump of the bull with his bare palm as if to kill flies.

The water of the stream looked much clearer as the days became cooler. The boy came to the fork in the road, tried walking up the other path, stopped by the reed bushes and looked across toward the village where the girl lived. The village looked very close in the crystal air of autumn.

According to the grown-ups, her family was moving tomorow to Yangp'yŏng to run a small store. The boy felt the walnuts in his pocket with one hand, and with the other mechanically lopped off reed tops.

Alone that night, he was still going over the news of the Yun family's move. He tried to decide whether he should go to the departure or not, and if so, would he be able to see her . . .

He was half dozing when he heard a voice.

"What a thing to have happened!"

Father was back.

"My, the Yuns are in a bad way. They had to sell all the estates they owned and then the house they've lived in for generations. And now they had to have that young girl die on them . . . "

There was only the light of the kerosene lamp, and threading her needle, mother said, "She was their only great-granddaughter, wasn't she?"

"Yes, they had two young grandsons but both died a long time ago."

"How unlucky they are with children!"

"That is just what I was going to say. She's been sick for some time but I hear they could hardly get as much medicine for her as she needed. But, you know, she must've been a strange child. Believe it or not, just before she died, she said, 'When I die, please bury me in the clothes I'm wearing now.'"

by Chŏn Kwangyong

Kapitan Lee

r. Yi Inguk emerged from the oper-
ating room and flopped down on the
sofa in the reception room. He took
off his rimless glasses with platinum
earpieces to wipe his brow. As the perspiration running
down his spine dried, fatigue sank into him. Two hours
and twenty minutes. Surgery on a stomach growth; the
patient was still in a coma.

Today's operation left a bitter aftertaste; the usual
good feeling was gone.

He remembered the record he had set: the shortest
time for laparotomy in the days of the Japanese occupation, when miracle drugs were scarce. Such simple things
as appendicitis or phimosis could be turned over to the
young physicians, but not the major cases. The patients
insisted that Dr. Yi himself undertake those operations.
This only served to flatter him and left a pleasant sensation of wielding a scalpel expertly.

Translated and abridged by Peter H. Lee

Dr. Yi's hospital was located in a densely populated neighborhood. His clientele consisted of patients turned over by the crowded, first-class university hospitals. As a hotel clerk instinctively determines after scrutinizing a guest's dress which room he should be assigned or whether he should be refused without hesitation, Dr. Yi's hospital had two traditional traits—that the premises be clean without a speck of dust and that his fees be almost double those of other places. The initial examination of a new patient consisted of an estimate of his financial capacity. If the patient appeared unable to meet the cost, Dr. Yi's nurse turned him down. For the most part, a preliminary checkup of light cases was handled by the young doctors. Dr. Yi's job was to hand out a final decision, taking into account the patient's symptoms and his financial means. Credit was out of the question unless the patient was a friend or a bigwig. Even if credit were allowed in some cases, his twofold examination of symptoms and finance was a creed and secret to his career of half a lifetime, resulting in no outstanding fee or deficit. It was no accident, therefore, that during the Japanese days his clientele was mainly Japanese and was currently the privileged or moneyed class.

In the morning, the doctor's day began in the consultation room, where he dusted the windowsills and the desk top with his fingertips, staring with unblinking deep eyes behind his rimless glasses. The nurse would suffer the whole day if he found one speck of dust. His regular patients never failed to express admiration for his spotlessness.

At the time of the January 4 retreat, Dr. Yi came across the Thirty-eighth Parallel carrying only a bag containing a stethoscope. No sooner was the capital regained than he rented a room and set up his practice. Today he owns a two-story tiled structure in the heart of the city, where one p'yŏng of land is worth five hundred thousand hwan. In addition to surgery, he has added such other departments as internal medicine, pediatrics, and obstetrics. The management of each was up to individual doctors, but Dr. Yi was the director.

Dr. Yi pulled his eighteen-carat gold watch from his vest pocket; it was 2:40 P.M. Only twenty minutes to the appointment he had with a Mr. Brown of the U.S. Embassy. The watch had a history of its own. Every time he looked at it, he was reminded of an incident akin to a miracle, a relic of his evacuation, together with his house-call bag. The old bag disappeared without a trace, replaced by the new one given him by a GI doctor, but the watch was a memento which shared his fateful escape from the North—a companion of his life, as it were. Even at night, he did not leave it beside his pillow or in its pocket. Only after he had secured it in the emergency cabinet containing his registration papers and savings book did he go to bed. He had good reason to. The watch, with his name inscribed on the back, was his proud graduation prize from an imperial university.

For the subsequent thirty years, everything changed around him but the watch. Gone was the rosy-cheeked, proud youth of twenty. Not only was half of his hair grey, but the wrinkles on his forehead were etched deeper. Days of Japanese control, imprisonment under the Soviet military occupation, the war, the Thirty-eighth Parallel, the U.S. Army, how many crises did he manage to escape?

It is a miracle that the seventeen-jewel Waltham watch had kept time through such tribulations. After checking the time, he would listen to the ticking, his half-closed eyes shrouded with miniature views of his past. Pressed by an irresistible impulse, he recalled anew the day when he changed from the square cap and close-buttoned jacket of a student into a business suit.

Dr. Yi Inguk remembered the letter he had put in a drawer just before the operation. Nami, his daughter now in the United States, whose Japanese name was Namiko—after the liberation he called her simply Nami for obvious reasons, and "ko" was dropped from the residence registry. Nami-chan—her image floated up to his mind along with the memory of happy days. Nami had been the joy of the family. Now that she too had left him, Dr. Yi—despite the fact that he was remarried—could not suppress occasional empty feelings. His first wife had died at the Kŏje prisoner-of-war camp, and he had no idea of the fate of his son. He often tried to brush aside the generation gap that separated him from his second wife, Hyesuk, who was twenty years younger. In contrast to Hyesuk's elastic body, his wrinkled skin made his entire body shrink. A one-year-old baby born to them was now his only flesh and blood—with a future as hazy and uncertain as it was distant.

With great expectation and curiosity, Dr. Yi opened the air letter. It was the answer to his previous letter in which he neither consented nor opposed Nami's plan to marry an American. He pushed the letter to the desk's corner. He reflected that the affair might have begun even before her departure from Korea. His daughter was studying English literature at a university, and her husband-to-be gave her private lessons, obtained a scholarship, and found a sponsor for her. It was not by chance. But was it not her father who had maintained—in accordance with the trend of the times—the importance of study abroad in the

States? When a foreign professor majoring in oriental studies admitted that he wished to marry a Korean girl, who had expressed his approval, without thinking, that that was an excellent idea? As he clenched his ivory pipe in his teeth, he closed his eyes. He was angry and unbelieving. "A big-nosed son-in-law!" The mere thought was enough to make his blood flow backward. "A dirty wench, finally . . ." He gave a mighty cough in disgust. He remembered the Japanese days when the theory of marriage between Japanese and Koreans was an unassailable proof of the oneness of two peoples. At that time, he did not think it slanderous or humiliating. Didn't he look upon it as a matter of fact or, in some respects, as a matter of superiority? But this time . . .

He ruminated on his daughter's words: "Is there a boundary in love?"

How trite! Daddy too had during his school days mastered such a trend of thinking. Arrogantly, you intend to preach to daddy? Why can't you be a shade more frank? So you wish to offer yourself as a touchstone of international marriage.

"Anyway, you said you would come over soon, so I'll follow your wishes as to the final decision. But . . ."

So if father does not show up, you want to go ahead with your plan?

Dr. Yi, calling to mind the theory of heredity he knew, shook his head.

"A white offspring!"

The very thought was repulsive.

He picked up the picture he had flung aside. A great stone structure looking like a campus, numerous couples walking in the garden—with this as background, his daughter and the American professor posed smiling with arms around each other.

"Hum, they've had a good time, eh?" With a groan he stood up.

I'll meet Mr. Brown and ask him—I'm going any-way—to rush the papers through. He was anxious to con-firm the State Department invitation, which was sup-posed to offer the best terms.

He crossed over to the living quarters where Hyesuk was.

"Nami says she'll marry for sure."

"Is that right?"

Dr. Yi divined in her voice a lack of feeling or of bewilderment. He had hitherto refrained from discussing in front of Hyesuk his children by his first marriage. On the other hand, the indirect stimulus for Nami's study abroad might have been the family atmosphere—he har-bored a guilty conscience. Nami had never once called Hyesuk mother, and Hyesuk had never conducted herself as a mother to Nami. Delicate strains lay concealed in the relationship of Nami and Hyesuk.

"I'll help you if you wish," said Hyesuk the first day she met Dr. Yi in Seoul. At first, Hyesuk did not know the doctor's wife was dead, and Dr. Yi did not bother about Hyesuk's status. But Hyesuk left the university hospital and moved to Dr. Yi's. But as their love deep-ened, Dr. Yi wished first to sound out his daughter's opinion. The daughter was sympathetic to his loneliness. Accepting the fact that the chores of tending her father were too much for her and that Hyesuk was the only one to look after him, the daughted expressed her approval on the spot. But as time passed, Hyesuk and Nami drifted further apart until Hyesuk too began to look upon Nami as an obstacle to a normal family life.

"Seems she is getting close to that American professor," observed Dr. Yi as if to himself, without looking into Hyesuk's eyes.

"What can we do? We have to follow her wishes," said Hyesuk unconcernedly.

"Well, I suppose so, but . . ." He just clucked his tongue and could not go on.

The doctor could not suppress a compulsive concern for Nami as if it were all his fault, even as he was stimulated by the young body of his wife as she offered her breast to the crying baby.

It would take twenty years more for that little thing to grow to be a companion like his son Wŏnsik and his daughter Nami. By then he would be a grandfather of seventy.

Today, medicine has increased the average life span, excluding the possibility of sudden death by diseases like cancer. But here I am, a physician, unable to guarantee my own life. Didn't I kill my own wife before my very eyes as easily as letting a bird get away?

Come what may, I'll have to see that brat through college. Time is time, so I should see him through study abroad in America. And come to think of it, it is not so terrible to have a marriage connection with an American. At least, they live better. It's only because of face, he grumbled, not knowing whether it was self-consolation or resignation.

"Will you wrap up that thing?" His voice had calmed down.

"What thing?" The wife only turned her head and asked, her breast still feeding the baby.

"I mean that vase." He indicated an antique on the dressing table.

"Where are you going to take it?"

"To Mr. Brown of the U.S. Embassy. I owe him a lot . . ."

Dr. Yi emerged slowly from his entrance hall with the parcel his wife had wrapped up neatly.

Whichever way you looked at it, it was a miracle. Complex recollection repeated intermittently, swirling and lashing fear and emotion. Always, it seemed yesterday—so fresh and so vivid.

End of August 1945.

The whole world was still in the vortex of a whirlpool as a result of the sudden liberation. It was after the dog days but still unbearably hot. Sleep did not come to the anxious, fretful Dr. Yi these few days. Not a sign of a patient, where so many had flocked, not a telephone that rang without end. The wards had been bare since the last peritonitis patient, a Japanese bureau chief of a provincial government, had left. The worried assistants and pharmacists had all departed, saying they were going to visit their hometowns. Only Hyesuk, the Seoul-born nurse, remained to keep what to all intents was an empty house.

In his ten-mat room upstairs, the fretful kimono-clad doctor threw down his fan and rose. He went to the bathroom and doused himself with cold water. A tingling cold ran down the back of his spine, and he felt light. Even while he dried himself with a towel, he could not wash away the tedium that weighed on him.

He went over to the window and looked down on the streets. The milling crowds were still surging back and forth in the midst of commotion. Across the street he could make out the white outline of the words inscribed on the iron shutters of a tightly barred and bolted bank.

"Down with pro-Japanese traitors and reactionaries!" The twofold circle splashed in red remained distinctly in the doctor's eyes. The shudder he had felt for the first time toward dusk of the previous day assaulted him again. At that moment, Dr. Yi quickly turned his head away. "Surely, that doesn't apply to me," he said to himself, picking up the fan again.

While he was gazing at the slogan, his eyes met the young Ch'unsŏk's, whose flushed face, wearing a wry smile, bordered on contempt or excitement, and that face kept assaulting him. Dr. Yi felt uneasy, as if he had spied a spider's web on a dark night. However much he tried to wipe the image away from his mind, it clung to him like a leech.

The event had taken place six months ago. A seriously ill patient, out on bail from a police cell, was carried in on his back. A young man, of skin and bones, with vacant eyes, he was hardly able to move. He was examined while supported by a nurse. Even while making out the faint breathing through the tubes of his ivory-tipped stethoscope, Dr. Yi's mind wandered on a crossroad of final diagnosis. "Am I to take him in? Or should I refuse?" The patient's offensive face and his companion's sloppy dress told the scale of their existence. There was a more disturbing point: to admit a person who had committed an offense involving dangerous thoughts to an official city hospital where Japanese officials came in and out at pleasure was unthinkable. A structure built with much labor as a model citizen of the empire—commonly acknowledged to be so by himself and others—could not be allowed to crumble in one day. He reached an instant decision. He gave the patient first aid and sent the two away on the justifiable grounds that there was no room. Later he learned from the nurse that the patient's house was in an alleyway across from the hospital. But that was nothing unusual, and he gave it no second thought.

But some days ago when he and Hyesuk, caught in the excitement, had come out to watch the liberation parade at the end of the citizen's rally, among the marchers his eyes met with those of the same young man, now wearing the armband of the Self-Defense Corps. The young man glared in Dr. Yi's direction, his eyes glinting with bloodthirsty rage. Dumbfounded, he could not make out what it was all about until Hyesuk reminded him of the earlier incident. Dr. Yi looked around furtively and crawled back into the hospital. Thenceforth he had avoided the streets as much as possible, only to run into the young man one night in front of the slogan painted on the bank.

Suddenly, an uproarious sound came from outside. Lying on the bed with his hands behind his head, Dr. Yi was lost in a thought whose head or tail he could not make out. He sat up and listened in the direction of the streets. The clamor grew louder. Unable to allay his anxiety, he leaned over, crouched low on the bed, to look out the window. People were milling about and cheering on the pavement, holding Korean flags and red flags.

"What can it be?"

He settled back on the bed, cocking his head to one side.

Sounds of hurried footsteps came up the stairs and Hyesuk ran in.

"It seems the Soviet Army has entered the city." She was breathless. "Everybody's in a stir."

He lay flat on the bed without a word, only blinking his eyes. The radio had foretold in the past few days that the Soviets would arrive on this day. So they had indeed, he thought. He remained motionless, staring out the window after Hyesuk had gone downstairs. Then a sudden thought struck him, and he got up with a jerk. He opened the closet door and produced a picture frame:

"Model Japanese-speaking family."

He had stowed it away on liberation day and had forgotten all about it. Opening up the back of the frame, he took out a thick sheet of paper that looked like a restaurant permit, and tore it to shreds so that not a word might remain intact. Back in the old days, this sheet of paper proved adequate to guarantee smooth commerce with the Japanese. A sense of regret flashed through his mind . . . a patient unable to speak Japanese seldom showed up in the hospital. And Dr. Yi spoke only Japanese at home and abroad. After the liberation, of necessity he had to employ his native tongue, which, he found, was inadequate in making himself understood. Taking the initiative and setting an example, his wife was of immeasurable help; his children too kept the practice. How elated the family had been when it was awarded this sheet of paper, as if it were a happy event!

"I believe you speak Japanese even in your dreams. Nothing less could have earned you such an honor," said the branch officer of the National League of Total Efforts with a smile. At the moment he reflected how fortunate he had been to send his children to Japanese schools, starting from primary education.

The doctor heaved a deep sigh. He felt a renewed gratitude for the goodwill of the manager of a branch bank who allowed him to withdraw all the savings from his account. If I hadn't had that cash . . . the mere thought chilled his spine. With this sum, whatever the form of government, his household would not be affected, not before half the city shall have been touched. He mumbled to himself, thinking of the safe in the chest of the inner room. He had a vague expectation that no matter what took place he would emerge unscathed.

The agitation and clamor at dusk seemed enough to shake the earth's axis. The mob exploded into loud cheers; "Manse!" shouts continued without end. His wife, who had gone out to investigate the state of affairs, returned.

"The tank brigade is in, and the streets are overflowing with an avalanche of people. What're you doing inside?"

"Doing what . . . ?"

"Go out and see. The big-nosed are in."

In the dark her voice was impassioned, but was it a strong emotion or confusion?

"Woman is foolish and yet audacious . . . " Casting a steady glance in her direction in the dim light, Dr. Yi clucked his tongue.

"You haven't turned on the light." She switched it on. The hundred-watt light proved too bright for the doctor.

"Why on earth did you put the light on?"

"Why not? It's dark; let's go out and see!"

Dr. Yi followed her out with a blank face. Dazzling glare of headlights—the tank brigade filed past endlessly. Avoiding the glare, the doctor leaned against a tree. Amid unending cheers and applause, the tanks slowly rolled past along both banks of the river. Occasionally the closely cropped soldiers lifted a hatch cover and waved their hands, shouting "hurrah!"

Dr. Yi kept on staring vacantly, neither applauding nor cheering, holding the illusion that he had nothing to do with the foreign troops. He only looked about him, in case his behavior was being watched. But all attention was on the tanks, greeted with shouts of "Manse" at the tops of voices.

"It will work out somehow or other," he said calmly and returned home.

Over the radio, a folk song, then a march was followed by a proclamation from the commander of the Occupation Forces. The doctor approached the radio and was all attention.

"We positively guarantee to secure the lives and properties of the citizens. Be at ease and stick to your posts. Arms are prohibited. Turn over shotguns, Japanese swords, and all manner of weapons at once!"

The thought of his hunting gun in the chest suddenly struck him. Was he to surrender that too? The latest model English double-barrel, his well cared for prize article, which he had never once lent to others?

He turned the dial. What are they doing in Seoul? It was the same. A folk song or a march, a speech by someone of the National Construction Preparatory Committee.

What was going to happen anyway? He had no way to allay his anxiety.

In the first days after the liberation, he was calm and composed, but his friends seldom showed up after the entry of the Soviet troops. Of course he ruled out any possibility of his going about inquiring after them.

After dark, his son and daughter returned, one from middle school and the other from primary, chattering about the tanks and Russians. The stories grew as they were joined by Dr. Yi's mother and Hyesuk, heedless of the father's concern. Dr. Yi quietly rose and went upstairs. What will future developments be, he wondered— boulders blocking his path? In the midst of entangled thoughts that refused to unravel themselves, Dr. Yi stared vacantly at the ceiling, clinging to a faint hope. Pangs of regret or pricks of conscience were out of the question.

"North Korean Students in Russia Escape to West Germany."

Such were the headlines in bold type, like reports of moves in a chess game. A foreign dispatch occupied the left side of the page, with a picture as large as the palm of the hand. Dr. Yi glared and pushed his glasses up the bridge of his nose. His eyes were trying to focus on the type, and the image of his son floated up in his mind. Had he coerced his son to go abroad to study in Moscow? He had little in his favor in terms of class and profession, except that he had graduated from high school and entered a university. Then, as now, Dr. Yi was confident of his secret of a successful life.

"Look, son, study Russian diligently!"

"What for?" retorted the son suspiciously.

"Wŏnsik, it can't be helped. Under the Japanese occupation, Japanese was the tongue to master, but now it's Russian. A fish can't live out of water, so it must learn to live in it. Take up Russian!"

The son did not seem particularly impressed.

"Don't tell me you can't at your age. Why even I can manage some halting conversation."

"Don't worry." The son's reply inspired Dr. Yi's confidence.

"Can there be any difference just because they have big noses?" The doctor continued with a profound expression.

"Only learn to communicate and it's all the same, I'm sure."

In the end, the doctor had managed to secure a Soviet scholarship for his son on the basis of a recommendation from an important party member known through Major Stenkov.

"Let's live like average people," his wife said. "The safest way is to be inconspicuous. Consider, we have barely escaped one crisis. Now you would push him into the heart of 'Raise the red flag' and all the rest of it. What will come of it?"

"How little you know. There's no catching the tiger unless you enter his lair. Whatever the world may be, let's do all we can to get the best of it."

"But to send a child like that as far as Russia?"

"Why, even middle school kids are desperately struggling to go. Why not a college boy?"

"But who'll know what things are to come?"

"Idle worry! Those rascals who are apt to pick on me will be silenced when my son returns with a Soviet education. Let's live proudly once again."

So he had high-handedly consoled his worried wife and carried through his intention. "Hmmm, even the families of revolutionaries find it hard to crack this nut, and that's just what I've done. I, the pro-Japanese Dr. Yi Inguk. What do you say to that?"

The son had sent letters in a continual stream, saying that he was getting along well, but since the outbreak of war and up to the retreat, no news had arrived. One could attribute his wife's death to her anxiety for her only son, exiled in a no-man's-land, the doctor thought.

Dr. Yi scrutinized every word in the paper, hoping to find some tidings of his son, but to no avail. "What in the world is he doing?" Dr. Yi muttered. "Can't he include himself in the ranks? Man must know how to take the initiative and to adapt himself to circumstances."

He folded the paper and rolled it up at random. "The

swift steed is born of a creek, but my son is not up even to his daddy." He clucked his tongue.

And, in the next instant, another thread of thought: "Can it be that he's wavering because he doesn't know his family has come south? But news of us must have reached him by now, and he must feel tacit pressure. The lad's naïve, he's below average."

As soon as he alighted from the car, he spat on the pavement.

He remembered what Major Stenkov had said: "Dr. Yi, I guarantee it. Send your son to our fatherland, the Soviet Union." The major's voice seemed still to collide with his eardrums.

Dr. Yi was summoned the day after the Self-Defense Corps was changed into the Security Corps. He found himself kneeling on a cement floor, his lips blue, the lower part of the body paralyzed, his side aching. This was the greatest pain he had ever suffered in his life; but more than this, he was swirled in the grip of an approaching, unpredictable fate. Hearing the thud of footfalls back and forth and curses pouring down on him, he was unable to raise his drooping head, which was about to break. Only time flowed. And many thoughts he had hitherto suppressed began to nod their heads at him one by one.

"If I knew this was to happen, I could have hidden beforehand or even fled south. . . . But then, under these circumstances, who is to help me? Those who are in a position to do something are all in the same boat or will be sooner or later. Japanese! To whom can I turn now that the walls against which I've been leaning have all crumbled . . . "

"But surely somehow . . . " The vague hope did not

completely disappear in the moment of impending danger. "Lucky I was not included in the first round of people's trials. There's no way to learn about the fate of those dragged away. And what of those rumors about summary convictions? Only three more days and I may well have departed. It's all fate. And yet, there must be a way . . . "

"You miserable agent of the Japs!"

Startled, Dr. Yi lifted his head with a jerk. It was Ch'unsŏk, glaring at him, wearing an armband over the clean Japanese military uniform.

The doctor did not even have the strength to look back. "It's death," he thought.

"You stepping-stone for the Japs!"

A kick from a Japanese army boot at his side.

"Let's see you die, dog!"

Kicks rained all over his body, front and back.

The doctor screamed as a shock ran through his spine, and he collapsed in a daze.

Pulling at his shoulder, they tried to make him sit, but his body would not respond, and he fell to one side.

"So you would sell your people and your fatherland! You dog! It's the firing squad for you. The firing squad!"

The words came to him as in a dream. Dr. Yi did not know how much time had fled when he became aware of the rustling sound of someone touching him and of the clink of metal. A pair of hands with a yellow mass of hair pulled out his watch by the chain. He instantly took tight hold of the watch pocket, staring at the owner of the hands. A blue-eyed close-cropped Soviet soldier grinned, showing all his teeth, and grabbed the end of the chain. With all his might Dr. Yi shielded the pocket with his hands.

"Huh, Yaponski!" His reaction angered the blue-eyed soldier.

"Spare me just this."

Unable to communicate by words, their hands and eyes confronted each other. At length, the soldier flung the doctor's hand aside and grabbed the watch. The chain was broken, leaving the ring dangling at the tips of the doctor's fingers. The soldier disappeared.

"Death and a watch . . . " The doctor grumbled to himself.

The image of the soldier who had two wrist watches up each wrist and yet had need to take his precious pocket watch became carved vividly in his memory.

The cell was full. But distinctions between the old-timers and newcomers were clear by the positions they occupied, and within a month Dr. Yi was two-thirds of the way up the ranks of the former, moving slowly away from the stool bucket. All day long he was silent. Great uneasiness prevailed, for as surely as the informers planted in their midst left, the complaining ones were called out only to return half-dead. Within a day or two, however, the prisoners were able to adjust themselves by whiling away their time, airing yet more grievances and talking of food.

Dr. Yi remained silent, not because he did not wish to expose his crimes, but because he knew that silence was the best policy.

The doctor picked up the Russian conversation book the student prisoner had left behind upon his release during the night and pored over it. His spine ached, and his ribs pained, he feared they might be past healing. The weather grew perceptibly colder in the morning and evening, and he could not allay his anxiety, despite efforts at resignation. He kept up with his Russian primer even as his ears took in all the exchanges of his cellmates. They were making estimates of the sentence each was likely to draw, and the doctor was startled at the enormity of his crime. Seven years for one who had sold rice stocks of the Grains Association; ten years for one who had rounded people up for forced labor. Ostensibly, judgments were based on law, not on emotions, but what laws were there in such a confused time? Against their taste, and it was the firing squad for sure . . .

"Pro-Japanese, traitor to the people, refusal to treat an anti-Japanese fighter, a spy for Japanese imperialists . . ."

His crimes were uncountable. If he were to be sentenced according to this list the investigators had toted up, the least he could expect was life imprisonment. More probably, death.

The doctor looked around the cell and heaved a deep sigh.

Sunlight the size of a handkerchief came through the ventilator hole at the eave, then lengthened like a bamboo stick, shimmered like a thin thread, and disappeared. Through the lattice, he saw in the far distance an autumn sky which brought on forgotten memories in a heap; his heart ached. How eternal his separation from the outside world!

What can we do? What did you expect of a colonized people? Of what use was the best talent—swiftest feet and flying wings? Were there any who had not flattered the Japs? A fool is he who did not eat the proffered cake. We're all cut from the same cloth, eh?

By rationalizing his excuses, the doctor was able to relieve his anxieties.

Then, too, there was the thin ray of hope in the expression of a consultant during the final interrogation session yesterday. A somewhat forced self-solace and yet!

What was the name? Major Stenkov? An officer with a wart on his cheek. The major had taken particular note of his occupation. "Doctor, doctor," he had repeated, cocking his head. The sudden expression that came over his face—an auspice of a miracle?

Dr. Yi opened his eyes, startled by a groan. The dim light in the corridor filtered through the iron bars, weaving a pattern across the cell. He looked up in the direction of the ventilator hole. The sun had not yet risen, and it was dark.

The smell of fresh dung assailed his nostrils. On one of his trouser legs. He touched it and brought his hand to his nose. He retched—it was dung all right.

The lad beside him was continuing to groan. The doctor peered closely. The lad's buttocks were wet. Diarrhea, he thought.

The doctor shook the bars and called out for the member of the Rehabilitation Corps.

"What?" came an indistinct voice aroused from sleep.

"Patient, look, look at this!"

In the light behind him, only the round outline of the man's face beneath a cap emerged. The doctor pointed a finger to the young man's buttocks. "It's blood, blood," he exclaimed, suddenly aware of the red that glowed. "Dysentery," he added in a louder voice, prompted by his occupational knowledge.

"Dysentery?" repeated the voice from the outside in an unconvinced tone.

"There's blood in his stool. See for yourself," the doctor insisted, raising his voice.

"Ah, indeed . . . "

In the clamor, the other prisoners one by one opened their eyes and each exclaimed.

"Dysentery is contagious, contagious."

"Contagious, you say?"

Only then did the guard open the cell door.

Some time later, the youth was isolated, and the prisoners took their time cleaning up every trace of the dung. By the time it was all over, they could not go back to sleep.

Two days later, two or three other similar cases were reported in another room. As days passed, patients grew. the doctor pondered: nine out of every ten would surely die. He was seized with concern.

One evening, he was summoned to the consultant's office.

"Comrade, for the time being work in the first-aid treatment room!"

A miracle—a bolt from the blue! The doctor doubted the interpreter. A ray of hope leapt to his eyes as he stared alternately at the Soviet officer and the interpreter.

"Is it understood?"

"Yes," replied the doctor composedly in order to suppress the elation. The doctor clenched his teeth so as not to betray his feeling.

Every time he saw a corpse dragged away, Dr. Yi felt that it might very well have happened to himself. "Doctoring is my mission," he told himself over and over again.

He did his utmost for all the patients under his care. Thus, with this as a turning point, his skills were brought to the special attention of the consultant. For all that, he had no way of knowing what punishment was awaiting him. He learned belatedly that to let a "thought" prisoner die in a cell will result in an interrogation of the one responsible. He wanted to make the most of his excellent opportunities. Even if I die, I won't regret anything, he thought.

How to extricate himself, once and for all, from an invisible confinement? Even as he treated the patients, he thought constantly about the wart the size of a duck's egg on the major's left cheek. A natural deformity, but the fact that he had advanced to a high rank must mean either that his party spirit was strong or that his war record was exceptional.

Hold on to that wart and surely he would find an opening through which to emerge alive! He applied what crude knowledge of Russian he had to exchange greetings with Stenkov whenever he appeared on an inspection tour. To be sure, books were banned except for the party literature and Russian-language texts. The doctor therefore memorized the Russian primer as if it were the key to his salvation.

The opportunity came with the Christmas drinking parties. Major Stenkov appeared on his usual inspection tour, his face aflame.

I must not let this chance pass, Dr. Yi decided.

As Stenkov approached the room of the Soviet officer whose appendicitis had developed into peritonitis and whose sutures he was removing, with words in Russian and hand gestures, Dr. Yi made it clear that he was willing to operate on the wart.

"Khorosho!" ("Good!") said Stenkov several times in rapid succession.

Several times thereafter, with an interpreter between them, the doctor had opportunities to express his views about how he would go about the operation. He spoke convincingly, remembering the wart of the Japanese major he had successfully removed. I neatly performed a medical feat, defeating the hospital staff of the entire Keiō University. He talked thus to himself, gambling his life on this undertaking.

A series of preliminary diagnoses was undertaken
with a Soviet military doctor as a witness. Then the big
day came.

The doctor arranged to have all his familiar tools
brought over from his own hospital. Three Soviet assistants were at hand, but it was he who wielded the knife.
To him these doctors of a field hospital were but mere
novices. He treated them as if they were his own assistants
at his hospital. With the scalpel at hand, the operating
table was his kingdom on his own authority. But that
written pledge he had signed just before the operation
momentarily clouded his concentration: "The firing squad
in case of failure."

Even though he appeared self-possessed, the patient's
face was tense, but that lasted only three minutes after
anesthesia. The nurse kept wiping the endless beads of
perspiration off the doctor's forehead with a cotton pad.
The clank of metallic instruments and the rhythm of
human breathing under a bright reflector broke the suffocating silence in the room.

The operation was over in a shorter time than he had
anticipated. When the doctor took off his gown, he was
wet with sweat.

On the day of his discharge, Stenkov grasped both
hands of Dr. Yi and shouted, "Kapitan Lee, spasibo!"
("Thank you!")

The doctor flashed his widest grin. He felt a liberation from the mind's prison.

"Odin, odin, ochen'khorosho!" ("Number one, number one, very good!") declared Stenkov, holding a thumb
aloft to indicate that he thought the best of the doctor,
tapping him on the shoulder.

The following day, Stenkov called Dr. Yi into his

office. He offered his hand in a most polite handshake, and that was the first time.

"Can enemy confront enemy and make a hundred-eighty-degree turn like this? Even the yellow-haired ones are human in their hearts!"

"Beginning tomorrow, you may attend to your regular duties from your home."

The doctor heaved a great breath, as if a clogged dike were bursting open.

This time the doctor took hold of Stenkov's hands, "Spasibo, spasibo!"

"Have you no favors to ask of me?"

The thought of the watch came at once to his mind. Was it wise to bring the subject up at this time and place? Wasn't it too trifling? He still had a lingering affection for the watch and was resolved to lay bare all that he felt about it though the chances of recovery might be nil. With the help of the interpreter, he set forth in minute detail every particular of the incident, including the time and place.

Stenkov listened with a strained expression on his face, all the while stroking the cheek on which the wart had once been.

"No need to worry, Doktorr Lee. The great Red Army is incapable of any such deed. It must be a mistake. I will bear the responsibility."

Doubt assailed the doctor once again as he stared at the profound expression on the major's resolute face. "Have I bungled up everything, needlessly?" He suppressed uneasiness and regret.

"Rest easy, Doktorr Lee," Stenkov guffawed and allusively closed the issue.

The doctor returned home, released from the threshold of death.

He remembered what the interpreter had told him: Major Stenkov had marveled at his ability to express himself in Russian in so short a time.

The car came to a halt before the residence of Mr. Brown. The sight of the Stars and Stripes reminded Dr. Yi of the Red flag and the returned watch. He was led into the drawing room, and while awaiting the host he examined the room. He had been indebted to the embassy official since his daughter went to the States three years before, but this was the first time he had visited the man in his home.

One wall was stacked with such Korean classics as the *Veritable Record of the Yi Dynasty, Unofficial Histories and Notes of the Eastern Country;* and along another, old books in cases were piled up neatly. On the desk in front were a golden Buddha statue and several antique pieces. The ashtray atop the table in front of the twelve-panel screen inscribed with Chinese seal characters was an old white celadon.

The doctor's face felt hot at the thought that each article must have been brought by someone. He turned an eye toward the inlaid Koryŏ celadon he had brought with him. He would certainly miss the article, but he had never once reproached himself for contributing to the draining away of national treasures. Rather he vacillated: Brown has so many precious things, one more wouldn't make him cherish it!

As soon as Mr. Brown entered, the doctor offered him the present, smiling. The host in turn smiled expansively as he unwrapped the package. "Thank you," he said as if unable to conceal his delight. "It's a very valuable gift, indeed."

"Not at all. It's merely an expression of my goodwill."

With a satisfaction following upon a relieved feeling, Dr. Yi agreed. Listening to Mr. Brown's talk, half in Korean and half in English, he gave himself up to a sense of contentment.

"Where did you learn your English, Dr. Lee?"

"During the Japanese days in the Japanese way. For instance 'Zatto is ah catto'."

"But your pronunciation is excellent now. You speak grammatically correct standard English."

He instantly recalled what Stenkov had said about his Russian. He noted that Mr. Brown, English-born, did not roll his "r's."

"I've been receiving private lessons for some time."

"Is that so?"

The doctor felt proud of his linguistic skills.

Mr. Brown returned from the kitchen with a tray of foreign liquors. "Please help yourself!"

As he watched Mr. Brown's face, the doctor recalled Major Stenkov, who felt good only when he had had a long draught of vodka, even if he had to take it straight.

Sipping his glass of Scotch—his high blood pressure compelled him to be moderate—he waited to hear what Mr. Brown had to say.

"I've heard from the State Department."

The doctor was overwhelmed with joy but controlled himself. Instead, he shook hands slowly and gravely. "Thank you, thank you," he said again, recalling Stenkov after the successful operation.

Sincerity moves heaven, thought the doctor in high spirits, reflecting the fact that his practical wisdom had worked even with the Americans. Mr. Brown seemed to be happy as he kept on caressing the celadon vase and emptying his glass.

"I'll entrust everything to you during my stay in the States."

"Please do. I shall write you a letter of introduction when you leave."

"Thank you."

"The United States may have a short history, but it is a paradise on earth. I hope you will help better friendly relations between the two countries."

"Thank you."

The doctor took his leave with a promise to join his host in a hunting excursion to the demilitarized zone. Reminded of his English double-barreled hunting rifle, he drew a picture of the dark blue barrels in his mind, and his body felt as light as a feather.

He had been worried a short while ago about the results of the operation he had conducted on the patient with the stomach growth, but the gloom left him. He was full of hope and aspiration. He had completed his physical checkup and had arranged with the Foreign Ministry to process the papers the very day word came from the State Department. Within a week he would leave; he remembered Mr. Brown's assurance.

He thought with disdain of those young fellows who, without clinical experience, but with just a university degree were prone to show off by a mere trip to the States as if they had caught a star! "Well, I shall return and we shall see!"

Again the images of his daughter Nami and his son Wŏnsik leapt into his mind. He gripped his hands in tight fists and his face shivered. Then a wry smile spread over his face.

"Hum, I who lived through those molelike Japs and prickly Russkis, what are the Yankees to me? Let revolution come, let the state change hands. None shall block a loophole for Dr. Yi Inguk. Considering how many have flown higher, what can possibly happen to me?" He wanted to shout at the void.

"Well, then, shall I go to the airlines and check on the flight schedule?"

Clamping a Florida cigar slantwise in his mouth, he hailed a passing taxi. "Bando Hotel," he told the driver, plopping down into the bouncy cushion.

The clear autumn sky through the windows seemed bluer and higher than ever before.

The Author

Chŏn Kwangyong was born in Pukch'ŏng, South Hamgyŏng, on March 1, 1919, earned a degree in Korean literature from Seoul National University (1951), and remained to obtain his M.A. in 1953. Since then he has taught at the same university, where he is professor of Korean literature.

His first story appeared in 1939, but his literary career began in 1955 with the publication of the story "Black Hill Island." In his earlier works such humble, isolated characters as a fisherwoman and a miner were allowed to express their isolation and poverty, as well as occasional zeal for life. The setting of the next group of stories is a decadent, corrupt society that sought only profit and power. The characters were made to compare such a world to a dumping ground or a dung hill. But again, Chŏn did not fail to register their attempts to leap from their miserable condition, testifying to their dream of attaining a sense of human dignity. In these and later stories, Chŏn skillfully arranged characters into symbolic relations with each other and presented a tension between their psychological states. A compressed style and concise yet sensitive sentences helped create a rapid flow and a sense of tension.

"Kapitan Lee," first published in the journal Sasanggye *in July 1962, was nominated the same year for the Tongin Prize. The story traces a human type during Korea's tragic years of servitude under the Japanese. Some, like Ko Hyŏn and his father ("Flowers of Fire"), revolted in spirit and by action; others, like Yi Inguk, cultivated the secrets of a successful life only to protect themselves. From the moment Yi receives a watch as a prize, he begins to venerate the oppressor as a chosen people and develops a slave consciousness. A slave unable to revolt against his master denies himself tomorrow and seeks a comfortable life day to day. Opportunism engenders an illusion that he too belongs to the world of the dominators. Like a chameleon, Yi changes his color and lives in a world of infamy and lies. An epitome of a sad human type, Yi is nevertheless not alone to be blamed for his hypocrisy and baseness. Yi's worldly wisdom deserves at once our scorn and our compassion.*

by Kang Sinjae

The Young Zelkova

He always smells of soap. Well, not quite. Not always anyway. He gives off a soapy odor whenever he steps out of the bathroom after dousing himself with water upon return from school. So I know without looking that he is coming near, even if I am sitting still at the desk, facing the other way. I can even guess what kind of expression he is wearing or what sort of mood he is in.

After changing into a T-shirt, he saunters into my room to flop onto the sofa or to stand leaning with his elbow against the window sill, flashing a smile at me.

"What's new?" he asks me.

He smells of soap when he says that. And I know that one of the most saddening and tormenting moments has come upon me. A tingle spreads in my heart along with the mild fragrance of soap that his body emits—this is what I would have liked to say in reply. Then he gazes

Translated by Song Yoin

at me, wide-eyed. His eyes seem to be spying on my feelings or beckoning me to cheer up, smile, and be gay. Or else they could be nothing more than an indication of his cheerful mood. Which is it exactly?

I cannot help gazing into his eyes, focusing all my sorrows, pains, and wisdom at one point in each pupil. I am anxious to know how I appear to him. Just like the sound of the breakers that wash the rocks on the shore day in and day out, this one obsession of mine lashes my heart and sets my body and soul on fire. No matter how hard I try every day, I cannot find out. I cannot fathom the meaning of his gaze. Only my sorrows and torment turn into something so heavy that it sinks to the bottom of my heart. And then I realize that, after all, I must return to being what I apparently am, his younger sister with nothing on the surface to be awkward or uneasy about.

"Is that you?" I ask him in a cheerful voice as if he wanted it that way. I know how ungraceful it is to be anything but cheerful in a situation like this. Relieved at my cheerful voice, he stretches his legs saying, "Yeah, I'm dead tired. How about bringing me something to eat?"

"Gee, you sound impatient. I just got a breakthrough on my English composition homework and I've been scribbling along . . . " I mumble as I sit back from the desk.

"Let me see whether you show any promise of becoming a woman writer." He leans forward, reaching for my notebook.

"My goodness, no!" I hide the notebook under a stack of books and go downstairs to fetch some food from the refrigerator. As I put a frosty bottle of Coke, crispy crackers, and some cheese on a tray, my heart begins to throb with secret joy. Why should he come to my room to ask for food? He always bypasses the refrigerator on his way and badgers me to fetch food for him. Certainly he is not too lazy to open such a simple device; or if he wanted someone else to do it for him, he could easily ask one of the servants. At least that would be easier than making me work, putting up with all my grumblings, tardy movements, and spilling and dropping things. (Somehow I am not adept in these things. I try to be neat and prompt, but in vain.)

When I return with the tray he is sitting down with his face half turned, peering through the window at the rose bush outside. Now he is in such a pensive mood that his eyes look placid and relaxed, unlike the ones I am used to. His tanned face and finely chiseled features viewed from an angle appeal to me. Even the side of his countenance that he would rather not reveal to me looks attractive. His head is shaped like that of Apollo, and a few curly hairs are drooping over his forehead.

"They say curly hair means a violent temper," I once said to him.

"No, not really, Sukhŭi. That's not correct," he replied in all seriousness to what I meant as a mere joke.

After repeating the routine of sitting down for relaxation in my room, he sprang to his feet, saying, "How about a game of tennis?"

"Fine."

"No. Wait. Didn't you say you're having midterm exams from tomorrow?"

"That's all right. It doesn't bother me."

To tell the truth, I didn't have any exams or anything like that. I pulled a pair of white shorts and a blue shirt out of the upper drawer of my bureau.

"You might flunk," he said as he stepped out of the room to pick up his racket.

The sun's rays were warm, but a cool breeze kept the fresh green leaves in the yard stirring. We walked to the fence at the foot of the hill in the back. Turning the corner where the stone wall has started to sag, we slipped into our neighbor's courtyard. By "our neighbor's" I mean the property belonging to the old royal household, most of which is an idle tract of land except for a couple of tile-roofed houses in the distant corner.

The residents of the old tile-roofed houses sweep and clean the yard religiously every day so that it is kept as clean as the *ondol* floor.[1] "It's a shame so large a piece of land should lie idle," I said one day, sitting on the stone fence, looking down at the yard. "We should make a tennis court here. Don't you think it's a good idea?"

At first he didn't go along with me, but later he gave in, and we walked over to the house to consult with the warden of the property. The following day, we drew lines by sprinkling lime. A few days later, we set up a net and leveled the ground to turn it into a regular tennis court. The warden couldn't have anticipated that so much work would be done on his property. If he should complain, we were ready to give it up any time. So we worked with more hesitation than dispatch.

But the silver-haired, good-natured old man of the house, not only did not express his displeasure but from time to time watched our games, leaning on his walking cane. On one or two occasions he spotted me climbing over the stone fence and appeared to be about to reprimand me, but said nothing. Perhaps he thought that I wouldn't abide by his instructions anyway. At any rate, the yard was our favorite playground.

As a physics major in college my brother was under

constant pressure to keep up with his studies. But he was
no bookworm to shy away from games. Although I had
played tennis even before I joined his family, I owe most
of my sophisticated skills to him. I was so happy to learn
that he could play tennis better than the coach at my
school in the country.

Dull brains do not appeal to me, nor do people with
little or no athletic inclination. Athletic games enable us
to taste the joy of life. There is nothing so sweet as the
air we breathe while we jump around in pursuit of the
ball. But that day, I was in the poorest of condition; I
was not playing well, I relied on his ability to adjust his
pace to mine and skillfully to lead me to finish each
game.

"Shucks! I ought to be playing better than this. I
wonder if I am deteriorating."

"You're playing quite well. How would you like to
play a game with Chisu before it gets warm?"

Soon after the sky turned lilac we picked up our
balls and headed toward the valley where there was a
spring of medicinal water. The water seeping through
cracks in the rock was so cold it chilled my teeth, and it
tasted of minerals. We scooped the water in our cupped
hands and guzzled it down our thirsty throats. Our manners added a jarring note to the scenery there: the willow's
light green leaves drooping over the rock and the clusters
of red blossoms on the lone branch of a nameless tree.
It's a pity we've never learned to improve our manners.

"Drink a lot! Spring water might do you some good."

"What good?"

"For one thing it might improve your tennis."

But this time there was a little gourd dipper at the
side of the well. The old man must have put it there.

"From today on we have to drink nicely."

"The mountain god is watching us."

So we took the rest properly. And then he bent down to scoop a gourdful of water. He put the dipper close to my mouth, looking serene and strange. The face I saw then was one I had never seen before, one that was totally of his own. I had a sip and looked up at him. He slowly drank what was left in the dipper. As he put the dipper back where it was, he appeared to be overtaken by a gush of emotion in that short span of time. He didn't look toward me. All of a sudden, I was seized by confusion. But there was something that never eluded me in that confusion. Happiness.

I walked along the stone fence with a racket on my shoulder. "Brother," for that is what he is to me in terms of formal kinship, but it was a symbol of irrationality and unreasonableness. My existence was entangled in that irrational and unreasonable relationship!

I jumped down from the stone fence, which is taller than I am, and walked straight into the garden without looking back. I walked barefoot, with a pair of tennis shoes in my hand. The turf was so smooth and tender that it tickled but slightly, and I felt like taking my stockings off too.

"How would you like to have your feet shod so you can go anywhere without shoes?" he said to me whenever he found me barefooted.

"Walking barefoot on the grass takes me back to my hometown. It makes me feel as if I've reclaimed myself."

On an afternoon like this my mutterings would give way to a surge of mixed emotions so that I would purse my lips like a grandmother and remain taciturn. I come to the terrace, looking glum. The purple carpet in the spacious living room, the large pieces of furniture in an impressive array, the mysterious calm that reigns in it, the peonies in full bloom around the house, the fragrance of lilacs, the deepening odor of the fresh green plants— all these make me perceive painfully the meaning of my existence afloat in that ethereal purple air.

The brief moments of cheerfulness and happiness I have experienced cannot be mine for long; aren't they manifestations of my own sorrows and torment? I am at a loss. Such terms as "younger sister" and "elder brother" evoke hatred and terror in my mind. I abhor them. The joy and happiness I have been groping for are not permissible in this category of kinship.

There was something pathetic about my daily illusions of myself as a lone figure in the ethereal purple air. I no longer had the courage to be beside him. He would blink his eyes and crack a joke. He would bid me to cheer up, smile and be merry, without explicitly saying so. This is all he could do for me.

Today I felt more miserable because my heart had been filled with bliss. I stood there for a while. As I stepped onto the shiny wooden floor, puffing out my cheeks, I left my footprints along the way. Soiling the clean floor gave me an ironic pleasure.

After taking a bath, I stole a glance outside the window while dressing. I saw him sitting on a bench under the wisteria. He looked lonesome, with his elbows on his knees and his eyes riveted on the laurel bush. Could he be suffering too, even a little? Well, what could he do? I said to myself. For no obvious reason, I became cruel to him.

I sat down in the corner of my unlit room and looked out at him. He stood up when darkness began to lap him; he stood there for a while, his face turned toward the window of my room. I kept the room unlit and did not go down for supper. Instead, I picked up the glass of

Coke he left unfinished. I brought my lips to the rim of the glass just as his lips had touched the rim of the gourd dipper in which I had left some water at the well.

How should I address him? Destiny compels me to call him "brother." I was escorted to this place by Monsieur Lee one day late in winter two years ago, when houses in Seoul were glittering like ice candies with snow and ice piled on tops of their roofs. My mother introduced the young man to me then. "Sukhŭi, I would like you to meet your brother. His name is Hyŏngyu."

I gazed at him standing on the purple carpet. Mother continued, "He's a top student at the College of Arts and Sciences of Seoul National University. I know you've been called a gifted girl in the country, but now that you're in Seoul, things will look a bit strange. I want you to get along well with him." Although she said this in a gay tone, a shadow of fear hovered about her as she gazed into the young man's eyes.

He wore a brown V-neck sweater with collar of his shirt, a shade lighter, turned up over the neckline. His thick eyebrows were spaced wide apart so that they gave an air of intimidation. His eyes were cool and yet generous and poised, betraying wit and self-confidence. The overall contour of his face was one of neatness tempered by vigor and tenacity. Only the soft and delicate lines of his jaw and neck were exceptions.

"Of medium height and build, he does look like a prodigy," I rated him to my self, although I was not so foolish as to evaluate a man on his physical appearance alone. When I stared at him, he wore a faint smile on his lips, narrowing his eyes as if dazzled by the sun. The smile was an awkward but sturdily individualistic one. Perhaps he was reading my heart as I was trying to size him up. I grew tense at being subjected to his keen observation.

What he said then was quite simple. "It's a pleasure to have you with us. We've been much too lonesome in this house." He shook hands with me.

This was evidence enough that he took me for a child and that he wanted to honor my mother's feelings. Relief and gratification surged on my mother's face, as if to vindicate my observation. I viewed the relationship of Hyŏngyu to mother as being pretty much an artificial one that could be upheld only with minute consideration.

Monsieur Lee, a man of easygoing nature, didn't seem to take things seriously. With a smile on his face, he kept glancing at us, reminding us time and again that I must be tired from the journey.

At any rate, from this time on, the young man has been calling me by that easy and simple name, Sukhŭi— sometimes simply, "Hey, Suk!" And he has been generous to me to the point of making me feel embarrassed from time to time.

Lately, important changes have taken place in his relationship to me, such as his coming into my room to ask for food and to ask me to dress wounds on his fingers.

Friendly and unreserved as he was to me, I could never for the life of me bring myself to call him "brother": in the beginning, because we were total strangers, later because of other reasons. To call him "brother" was many times more difficult than to call Monsieur Lee "father." I was not sure whether I was obstinate or sheepish. Both he and mother understood my predicament, for they phrased their questions in such a way that I did not have to struggle to avoid using the term "brother" in my replies. The only person who added relentlessly to my predicament in this regard was Monsieur Lee.

I changed a good bit in many ways during my first year in Seoul. I grew taller and learned to look stylish, and my complexion turned fairer. Last spring, I was crowned queen of E. high school and reigned one whole day over campus activities. I felt that my bust measurement fell short of the title, but the votes were overwhelmingly in my favor and I was amazed. Of course mother was extremely pleased, and Monsieur Lee bought me an expensive watch.

But Hyŏngyu didn't have much to say, not even a joke. All he said was that he wanted to congratulate me and he said that in an awkward and self-conscious manner. And I liked him for it.

Also, my personality had appreciably changed. I felt things more intensely in this new and quiet atmosphere than in the country, where I used to have a lot of friends to play and sing with.

I now understand what *joie de vivre* means. The atmosphere in the new home is pleasant and cozy with a touch of romantic air emanating from the relationship between mother and Monsieur Lee. I like the suburban setting of the home, in the woods away from the center of Seoul, and this old ivy-mantled brick house itself, in which Monsieur Lee is said to have lived alone for years.

Hyŏngyu is well mannered and courteous toward mother, and Monsieur Lee is content so long as I look healthy and happy. A professor of economics at a private university, he is a little chubby and looks every inch good-natured. Even though he has nothing to do with France or the French, I call him Monsieur Lee because he reminds me of the hapless father in a French movie I saw.

But Monsieur Lee is not hapless; in fact, he is quite happy now. It is possible, though, that such a good-natured person may become wretchedly miserable if thrown into adverse surroundings.

In the tragedy of a young man like Goethe's Werther there is acute beauty; in the sorrow of a man like Monsieur Lee, nothing but wretchedness seems to prevail. How fortunate for him to have the companionship of my mother!

Mother looks happy even though she spends most of her time cooped up in our new house. Her voice, which was noted for being tender, has grown more so. She must be harboring a sense of guilt in her newly acquired happiness, for she refrains from going out or even from laughing aloud. Nevertheless, she is always well dressed and her light makeup is pleasing.

But there was something unexpected here which tormented me. It was my feelings toward Hyŏngyu that bore down on me day and night. When the crushing feeling was too painful to bear, I wished I hadn't come here. But such a feeling did not last long. I shudder to imagine my life without ever meeting a man like Hyŏngyu. Just meeting him has made me happier than any other woman on earth. I wouldn't trade the happiness of being near him for anything in the world.

It is true that I am at the same time sad and restless. To be more honest, my feelings keep changing every minute. The absence of Monsieur Lee, who is now traveling overseas, is a welcome relief, for I don't have to greet him every morning, looking royally happy, or go downstairs for supper on schedule.

"Mother, you know I don't like fixed schedules," I said immediately after Monsieur Lee had departed on his journey. "I want to eat when I feel like eating, and

I don't want to eat when I don't feel like it. So will you please excuse my manners as long as he is away?"

While the well-mannered Hyŏngyu was keeping mother company in the dining room, I sat by the window, staring blankly into the darkening sky. There was a faint glimmer of the river flowing beyond the vast plain dotted with small houses, patches of woods, and shimmering lakes. The river was as whimsical as the weather, glittering like platinum one day and becoming shrouded in fog the next. When the sky turned from purple to light grey, the river merged with the soft grey of the hanging clouds.

Viewing the dark river, I thought I must extricate myself from the confusion of tangled emotions. I couldn't let my whims be my guide, nor could I make any sense out of my conflicting claims. I was not bound by any sense of guilt in loving Hyŏngyu. That was out of the question. But to betray mother and Monsieur Lee in that sense was tantamount to ruining the lives of all four of us. I trembled at the dismal and horrible connotation of the word "ruin."

Before moving to this new home, I had lived in the country with my maternal grandparents. Until three or four years before that, mother used to live with us, but after she left for Seoul there were only three of us, my grandparents and me. We had a few workers and several watchdogs for the orchard. One of the dogs, a Chindo, was my pet. But I was always unbearably lonely, especially after mother went to Seoul.

Even when mother was with us I really didn't feel that our life was reassuring or joyful. It pained me that mother, a beautiful young woman, should devote all her time to the monotonous routine of a rural home. Although she usually had on her lap beautiful pieces of cloth or woolen yarn to make or knit something for me, and spoke about me often, I felt unhappy and uneasy about her.

If only she would stop sewing or knitting for a change and act like other mothers—shouting at me or scolding me under the pressure of household chores or of carrying a baby on her back—and live a life of her own, I would be content.

I cannot recall when mother began to live a shadow-like life. It was already like that about ten years ago when the Korean War forced us to move to my grandparents' place. I remember it was like that even before the war, when I started elementary school in Seoul.

I know nothing about my father. Someone had once told me that he was dead, but I never really believed that. It was only after the war, when grandmother told me in a convincing tone, "Your daddy has passed away," that I tended to believe it was true.

Probably my parents were separated when I was a baby, and the eventual death of my father made the separation permanent. At any rate I have no more information, curiosity, or feelings of any kind about my father. All that I have inherited from him is my surname Yun, which is nothing unique.

I have no idea how Monsieur Lee, then a refugee in the area, happened to visit my grandfather's orchard. I remember sitting on the branch of a tree one day, munching an apple, when a chubby gentleman, a stranger, walked into the yard. He stopped at the main gate for a while, took off his hat, and proceeded inside, hat in hand. As he was passing under the tree, I threw apple seeds in front of him, but he merely glanced up at me without a smile and walked away. He looked somewhat confused.

When I was later introduced to him inside the house, he appeared ignorant of the prankish welcome I had extended to him from atop the tree. He left before the day was over; and my grandparents had something very important to mull over. I often found mother taking a walk at night alone in the apple orchard.

Monsieur Lee paid one more visit to us, and mother went to Seoul shortly thereafter.

"We should have arranged her first marriage like this," said grandmother in a soft but tearful voice to grandfather in the adjoining room. "And then it wouldn't have been so hard for the child." I was shocked.

"If so, Sukhŭi wouldn't have been born to begin with."

"It's all a matter of luck. We couldn't blame Kyŏngae for her poor judgment in the past."

Hearing my grandparents refer to mother by her maiden name instead of the usual "Sukhŭi's mommy," I grew curious about her childhood and giggled. I no longer had to endure the sorrow of glancing at mother sitting like a shadow, mending my blouses or sweaters.

Although I was pleased that she had become appreciably happier, there was no denying that I myself was bitterly lonesome. So I sang aloud day and night; I sang on my way home from school, turning round the bend of the hill nearby; I sang in the garden where the crimson balsams were in full bloom.

"If you sing so loudly, people may laugh at you," grandmother said.

Two years ago, when Monsieur Lee came down late in the winter and insisted on taking me to Seoul, no one was more surprised than I. The old couple appeared hesitant at first, but soon gave in to the persistent demands of Monsieur Lee. But they looked dejected.

"More than anything else, her mother wants it that way," Monsieur Lee said to them in a serious tone. "She has never said so, but I know how earnestly she wants her."

I couldn't help smiling. My grandparents appeared fully convinced and were ready to consent as soon as Monsieur Lee should stop pleading. But he kept on as if they were dead against releasing me. When he stole a glance at me while talking, I nodded my own approval. At this gesture, he stopped talking, flashed a grin, and took out his handkerchief to wipe his forehead.

Thus I was transferred to E. girls' high school in Seoul. I ponder: Monsieur Lee and mother are man and wife. If I find it difficult to call him "father," it is because I am not used to uttering such a word.

I not only like him but also feel a kind of paternal tie toward him—a feeling of protective tenderness several times more powerful than toward my grandfather. But he is no blood relation of mine. Nor is Hyŏngyu, for that matter. Hyŏngyu and I are totally unrelated. The crux of the matter is that he is a man of twenty-two, and I am a girl of eighteen. Why can't I accept these facts?

I wouldn't want to release Hyŏngyu to anyone else; nor do I intend to offer my love to anyone else. I know that what binds us together must not be my being his "sister." I wish he would feel the same as I do—if not the joys, at least the agonies!

I cannot shake off trivial memories, expressions, or suggestions that seem to be responsible for my suffering. Would it be possible for me to become happy? Doesn't happiness stand for something for which a human being is born? The fragrance of the blossoms wafted into the room, shrouded in the darkness of an early evening. Lying face down on the bed, I finally broke into tears.

"Sukhŭi, here's something I've picked up for you," mother said Sunday morning when she saw me downstairs. She was sitting on the sofa, holding an envelope in her raised hand.

"What is it?" I said, stepping close to her. "Where did you pick it up?" I was a little embarrassed, but I couldn't help being inquisitive. I tried to take the letter away from her.

"Wait, sit down over there." She tried to conceal her momentary strain as she pointed to a chair in front of her. I sat down, trying to control my giggles.

Chisu is a cabinet minister's son. He lives in a mansion ridiculously surrounded by a Great Wall of China at the foot of a hill. Burly and unsophisticated, Chisu is a medical student and a friend and tennis partner of Hyŏngyu's. He drives a jeep every morning, delivering his brothers and sisters to kindergarten and high school. He gave me a lift in his jeep twice: once when I was with Hyŏngyu and had no excuse to turn down the offer and another time when I was walking home from downtown and couldn't possibly refuse a ride without appearing foolish.

On my second ride I said, "I don't see any little ones today."

"Those who come to my stops on time get a ride, but those who don't are left to their own devices," he replied. "You see, my jeep runs on schedule like a train."

I didn't consider it funny that this simpleminded young man should have sent me a delicately worded love letter. What was funny was mother's serious concern about the matter.

"Well, I wonder where you picked it up."

"On the bench under the wisteria tree."

"That's right. That's where I left it."

"Listen, Sukhŭi. You ought to be more careful. Don't you realize how careless you are when you get through with your tennis? It's always your brother who brings the rackets in." I smiled in acknowledgment. She continued, "Don't you think you're being discourteous to the man who sent the letter?"

"I certainly do, mother. You're right," I said, grabbing the letter.

"Is it something important, something your mother shouldn't read?"

"No, not at all. You may read it. Would I have left it there if it were something you shouldn't read?" I grew a bit annoyed.

"I am relieved. The fact is, I've already read it."

"My goodness, mother!"

"What I want to speak to you about is this. I wish you would consult me whenever things like this happen to you, instead of trying to solve them by yourself—you can at least tip me off about what's going on."

Meanwhile, I grew melancholy and wanted to leave as soon as possible.

"You realize that mom is on your side, don't you?"

"Certainly," I gave a halfhearted reply, walking slowly outside. I wondered how she would feel about being on my side if I had said to her, "I am in love with your son."

It was something mother couldn't help, something Monsieur Lee couldn't help, either. I stuffed the letter into my pocket and walked down the grassy slope, drenched to my knees in the morning dew. I trudged on toward the swamp in the distance, along a trail least likely to have people on it. I walked past the patch of acacias, barley fields, and wild bushes.

My relationship with Hyŏngyu about this time had

reached a stage more pessimistic than at any other time. I tried to avoid seeing him. It was an unbearable pain to laugh, exchange jokes, and then part as though nothing had happened. I grew temperamental even when he didn't say anything unusual, and then he would turn away.

Birds were chirping overhead. The sky was dark blue like the deep ocean, and the leaves glittered in the sun. It was high summer. The oak forest concealed the swamp, and I sat down on the grass, brooding, with a hand propping up my jaw.

Should I become a world-renowned ballerina and stare at him from the stage, glittering like jewels? (I didn't pay much attention to my ballet instructor, but I remember her telling me to be ambitious.) I imagined him sitting in the audience, accompanied by an unattractive wife, and becoming heartsore at seeing me on stage. This kind of fancy—my bright idea—disappeared as rapidly as foam on water. And a new kind of fancy took its place: I ought to be thankful just to have a chance to serve him like a maid, expecting nothing in return. Soon teardrops fell on my toes before I became really sad.

I rose to my feet to go back home. Then I heard a rustle in the bush behind me. A slim hound on a leash nosed its way out of the bush, followed by Chisu. He was wearing a light grey sports shirt that matched his robust physique. From behind him darted a boy and a girl, each about ten years of age. Chisu was taken aback to see me there, but soon collected himself to greet me with a smile, showing a row of white teeth.

"Where have you been? Taking a walk?"

"Yes, I'm on my way home now."

The children started playing hide-and-seek, running round the two of us. Chisu stopped the boy and handed the leash over to him, motioning him to go ahead of us.

Chisu and I walked together silently for a while. While we were passing by the acacia forest, he asked me abruptly in an embarrassed tone, "Have you read my letter?"

"Yes, I have."

"Aren't you going to give me a reply?"

"Yes, but I don't know what to say."

He nodded his head impatiently, blushing up to his ears.

"But you understand how I feel about you, don't you?"

I said I did. And to change the topic I told him that Hyŏngyu wanted to play tennis with him soon.

"Certainly, I'll be there," he replied with renewed vigor. He started whistling. I heard him whistle all the way until I reached my doorstep. Brushing off an insect that was crawling on my shoulder, he said, in a sad tone, "I've had a wonderful time today. Thank you."

"Good-bye. Don't forget to practice a lot. Our team is quite good now."

He nodded blankly, biting his upper lip as if absorbed in some other thoughts.

I ran up the narrow flight of stone-tiled stairs toward my room, whistling all the way as Chisu did. I needed to keep my spirits up no matter what happened. The sleeves of my blouse and hem of my skirt were damp with dew and smelled of grass. I pushed open the half-closed door.

Unexpectedly, I saw Hyŏngyu standing there facing me. He normally didn't come into my room when I was not in. But this was not what really surprised me; rather, it was his deeply disturbed countenance. In front of his stormy appearance, I faltered, not knowing what to do.

"Where have you been?" he said in a low but firm voice. I didn't answer.

"Did you leave the letter there as a favor to me, so that I could read it?"

He stepped closer and closer until his chest nearly touched my face. I remained silent.

"Where have you been?"

I kept my mouth pursed tight. I was in no mood to speak up. In a flash, he raised his hand and slapped me in the face. A flame shot up inside me. Tears filled my eyes. But he walked out of the room without turning around.

I glanced outside the window absentmindedly. I saw Chisu in that light grey shirt trudging along the trail in the woods. And the place where he had brushed the insect off my shoulder looked as vivid as if it were within the reach of my hands.

My body tingled as if shocked by an electric current. I understood why Hyŏngyu had lost his temper. Happiness swelled in my heart, and I felt like bursting. I threw myself down on the bed, curled up like a shrimp, lest the pulsating stream of happiness leak out of my body.

What should I do?
We took a walk in the woods at night.
We held each other's hands in the dark.
And I let him hold me in his arms.
What should I do?
The answer to this question becomes more and more obscure. At any rate, I ought to stop going to the woods. This is all I can say now with confidence.

Arriving home from school one afternoon, I was told to go directly to see mother in her room. I was worried because I hadn't been greeting her whenever I left or returned home.

"Are you back now? You look pale. Is anything the

matter with you?" Mother put her hand on my forehead. "Your brother comes home late in the evening, and you're hard to see unless I call for you . . . "

She smiled softly, apparently unaware of what was going on. And she went on: "According to his last letter, it looks as though I might have to go to the United States. If I go there, I'll be away for a year or so. But I wouldn't want to leave your brother and you behind. So I've written him several times that I'd rather not go, but you see . . . " She turned her face away.

"What do you think? Your brother has agreed to my going," she said, gazing into my eyes.

"It's all right with me, too," I replied, wondering what would happen to us in that event.

"I appreciate it. I'll take up this matter in detail with you tomorrow. Shall we ask grandmother to come and live with you? Still that wouldn't improve the security of the family . . . "

Grandmother, whose back is bent with age, would be of little use. What would happen in this house if mother went away? The thought of living alone with Hyŏngyu appalled me. Things, fateful things that no one could prevent, not even I could prevent by staying away from the woods, were bound to take place. I couldn't sleep. My nerves bled at the slightest touch like a fresh wound. As days went by, I couldn't bear it any longer. I left Seoul, insisting that I must be away for a while at grandmother's.

I made up my mind never to go back there, nor to return to school. I felt that it was best to look upon it as the end of a chapter in my life. It would be as painful as carving out a piece of my own flesh; but could I conceive of any other plan?

I made it a rule to often climb the mountain behind our house. An hour or so of climbing brought me to a Buddhist nunnery. That was not my goal, but past the nunnery, up on the crest, I found a place for myself where a thicket of roses and fresh green trees stood in the rushing wind. I would sit there in the wind. Between the trunks of young zelkova trees wafted the light fragrance of wild roses.

I plucked white blossoms, many of them, and put them on the lap of my turquoise dress. Under the dazzling sky the blossoms quickly lost their sheen and began to wilt.

Then I looked up. The next instant, I jumped to my feet in spite of myself. It was Hyŏngyu, climbing up the steep slope. He looked disturbed as he once was before, with his lips pursed tight. The tight lips made him look more sad than angry. When he halted within several feet of me, I was overtaken by an illusion that I was rushing out to him spontaneously. Actually, on the contrary, I was holding on to the trunk of one of the trees.

"Well, Sukhŭi. Don't let go of that tree. Hold on to it and listen to me," he said, retreating a few steps. He now looked miserable.

"You must come back and go to school. You must forget everything and study. I'm going to do exactly the same. We ought to be separated. We should study separately. Mother will need some money for her trip, so I suggested that she lease the house.

"I've decided where I'm going to stay. You can go to one of mother's friends. Sukhŭi, we must live apart, but that does not mean that there is no way out for us. Do you understand me?" he said, with his feet planted firmly on the ground. I was trembling, clinging to the zelkova.

"What happened in the woods at that time was really

something that couldn't be helped. We can never forget nor ignore it as long as we live. We're parting to meet again. There's bound to be a way out. Such as going abroad . . . " He wiped tears away with the back of his clenched fist.

"Do you understand me, Sukhŭi?"

I nodded with tears in my eyes. After all, my life had not come to an end. It was all right for me to keep on loving him.

"Now, won't you promise you'll come back tomorrow, the day after tomorrow, or as soon as possible?"

I nodded.

"Thank you so much."

He forced a smile on his face. Then, turning around, he ran down the slope. The wind blew against me. Embracing the young zelkova, I laughed. With tears streaming down my face, I was laughing till my laugh rang through the sky. Ah, it was all right for me to keep on loving him.

The Author

Kang Sinjae was born on May 8, 1924, in Seoul and attended Ewha Women's University. Since making her literary debut in 1949 she has published a dozen novels, some fifty short stories, and several plays, and won prizes in 1959 and 1967. One of the recurrent themes in her works is the destiny of woman in love and marriage; some heroines submit to convention, but others escape from family or into the recesses of their minds. Her beautifully chiseled sentences and paragraphs, skillful ex-

ploration of human emotions and actions, sensitive responses to colors, smells, and natural scenes that often figure as motifs of narrative make her one of the most readable women writers today.

"The Young Zelkova" was first published in the journal Sasanggye for January 1960 and was subsequently made into a movie (1968). Narrated by the eighteen-year-old Sukhŭi, the story concerns her relationship with her new stepfather's son from his first marriage. Sukhŭi follows her mother into her new home when the latter remarries and meets Hyŏngyu, her mother's new "son." Instead of accepting the bond artificially imposed by convention as brother and sister, they fall in love as man and woman. How they solve the differing claims of society and personality, convention and spontaneity, is told refreshingly from a girl's point of view.

by Yi Hoch'ŏl

Midnight

t was a May evening. They had heard again that the elder daughter would be coming home at midnight, and now they were awaiting her arrival. No one paced the floor, but an air of expectation reigned. The master of the house, over seventy years old, sat neatly clad in light purple silk Korean clothing on the sofa in the drawing room. He had once been president of a bank and since his retirement as an emeritus director still drew enough pension to maintain the household. Although tidy in appearance, he looked somewhat unstable and frail, a dullard, without the strength to stand by himself. He was almost deaf, but his fair, broad face and complexion made him look younger than his years. On either side of him sat his daughter-in-law, Chŏngae, and his younger daughter, Yŏnghŭi. He disliked the way his daughter-in-law usually dressed in traditional Korean clothes; this evening, therefore, she had put on a spring sweater and black, narrow

Translated and abridged by Peter H. Lee

slacks. His younger daughter wore a one-piece dress. The two women looked like two friendly sisters. Chŏngae supported the arm of the old man while Yŏnghŭi lounged with her chin propped on her hand. All three gazed at the dark front yard through the broad window.

There was little light outside. A gentle breeze rustled through the aged trees around the yard. The sky spread above the eaves and the stars glittered, but the yard was dusky and desolate and the whole house was quiet, almost dead.

Clang, bang, clang, bang.

Now and then the echo of something striking metal sounded in the distance. It was like the noise of a hammer pounding on red-hot iron at a smithy or a workshop down the road. But, there was no smithy or workshop nearby. The sound must have come from afar.

Clang, bang, clang, bang.

The monotonous sound penetrated the quiet, empty night air and pierced the body, setting one's nerves on edge.

"What is that sound?" Yŏnghŭi asked, knitting her brow.

"I wonder what it can be?" Chŏngae replied vaguely.

"There aren't any workshops around here."

Chŏngae nodded.

The hammering continued intermittently. If one listened carefully, he would realize that the trees were swaying, not because of the early summer night breeze, but because of the reverberation of the thudding sound. The noise seemed to cleave to the cracks in the walls of the room. A certain pathos lurked in the ceiling just above the fluorescent light. Mother, now dead, was free from the painful management of this declining, debased household. Clang, bang, clang, bang—eventually this sound would cause the house to crumble. The snake, the guardian of the house, would soon wriggle out of a prolonged hibernation. Then would come the feast, surely the last, and the members of the family would depart without regret.

Suddenly Yŏnghŭi burst into laughter, shrill and affected. Chŏngae was startled.

"Sister, do you know what I've been thinking?" she exclaimed. "When I see you supporting father's arm, you don't look like an in-law, but a real daughter."

Chŏngae was a bit embarrassed. Of course, the old man did not hear the remark. He was fingering the mole on the tip of his nose.

Yŏnghŭi continued to jabber in her shrill voice, and appeared to be irritated. She kept on gibbering to drown out the metallic sound that went on at even intervals, once every thirty seconds. It was a tense thirty seconds; the sound crept into Yŏnghŭi's voice producing a strange resonance in her speech.

"So our home is not entirely undemocratic. It's good to see you getting along so well with papa." After a pause, she went on in a louder voice, "But don't you get tired of it all? I mean, it seems that something is amiss, making everything empty—a big nail, a pillar, or something like that. Don't you feel that way?"

Chŏngae seemed to resemble her father-in-law. She too had become a dullard—but in a different way. She seemed to believe that dialogue was not meant to scratch the nerves, to drive the idle to recall things forgotten, or to waste time on the useless past.

"Is it midnight again tonight?" Yŏnghŭi asked once more. She went on, "Is my brother still upstairs?" Then she realized, "Oh, he hasn't come home yet, has he?"

She was referring to Sŏnjae. They were not engaged

yet, but they were almost resigned to it. Everybody expected it. She only knew him to be the younger cousin by marriage of her elder sister, who had married twenty years ago and since lived in the North. Sŏnjae had come to the South during the great retreat in January 1951. He had undergone many dire hardships and had gradually become part of the family. Mother, who died three years ago, had looked after him tenderly and sympathetically, probably because he was the cousin-in-law of her own daughter. But at seventy, mother was senile, and she asked him again and again about her daughter. On her deathbed, although everybody was present, mother seemed to be relieved only after she made sure of Sŏnjae's presence. Perhaps she regarded him as she did her own daughter. After her death, he occupied the corner room upstairs. For a while he paid for the room, but no longer. At first, Yŏnghŭi considered him untidy and even uncouth. She thought herself illfated and unfit to marry but, without realizing it, she gradually became used to him. However, she never was very close to him and could never find out whether he really worked at a fisheries company.

"Why does it have to be midnight?" Yŏnghŭi asked.

"I have no idea," answered Chŏngae.

"If she really came home, how nice it would be!"

"Wouldn't it?"

"But the whole business is so ridiculous," said Yŏnghŭi as if wanting to laugh. Then she changed again and went on playfully.

"Let's break up. Each of us shall find some way to continue living. Let's all go our own way. It would be easier and far better that way." She looked up seriously as though really planning to go away.

At that moment her brother Sŏngsik came down the stairs and peeped into the room through the door which opened into the hallway. Meeting their eyes, he turned to Yŏnghŭi:

"What are you sitting there like that for?"

She grinned at him and threw stinging words:

"You still in your pajamas? Don't you see that we are again waiting for your sister?"

Without a word, Sŏngsik sat in the chair opposite the old man.

"It's to be midnight again," Yŏnghŭi went on without a pause. "Aren't you going to wait for her with us?"

Sŏngsik said nothing and opened the paper.

"Since you are the young master of this house, you must wait along with us. Isn't that right, Chŏngae?" Then turning to the old man, she shouted, waving her hand:

"Papa, brother has come down to wait with us."

The old man was startled, and although it was unlikely that he understood what she said, he nodded.

Her brother did not show it expressly, but she knew that he disdained her relationship with Sŏnjae. Perhaps he was contemptuous of him. She felt humiliated by her brother and consequently felt more closely attached to Sŏnjae.

"Did he tell you when he would be back tonight?"

Sŏngsik shook his head, frowning.

"Do you realize that every word I say annoys you?"

Sŏngsik's glasses cast a chilly reflection.

"Do you know why I say that? Of course, you do. I have been setting you against Sŏnjae in many ways. You are so affected and priggish." Sŏngsik did not say a word. "You're thirty-four, pale with bony legs, in pajamas day and night. You intended to study music, but graduated from the College of Fine Arts. You have no mind to get a job since you've been to America a couple of times.

You've nothing to do in particular, yet you are vaguely dreaming of becoming a composer. Is there anything else to add to your description?"

Only the glasses flashed again.

Yŏnghŭi went out of the room into the hall.

The clanging noise had been forgotten for a while, but now it intruded again, a hard, metallic sound. Shaking the whole hallway, it fell on her even louder and heavier than it had in the room. She smelled carbide and noticed that the bathroom door was open and the light was on inside. She moved to turn it off, but thinking that it might be better left on, turned back.

The rumor of her sister's return home from the North at midnight was only a vague expectation, not the sort of thing demanding a second thought. They had been accustomed to waiting for so long now that it was difficult to remember when it had begun. Father had been deaf for the last two years and then had become almost mute. He made himself understood with his hands and facial expressions even though he could have spoken. He slowly became dull. When the cord of control that had governed the household snapped, only the housemaid grew freer, livelier, and more impudent. She probably considered Sŏnjae the softest of all the members of the family, for she often addressed him jokingly. This irritated Yŏnghŭi. The maid often went out in a gaudy one-piece dress and painted her bloated, slightly pockmarked face. At the time of the April revolution and the May military coup, she was gone for the whole day. She had not joined in the demonstrations of course, but had returned to tell wild tales about the events of the day.

Yŏnghŭi stealthily opened the kitchen door.

"Why has it got to be midnight?" the maid grumbled. "Why not at noon? There should be at least some sense even in madness."

Yŏnghŭi lashed out.

"What! What on earth are you talking about?"

The maid turned toward her and only giggled.

"I say, what are you talking about?"

"Why, nothing, miss!"

"You're living in this house, so why not count yourself one of the family? Can't you be more obliging? Can't you? You think we are all as stupid as you are?"

"I didn't say anything, miss. I was just talking to myself."

Her brother was still reading the paper over his thin silver-rimmed spectacles. In his hand he held a can of Coca-Cola. His thin, pale legs stuck out from the bottom of his rolled-up pajamas to reveal hair and blue veins.

The old man sat just as before. Chŏngae looked sad and pathetic, as she always did when she sat near Sŏngsik. She tried not to look at her husband and turned her head slightly aside. Yŏnghŭi never understood how Chŏngae could be so attentive to her father-in-law and herself while she evaded and turned away from her husband, who should be the most important person to her.

Just then the big clock on the wall began to strike ten. The chime upset the room with its heavy echo. The walls seemed to swell and shrink as the notes came and went. Yŏnghŭi flopped down before Chŏngae, buried her face in her lap, and snickered at the way her father stared vaguely into the air. With the last sound of the clock, she sank into silence for a while. Then she lifted her face and started talking in a low, composed tone that gradually grew louder and more vehement:

"Sister, are you going to be like that forever? Aren't you bored? Look at your husband, my brother. He is hopeless, always in pajamas sipping Coca-Cola."

Chŏngae and Sŏngsik lifted their heads at the same time. The paper slipped from his hands. The glasses gleamed in the light again. When Chŏngae's eyes met his, she immediately turned frigidly away. Frowning, she said, "Don't start that again." Yŏnghŭi sat up on the floor on her knees and grasped Chŏngae's hands.

"Papa is now a cripple. What is it that we are trying to preserve so desperately? I'm twenty-nine. Have you ever considered the fact that I'm an old maid? Now you're virtually the mistress of this house, aren't you? The honor and tradition of this family . . . Chŏngae, sister, why are you trying so hard to maintain this house?"

Sŏngsik put down the Coca-Cola can and took out a cigaret. Though an expert at lighting cigarets, his long, thin fingers trembled just perceptibly. He was no longer a husband to Chŏngae or a brother to Yŏnghŭi: the only noticeable thing about him was the cold, gleaming spectacles.

"For God's sake, don't start that again," Chŏngae said.

The old man, who was looking at the clock, did not understand and glanced at Yŏnghŭi with his usual wide, vacant eyes.

"For heaven's sake, let's leave this house and move somewhere else. We can buy a small house in the suburbs . . . and leave this rented house. Then Papa may rest in eternal peace as soon as possible, and you may get a divorce . . ."

"And then let's get rid of the maid, and we two . . ." Yŏnghŭi's voice changed to a whispering, whining tone.

"I'm getting more and more confused. You know what kind of a situation I'm in. You just can't pretend not to know anything about it. It is not something that can be left as it is. You just can't go on taking everything for granted."

Clang, bang, clang, bang.

The hammering sound again penetrated through the cracks in the walls.

The maid opened the door. Yǒnghǔi was holding Chǒngae's hand. Sǒngsik was still poring over the paper, though not really reading it. The old man sat looking out into the dark as before. In this manner they each waited for someone. The old man was waiting for his elder daughter; Chǒngae was waiting for the elder sister-in-law she had never met; Yǒnghǔi and Sǒngsik were waiting for their sister. All were expecting her, but none was really conscious of waiting. In fact, were it not for this sense of waiting, they would not pretend to fulfill their assigned obligations in the family. Though they were acustomed to waiting, now they felt the weariness that comes with boredom. Yet they had enough reason to be bored. The ceremony of waiting, however, revealed in a way that the old man was still master of the house. If he insisted that his daughter was coming home, they had to be ready to welcome her. As they waited, it seemed to them that she really would appear.

The maid stood in the doorway for a while. Although she had a sudden impulse to laugh, she merely said, "Miss, he is expecting you outside." Yǒnghǔi, startled, scrambled to her feet and went out of the room, smoothing down the hair at the back of her head.

Coming out of the lighted room, she found it pitch dark outside. She shuffled slowly in her rubber shoes toward the gate and opened it. The lane was empty and straight, and down at the corner where it met the main road the lights of the small shop shone cozily. The shadows about her began to swell. Unlike fluorescent light, the reddish light of the shop had a warm tranquility. Yŏnghŭi knew she was longing for something.

Someone was standing against the wall beside the gate. It was Sŏnjae, dead drunk as usual. She knew this instinctively and was revolted by it. Then, slowly, she felt a sweet sensation spreading through her body. She liked Sŏnjae far better when he was drunk than when he was sober. Biting her lips softly, she went over behind him and placed her hand on his shoulder. She thought her gesture warm.

"You're drunk," she said. "Why do you call me out instead of coming in yourself? What's there that stops you? It doesn't become you at all." He gave a meaning-less smile and half turned around, saying remarkably distinctly for a drunken man:

"I'm drunk. Do I look funny? Do you think I'm funny? Well, I've got something to straighten out with you."

"No need to straighten anything out with me."

Yŏnghŭi smiled sullenly and clasped her fingers. Sŏnjae staggered in the dark and said:

"Let's leave this house, this very moment. What do you think?"

"I'm all for it. We'll be leaving this place sooner or later anyway," she said quietly. "Let's go away tonight, right now." She laughed lightly.

"I'm serious. I mean it," he said.

She did not know exactly what he was serious about, but she felt that he was serious.

The banging came again. It was not as irritating as before, now that she heard it standing outside in the dark with drunken Sŏnjae.

"I'm serious—I mean it," Sŏnjae repeated.

"I know you are," whispered Yŏnghŭi.

She listened to Sŏnjae's words which in fact echoed her own usual remarks to Sŏngsik and Chŏngae. To a drunken man words were quite futile, she thought.

Suddenly Sŏnjae bent his head forward and, retching once or twice, started to vomit. She quickly cupped her hands to his mouth, and the sticky liquid flowed into them. She giggled absently and, throwing it aside, rubbed her palms on the wall. Even in the dark she could see tears in his eyes. She wiped them away with the back of her hand. Sŏnjae smiled again doubtfully. She supported him with one hand and patted his back with the other. At the moment she felt an indescribably sweet melancholy spreading through her body. The weight of a grown man was heavy on her and she was ready to embrace him. She knew then the inevitability of her feelings and what they would lead to. Slowly passion overwhelmed her. She laid her cheek on his broad back, still patting it with her hand. She could feel the solid warmth and the heavy pounding of his heart. The stars shone brightly among the trees.

Clang, bang, clang, bang.

Now the noise seemed to have lost its sharpness coming from far away. It took a sinewy man to make such a noise—he would be hammering a piece of iron. Sparks would be flying from the hammer, and the people nearby would be sitting around in their yards, gossiping about the people in the neighborhood. When darkness falls on a May night and stomachs are no longer heavy, people sit around and talk. There would be the red glow of a few cigarets.

"Do you hear that noise?"

"What noise?" Sŏnjae stammered.

Her ear being buried in his back, she felt his voice vibrate through her whole body before reaching her ear.

"I mean that metallic sound."

Sŏnjae tried to listen for a while, then said:

"Yes, I can hear it now. Why?"

Yŏnghŭi helped him into the house and, sitting him on the bottom step of the staircase, went into the drawing room. Father turned and looked at her. Chŏngae gave her a sad smile. Sŏngsik was still buried behind the paper.

"He's drunk again," said Yŏnghŭi. The very next moment she regretted her words for she was aware that when a man comes home drunk, a woman usually complains about it. Chŏngae smiled again without a word. Yŏnghŭi blushed slightly, for Chŏngae's smile told her that she knew everything. The maid abruptly opened the door and trying to suppress her laughter said:

"Oh, miss, he did it in the hall."

The whole house immediately reacted as if something had really happened. Yŏnghŭi dashed out of the room; the maid ran to the bathroom. The door banged. The lights in the hall flashed on. Water gushed from the faucet. The maid was in a hilarious mood, and the drawing room was almost empty now.

At last Chŏngae looked at her husband, but she could only see the cold glasses. A shudder ran down her spine as she contemplated him. The old man turned toward the noisy hall and looked at his daughter-in-law inquiringly. She pointed upstairs to let him know that Sŏnjae had returned. The sound of gargling came forth from the bathroom and was followed by the creaking of stairs. Chŏngae listened attentively to the sound as though trying to keep it fast in her memory. Somehow she liked Sŏnjae as he was now. She listened to the laughter of the maid, who was helping Yŏnghŭi take Sŏnjae upstairs. Then the thuds of rolling and Yŏnghŭi's suppressed laughter. In a moment all became quiet again. The door upstairs closed. The maid's voice was heard, followed by the sound of her footsteps on the stairs. Sŏngsik slowly got up on his feet and turned toward the door without a word.

"Sŏngsik," she called to him, "are you going upstairs?"

He turned toward her for a second, and then left the room. She suddenly became irritated, trembling without knowing why. It seemed to her that he was climbing to a height far beyond her reach and that the ascent would take hours. She closed her strained, tired eyes, holding fast to the arm of the old man whom she momentarily regarded as her own father.

The maid opened the door again. The light was pale and cold. Chŏngae, who was crying, lifted her head. The old master of the house was still gazing at the yard. The maid stood there for some time, and as she was about to close the door, Chŏngae asked:

"Isn't Yŏnghŭi coming down?"

"She says she'll be down in a while, ma'am."

"What is she doing up there?"

The maid was silent.

"Never mind."

The maid wondered whether she really understood, whether her mistress knew all about it. Their eyes met, and they stared at each other. The old man looked at them alternately. For an instant his eyes appeared clear and sharp.

Yŏnghŭi seldom had been in the small shabby room. She could smell the manly odor and wondered whether she should turn on the light. She laid Sŏnjae on the bed in the dark and opened the window, which looked out over the front yard. The room was not entirely dark, since light reflected from the drawing room downstairs. She was still excited and wanted to remain so. Before the feeling left her, she wanted to get it over with. She slipped out of her dress and, sitting down on the edge of the bed, shook him.

"Wake up, Sŏnjae. Open your eyes and don't go to sleep."

He groaned and waved her away. When he opened his eyes and saw her there, he was surprised and for a moment fixed his eyes on her in silence. Then he embraced her in an easy manner. She let herself go and whispered and caught the smell of his hair, wet with sweat.

"I don't want you to be drunk—not on an occasion like this."

Sŏnjae remained half-conscious, but he was slowly recovering.

"Now pull yourself together. You should be wide awake. Otherwise I'll regret it."

"I'm all right. I'm quite sober now," said Sŏnjae at last.

Clang, bang, clang, bang.

It still went on. This time it seemed much closer. The open window looked like a hole drilled by the sound.

"Don't be drunk," she said again.

"I'm quite sober."

Yŏnghŭi felt a thrill.

"Really, you shouldn't be drunk. You must be sober and wide awake. Try to take in every bit and feel it."

He turned around and held her in his arms, causing her to roll about and lie beside him. Both lay comfortably side by side.

"What day is it?" whispered Yŏnghŭi.

"I don't know."

"Don't you even know the date?"

Like most men, Sŏnjae was impatient: she wanted to prolong the sensation.

"Don't be impatient—be easy now. Let's have a talk first." She embraced him as he was preparing himself. He scrambled up in the dark like some tortoise rising with its own shell.

"Let's talk first."

"Talk about what?"

"What's the date today?"

"I don't know."

"You must know."

He was silent.

"My sister is supposed to come home tonight."

He kept quiet.

"It's true. Aren't you also frustrated, Sŏnjae?"

Her voice became pathetic and faint, and she closed her eyes.

"All of them have lost something—left something important behind them. They're all in pieces, all scattered. Isn't that so? That's why you're frustrated."

She opened her eyes for a second and could see the May night through the open window. She felt shy and shut her eyes again.

"Oh, don't behave like that! I must go downstairs and wait for my sister with them. Let's not do anything that'll embarrass us tomorrow morning. We're not going to be clumsy, are we? It's true that women are more beautiful than men. You can see it at a time like this."

She chattered continuously.

"It has been chasing me, and I have been trying to escape it all evening. I am so afraid to face it myself. I mean that hammering sound, that hard metal sound."

Elder daughter, dressed in a sailor suit, is with her children. The bright white color smells of the sea. With a tennis racket in one hand, she clings to her father with the other saying, "Papa, we won, we won!" "How did you win?" asks her father. Then she swings the racket and says, "We won like this, of course." The house is alive with her presence. Every door flies open and slams shut. Sŏngsik sharpens a knife on the grindstone. The stone and the knife glisten in the bright sunshine. Everything is shining. The front gate is wide open. The wind blows in and out unchecked. The trees in the yard are sleek and luxuriant, and the mixed smell of earth and leaves is fragrant. Spotty lies in the middle of the yard. Contented, he does not bark; Yŏnghŭi totters toward the dog and kicks him. The dog looks up at her with a contemptuous air, but he steps aside. She laughs cheerfully and gives him another kick. Now angry, he looks askance at her and barks, imploringly, resentfully, as if complaining about the undeserved kicks. Yŏnghŭi laughs again, and the dog, yawning, wags its tail.

"I want to pass water." The maid stands at the door, smug and insolent, with the smell of a sour apricot. The wife, with her black hair, is picking roses in the garden. Her waist is plump. Yŏnghŭi, crying her heart out on the cane chair, is left to fill the whole house with her loud sobbing. Elder daughter, in her sailor suit, is talking to my wife, "Mama, we must plant some lilacs in the garden." "Yes, dear, let's plant some," answers my wife confidently. "Let's have some by all means. We can always do what we want to." The old maid passes by at the corner of the yard. The wife asks her, "Where are you going?" The old maid flinches and mumbles, "I want to urinate, daughter-in-law, I want to pass water."

Mother is perched on the mulberry tree. The strong

smell of the mulberry field assails the nostrils. The red sun hanging on the western hill is enormously big. "Mama, look at the sun." She pretends not to have heard. "Look at the sun, mama." The sun seems to be much nearer than when it is in midheaven. It looks as if it will grow tall and stretch out its arms and legs to run toward them. The shadow of the western hill is rushing toward them, and the prostrate barley field sweeps up its head in the shade. The magpie's nest on the gingko tree glitters. Father, who has been crying over his departed mother, comes down to the yard and is still crying. Mother's disheveled hair is long and unbecoming to her. A black-bearded man on the roof emits a strange yell. The four quarters shake. Father, who has been crying below, looks up at the man. The neighbors gather around noisily. Clad in white robes and horsehair hats, they come and bow one by one. The house smells of boiling noodles. The noisy gathering compensates for the desolate atmosphere. Yet, the death of mother makes everyone sad. Father is still crying. Father, don't cry. After twenty years' absence she returns in a western dress. But he cries all the more sadly. Don't cry, father, please don't . . .

Yŏnghŭi opened the door. "Are you asleep, brother?" she asked. "Don't go to sleep. You must wake up." Sŏngsik, stretched out on the bed, glanced at her. Without his glasses he looked much leaner. The bluish light was as cold as the deep sea, and the size of the room made the ceiling appear much higher. Sitting on the edge of the bed, she called him tenderly, but he did not answer.

"Brother!"

His eyes grew a little bigger.

"How do I look now? Brother, I am married."

Sŏngsik was looking for his glasses. To avoid his

eyes, she picked them up and handed them to him. Even
after he had put on his glasses he seemed unable to keep
himself steady.

"Things would have drifted that way anyhow. There
was no other way out. Each has only his own problems
now. Don't you think so? I just don't know how we all
have become like this."

Sŏngsik looked up at the ceiling.

"Don't you have anything to say, brother? Don't you
have any feeling about anything at all? For heaven's sake,
can't I ever make you talk?"

Sŏngsik kept gazing at the ceiling without a word.
Yŏnghŭi gave a bitter, unrecognizable smile.

Again the metallic sound came sharply. Yŏnghŭi
shuddered.

Sŏngsik was smoking a cigaret now.

The night grew pale and transparent as it wore on.
The lights in the room became whiter. The old man
continued to finger the mole on his nose. Sŏnjae and the
maid fell asleep in their own rooms, fully clothed. Yŏnghŭi, now changed into pink pajamas, tried on a pair of
sunglasses. Chŏngae sat staring at the ceiling.

Clang, bang, clang, bang.

The metallic sound became clearer now, no longer
at intervals, but at a quicker tempo. It sounded like a
patrol, with a considerable force in battle array behind it.
Yŏnghŭi, still playing with the sunglasses, said:

"Really, what is that sound?"

"I have no idea."

"I don't think there is any workshop around here."

Chŏngae did not answer.

"Don't you get a strange feeling when you hear that
sound?" Yŏnghŭi said, putting down the glasses.

"What kind of strange feeling?"

"Well, I don't know how to put it, but a sort of feeling that something different and vigorous is gradually swelling up and will at last swallow us up. . . . It sounds ridiculous, but . . . " Yŏnghŭi started humming feebly, tapping a rhythm with her foot. Chŏngae frowned a little. Yŏnghŭi abruptly began to talk again:

"Why are we sitting like this without going to bed? It only bores us. But, if we retire into our separate rooms, we're so lonely and so scared that even the sound of falling leaves frightens us to death. When I come down to this room in the middle of the night, there are always a few people sitting around like this under the bright lights. How nice it would be to have a sound sleep just for once!"

She appeared to want to talk endlessly.

"Have you ever had this kind of feeling yourself? You know, one evening when we were young we had the ancestral ceremony. A lot of women worked in the kitchen, and the floor of the room was so hot from the fire that was kept burning to cook all the food. Children, tired from their play, fell asleep with nobody around to look after them. Then later, when I awoke, I found the light had been left on, and the floor was still very hot, and I had been asleep alone in the room while others were busy in the kitchen, in the hall, or out in the yard. Of course, I had been sleeping with my clothes on. Everywhere else people were bustling about but there it was so quiet with nobody else in the room. I felt so lonely and deserted I wanted to let them know that I was alone. Finding no way to tell them, I worried so much and felt so helpless . . ."

Chŏngae still kept silent.

"Some people are said to feel bizarre on a clear night

like this. They say it helps to play the role of an Anna Karenina or a Jean Valjean, but I wonder. Still, I would like to try it myself. Oh, dear, it's already quarter to twelve."

The old man, fingering the mole on his nose, looked like an insistent child. His hand was wet with perspiration, and he was more irritated than he had been earlier in the evening. Now and then he appeared frightened and opened his eyes to stare wildly at Yŏnghŭi and Chŏngae in turn. His look was strangely piercing. Yŏnghui followed the old man's eyes wherever they moved, and Chŏngae also pursued them in her vague way. Undoubtedly he was still master of the house.

"Sister, how on earth have we become like this? You know, in the night you lie awake for a long time, thinking of so many things—this kind of situation we're in now, for example. How things have changed in this house! Let's think about it seriously—people in such a condition do think about it seriously, don't they? In a corner of one's mind, one counts—one, two, three, four, five, six, seven—a simple, easy, unending calculation. Looking out at the night sky, but, in another corner of the mind, one deliberates painstakingly—how things were in the household a year ago with father, Sŏngsik and you. And how about two years ago? Everything seems to have been all right. However, when I trace back ten or twenty years and compare those days with things of a year ago, and then of today, I know that there's a big difference, and I can see definite changes."

Yŏnghŭi's voice was serene and unusually charming. Chŏngae sat with her head lowered in silence and her hand to her brow. Yŏnghŭi, her chin on her hands, stared at the ceiling while she spoke. But now she stared at Chŏngae.

"Goodness, are you crying, sister?"

It was quiet for a while.

Clang, bang, clang, bang.

Somebody was coming down the stairs, and although he was stepping carefully, the noise was so loud the whole house seemed to quiver. It sounded like someone descending from far, far above. I shouldn't have put out the light in the hall, Yŏnghŭi murmured to herself, trembling all over. She thought it would be better to imagine a figure coming down in the light rather than in the dark and that it did not matter who it was, although it was probably her brother.

The door opened and Sŏngsik came into the room. He could not stand the loneliness upstairs.

"Have you been awake?" asked Yŏnghŭi in a caressing, affectionate voice. Sŏngsik did not know what to say. He was timid and evasive, looking alternately at Chŏngae and Yŏnghŭi.

"Brother, she knows it, too," Yŏnghŭi said. "I told her everything. Is there anything to make a fuss over?"

It was strange that when she was with Chŏngae her voice was as soft and fine as silken thread, but with Sŏngsik it tended to be cold, sharp, and bitter. Sŏngsik seemed to smile meekly behind his cold glasses. Impulsively Yŏnghŭi said:

"Are you smiling, brother?"

He made no answer.

"You did smile just now, didn't you?" She forced herself toward Sŏngsik and, sitting before him, grasped his knee and demanded again.

"Did you really smile?"

As if attempting to dust himself off, he tried to retreat. Chŏngae looked at them blankly.

At that moment the clock began to strike twelve,

and all three turned their eyes toward it. The room became astir. Then all turned their eyes on the old man, who became bewildered and looked at each of them in turn. The door opened and light was reflected on the white wall across the hall. The clock had stopped striking, and all four turned their eyes toward it. Everything was quiet. The maid slowly emerged from the left corner, laughing in a queer voice, which perhaps meant that she was sorry.

"I've been to the bathroom," she said.

Then, as if in a fit, Yŏnghŭi dashed toward the old man and pointing at the maid with one hand while helping the old man up with the other, shrieked:

"Look, papa, sister has come home now. It's midnight and she has returned. Now we have the real mistress of the house. Aren't you glad, papa? It's going to be all right now, isn't it?"

This time the maid laughed without restraint.

"It's true, papa. Sister has come back. Look! You've been waiting for her for such a long time, haven't you?"

Yŏnghŭi's eyes burned with hatred as she shouted and glared at the maid. The old man, supported by Yŏnghŭi, waved his hand in the air as if either to motion her aside or to beckon her to come in. Sŏngsik and Chŏngae stood not knowing what to do.

Clang, bang, clang, bang.

The metallic sound would continue all through the night.

The Author

Yi Hoch'ŏl was born in Wŏnsan, South Hamgyŏng, and came to the South in 1950. "Midnight," first published in the journal Sasanggye *in July 1962, subsequently won the Tongin Prize. His acclaimed novel is* Petit Bourgeois *(1964–1965), which is set in Pusan, Korea's temporary capital during the war.*

The setting of "Midnight" is one May evening, from dusk to midnight. Except for the act of waiting in the quiet, stuffy living room, little else takes place. The first conflict is that between the characters; what binds them together is the act of waiting for the family's elder daughter. But it is an empty action, done only from force of habit, for all know the futility of waiting. Yŏnghŭi's zeal for change and revolt against inactivity finds solace in Sŏnjae, a normal, active man. But they too have their communication problems, as their dialogue shows. The real conflict that runs through the story comes from the metallic noise from an ironworks or a smithy, inauspicious and provocative sounds. They are, as one Korean critic has pointed out, a symbol of the onrush of the machine age, portending a downfall for the family, like the falling trees in Chekhov's Cherry Orchard. *Modern society, which demands systematization and collectivization, denies man his freedom and individuality. But the victims of such a society are only those who are consciously aware of its threat. Like a gimlet the sounds bore a hole in Yŏnghŭi's mind, but fail to create reverberations in others. Only Sŏnjae and the maid come out intact, as normal human beings unaware of the meaning of the sounds;*

others are outsiders trying in their various ways to shut off the march of modern civilization. In the end, the miracle does not occur: the one who appears at midnight is none other than the maid, not the elder daughter, the hope of restoration of the family. There is no escaping reality. The story ends with a loud clang.

by Sŏ Kiwŏn

The Heir

 t was the monsoon season; rain was pouring down heavily, but he did not hear it. As he read to Sŏkhŭi, he was conscious of the smell of straw emanating from his cousin's hair.

"Why did the man leave his home? Sŏgun, brother Sŏgun?" asked Sŏkhŭi. They had come to the part of the story—the end of the first chapter—where the hero leaves home.

"Won't you let me break off here for today?" he asked her, closing the book. But she pestered him to go on, twisting at her waist.

He opened the book again and trained his eyes on the printed letters. On his cheeks he felt a blush appearing. He wished she would leave his room now. To be alone in a room with her made him uncomfortable.

Through the driving rain, he heard his grandfather's voice calling from across the courtyard.

Translated by Kim Uch'ang

"I think grandfather's calling me." He raised his eyes from the book and strained his ears. Sŏkhŭi seemed not to care, whatever the old man might be wanting. She stared at his half-turned face intently. The call came louder.

"Coming!" he answered with a formal, grown-up voice and, leaving the room, put on the polite manner of a boy called to the presence of his elders. His name, Sŏgun, sounded much the same, in the inarticulate pronunciation of the paralytic old man, as those of his two other cousins, Sŏkpae and Sŏkkŭn. Often they answered to the old man's call together. His cousins, however, had not been seen around the house since morning.

"Greet the gentleman here," ordered the old man in the smoke-filled room, even before Sŏgun finished closing the double door. He bowed to the stranger who, like his grandfather, was wearing the old-style horsehair head-gear. Sŏgun blushed as he did so, for he could never perform a kowtow without feeling embarrassment. He could not help feeling a momentary sense of disgrace whenever he had to kneel down on the floor with hands folded on his forehead.

"A fine looking boy he is! Sit down." The stranger spoke in a low voice, caressing his long beard, which looked like the silk of an ear of corn.

"He takes after his father. Do you remember my son?"

"Yes," answered the stranger, and then, to express his sympathy, he clucked his tongue.

Seated respectfully with bowed head, Sŏgun listened to them while they talked about his dead father. He stole a glance at his grandfather. The old man seemed to be reluctant to satisfy the other man's curiosity. The old man seemed to have mixed feelings of pity and resentment about his son, who had died in a strange place.

"You may retire now," said grandfather.

The rainwater had gathered into a mud pool in the courtyard. The rain was not likely to let up soon. Standing in the gloom of the entrance, he looked across toward his room, where Sŏkhŭi was waiting for his return. He had a pale forehead and long black eyebrows. Bashfulness lingered between his brows, which he narrowly knit, as if from biting a sour fruit.

To shelter himself from the rain, he stepped gingerly along the narrow strip of dry ground under the eaves. He entered the storeroom next to the room that stood beyond the garden, filled with the tepid warmth of straw decaying in the damp. The rafters stood out darkly from the mud-coated ceiling. He could smell the acrid odor of mud as the rats raced about the room. He looked up at the window set high in the wall. The paper was torn here and there, and a grey shaft of soft light entered, as at the dawn of a rainy day. The storehouse was divided into two sections. One of them served as a barn where farming tools lay scattered all around. Winnows and baskets hung on the wall where the corn stalk wattles showed amidst the mud plaster. It was damp and stuffy in the poorly ventilated storehouse.

Sŏgun picked up a weeding hoe and made a hoeing motion in the air a few times. A weeding hoe with its long, curved neck always amused him. He thought there was something attractive in its curious curve. Looking around the room, he saw the connecting door to the other section of the storehouse. There used to be an iron lock on the door ring. To his surprise, however, the rusty lock had come loose. His heart throbbed.

This room had been an object of curiosity ever since he came to the country house—a vague fear and mysterious expectation mixed in his curiosity. Perhaps it was not right for him to enter the room without his grandfather's or uncle's permission. He hesitated a moment in front of the half-locked door, then finally took the lock off and stepped into the room. He assured himself that he was the heir of the family and was entitled to have a look at what was lawfully his. In fact, the word "heir" as it was said by grandfather did not sound quite real to him. But now the boy once again uttered the word to himself.

Inside this part of the storehouse, it was darker than in the barn. There was a window the size of a portable table, but it opened on the dark entrance, providing no more illumination than a pale square of light like the night sky. There were soot-colored paper chests stacked one upon another on a corner of the shelf. He tiptoed to the shelf. At every stealthy step, the floor squeaked. Old books, tied up in small bundles with string and stacked high, were keeping a precarious balance. But the books interested him little. His attention was on the soot-colored paper chests. He did not hear the rain outside. The day after his arrival here, grandfather had taken him to this room. From among the paper chests, the old man opened the one that best kept its shape. Taking out a scroll he said:

"This is a *hongp'ae,* which the king issued to those who passed the civil service examination."[1]

"What is a civil service examination?" asked Sŏgun.

"You had to pass it if you were to get an official position."

"Did you take it, grandfather?"

"No, I did not."

"Why not?"

"By the time I was old enough for the examination, the Japanese were here, and the examination was banned."

There was embarrassment in the old man's tone. Later he found out that his grandfather as a youth had led a dissolute life and did not apply himself to study. It was not because of the Japanese but because of his own laziness that the old man failed to take the examination. All this he learned from his aunt, who having heard it from her mother-in-law, passed it on to him like a family secret. The boy had a good laugh out of it.

"You are the ninth heir of a family with as many as five hongp'aes," the old man would say. But hearing his grandfather, the boy would picture a young man with a rambunctious crew of his schoolmates who abhorred books, juxtaposed with the present figure of his grandfather. Thinking about this amusing incongruity when he was alone, he would laugh to himself.

He carefully took down the paper chest his grandfather had shown him. It was full of scrolls. He ransacked them to see if there was anything else in the chest. But there was nothing except the grimy scrolls. He unrolled the one his grandfather had called hongp'ae, which looked like a sheet of flooring paper dyed red. A precocious boy who read difficult books beyond his age, he deciphered the faded characters. He found the three characters which made up his ancestor's name. They looked familiar to him.

He rolled up the paper and put it where it had been and shut the lid of the chest. Then he took down a leather case from a peg on the wall. It was a roughly made thing, heavy as an iron trunk. The old man told him it was a quiver. There was a broken brass lock on it like the one on the rice chest, though smaller. The key was hanging on the corner of the case, but he did not need to use it.

Among various trinkets and knicknacks, he caught sight of a small wooden box. Out of the box he took a pair of jade rings strung together. The jade was a soft milky color.

He had no idea what these rings were for. The holes in the center would be too small even for the little finger of Sŏkhŭi. Maybe a kind of ornament for ladies, he thought.

He clicked the pieces of jade one against the other. They gave off a clear, sharp sound. Repeating the clicking several times, he listened to the sound intently. Then he strung the pieces together and put them into his pocket. His legs trembled. But hadn't he been told that everything there in the room was lawfully his? As he closed the leather case, his pale hands shook. He did not look into the other relics. He stole out of the room. The rain was beginning to turn to a drizzle.

At every mealtime, Sŏgun sat alone with Sŏkpae at the same table with his grandfather. The country cooking, which was so different from what he had been used to in the city, tasted bitter. What was more, the boy hated to sit close to Sŏkpae, their shoulders nearly touching. He felt repelled by the occasional contact with the other boy's skin. Sŏkpae, two years his junior, was an epileptic. That his cousin looked like him disgusted him. As he looked at Sŏkpae, a secret shame seemed to stir in him.

It was not until a week after his arrival that he had found out about Sŏkpae's condition; the fit occurred at dinner time. The shredded squash seasoned with marinated shrimp gave off a foul smell. The soy sauce in the dark earthenware dish was no better. To swallow the squash, he had to hold his breath. A sense of loneliness choked him when he thought that he would be spending countless days from now on in this house, eating this food. Suddenly Sŏkpae fell over on his back, his spoon flung to the floor with a jangling sound. His eyes showing white, his foaming mouth thrust sideways, he struggled for air. Frightened, Sŏgun sat back from the table. The old man put his spoon down and sighed, turning away. The veins stood out in his eyes, either for grief or anger. Perhaps he was trying to keep the tears back.

Sŏkhŭi came in to serve the rice tea. Sŏgun felt pity for her. Perhaps the pity in his eyes touched her. He could see her eyes become moist. She hurriedly turned away and went out of the room.

Suddenly his uncle shouted angrily: "Take away the table!" He was moaning.

"What's the matter with you? Is he not your son, sick as he is?" Grandfather checked the outburst of the uncle. The uncle sat silently; a blue vein showed in the middle of his forehead.

"Don't be frightened, Sŏgun. He worries me so." His aunt tried to placate him in a tearful voice. Sŏgun wanted to run out of the room. But he felt that he had to see it through with the other members of the family until the fit was over.

Stiffness began to go out of Sŏkpae's twisted limbs, and he was breathing with more ease, but was still unconscious. He became soft like an uncoiled snake or a lump of sticky substance liquefying.

The boy gulped down some of the rice tea and left the room. The midsummer sun was going down, the clouds glowing in the twilit sky. Clear water, bubbling up from the well in the courtyard, prattled along in a little stream. They said a huge carp lived in the well among the moss-covered rocks.

His great-grandfather, returning from a long exile, had settled down here by the water, as his grandfather told the boy the story. Five ginkgo trees stood in line, dividing the path leading to the village and the outer yard.

"I wish he were dead!" Sŏkhŭi's sharp-edged voice came from behind his back. He wondered a moment whom she meant, but he did not care whom she wanted to be dead. He was feeling desolate enough to take it calmly, even if it were himself she was referring to. He watched Sŏkhŭi as she came near. He tried hard to be casual, but he felt as if he were choking; she looked grown-up, more grown-up than himself. She was smiling.

"Cousin Sŏgun, tell me about Seoul."

He did not answer. He merely smiled. Sŏkhŭi sat on one of the rocks by the well and stretched her skinny, red legs.

"I am the second tallest girl in class." She giggled, ducking her head. He wanted to find out more about her brother's illness, but he felt she feared to be questioned about it.

"You will be going to middle school next year. Perhaps the one in the county seat, right?" he asked.

"Grandpa won't let me go," Sŏkhŭi said in a thin angry voice.

"I suppose not," mumbled the boy.

"You don't know anything." Sŏkhŭi rolled her eyes and was going to add something, then seemed to give up. The air did not stir. Evening was coming on. A dry coughing broke the spell which had hovered over the scene. He recognized the dry coughs of his grandfather, which he heard early mornings, while still in bed. His eyes searched around in the gathering dusk.

The smell of wild sesame seed oil came drifting by;

they must be frying something in the kitchen. He saw the white steam rising inside the dimly lighted kitchen. Grandpa had told him to get some sleep until called. Both his male cousins, Sŏkpae and Sŏkkŭn, seemed to like memorial services very much. They would poke their heads into the kitchen and get shouted at by their mother.

This was his first experience with sacrificial rites for the dead ancestors. He remembered his mother reminding his father about the rites and worrying. She would ask him if they shouldn't send some money to the country house to cover part of the expenses. Then his father would snap out sharply between his teeth: "How could we when they're having these rites every month of the year!" Sŏgun now seemed to understand why his father was so bitter about these rites. His uncle also looked angry and gloomy while getting the table and plates ready for the ritual. He could see his uncle considered these ancestral rites a burden.

Calming his restless spirit, he gazed at the tilted flame on top of the wooden lamp post. He made his bed and lay down, but sleep eluded him.

Sooty flames rose from the two candles burning in the discolored brass candlesticks set on either side of the sacrificial table. Through the thick wax paper covering the foods on the table came the pungent smell of fish. The grandfather, unwrapping a bundle of ancient hemp clothes, took out a long ceremonial robe and put it on.

The dusty robe wrapped around his thin old body, the old man knelt down before the sacrificial table and respectfully kindled the incense in the burner. Thin wreaths of bluish smoke began to writhe up from the age-stained burner. The stink from the fish on the round flat plate filled the room.

"The meat dishes should be set to the left. When will you learn the proper manner of setting the sacrificial table?" The man reprimanded his son and, holding up the sleeve of the robe with one hand, rearranged the dishes on the table with his free hand.

"This is for an ancestor of five generations ago," he told the boy for the third time this evening. The two elder men in the ceremonial robes made low bows; the children in the back rows did the same. Sŏgun nearly burst into laughter at the comic sight of the big flourish with which they brought their hands up to their foreheads before each kowtow. Yet his cousin Sŏkpae had a certain grace when he performed sacrificial bows. His soft and elastic body, unlike Sŏkkŭn's, fitted into the role with natural ease.

Sŏgun brought his hands up to his breast, but dropped them; Sŏkpae was bowing away ecstatically, flourishing his two limbs, which looked longer than his torso, as if performing a dance.

Grandfather cleared his throat, coughing a few times, before he started reading the prayer to the dead in a low, tremulous voice. Finished, he started keening, followed by everybody else. The grandfather's keening was the loudest and the saddest. The uncle was mumbling something in a low indistinct voice.

Sŏgun remained still, his eyes and mouth shut tight. Yet he was not indifferent; he was tense and felt an unexplainable chill running down his spine. He half opened his eyes and looked up surreptitiously. Insects had gathered around the candle flames, which cast their shadows over the sacrificial table. He had an illusion of a strange figure squatting in the gloom behind the tablet bearing the ancestral name.

When he died, his father became like a stranger, the

way he heaved a last chilly breath toward him. Sŏgun had had to draw his hand by force out of his father's tightened grip. He feared that the hand would come and grip him again. He could not bring himself to touch his father. He could not cry. But when he came out of the death chamber, an inconsolable sorrow seized him, and he cried with abandon.

The boy closed his eyes again. The keening went on. His body shook from suppressed crying.

When the rite was over, Sŏgun went out to the well. Stars glittered in the night sky between the clouds. The pale starlight played on the ripples in the well. He dipped his hands in the cool water. He washed and rubbed his hands until he thought he had scrubbed the last odor of the rite from his hands.

"Sŏgun!" His grandfather called him.

In the hall were placed three tables, around which sat all the family. "We are going to partake of the ancestral food and receive the blessing of the ancestors," said the grandfather, pointing with his chin to the seat opposite him for Sŏgun. The bronze rice bowl that had been placed on the sacrificial table was now set in front of the old man, almost touching his beard. Sŏgun could still see, in the center of the heaped rice in the bowl, the hole which had been dug up by the brass spoon in the course of the rite.

Sŏgun tried a sip from the brass wine cup his grandfather handed to him. He grimaced. Making much noise, everybody ate a bowl of soup with rice in it. The grandfather seemed displeased that Sŏgun did not eat like the others. He excused himself from the table, saying he had a stomachache, and returned to his room.

"How like his father!" he heard the old man say in a cracked voice.

The grandfather, donning the new ramie cloth coat the aunt had finished for him overnight, left for town early in the morning. The boy waited until he was sure his cousins were all safely out playing and then took his suitcase down from the attic storeroom. He took stock of its contents. The first time he was engaged with his things in the suitcase after he came here, his cousins stuck their noses in and pestered him. He wanted to keep his things to himself. In the suitcase were several novels, his school texts, a glass weight with a goldfish swimming in it, a telescope made of millboard, and a wallet which his father had given him the day before he died. They were all very dear to him. He placed on his palm the jade rings he had taken from the storeroom on that rainy day. He listened to the music the milky jade made when clicked together. The sound was as clear and sharp as before. The sound, in fact, had improved with the weather, which had cleared in the meantime.

Somebody came into the room, unannounced.

"What are you doing?" It was Sŏkpae.

"Just checking on my things," the boy answered, very much confused and concealing his hand with the jade rings behind his back.

"Are you going somewhere?" asked Sŏkpae, drawing near.

"No."

Sŏkpae sneaked an eager look into the suitcase and then, grabbing at something, said:

"Won't you draw a picture of me, please?" The object Sŏkpae took hold of was a half-empty case of pastels. Sŏkpae's slit eyes winked at him.

"Oh, well." Sŏgun was pleased; he wanted to boast of his artistic talent. He felt much relieved that his cousin did not suspect anything. He spread out a sheet of paper on top of his suitcase and made Sŏkpae sit facing the doorway. He picked up a yellow crayon, taking a close look at his cousin. Sŏkpae sat, putting on an air of importance with his lower lip solemnly protruding. Sŏgun looked into the other boy's eyes and sat unmoving for a while, absorbed.

He felt dismay at a face that was so like his own. If Sŏkpae's features were taken separately, they would not noticeably resemble those of anyone in the family, let alone Sŏgun's. However, when Sŏgun looked at the other boy's face, it wasn't as though he were looking at a face other than his own.

"Aren't you going to draw?" Sŏkpae asked, only lowering his eyes.

Sŏgun began to draw. Sŏkpae's skin was darker, his features duller and fatter. From time to time, he slipped out a red, pointed tongue and licked his lips. Suddenly Sŏgun found himself wishing that Sŏkpae would have his fit there and then. A mixture of fear and curiosity came over him. He deliberately took time with his drawing.

"Here you are." The boy handed the finished picture over to his cousin, blushing.

"Why, it's you, not me, you drew!" Sŏkpae muttered.

"It's not true. It looks exactly like you!" he retorted angrily.

"Will you write down my name on this?"

He picked up a black crayon and wrote down the name.

Finally the grandfather found out about the missing jade. Sŏgun was sitting with his legs dangling on the low porch in back. The air was filled with the fragrant scent of balsam flowers, and beyond the mud wall towered the jagged ridges of the Mountain of the Moon against the cloudy, grey sky. In the direction of the courtyard, he heard the grandfather's querulous voice. Now being used to the old man's intonation, he could follow the old man as he bawled out in fury.

"Why, you ignorant ones! You think it's a toy or something, eh?"

"Oh, please, father. I will take it back from the boy as soon as he comes home." His uncle tried to pacify the old man.

"It is all because you are so ignorant. You should have raised your boys to act like a gentleman's offspring. Instead, what you have now, eh?"

The old man did not attempt to choose his words in chiding his son, even when children were present. Sŏgun's heart sank. It was clear that Sŏkpae was being suspected of stealing the jade rings from the storeroom.

"That he could get so upset over such trash, after he has sold off every bit of property of any worth!" His uncle muttered after the old man disappeared into his quarters. Sŏgun trembled all over. He could not walk out of his hiding place and face the family. When he thought of what would take place after Sŏkpae came home, he felt an impulse to rush out to his grandfather and tell him everything. But still he could not move.

"I say, do you know what that is?" grandfather, coming back, said now in a mocking voice.

"You told us it was jade beads, didn't you?" his uncle said.

"So you think it is just like any other jade, eh? It is no less than *tori* jade,[2] you hear?" The old man did not spare his son in taking him to task, as if they were not father and son but strangers to each other. Sŏgun did not know what jade beads were. They would not bring much money on the market, but they must still mean a great deal to his grandfather, the boy guessed.

He went out to the yard, dragging the rubber shoes which were too big for him. He was counting in his mind the money his father had left him along with that wallet. He thought he had enough to pay for board and room for four or five months. After his father died, his house, where he had a sunny study room, was sold by his uncle. He kept only the scuffed leather wallet and the bills in it.

"Let's go fishing together later on," said Sŏkhŭi, coming out to the yard with an armful of vegetables from the farm.

"It looks like rain again," he said.

Sŏkhŭi squatted down by the well and started washing the radishes.

"Pretty, isn't it?" Sŏkhŭi held out her wet hand, wiggling her pinky to draw his attention to it. He noticed that it was dyed with balsam flowers. As he looked at the finger, she bobbed her head, puffing her cheeks, as she often did when she felt bashful. She was smiling. Sŏgun threw his head back and laughed like a grown-up. Looking at her from the back, in her white blouse and blue skirt, he could not think she was a cousin younger than himself.

"Do you know, Sŏkhŭi, what jade beads are?" asked Sŏgun, lowering his voice.

"Did you see the buttonlike things on grandfather's headgear? They call them *kwanja*,'" Sŏkhŭi whispered back.

"They are not jade, are they?" He expressed his doubt.

"You hate my brother, don't you?" Sŏkhŭi too must be suspecting Sŏkpae of stealing the jade rings.

"Why should I?" Sŏgun feigned ignorance.

"I heard grandpa once say there has been no one else like him in the family." Sŏkhŭi looked up from her work, stopping her washing for a moment.

Sŏgun did not say anything. What he had just heard hurt him somehow.

"Do you know he had his head cauterized with moxa?" said Sŏkhŭi wearily.

Sŏgun stood up and, leaving Sŏkhŭi to her work, walked toward the stream. He kicked at the small rocks on the roadside.

Rain started again toward evening; thunder clapped and rain began to pour down in streaming showers. It was only then that the house became topsy-turvy. The old man kept pacing back and forth between the inner and the outer wings of the house, oblivious to the down-pouring rain soaking his clothes.

"Where's your father? Of all the misfortunes of man!" The old man kept saying the same thing, wiping away the raindrops running down his beard. Sŏgun guessed the cause of all the commotion in the house. He saw in his imagination Sŏkpae's helpless body whirled in muddy torrents and then dashed against the rocks. His upturned eyes and foaming mouth were covered with the muddy water. "Grandfather, oh grandfather! I didn't steal them!" But mud water filled his mouth, and not a moan came out of him. Sŏgun hugged his shaking knees. The uncle, who had just come back from the search, was going out again, this time taking Sŏkkŭn along with him.

"Let me go with you," asked Sŏgun.

"We don't need you." His uncle looked at him out of the corner of his eyes.

"I want to go," insisted Sŏgun.

"I said we didn't need you," his uncle flung back an answer with anger in his voice.

The old man groaned with agony and said, "You had better take several men along with you."

"All right, all right," answered the uncle, exasperated.

The moldy smell pervaded the room. A millipede crawled up the door frame and then down into the room. The sound of rain did not reach him. He thought he ought to walk over to the male quarters and keep the old man company. He did not have the courage, however. He lit the lamp. He felt his forehead with his hand. Probably his hand was feverish too. His forehead felt almost cold against his palm. He felt a chill running down his back. He was too sick to sit up and wait. He made the bed and lay down.

He could hear the light, pleasant music of the jade rings in the rain. For a moment, he wished Sŏkpae's wriggling body would stiffen into a chunk of wood. He wished that Sŏkpae would never show up again. Even after he was gone from this house, Sŏkpae must not show up before the grandfather.

When he awoke from sleep, Sŏkhŭi was sitting by him. Her body, outlined against the lamplight, was almost that of a woman. He felt a cool hand on his forehead. He did not shake it off. The palm grew warm and sticky.

"Anything new about Sŏkpae?" asked Sŏgun, turning toward her.

"Sŏkkŭn came back alone," answered Sŏkhŭi. "Father went to the Mountain of the Moon with the village people."

Sŏgun remained silent.

"This happened before," said Sŏkhŭi. "Everybody

was terribly scared. Sŏkpae came back the next morning.
Even he himself didn't know where he had been."

The uncle came back toward midnight exhausted.

"Oh, that I might be struck dead!" The aunt wailed,
beating the floor with her fists.

Sŏgun spent a sleepless night. Early in the morning,
the villagers arrived with the news that Sŏmun Bridge
had been washed away overnight. It was a wooden bridge
on the way from the village to the county seat.

It was hard to tell whether his uncle was laughing or
crying. He was scowling darkly. He sat on the damp
floor and ordered the kitchen staff to prepare drinks for
the guests and called in the people who stood around in
the yard.

"Did you look into Snake Valley?" demanded the
uncle.

"He can't have gone that far," said a man from the
searching party, "and it rained so hard last night."

"The last time the bridge was washed out was five
years ago," said another man and suggested: "Hadn't
we better notify the police?"

The uncle stood up abruptly and, rolling up his
trousers, started out. The rest of the men stood up too
and, drying their wet lips with their hands, followed him
out. The uncle disappeared out the front gate. But he
seemed to have given up all hope.

"Oh, that I might be struck dead!" The aunt wailed
in the main room. Her usual heartburn had gotten worse,
and she had been fasting the previous day. When the
heartburn got too painful, she nearly fainted but never
forgot to exclaim: "Oh, that I might be struck dead!" as
though it were some charm she had to repeat. She was not
likely to recover from her mania unless Sŏkpae came

back alive. She would rather cling to her sobbing, cling to her suffering, than seek a release from it, Sŏgun thought.

Sŏgun could not help feeling that Sŏkpae had gone out in the rain because of him. If only he had not come here, everything would have gone on in this moldy house as it had before his arrival. He was responsible for the untoward change in it.

Dark shadow covered the courtyard. No one stirred in the house. The whole place looked deserted. There was only the sound of heavy raindrops falling on the rocks. The boy took up the jade rings in his hand and stole across the courtyard into the storehouse, shaking with excitement and fear. The rotten planks creaked and groaned under his light body.

He stifled an exclamation of surprise; a new lock was hanging from the quiver in place of the rusty old lock. The silver gleam of the new lock mocked him. A white, mean mocking was spreading all over the place: we have been waiting for you; we knew all along that you would come here to open the quiver again.

Sŏgun felt dizzy and had to lean against the muddy wall.

Sŏkpae's body was found lying among the rocks after the flood receded. It had once been as light and supple as a snake crossing the highway, but it was now as stiff and heavy as a water-soaked wooden tub, his once sleek skin turned dirty yellow by the working of the muddy water. His uncle loaded the body on his shoulders and carried it down the slope with unsteady steps.

Sŏgun thought he must go away from this house before Sŏkpae's body should come home. He must get away quickly because he could not face the dead body of someone virtually killed by him.

Sŏgun ran to his room and took down his trunk. He fished out the wallet his father gave him and put it deep into his pocket.

"Are you going someplace?" Sŏkhŭi's voice called from behind. He was startled but did not turn his head.

"Don't go, please. Don't go." Sŏkhŭi implored with tears in her voice. Sŏgun turned his head around and looked into her eyes. He shook his head sadly. His lips were trembling, and his throat choked so hard that he could hardly breathe. Sŏkhŭi was crying with her head lowered.

The smell of dry straw drifted from Sŏkhŭi's hair. Sŏgun walked out, leaving her alone in the room. The rain suddenly poured down in torrents. All he carried with him was an umbrella, the wallet with the scuffed edges, and the pair of jade rings. He started slowly toward the highway, all the time feeling with one hand the cool jade rings in his pocket. Rain soaked him. He heard the voice of his punctilious grandfather saying: "Everything in here is yours."

Once he reached the highway, Sŏgun started running.

The Author

Sŏ Kiwŏn was born in Seoul in 1930 and left the College of Economics of Seoul National University without taking a degree in order to serve with the Air Force during the Korean war. He was discharged as a captain in 1953. He made his literary debut in 1956, and in 1960 he won a prize from the leading journal Hyŏndae Munhak, *in which "The Heir" was first published, in February 1963. Currently Sŏ Kiwŏn is an editorial writer for the* Chungang Daily *in Seoul.*

He deftly portrayed the types of student soldiers in action in a war that failed to provide an inspiration for self-dedication, or in a postwar society fraught with contradictions and absurdity. Life devoid of dreams and hopes and the landscape of the mind's wilderness have been his recurrent themes. Often praised are his psychological depth and disciplined narrative technique. Built on the conflicts between the old and the new and the delicate relationships between Sŏgun and his country cousins and niece, "The Heir" is an ironic story probing into the awakening mind of an innocent boy, who fails to cherish the inherited values of traditional Korea, where the civil service examination system was the only path to worldly success. The red certificate and jade pendants, symbols of old Korea's social and political ills, are meaningless in postwar Korean society.

In his more recent novel, Revolution *(1965), which concerns the Tonghak Rebellion of 1894 that triggered the Sino–Japanese War, Sŏ continues his inquiry into the inherent contradictions of nineteenth-century Korea.*

by Kim Sŭngok

Seoul: Winter 1964

nyone who spent the winter of 1964 in Seoul is probably familiar with those wine shops that appeared on the streets at nightfall, those stalls into which one stepped off a freezing, wind-swept street by pushing aside a flapping curtain. Inside, the elongated flame of a carbide lantern danced in the wind, and a middle-aged man in a dyed army jacket served up Japanese hotchpotch, roasted sparrow, and three kinds of wine. It was in one of these wine shops that the three of us happened to meet that night: myself, Kim; a bespectacled graduate student named Ahn; and a man who was about thirty-six years old and obviously poor, but about whom I could tell little else. In fact I didn't care to know any more.

The graduate student and I began a conversation and when the introductions were finished I knew that his name was Ahn, that he was twenty-five, was majoring in

Translated by Peter H. Lee

a subject I had never heard of and was the oldest son of a rich family. He, in turn, learned that I was twenty-five and had been born in the country. After being graduated from high school, I had applied to the Military Academy but had failed and so had enlisted in the army, where I had caught gonorrhea once. I was now working in the military affairs section of a ward office.

With the introductions completed there was nothing else to talk about so we quietly drank our wine for a short time. Then, as I picked up a charred sparrow, an idea occurred to me. After silently thanking the sparrow, I began to talk.

"Do you like flies, Mr. Ahn?"

"No, I've never—" he began. "Do *you* like flies, Mr. Kim?"

"Yes," I answered, "because they can fly. No, not just that. It's because they can fly, and at the same time they can be caught in one's hand. Have you ever caught in your hand something that can fly?"

"Well—just a moment." He gazed at me blankly from behind his glasses for a while, then screwed up his face a bit and said, "No, nothing—except flies."

Since the weather had been unusually warm that day, the frozen streets had turned into mud. But with nightfall the temperature dropped again and the mud began to freeze beneath our feet. My black leather shoes couldn't block the chill that rose from the ground. A shop like this is all right for someone who thinks he wants to stop for a quick drink on the way home, but it's no place for leisurely drinking and chatting with the man standing beside you.

Just as this thought was running through my mind, my bespectacled companion asked a commendable question. "He's quite a fellow," I thought and urged my cold-benumbed feet to hold out a little longer.

"Do you like things that wriggle?" he asked me.

"Yes, indeed," I answered with a sudden feeling of exultation. Reminiscences, whether sad or happy, can make one exultant. When memories are sad, one feels a quiet and lonely kind of exultation; when they are happy, the feeling is one of boisterous triumph.

"After I failed the examination for the Military Academy, I stayed for a while in a rooming house in Miari with a friend who had failed his college entrance exams. Seoul was a strange city to me. My dream of becoming an officer had been shattered, and I had fallen into deep despair. I felt I would never get over my disappointment. As you probably know, the bigger the dream, the greater the despair when you fail."

"About that time, I became intrigued with crowded morning buses. My friend and I would hurry through breakfast, then run, panting like dogs, to the bus stop at the top of Miari Ridge. Do you know the most exciting and marvelous things to a country boy's eyes when he first comes to Seoul? The most exciting thing, let me tell you, is the lights that come on in the windows of buildings at night. No. Rather it's the people moving about in the lights. And the most marvelous thing is finding a pretty girl beside you, not a centimeter away, on a crowded bus. Sometimes I would try to touch a girl's wrist and rub against her thigh. Once I spent a whole day riding around, transferring from one bus to another, trying to do just that. That night I was so tired I vomited."

"Wait a minute," Ahn interrupted. "What's the point?"

"I was going to tell you a story about liking things that wriggle. Please listen."

"My friend and I threaded our way like pickpockets into a crowded bus at rush hour and stood in front of a young woman who had found a seat. I grabbed a strap and leaned my tired head on my arm, then slowly let my eyes come to rest on the girl's stomach. At first, I couldn't see it, but in a few moments my eyes clearly detected the quiet rising and falling of the girl's stomach."

"Rising and falling? Because of her breathing?"

"Yes, of course. The belly of a corpse doesn't move. Anyway, I don't know why seeing the movement of that woman's stomach on the bus that morning delighted me so much. I really loved that movement."

"That's a very lewd story," Ahn said in an odd voice.

That made me angry. I had memorized that story in case I should ever get on a radio quiz show and should be asked, "What is the freshest thing in the world?" Others might say lettuce or a May morning or an angel's brow. But I would say that movement was the freshest thing.

"No, it's not lewd," I responded firmly. "It's a true story."

"What relationship is there between not being lewd and being true?"

"I don't know. I don't know anything about relationships."

"But that movement is just a rising and falling, not wriggling. It still seems to me that you don't love things that wriggle."

We both fell silent and just stood there toying with our glasses for a while. "All right, you son of a bitch," I thought, "if you don't think that's wriggling, it's all right with me."

A moment later, Ahn spoke again.

"I've been thinking it over, and I've come to the

conclusion that your up-and-down movement is a kind of wriggling after all," he announced.

"Yes, it is, isn't it?" I was pleased, "It's undoubtedly wriggling. I love a woman's stomach more than anything. What kind of wriggling do you like?"

"Not a kind of wriggling. Just wriggling itself. For example—to demonstrate—"

"Demonstrate? A demonstration? Well, then—"

"Seoul is a concentration of every kind of desire. Understand?"

"No, I don't," I answered in a clear voice.

Our conversation broke off again. This time the silence continued for a long while. I lifted my glass to my lips and when I had emptied it I saw Ahn, glass at his mouth, drinking with closed eyes. I thought, a little sadly, that it was time to leave. So much for that! I was considering whether to say "Well, see you again sometime," or "It's been interesting," when Ahn suddenly grabbed me by the hand and said, "Don't you think we've been telling lies?"

"No." The idea annoyed me a little. "I don't know about you, but everything I said was the truth."

"Well, I have the feeling we've been lying to each other." He blinked his reddened eyes a couple of times inside his glasses. "Whenever I meet a new friend about our age I always want to talk about wriggling. So, we talk, but the conversation doesn't last five minutes."

I felt I could understand what he was talking about, but only vaguely.

"Let's talk about something else," he said.

But I wanted to give a hard time to this fellow who liked serious conversation so much, and I also wanted to exercise the drunk's privilege of listening to his own voice a bit. So I started to talk.

"Among the street lights in front of the P'yŏnghwa Market, the eighth one from the east end isn't lit."

I became excited as I saw that Ahn looked a bit stunned, so I went on.

"And among the windows on the sixth floor of the Hwashin Department Store, lights appear only in the middle three."

But this time I was taken aback, because Ahn's face began to glow with a look of delight. He began to speak quickly.

"There were thirty-two people at the West Gate bus stop. Seventeen of them were women and five were children. There were twenty-one youths and six old people."

"When was that?"

"At 7:15 this evening."

"Ah," I said. A feeling of desperation came over me for a moment, but I quickly recovered and plunged on.

"There are two candy wrappers in the first trash can in the alley beside the Tansŏng Theater."

"When was that?"

"As of 9 P.M. on the fourteenth."

"The walnut tree in front of the main gate of the Red Cross Hospital has one broken branch."

"At a certain tavern on Ŭlchiro Third Street there are five girls named Mija, and they're known by the order in which they came to stay there—Big Mija, Second Mija, Third Mija, Fourth Mija, and Last Mija."

"But other people know that, too, Kim. You're not the only one who has been there."

"Oh, yes. You're right. I hadn't thought of that. Well, I slept with Big Mija one night, and the next morning she bought me a pair of shorts from a woman who came around selling things on credit. By the way, there was

110 wŏn in the half-gallon wine bottle she uses for a bank."

"That's more like it. That fact belongs only to you."

Our manner of speaking showed increasing respect for each other. "I—" we would both begin speaking at the same time, and each would yield to the other.

This time it was his turn.

"In the West Gate area I saw a streetcar heading for Seoul station send sparks flying five times while it was within my field of vision. That was the streetcar passing by at 7:25 this evening."

"You were in the West Gate area tonight?"

"Yes, that's right."

"I was around Chongno Second Street. In the Yŏngbo Building, there's a fingernail scratch about two centimeters long just below the handle on the door to the toilet."

Ahn laughed loudly. "You made that mark yourself, didn't you?"

I was ashamed, but I had to nod my head. It was true. "How did you know?"

"I've had that experience, too," he replied. "But it's not a particularly pleasant memory. It's better to stick to things we happen to have discovered and secretly stored away in our memories. Manufacturing things like that leaves an unpleasant aftertaste."

"I've done many things like that and rather—" I was about to say I enjoyed it when a feeling of dislike for the whole thing welled up inside me; I just stopped without ending the sentence and nodded agreement with his opinion. Then a strange thought occurred to me. If there had been no mistake about what I had heard some thirty minutes earlier, the fellow in the shiny glasses standing beside me was surely the son of a rich family and was a highly educated young man. Then why did he now seem so uncivilized?

"Ahn, it's true that you come from a rich family, isn't it? And that you're a graduate student?" I asked.

"Well, you can call a man rich when he has about thirty million wŏn in real estate alone, can't you? But, of course, that's my father's property. As for being a graduate student, I have a student ID card right here." As he spoke, he rummaged his pockets and pulled out a wallet.

"An ID card isn't necessary. It's just that there's something a little strange. It just struck me as a bit odd that someone like you would be in a cheap wine shop on a cold night talking to someone like me about trivial things."

"Well, that's—that's—" he began in a heated voice. "That's—but there's something I want to ask you first. Why do *you* roam the streets on such a cold night?"

"It's not a habit. A poor man like me has to have a little money in his pocket before he can come out on the streets at night."

"Well, what's the reason for coming out?"

"It's better than sitting in a boarding house and staring at the wall."

"When you come out at night don't you have a feeling of richness?"

"A feeling of what?"

"Well—something. Perhaps we could call it 'life'. I think I understand why you asked your question. My answer would be this: night falls, and I leave my house and come out on the streets. I feel like I've been liberated from everything. It may not actually be so, but that's the way I feel. Don't you feel the same way?"

"Well—"

"I'm no longer among things; rather I watch them from a distance. Isn't that it?"

"Well, somewhat—"

"No, don't say it's difficult. In a manner of speaking, it's as if all the things that are constantly sweeping past me during the day are stripped bare and completely exposed before my eyes at night. Don't you think there is some meaning in that? Looking at things like that and enjoying them, I mean."

"Meaning? What meaning? I don't count the bricks in buildings on Chongno Second Street because there is some meaning. I just—"

"You're right. There is no meaning. No, maybe there actually is some significance, but I don't know what it is yet. Since you don't know the significance either, let's go out and search for it together sometime. And we won't intentionally create some significance for it either."

"I'm a little confused. Is that your answer? I'm a bit puzzled. All of a sudden this word 'meaning' appears."

"Oh, I'm sorry. Well, my answer would probably be that I come out on the streets at night because I feel a sense of fullness." He lowered his voice and continued. "You and I took different routes and came to the same point. If by chance it's the wrong point, it's not our fault."

Then he spoke in a jovial voice. "Say, this isn't the place for us. Let's go somewhere warm and have a proper drink, then call it a night. I'm going to walk around a while and then go to a hotel. Whenever I come out at night to wander around on the streets I stay at a hotel. That's my favorite plan."

As we reached into our pockets for money to pay the bill, the man beside us—who had put down his glass and was warming his hands over the coal fire—spoke. He seemed to have come in more to warm himself than to drink. He wore a fairly clean coat, and his hair, neatly combed and oiled, glistened in the fluttering light of the carbide lamp. Although I couldn't tell much, he seemed around thirty-six and had an air of poverty about him. Maybe it was because of his weak chin, or his unusually red eyelids. He just aimed his words in our direction, addressing neither of us in particular.

"Excuse me, but would it be all right if I joined you? I have some money with me," he said in a weak voice.

From that weak voice, he seemed to want sincerely to go, although he was not begging. Ahn and I looked at each other for a moment.

"Well," I said, "if you've got the price of the wine—"

"Let's go together," Ahn chimed in.

"Thank you," the man said in the same weak voice and followed us out.

Ahn's expression indicated he thought this a strange turn of events, and I, too, had an unpleasant premonition. I knew from experience that one could have an interesting and enjoyable time with someone he met unexpectedly over a glass of wine. These strangers virtually never came on with such weak voices, though. They were boisterous and overflowing with joy.

We suddenly forgot what we were going to do. A pretty girl beamed a lonely smile from a medicine advertisement stuck on a telephone pole and seemed to say, "It's cold up here, but what can I do?" A neon sign advertising liquor flashed incessantly on top of a building, and beside it another one advertising medicine would light up for long periods and then, as if it had forgotten, hurriedly go off and back on again. Here and there beggars lay like rocks on the hard-frozen street and people walking hunched over intently passed swiftly by those rocks. A piece of paper driven across the street by the wind landed at my feet. I picked it up and found it was an ad for a beer hall touting "Service by Beautiful Hostesses" and "Specially Reduced Prices."

"What time has it gotten to be?" the listless man asked Ahn.

"It's ten till nine," he answered after a moment's pause.

"Have you had supper? I haven't eaten yet, so why don't we go together. I'll treat you," the man said, looking at each of us in turn.

"I've already eaten," Ahn and I replied at the same time.

"You can have yours," I suggested.

"I'll just skip it," he said.

"Go ahead and eat. We'll go with you," Ahn said.

"Thank you. Well, then—"

We went into a nearby Chinese restaurant, and when we were seated in a room the man again urged us politely to have something to eat. We declined again, but he suggested once more that we have something.

"Is it all right if I order something expensive?" I asked, trying to get him to withdraw his offer.

"Yes, by all means," he said, his voice sounding strong for the first time. "I've made up my mind to spend all the money I have with me."

I thought the man must have some secret plan in mind and felt somewhat uneasy with him. Nevertheless, I asked for chicken and some wine, and he gave the waiter our orders. Ahn looked at me in amazement.

At that moment, I heard a woman's warm moans coming from the next room.

"Won't you have something, too?" the man asked Ahn.

"No, thanks," he declined abruptly in a voice that seemed sobered.

Silently, we turned our ears toward the moaning sound that was growing more urgent in the next room. The faint rumble of streetcars and the sound of moving automobiles, floating in like the rush of a flooding river and now and again a call bell demanding service rang somewhere nearby. Our room, however, was wrapped in awkward silence.

"There is something I would like to tell you." The man began speaking, apparently in better spirits. "I would be grateful if you would listen to what I want to say. During the day today, my wife died. She had been admitted to Severance Hospital—"

He looked at us searchingly as he spoke but there was no sadness in his face.

"Oh, that's too bad."

"I'm sorry to hear that."

Ahn and I expressed our sympathy.

"We were very happy together. Since she couldn't have children, we had all our time to ourselves. We didn't have a lot of money, but when we did get a little we would travel around and enjoy ourselves. During strawberry season we went to Suwŏn, and when the grapes were ripe we went to Anyang. During the summer we went to Taech'ŏn, and in the fall we visited Kyŏngju. We saw movies in the evenings and went to the theater whenever we could."

"What was wrong with her?" Ahn asked cautiously.

"The doctor said it was acute meningitis. She had had an operation for acute appendicitis once and had been sick with pneumonia once and got over those all right. But the next bad attack killed her—she's dead now."

The man lowered his head and mumbled something. Ahn jabbed my knee with his finger and winked a suggestion that we leave. I felt the same way, but just then the man raised his head and continued talking so we had no choice but to stay.

"My wife and I were married year before last. I met her by accident. She mentioned once that her home was in the Taegu area but we had no contact with her family. I don't even know where her home is. So, there was nothing I could do." He dropped his head and mumbled again.

"There was nothing you could do about what?" I asked. He didn't seem to hear me. After a few moments, though, he looked up again and, with eyes that seemed to be pleading, continued to talk.

"I sold my wife's body to the hospital. I had no choice. I'm just a salesman, selling books on the installment plan. There was nothing I could do. They gave me four thousand wŏn. Until just before I met you, I stayed around the wall outside Severance Hospital. I tried to figure out which building housed the morgue with her body in it but I couldn't. I just stood by the wall and watched the white smoke coming out of the chimney."

"What will become of her? Is it true that students will practice dissection on her, splitting her head with a saw and cutting her stomach open with a knife?"

We could do nothing but keep quiet. The waiter brought dishes of pickled radishes and onions.

"I'm sorry to have told you such an unpleasant story, but I had to tell someone. There's something I'd like to discuss with you—what should I do with this money? I'd like to get rid of it tonight."

"Spend it, then," Ahn replied quickly.

"Will you stay with me until it's all gone?"

We hesitated before answering.

"Please stay with me."

We agreed.

"Let's spend it in style," the man said, smiling for the first time since we had met. His voice, however, was just as enervated as before.

When we left the Chinese restaurant all three of us were drunk, one thousand wŏn was gone, and the man was crying in one eye while laughing in the other. Ahn was telling me that he was tired of trying to get away from the man and I was muttering, "You put the accents in the wrong places! The accents!" The streets were as cold and empty as those of colonial settlements in the movies, the liquor advertisement was flashing as relentlessly as before, and the medicine sign glowed when it could overcome its indolence. The girl on the telephone pole was smiling, "Nothing new here."

"Where shall we go now?" the man asked.

"Where shall we go?" Ahn asked, too.

"Where shall we go?" I echoed.

But we had no place to go. Beside the Chinese restaurant we had just left was the show window of a shop selling imported goods. The man pointed toward it and pulled us inside.

"Choose some neckties. My wife is buying them," he bellowed.

We picked out ties with motley designs, and six hundred wŏn was used up. We left the shop.

"Where shall we go?" the man asked.

There was still no place to go.

There was an orange peddler in front of the shop. "My wife liked oranges," the man exclaimed, rushing up to the cart where the oranges were laid out for sale.

Three hundred wŏn was gone. We paced the area rest-
lessly while peeling the oranges with our teeth.

"Taxi!" the man shouted.

A taxi stopped in front of us. As soon as we got in,
the man said, "Severance Hospital!"

"No, don't go there. It's useless," Ahn shouted
quickly.

"No?" the man muttered. "Then where to?"

No one answered.

"Where are you going?" the driver asked with irrita-
tion in his voice. "If you don't have any place to go, then
get out."

We got out of the taxi. We still hadn't gone more
than twenty steps from the Chinese restaurant. The wail
of a siren drifted from the far end of the street and
gradually drew nearer. Two fire engines roared past us
at high speed.

"Taxi!" the man shouted.

A taxi pulled up in front of us, and as soon as we
got in the man said, "Follow those fire engines!"

I was peeling my third orange.

"Are we going to watch the fire?" Ahn asked the
man. "We can't do that. There isn't enough time. It's
already 10:30. We should find something more enter-
taining. How much money is left?"

The man searched his pockets and pulled out all the
money, which he handed to Ahn. Ahn and I counted it:
nineteen hundred wŏn, with some coins and some ten-
wŏn notes.

"That's enough," Ahn said, returning the money
to the man. "Fortunately, there are women in this world
who specialize in showing off the particular characteristics
that make them women."

"Are you talking about my wife?" the man asked

sadly. "My wife's characteristic was that she laughed too much."

"Oh, no. I was suggesting that we go see the girls on Chongno Third Street."

The man looked at Ahn with a smile that seemed filled with contempt and then turned away.

By then we had arrived at the scene of the fire. Another thirty wŏn was gone.

The fire had begun in a ground-floor paint store, and flames were now leaping from the windows of a beauty school on the second floor. I could hear police whistles, fire sirens, the crackling of flames, and streams of water striking the walls of the building. But the people there made no sound. They stood like objects in a still life, the flames giving their faces the appearance of being flushed with shame.

We each took one of the paint cans rolling around at our feet, set it upright, and sat down on it to watch the blaze. I hoped it would go on burning for a long time. A sign saying, "Beauty School" had caught fire, and the flames had begun to burn the word "school."

"Let's continue our conversation, Kim," Ahn said. "Fires are nothing. We've just seen in advance tonight what we would have seen in tomorrow morning's newspaper—that's all. That fire isn't yours or mine or his; it's our common property. But fires don't go on forever, so I'm not interested in them. What do you think?"

"I agree," I said, giving the first answer that came to mind and, all the while, watching the flames consuming the word "school."

"No, I was wrong just now," Ahn said. "The fire isn't ours; it belongs exclusively to itself. We're nothing to the fire. That's why I'm not interested in fires. What do you think about that?"

"I agree."

A stream of water leaped at the burning "school," and grey smoke blossomed where the water landed. The listless man suddenly jumped to his feet.

"It's my wife!" he screamed, eyes bulging, and fingers pointing at the glowing flames. "She's shaking her head wildly. She's tossing her head back and forth violently as if it were about to crack from the pain. Darling—"

"Head-splitting pain is a symptom of meningitis," Ahn said, dragging the man back to his seat, "but that over there is just fire being blown by the wind. Please sit down. How could your wife be in the fire?" Then he turned to me and whispered, "This guy is giving us a good laugh."

I noticed that "school" had caught fire again after I thought it had been put out. A stream of water was reaching for that spot again, but the aim was off, and the torrent waved back and forth in the air. The flames licked vigorously at the letter *B*. I was hoping the Y would burst into flames, too, and that I alone among all the spectators would have known the entire process of the sign's burning. But then the fire became like a living thing to me, and I took back the wish I had made moments earlier.

From where we sat crouching, I saw a pure white object fly silently toward the burning building and drop into the flames.

"Didn't something just fly into the fire?" I turned and asked Ahn.

"Yes, it did," he answered and then turned to the man and asked him, "Did you see it?"

The man was sitting silently. At that moment, a policeman ran toward us.

"You're the one!" he said, grabbing the man with one hand. "Did you just throw something into the fire?"

"I didn't throw anything."

"What?" the policeman demanded, drawing back as if to hit the man. "I saw you throw something. What was it?"

"Money."

"Money?"

"I threw some money and a stone wrapped in a handkerchief."

"Is that true?" the policeman asked us.

"Yes, it was money. He has the idea that his business will prosper if he throws money into a fire," Ahn explained. "You might say he's a little odd but he's just a businessman who would never do anything wrong."

"How much was it?"

"A one-wŏn coin," Ahn answered again.

After the policeman had left, Ahn asked the man, "Did you really throw money?"

"Yes."

"All of it?"

"Yes."

We sat there for quite a while listening to the crackling of the flames. After a time, Ahn spoke to the man.

"You've finally used up all the money. I guess we've kept our promise, so we'll be going now."

"Goodnight," I said, bidding the man farewell.

Ahn and I turned and started to walk away, but the man followed us and caught each of us by the arm.

"I'm afraid of being alone," he said, trembling.

"It will soon be curfew time. I'm going to find a hotel," Ahn said.

"I'm going home," I said.

"Can't we go together? Please stay with me just

tonight. I beg you. Please come with me for just a little
while," the man said, shaking my arm like a fan. He
was probably doing the same to Ahn.

"Where do you want us to go?" I asked.

"I'll get some money at a place near here, and then
we can all stay together at a hotel."

"At a hotel?" I asked as my fingers counted the
money in my pocket.

"If you're worried about the cost of the hotel, I'll pay
for all three of us," Ahn said. "So—shall we go together?"

"No, no. I don't want to cause any trouble. Just follow me for a little while, please."

"Are you going to borrow money?"

"No, it's money that's due me."

"Near here?"

"Yes—if this is the Namyŏng-dong area."

"It certainly looks to me like Namyŏng-dong," I
said.

With the man leading the way and Ahn and I following, we moved away from the fire.

"It's too late to be going around collecting debts,"
Ahn told the man.

"But I have to get the money."

We entered a dark alley and turned several corners
before the man stopped in front of a house at which the
light at the front gate was lit. Ahn and I stopped about
ten steps behind the man. He rang the bell. After a while,
the gate opened, and we could hear him talking with
someone inside.

"I'd like to see the man of the house."

"He's sleeping."

"The lady, then."

"She's sleeping, too."

"I must see someone."

"Wait a minute, then."

The gate closed again. Ahn ran over to the man and pulled him by the arm. "Forget about it. Let's go."

"I've got to collect this money."

Ahn came back to where he had been standing. The gate opened.

"Sorry to bother you so late at night." The man stood facing the gate, head bowed.

"Who are you?" a woman's sleepy voice inquired from the gate.

"I'm sorry to have come so late, but—"

"Who are you? You look like you're drunk."

"I've come to collect a payment on a book you bought." The man suddenly screamed. "I've come for a book payment." Then he put his hands on the gatepost, buried his face in his outstretched arms, and burst into tears. "I've come for a book payment. A book payment—"

"Please come back tomorrow." The gate slammed shut.

The man went on sobbing for a long while, occasionally muttering, "Darling." We remained ten steps away waiting for the crying to end. After some time, the man staggered over to us. The three of us walked, heads lowered, through the dark alley and back out onto the main street. A cold, strong wind was blowing through the lonely streets.

"It's awfully cold," the man said, sounding worried about us.

"Yes, it is cold. Let's hurry to a hotel," Ahn said.

"Shall we each get a separate room?" Ahn asked when we had arrived at the hotel. "That would be a good idea, wouldn't it?"

"I think it would be better if we all shared one room," I said, thinking about the man.

The man was standing there blankly as if he didn't know where he was and looking as if he just wanted us to take care of things.

When we entered the hotel we experienced that same awkward feeling one gets when he leaves a theater after the show is over and doesn't know what to do next. Compared with this hotel, the streets seemed narrow and confining. All those rooms separated by the walls, one after the other—that's where we had to go.

"How about sharing a room?" I said again.

"I'm exhausted," Ahn said. "Let's each take a separate room and get some sleep."

"I don't want to be alone," the man mumbled.

"You'll be more comfortable sleeping by yourself," Ahn said.

We separated in the hallway and headed for the three adjacent rooms indicated by the bellboy.

"Let's buy a pack of cards and play a hand," I said before we parted.

"I'm completely exhausted. If you two want to play, please go ahead," Ahn said and stepped into his room.

"I'm dead tired, too. Good night," I said and went into my room. I wrote a false name, address, age, and occupation in the register and drank the water the bellboy had left, then pulled the covers over myself. I slept a sound and dreamless sleep.

Early the next morning, Ahn woke me. "The man is dead," he whispered, his mouth close to my ear.

"What?" I was suddenly wide awake.

"I went into his room just now, and he was dead."

"Dead—" I said. "Does anyone else know?"

"No, it looks like no one knows yet. We had better get out of here quickly before someone notices."

"Suicide?"

"No doubt about it."

I dressed hurriedly. An ant was crawling along the floor toward my feet. I had the feeling the ant was going to seize my foot, so I hastily stepped aside.

Outside, fine snow was falling in the early morning. Walking as quickly as we could, we left the hotel behind.

"I knew he was going to die," Ahn said.

"I couldn't have guessed it," I said truthfully.

"I was expecting it," he said, turning up the collar of his coat, "but what could I do?"

"There's nothing we could have done. I had no idea—"

"If you had expected it, what would you have done?" he asked me.

"Damn! What could I have done? How were we to know what he wanted us to do?"

"That's right. I thought that if we just left him alone he wouldn't die. I thought I was trying my best and that that was the only way to handle it."

"I had no idea he was going to kill himself. Damn! He must have been carrying poison around in his pocket all night."

Ahn stopped by a bare tree that stood beside the street gathering snow. I stopped with him. With a strange look on his face, he asked me, "Kim, we're distinctly twenty-five years old, aren't we?"

"I certainly am."

"I am, too. That's certain." He tilted his head slightly. "I'm frightened."

"Of what?" I asked.

"That 'something'. That—" He spoke in a voice that was like a long sigh. "Doesn't it seem like we've become very old?"

"We're just twenty-five," I said.

"Anyway," he said, extending his hand. "Let's say good-bye here."

"Enjoy yourself," I said, as I took his hand.

We parted. I dashed across the street to a bus stop where a bus had just pulled up. When I boarded it and looked out a window I could see, through the branches of the naked tree, Ahn standing in the falling snow deep in thought.

The Author

Kim Sŭngok was born in Osaka, Japan, in 1941, and was graduated in French literature from Seoul National University. He made his literary debut in 1962 and published a collection of short stories in 1966. "Seoul: Winter 1964," first published in the journal Sasanggye *in June 1965, was nominated for the tenth Tongin Prize.*

Kim excoriated the intellectual timidity and the repetition in technique and theme in contemporary Korean fiction, and effected a renovation in sensibility. A superb creator of atmosphere and tone, his narrative sophistication and satirical brilliance have delighted readers. A meretricious and selfish society is often set against the purity and innocence of childhood dreams, "a mirage in the splendid kingdom." The shattering effect of the intrusion of the impure into the world of dreams and the character's incapacity to come to terms with contemporary actuality have been his chief concerns. His fascination with the possibility of language at times gets out of hand as, for example, in the dialogue in the beginning of the story (although its aim is to drive home the inadequacies of everyday words and the impossibility of a real dialogue).

Purporting to portray the inaction, self-deception, and boredom of the alienated generation, "Seoul: Winter 1964" is about three characters: the narrator, Kim, a graduate student Ahn (both wanderers of the night in search of an escape from their absurd existences) and a middle-aged man who has experienced a great crisis and who comes to the realization that life is illusion and that man owns nothing. The three grope after the definition of man, his true situation in the modern world, but the story verges on allegory, as do other stories by Kim.

by Chŏng Inyŏng

Illusions of Nothingness

That man's gaze seems to seize the scruff of my neck. A big man with a stumpy nose. The face is dark, concentrated, balanced. The black, oil-slicked hair, glossy. And the exceptionally rich and large pupils . . .

I'm absorbed into that gaze. Not for these realities alone. I'm out of sorts and very uneasy. A relatively poised face, but one somehow giving an unpleasant impression. A face thickly encrusted with stupidity and doltishness. No, not for these reasons alone.

Well, then, why would his gaze disturb me so? I've quite casually sought out an empty seat in a tearoom, coming here to meet someone. Drawing out a cigaret and putting it in my mouth, I've surveyed every corner. I wonder if the person I planned to meet might possibly have arrived already. Lighting a match, I've let my line of vision absently go to the other side of the room.

There sits a man staring piercingly at my movements

Translated by Mark J. Belson

as a newcomer. At first nothing is visible save those large, raven pupils. As soon as these other things catch my eye— the jet-black hair, slicked with oil, the luster shimmering —I stop the hand bringing the match flame to my cigaret. I end by riveting my gaze on him.

He continues, however, to stare unwaveringly at me. He is zealously picking his nostril with the second finger of his right hand. His body buried deep in a cafe chair, he's stacking his legs one on top of the other. Propping the bit of arm with which he picks his nose on the armrest of the chair, he's letting his body lie aslant in that direction. It seems he just can't realize he's picking his nose. Absorbed in looking over at me, it appears his nerves aren't particularly active in the movements of his right hand.

Avoiding his gaze, I light my cigaret. It's quite a common thing after all. Absently staring over at others sitting around is an infelicity I also commit from time to time during moments of boredom in such places as tearooms. But he's eagerly burrowing into his nose as he stares on at me, isn't he?

I'd been in a complete absence of mind, and his gaze had lashed out at me. At the very start, I'd been vaguely out of sorts and uneasy. But with the flow of time his gaze had inflicted obvious pressure.

I look askance at him. But he doesn't alter his manner or stare a bit. As the number of times I look at him increases, I become seized with a deep, incomprehensible anxiety.

After all, I've never really done anything worthy of interest to anyone. This is simply because I've come to live as a somewhat stable person during these last five or six years.

Then again, if life is to be lived, there are bound to be occasional situations that do ensnare one in petty anxieties. Those coming from the hardships of life, those coming from infirmities and neuroses. . . . But I do seem to be a rather dull and simple human being by nature. I've just lived out my life from day to day in the midst of a most practical contentment.

Now that man sitting opposite me, sitting in that chair over there at a diagonal to mine, facing me, appears to be of a similar age. But, I'm seized with fear, a fear of sitting before a stranger harboring hostilities.

As I wait for the appearance of the person I've promised to meet, I purchase an evening newspaper, intending to shake off this fear as best I can. Spreading the paper open, I read it with a very self-composed air. But the print doesn't catch my eye. I'm holding the paper, but my nerves are racing toward the man.

I look at my watch after a bit and then turn my line of vision from the door to him.

Once more the dark face and the huge eyes fixed upon me, like those of a sphinx, the black hair glistening with oiliness. . . . It doesn't appear to me to be the face of a man. It takes on the reflection of a forbidding sphinx. Suddenly my heart starts to race.

To calm myself I shoot my gaze back to the paper. But my will is completely overwhelmed by his image.

Time passes, but the person I'd planned to meet doesn't appear. I grow anxious, my mood much like that of being cast off alone in a strange place. And that one man there, with whom I haven't even spoken, glares on at me.

I seem unable to endure much more of this. I have an illusion of that man springing up suddenly, grabbing my throat, and screaming out obscenities. Instinctively my line of vision returns to him.

My God, how can you explain this? He isn't a man.

Only his eyes, and his nose moving with the finger lodged in it, are fragments of a man. A complete sphinx. A brazenness without any humanity or good sense at all. I find I've suddenly gotten up, leaving the paper behind as I go out. He's coming after me in pursuit. The music of the place is instrumental; the monotonous, fast-tempo metallic sounds grasp the nape of my neck.

No sooner do I emerge from the tearoom than I forget my appointment and listlessly urge my steps forward. The late autumn streets are dreary and cold, much as if rain has poured down upon them. Pressing on, I consider the day a very luckless one.

I've returned home, eaten dinner, and lain in bed. Even so, the nose he had kept picking with his huge finger keeps rising before my eyes. Whipping my head, I've tried beating back that image. But his face and eyes have vividly appeared in inverse proportion to such efforts.

I collect my wits, determined to consider it all scrupulously. Why should I be like this? Why, at any rate, would one person of the streets, whom I'd completely overlook, seize me and cause me such anxiety? Would he be someone I'd seen somewhere? If not that, would he then be someone with whom I'd had some sort of relationship? Think as I may, no memory comes.

I can't even be sure if it's all on account of my having fallen into a life of mundane indolence.

That evening I'm being pursued by the man seen during the day. He has come after me wordlessly, one hand inserted in his coat pocket, one forever picking his nose. When I jump, he jumps after me; when I walk slowly, he too walks slowly. When I stop and look around at him, he glares at me with those raven pupils as if boring into my face. All the while he pursues me, keeping a distance of several paces.

I want to ask him why he is following me like this. But I'm needlessly afraid. My heart races on as I feel the necessity to escape this man's pursuit at all costs. Not one of the passersby on the street will help me. Everybody is just unconcernedly going his own way.

As best I can, I choose a street of many people, strenuously making for an escape. But he gives chase relentlessly, maintaining those several footsteps distant.

My sweat seems to shower. I keep squirming about but appear unable to shake his pursuit. Finally I'll die in his captivity. Die. Only death is securing a place in my mind.

Strenuous in my flight, I make out the entrance to an alley brightened by electric lights and lean in that direction with urgency. As I bend toward it, I look around behind me. His face is half visible. One eye and half a scrap of nose, half a scrap of mouth—I scream in terror and start lurching forward. No sound comes out. Before I've staggered more than a few steps, my body crashes into a wall. I fall with a thud. It's the entrance to a stranger's home. The closed gate in front obstructs me. I look around. The black shadow of the man stands four or five steps from the entrance to the alley. The dark face appears ashen in the electric light. Like viewing the face of a heavily made-up actor at a very short distance. A smile nestles on the corners of his lips. A smile . . .

I scream in terror. My startled wife wakes me up. My quilt is soaked with sweat. She sits by my pillow asking what I'd dreamt. Her eyes are sphinxlike as they look down upon me.

I calm myself, intent upon telling her about both the

dream and the man seen during the day. But the words don't come easily. For some reason, I'm overtaken by those hesitations that seem to come before admissions of great disgrace and sin. I vacillate several times, finally unable to tell her either about the dream or the man.

I'm unable to talk and after a while can only sigh deeply. It's a sigh of relief, guaranteeing at a moment of peril a secret that could have been divulged at the slightest slip. That evening I'm unable to get a wink of sleep. That man's huge black pupils and his scrap of nose flicker before my eyes throughout the night.

Very ill at ease, I begin to wonder if I haven't already become a victim of the most extreme of neuroses. Inevitably, however, I'm more consumed by the distress over the objective coercions of that nose and pair of eyes than by any concern for my own body.

The next morning. The day is still begun with the sun rising and the constant drone of the city increasing.

But I suddenly feel the day stretched out at length before me, and this new morning to be very alien. This one day. This one day in November 1965 seems to have no relationship to me at all.

Never in the course of my mundane life had I ever had any misgivings about meeting the new day. Usually, as one day goes, the next just comes; that one goes too and the one after comes. But now I seem to gaze at this intimation of the calendar as reality, having been unable to be conscious of it as such before this.

It amounts to the complete severance of time. I've come to feel time not as a flow possessed with a sense of continuity, but as a new rigidity cut piecemeal.

I feel the beginning of this severed time with the

morning drone of the city. The anxieties and nightmares which filled the hour previous to this point of departure. The gush of the shrunken mind before a certain self-confrontation. For all I know, that confrontation set upon me and incarnated by me as anxiety may have been with a fine human being. But as in his freedom, I allow myself in mine to accumulate apprehensions brought about because of him.

My day seems to spread before my eyes, weighted down by mammoth images of yesterday, which will not blot out at all. A deep, uncleansable swamp of doubt.

I've been drinking since morning; wine, not especially favored these past few years. No sooner do I gulp down several drinks in succession than a strange confidence takes hold of me. The anxiety bearing down on me since yesterday seems to take on a measure of visibility in proportion to my degree of intoxication, and appears to manifest itself before me. But this anxiety remains separate. It's only partially the wine-swollen chords of my consciousness quivering.

I drink several more cupfuls. My wife gazes at me with concern. It is a pleasure to behold such a wife.

"What is it?" her eyes demand. Even the woman's worried remarks strike me as peculiar.

I've gone to work, the wine beginning to wear off after two hours or so. But as it wears off, I feel yet another severance of time. Now a headache. I feel my head—the clinging oil-slicked hair. Instantly I recall the glossy oiliness of the man's hair yesterday. My hair is nothing but his hair. I go to a mirror. The face reflected there is clearly mine. Yet it is not mine. I shake my head. It seems to ache again. Maybe it's just my imagination. No. My head really hurts. The phone rings clamorously.

"Oh, yes, yes . . . what did you say? The tax office?

Yes, yes . . . well, we haven't quite adjusted all the records yet . . . we'll certainly have it all done by tomorrow afternoon . . . yes, yes, well then, we'll get on it."

The general affairs chief has put down the receiver and has hurriedly entered the company president's office. After a bit he has come out and whispered in my ear.

"A tax official said he'd be here tomorrow to look at the company records. The president says you're to prepare one more account book to be shown only to them . . . and you'll have to be quick about it."

He has frantically begun to set about his work. The gaze of that man yesterday instantly comes to mind.

"A duplicate set of account books." I'm dumbfounded. And my hands begin to tremble.

Normally there wouldn't be anything to such a matter. But I am evidently being chased by someone. My head hurts. Without a word, I put on my coat and go out. I'm completely unintimidated by the chief's angry face.

I've been in a tavern since the middle of the day. It seemed that by going there and drinking I could thoroughly relax myself. But there's no change, even after having emptied three or four cups. I don't know where that man of yesterday is. But the illusion that he is waiting for me to come out of this tavern suddenly chills my spine. Each time that happens, I empty another cup in one gulp.

By afternoon I am a mess. I am unable to steady my body. On the vague perimeters of my consciousness that man's strange eyes and nose still squat in a sort of demonic image.

I've completely forgotten about the company's duplicate set of account books. Before sundown I return home, dead drunk. Once in, I collapse.

There's no distinction between having dreamt or just

having slept on dullishly. This time, upon opening my eyes in the morning, two images fall upon me. One is the usual apprehensiveness grabbing me by the throat—that man's nose and eyes lumped into one—the other, the duplicate set of account books.

The office chief, perhaps thoroughly angry, may have dismissed me. Up to now I'd been a model employee, never absent from work. As if my destiny was indeed just to be a company employee, I'd never even tried indulging in far-fetched dreams. I was satisfied with the monthly wage I received, and I'd worked at my job enthusiastically. Thus the company I served had had absolute reign over my existence.

But suddenly that crumbled via a petty matter of hardly any relative importance at all. I demand more wine from my wife, who comes in with my breakfast tray and urges me to get up; as soon as the spirit of alcohol grabs me again, I lie back in bed. My wife appears at a loss. She's not even able to ask me if I'm ill, for she too knows that as I drink wine instead of eating there's really no reason for me to be ill. She can merely study my attitude.

Day after day I stayed drunk. It has been an anodyne, stilling my anxious consciousness like a narcotic. I lead a life of lethargic, dreamy indolence between my home and the taverns of the street. All the everyday relationships extant in the world have fled from me. My wife and the company and friends—everything has grown alien to me. I gad about the taverns alone. But, like a shadow, a dim companion to my consciousness remains. Seen before in the tearoom, it's that man's dark face, stolid, and ignorant in impression, with those black, boring pupils.

Not more than a week later the notification of my dismissal comes from the company. But I consider it unimportant.

I sit alone in taverns, gazing at filthy walls with dazed eyes, screaming inside. I've got to get free, I've got to free myself from this inscrutable, mysterious invader . . .

That man's black pupils treating me blasphemously, like an owl's eyes, like a dead fish's eyes. That disconcerting image grasping me by the neck.

Functioning sexually becomes impossible. That day too I'm drunk. My shirt, salted with sweat, must have been in wretched condition. I've not changed my socks in several days, and my shirt stays on until it blackens. How ludicrous the troublesome changing of clothes has become.

The girl takes me on, sweat-stained like this. She is smiling. The compensation of money. Her gruesomely sleek face is completely drenched in the electric lights. Adjusting my own obscured, turbidly discolored vision, without any reason I speak fatuously, "You deliberately affect being a woman." The girl shows embarrassment as she stands among the four walls that serve as her dressing area. "You, no—it's for the money." I'm already losing my smile. But she smiles on. This smiling is a sort of dialogue. I'm in agony. The agony of welling sobs forced back within one's breast. But the compulsion to spring forth rests in its place. The endlessly continuous sobs of one's consciousness. Then the following sham of the flesh. My flesh, acting antique, without desire, acclamation, triumph. I grow to feel my existence here before the girl become awkwardly craven. And I think of myself feeling this personal servility as shameful beyond measure. I flee her four walls out of an impulse to be effaced. My behavior is making my existence drift along like a balloon gliding through currents of air.

The night is a dark channel. The heavens are not visible. The countless lights of the city send their afterglow into the sky as grey mists form there to cover the stars. This hint perhaps of a storm coming. The man is there. Not a dark face. A crimson one. Eyes dead. Those eyes gazing at me like those of dead fish, like those of the blind.

I spring forward. But the man is everywhere. I run on panting, but suddenly stop. I have a strange premonition. But it's opaque. It merely brings me to a halt and makes me survey the area.

I calm myself and scrutinize the immediate vicinity. It's dark. Lights from shops in buildings spread out along the sides of the street. The hour is quite late, pedestrians few. The dark shadows of several shacks are visible before me, and there . . . I come to form an idea of what is there. It must be in that very vicinity. Several men totter out from among the shacks. "Good God, that tavern's wine is vile . . . moonshine, God, it's moonshine . . ." I enter an alley among the shacks from which they had emerged. Twice I turn bends of the street in darkness and then find a lighted eave. A door has been opened. I pass in through the opened shack door, a narrow space about the size of the entrance to an air-raid shelter. Beneath the space I hear the noisy sounds of people as soon as I arrive before it . . . ah, this is it! I bend at the waist and go down the staircase.

The entire area is an overcrowded basement of not more than ten square feet. The smell of alcohol flows over my face.

Wedged between people I empty a wine cup. Someone seems to be mocking me. Perhaps it's the mockery of the girl I'd fallen upon a bit before. Impotence. How absurd she must have found me. How the man must have laughed upon seeing my awkwardness before the girl. What sort of changes must have come over his stupid and doltish expression. I swallow several cups of wine in a row. Perhaps I can push back my fears this way. Perhaps I can somehow break the chains that bind me this way. The wine is vile. My stomach seethes; I can feel my face flushing immediately.

As a group exits, one of them mutters, "Well, let's be off; one grenade into the furnace here and all the tipplers get it." I look all around. The cement walls are quite stained, full of graffiti—grenades, grenades—ah, yes, no doubt. That man has come to the entrance. He's there. He's there, his stupid and doltish expression transformed into one of grief and bloodthirstiness.

Seoul was a city of death then. Arrest and execution were ceaselessly in motion everywhere. One day in September. News was that the tide of the war had changed and Seoul would soon be retaken. In truth I was not enemy to any side. The Communist forces had not molested a poor salary man approaching thirty, and even with admitting the eventual recovery by national forces, there was really no reason for me to be punished by them as I merely lay idly napping away at home. Yet I did feel this had to come to an end soon. It happened a certain September day. Without any reason I was escorted to an interrogation station in town, questioned, compelled to wait for trial before the people's court. My crime was espionage.

After having been interrogated on the third floor of a building in the heart of the city, I spent several days in the darkness of a small basement in the building. I didn't think of death at the time. There was no reason for me to die. Even they, believing in my innocence, acknowledged such. For all I knew, I just expected to be set free.

One day the man who had interrogated me came

down the basement steps. His eyes were carnal. "All of you will be executed this afternoon." Those were his words. And then he walked back up the steps.

There were five other men besides me clustered together in this provisional basement cell. All of us turned pale. Death soon approaching. We would hear the gunshots, feel the bullets tear into our breasts and die. Then wouldn't we be but corpses strewn on a street corner?

Time flowed on in anxious silence. All of us riveted our attention on the stairway entrance. The basement grew dark. A cavernous basement allowing no sun even during broad daylight. It was a hell of silence. Time was distended here like a balloon.

This temporal distention peaked. Frantic footsteps were heard at the head of the stairs. About the same moment, the door to the entrance opened. Then silence. An instant later something rather heavy came rolling down to the foot of the stairs. During the split second that the explosion hit our eardrums we realized one more was on its way down. We prostrated ourselves instinctively. The footsteps faded. Raising our heads after a moment, we surveyed the floor. A dim outline of metal—the safety pin of a grenade. A thought had instantly glanced off our minds. They'd planned on killing us by throwing grenades into this cramped basement. Contrary to their design, luckily not one of us had been killed. The first grenade had accidentally misfired, the second one exploded about halfway down to the bottom.

That afternoon Seoul was retaken by national troops, and we came out of the event as if waking from a nightmare. It had all been completely by chance.

Now. That man standing at the entrance to this basement is that man of the past. The one man who has followed me now for some ten days with his unnerving expression of stupidity and doltishness has been none other than that man of the past.

The fear that had just now seized me had clearly been brought out by that realization.

He is that man.

The man who had thrown the grenades and then had fled, believing us dead.

He gazes at me intently.

He had gazed at me in the tearoom with eyes that disbelieved seeing me for the first time in more than ten years, with eyes as menacing and abusive as during that interrogation.

I leave the place inebriated; not the victim of long ago emotionally facing a rediscovery of that valley of death from which I had miraculously escaped. A sort of manifestation. A manifestation being attested to by that man shadowing me now.

Evil cannot but be native to this cramped tavern, a public place of evil. They are selling moonshine here in this basement where we were to be drawn to our deaths, much like a daughter prostituting herself in a room where her mother has engaged in adultery. Isn't this a coincidence?

That man of that time in the past keeps after me ceaselessly. That man who'd been a Communist in a Lenin cap. Hadn't he openly glared at me? Doesn't he stand everywhere gazing and scowling on at me like some stranger? "Why shouldn't this man have died then? I clearly threw two grenades. And I clearly heard the explosion. It had been no hasty conclusion to assume there wouldn't be any chance at all that anyone would survive the explosions of two grenades in that tiny basement. Well then, how had he survived? Perhaps he's just someone else who resembles him. What with there being any number of people who could resemble him and what with all the time that's passed, I cannot really guarantee my eyes remember just what the man looked like . . ."

That man must have been vexed by such thoughts as he looked on at me that day in the tearoom while vigorously picking his nose. Those black pupils which seemed to bore, and that obstinate stare: they'd given me quite a bit of irrational uneasiness. The uneasiness of involvement in a self-confrontation that penetrates my other self. That stare tearing my existence down to nothingness.

As I stagger out, I recollect the monotonous, fast-tempo melody of the instrumental music I'd last heard at that tearoom. And I came to regard those metallic sounds as speaking for the mind of that man with the large dark pupils. They'd been sounds calling my existence into question. "You should have died, bastard. I don't believe you survived. Your existing isn't reasonable, it isn't reasonable . . ."

I pant as I scurry along night streets. He's behind, pursuing me, with his dark, digging stare.

His suspicions come after, intent upon seizing me by the scruff of my neck. "Your being alive now isn't reasonable, it isn't reasonable." A dialogue transmitted by his stare of suspicion . . . a dialogue without dialogue . . .

I've been feverish since that day. As if tormented by some febrile disease, I lie forever restless, my lips seething. No headache. The doctor has been unable to diagnose any physiological problem; it's just that I need rest. But feeling the constriction in my breast, I want to thrash about madly. This stupor—maddening, malarial—continues.

Someone appears to be forever tightening his hold upon my chest. It's like undergoing torture.

My hands fly into the void, attempting to beat off the dim, shadowlike fears and agonies that have fallen upon me. But they are nothing more than the ravings of a thread of my consciousness.

Is this then the ordeal of purgatory? The anguish of thrashing about in a sea of flames?

Such anguish and the stupor of my restless consciousness now make me unaware of any rupture in time. No, tranquil memories—my having swum in a flow of time to which that previous mundane indolence had lent itself—are there to the extent that they invade my mind in bits like distant, ancient myths.

Yet soon I lose even these piecemeal glimpses of my consciousness.

A state of absolute nothingness . . . have I fallen to this?

I'm rubbing my face on the cement wall of that basement tavern. The dampness is cool. The wall coarse. When a youth, I'd gotten simple pleasure out of sweeping a cement floor clean and scribbling on it. Suddenly my cheek hurts. The return of consciousness is like the exit to a maze. I collect my wits and lift my head. Blood is scattered on the wall. I touch my face. Blood. Fresh blood continuing to flow down my cheeks. I look around. Two men stand at a dusky distance. Panic-stricken expressions. Oh God, three fallen by my feet covered with blood.

I hold a blood-drenched kitchen knife in my hand.

No sooner are clamorous footsteps heard outside than dark uniforms are visible descending the stairs. Abruptly they seize and handcuff me. Only then do I hear the surly voice of the tavern mistress.

"Murderer, madman, murderer!"

Yet I feel a strange pleasure. My breast feels unburdened. As soon as I'm dragged from the basement, sunlight blinds me. I move several steps from the entrance and stop suddenly.

There stands the man. There clearly stands that expression, stupidity and doltishness all jumbled, an expression that shot its stare of suspicion at me in the tea-room. Wedged between many people, hands in pockets, those big black pupils gazing on at me. That glossy, oil-slicked hair . . .

Clearly the man.

A policeman shoves me on. I seem to smile over at the man as I'm being pushed along. A very strange smile. The muscles of my lips and face do not move.

The man quickly turns his head. No sooner does someone in the crowd yell out, "Madman, murderer! A bastard who's killed simply has to be killed . . ." then the throng grows noisy. Their dismal words follow me.

Those black pupils and the crowd's dismal words always seem to shadow me—like the wind glancing off a desert, like the sound of the last breath arriving at death.

The Author

Chŏng Inyŏng was born in 1933 in Okch'ŏn, North Ch'unch'ŏng, and was graduated in Korean literature from Sŏnggyungwan University in 1958. Since he made his literary debut in 1956 he has produced a series of problematic stories. "Illusions of Nothingness" was first published in the journal Hyŏndae Munhak *in January 1965.*

Since his maiden story, "Exitless Horizon," Chŏng has fondly dealt with moments of great crisis or extreme situations resulting in great violence, and his major concern has been man's search for definition of the self—in terms of the presence of others and against the evils of society. "A girl's babbling and a grandmother's tenderness," he once said, "have vanished behind the clouds of May. I must try to be coldblooded like a fish in the bottom of my existence." His farewell to lyricism, his audacious style, and his unusual topics make him one of the most difficult writers in Korea today. To him, literature is "an expression of freedom from anguish and solitude." One critic lamented the lack of dialogue in his stories as a form of despair, and the absence of faith in man as a refusal to compromise. Will Chŏng be able one day to reconcile history and man, and to rediscover hope and value in human relationships?

by Sŏ Chŏngin

The River

"It's snowing."

Inside a bus: the man sitting next to the window has a pale face. His head is half buried in the collar of a heavy black overcoat. His long hair clings close, like tendrils of a vine, behind his ears and above the nape of his neck and, around the whorl, a few stray wisps are sticking up.

"Yes. Sleet, in fact."

The man seated beside him, who has been contemplating the large flakes of dandruff on his companion's hair, also looks out the window. He has a deep voice. Apparently he likes to dress smartly. A white scarf guards his neck where it drops into a brown jacket. His sideburns look freshly trimmed. He begins to be more interested in the scene outside, where rain and snow are falling in a mixture. The bus is behind its departure time but shows no sign of budging.

"What? Oh, yes, sleet. To be sure."

Translated by Paek Nakch'ŏng

Behind them a very practical-looking man with a navy blue woolen cap pulled way down over his ears leans against a plump young woman seated by the window. Her swarthy face is heavily powdered. He strains to look out the window as if he felt called upon to touch the pane with his forehead. She feels stifled. The man's left shoulder is pressing her chest, but he shows no sign of discomfort. She, too, is remarkably patient. She decides to lean her head on the back of the seat. Her rich shining hair curves on the bare vinyl seat like a nude. The man in the brown jacket looks back at them. He envies the other man's luck. But the man in the back seat keeps gazing outside and shows not the slightest interest in anyone's looking at him. "It's sleet, all right," he only mutters. "Yes, it sure is sleet."

"Where were you inducted?"

The man shrinking inside the overcoat has a grudge against sleet. He was inducted at Shinyongsan, and sleet fell that day. To him it is incomprehensible how anyone could watch sleet falling and not think of induction. Wearing dyed, secondhand black-market fatigues and shabby old shoes, holding a grey vinyl bag, he thinks one could very well use a girl friend on such an occasion, and pictures, at a little distance from himself, a graceful maiden with sorrowful eyes—but, of course, there was nothing of the sort. Instead, he saw one of those prostitutes, typical of railway stations, who came out of a public latrine in the station square and, with disheveled hair and unsteady, crablike steps, disappeared among the wooden shacks nearby.

About twenty were inducted. Not a single person saw them off. No band, not even a flag. Only sleet. Every now and then, from beyond the station building and across the sky dotted with yellow puffs of smoke, there came the sharp whistle of a train, and he, saying to himself, "At last, the time has come for a farewell to Seoul," would look back at the shacks where the diseased prostitute had disappeared. Soon dusk fell, and when luxurious emotions such as regret and longing had become engulfed in tedium, a sergeant from the draft office finally showed up and led them into the train to Nonsan.

"I was called up in the province."

The man in the brown jacket sounds a little petulant. He looks sideways at his companion without changing his posture of looking behind. He seems disgruntled. But no law says you cannot talk about the day of your induction because sleet is falling outside. He continues in a softened tone:

"I was quite drunk when I entered the army—so drunk I had no idea what was going on. I shook hands with everybody—twice, three times with the same guys. I didn't care whose hand I shook. I would just grab one and shake it from head to knee and shout, sigh, nod, and repeat words of farewell for the hundredth time without listening to what he had to say or seeing who he was, and sing, and stamp my feet once I got on the train—and when finally I came to myself, what do you think I found? We had been packed into a freight train!"

The man in the woolen cap feels uncomfortable. He is a draft dodger. Any talk about Nonsan or going into the army is enough to make him neurotic. From looking out the window, he shifts his body back to straight up. The woman, liberated from his oblique pressure, also sits up straight and looks out the window. Of course, one does not propose to condemn all talk of Nonsan as such. Only one has heard far too much of it. Where could one meet a chap who would not get around to the subject sooner or later? How you got kicked by a PFC so hard that your

head crashed into a door; how suddenly the firing pos-
tures at rifle training became easier the moment the
trainees collected one Hwarang cigaret each for the sergeant; how you, as the head trainee of your company or
platoon or at least your squad, collected tributes for the
sergeants and officers but embezzled some of them and
had a grand time; how uninhibited were the dirty stories
that the sergeants used to tell; and so on. He ought really
to know more about that place than anyone who had
actually been there, and yet the word Nonsan calls up no
clear image in his mind. This is very unpleasant.

"How far are you going?"

There is no need to linger over an unpleasant thought.

"To Kunhari, sir."

The woman turns out to be more bashful than he
expected. A blush even spreads over her forehead; the
fine veins become visible under the skin.

"Where did you enter the army, Mr. Kim?"

The brown jacket feels uneasy that his neighbor only
gazes out the window impassively. Perhaps he had asked
the question not so much to get Kim's answer as to
launch on his own version of the Nonsan saga.

"Me? Oh, you mean, where I . . .? Well, I . . . "

Mr. Kim, the man shrinking in his overcoat, who has
just been picturing the scene of his induction, does not
feel like talking about it.

"Really? Isn't that interesting! We're going to the
same place."

The man in the woolen cap draws a little closer to
the woman, slipping his fingers beneath the cap to scratch
his head. She looks happy. Evidently she is not given to
expecting much. It will probably be easy to make her
happy.

"Is this junk of a bus ever going to leave?"

The brown jacket feels depressed. He throws an angry glance toward the door. Apparently the conductor is having lunch or something.

"Where is this bus going, I wonder?"

An upturned face wearing sunglasses looks up into the bus. Nobody answers. He tilts his head doubtfully and moves out of the narrow field of vision through the open door of the bus. The man in the brown jacket somehow feels consoled. These sunglasses—do people wear them of necessity or as a luxury? Probably not from necessity, in most cases. But to have the nerve to show off as luxury something you could get from a peddler for a mere hundred wŏn! He himself once thought of buying a pair at two thousand wŏn but, on second thought, settled for a used pair at one thousand. They are in his pocket right now, ready to be worn any time snow covers the ground.

Mr. Kim thinks of a blind man whenever he sees sunglasses. He used to be obsessed with the idea of going blind, wearing dark glasses, and becoming a masseur. He gets a battle wound in the eyes; he is laid up in an army hospital, his eyes bandaged; his girlfriend comes to see him but misses him by a split second; he wears the dark glasses of a blind man and, tapping the asphalt with his stick, walks the night streets sounding the masseur's flute; he hears a window open; a woman calls him; it is a familiar voice . . .

"Do you live there, at Kunhari?"

The man in the woolen cap cannot stand sunglasses. To him anyone with sunglasses is a police detective. And police detectives are after draft dodgers. Until he finally got fired from his post, he used to receive a "friendly call" from one of them every payday.

"Pardon me? Oh, yes, I do. What about you, sir?"

"Me? This is my first visit since they cut my navel cord."

"Ha ha ha."

The sound of her laughter spoils Kim's daydream. He can never picture himself as a blind man without pathos. But just when he has worked up his fancy to a climax, the sound of her giggling intrudes upon him. A plump woman, and himself the masseur. He feels no great chagrin. It wouldn't be too bad either to be massaging a plump young woman. The original version proceeds somewhat differently. The woman who has called him is his old sweetheart, and the one giggling is her husband; he massages the husband; she waits on them by their side but does not recognize him behind the glasses; he finishes the massage; she hands him some money which he puts in his pocket and goes out to the street again; he takes out his flute and starts to blow . . .

"So, they are starting at last, are they?"

A part of what looked like just another window in the front left side suddenly caves down to open, a gloved hand, which pulls in the head and unshaved chin of the bus driver, slips inside. A jacket follows the head, in its turn followed by a pair of old corduroy pants with the edges of the pockets frayed thin and white. Once seated, the driver puts one hand on the steering wheel and turns around toward the passengers. He seems displeased that there are so few heads. With a grunt he turns back and reaches out to start the engine. Apparently it is the passengers, who have waited for half an hour, who ought to feel guilty. Oh, why are there so few of us? If only there were a hundred packed like sardines into a bus whose legal capacity is forty-eight, the driver might feel a little guilty toward us!

"Hey, isn't it about time we moved a bit?"

The man in the brown jacket is watching the girl conductor come aboard, hips first.

"Yes, in a minute."

She has no intention of looking round to see who asked the question.

"You mean we're not moving yet?"

"Yes, we are, in a minute."

"Do you think this is a Chinese restaurant?"

"Why would I be in a Chinese restaurant?"

She looks round for the first time.

"You, you're a bear, aren't you?"

"Why would I be a bear? And what would you be, sir?"

"Me? Why, I'm your grandpa."

Now that the bus has begun to move, the man in the woolen cap can move sideways more freely, especially to the left. Each time he does so, the woman makes as if to move away toward the window. Then, as though in apology, she gives him a glance.

"Why are you going to Kunhari, sir?"

"Just for fun."

"Are you going together, the three of you?"

"Yes." He lowers his voice. "That man there is Mr. Kim, an old student. On this side is Mr. Lee; he is with the internal revenue service. As for myself, I taught at a primary school until recently. Pak is my name. Well, that's about all."

"It's an unusual group, isn't it? Are you friends?"

"We live in the same house."

"Oh, really?"

"Yes, really. Those two are boarding at my house."

Kim leans his forehead on the windowpane. The

vibration of the vehicle comes through to him, and he removes it.

"Well, it looks as though this bus can run like any other bus. I thought they built it just to stand around."

"It's all thanks to our conductor lady's shouting 'All right, go.' Isn't that so, my girl?"

Mr. Lee, in the brown jacket, is thinking that the girl's buttocks in the glossy, black nylon slacks are rather big. She is still angry with him. He takes a pack of chewing gum from his pocket. Mr. Kim is still looking outside. He always finds a running bus pleasant. It seems as if every problem were about to be solved.

"Do you know how to chew gum?"

Mr. Lee pulls out a piece of gum and pokes the girl's back with it. She looks back and grins at him.

"How can a bear chew gum?"

"What? Oh, ha ha! That's not bad. Bears play pretty good tricks, anyway. Well, take it. It's not going to do you any harm, is it?"

The girl takes the gum. Mr. Lee gives another to Mr. Kim sitting next to him and one each to Mr. Pak and the woman in the seat behind. Then he takes out the remaining one and unwraps it.

Mr. Pak and the woman are making friends fast.

"Have you always lived at Kunhari?"

"No, I used to live in Inchon."

"Oh, so you moved?"

"No, we just live there. With my mother and sister, the three of us just live there."

"In Inchon?"

"No, at Kunhari."

"Then there's nobody in Inchon now?"

"Why, yes, there is too—oh, but you don't have to know all these things."

"No, I guess you're right."

Of course not! Kim cannot help laughing to himself. Although he keeps looking out the window, he is
listening to everything that is said. He likes to pretend
that he sees nothing and hears nothing. To seem to know
when you don't and not to know when you do, it is quite
enjoyable. "Come, come, Mr. Kim, you are kidding me."
What do you mean? "Where were you between two and
five yesterday?" What do you want to know that for?
"No, you can't fool me. You can fool Mr. Pak, but not
me." Ha, ha, ha—he steals a glance at Mr. Lee. Lee may
be as smart as he likes, but what can he do as long as
you answer him with only laughter?

"Why don't you sit down, my girl? Standing is bad
for you."

"Oh, it's all right with me."

"I know it's okay now, but I mean it'll be bad later,
when the time comes for you to get married."

The girl blushes and takes an empty seat about the
middle of the bus. Mr. Lee grins contentedly. Even when
it means nothing at all, he is happy when he has a word
with a girl. He pulls his white scarf up out of his jacket
slightly and gently covers the tips of his ears. Then he
leans back in the seat, takes out a cigaret, holds it in his
mouth without lighting it, and directs his eyes outside the
window. Against a dull sky a few flakes of snow are
fluttering here and there. The two men in front sink into
thought. Only Mr. Pak in the back seat keeps talking to
the woman in a low voice. From time to time, discon-
nected sounds of laughter rise above the engine noise, but
it is impossible to catch what they are saying.

The bus stops in Kunhari. It is past three o'clock.

They, and several others, get off. The soaked dirt road seems to stretch on endlessly. The bus leaves at once.

"I wonder why the others don't get off here."

"Maybe they have no business here."

"Perhaps they have business at the next stop."

"Very likely. Just as we had no business at that place called Yulp'yong or something."

Kim is impressed by the sagacity of the other two. Only a while ago, those who got off looked strange to him, but now it's those who do not. Lee and Pak must be right in their inference.

The young woman is hurrying away at some distance. Mr. Pak runs after her. They are both short. The white-lettered motto, "Farmers' Co-op Must Thrive If Farmers Are To Prosper," forms the background. She steps aside from the road, giggling. They exchange a few words. Then she walks sideways like a crab and disappears behind the gate of a roadside house less than ten paces from where they were standing. The house has a sign, rather sloppily written on a thin pinewood board—"Seoul Chip" ("Seoul House Tavern"). Few people are in the street. Perhaps they are in their houses waiting for market day, which comes around every five days. The branch office of the Farmers' Co-op looks like a warehouse. The district office and the police station stand side by side—in close intimacy.

A countrified-looking young man, no doubt only a month out of the army, pokes his head out of the low shack of a barber shop to look at the strangers. A pharmacy is also housed there, and a beauty parlor; you can get a bridal makeup too, evidently. From a hole-in-the-wall store a transistor radio is blaring the re-run of a soap opera. Next to it is an empty lot and across the

clearing stands a building that looks like another warehouse but which must be the public hall. Every other
market day, an old film that has been to every nook and
corner of the country and has nowhere else to go will
turn up in this building, and people from the vicinity will
come to see it.

The three go around the corner of that building.
They stand at regular intervals and, in a single move,
begin to urinate. After long suppression, the water jets
out with considerable force. The place obviously is not
being so used for the first time. Mr. Kim, who has been
standing at one end, bursts into a guffaw. The other two
draw toward him, buttoning up their trousers, and follow with their eyes where he is looking. They see a pair
of shears drawn on the wall.

They walk back to the street. Coming towards them
is a middle-aged man who looks as though he would
know everything that happens around this part of the
country. Mr. Pak goes up to him.

"Excuse me, sir. Do you by any chance know of a
house where they are having a wedding? Their name is
Kim."

"Humph, you are looking for Kim Chabang's over
at the Rocks."

"Yes, sir, you are right. I think that's the name they
gave us, Rock village or something."

"Exactly as I said. Well, go straight down this road.
Before you have gone one-third of a mile, you will see on
your left a village of about fifty houses. That's Rock
village."

Finishing his words, he resumes his way and deftly
blows his nose by squashing his nostrils with a single
finger, first one side, then the other. The three look on

for a minute; then coming to themselves, begin to walk in the direction he had pointed. The main street ends abruptly, before they have walked ten paces.

Around ten o'clock that night.
They are walking out of Rock village quite drunk.
"The bride wasn't so pretty."
"She's nice and plump, though."
"That's none of your business, I say."
Each is shouting at the sky. Arms and legs are moving in every direction. They are walking in single file— Lee, Pak, Kim. They are not so much walking as just letting their feet move on. The shouting, too, comes in that order. Once they get out of the narrow lane into the road where the buses run, their steps become much less hampered. They swing to left and right with abandon.
"Say, what shall we do now?"
"Let's go back to our Seoul House."
"The last bus has gone."
"There's a Seoul House at Kunhari, too."
"I know that."
"Let's go, then."
"I've got no money."
"Was it scrap metal they gave you back there?"
"Yeah, I saw it, too."
"So what? They gave me a thousand wŏn for expenses."
"Good for you. We'll drink with that."
"Yeah, why is a tax official so hot on free booze?"
"Less than a school teacher, you bet."
"Can a student drink, too?"
"Yeah, he can drink more than the teacher, once he gets started."
"Okay, let's go."

They headed for the Seoul House, going one step backward for every two forward. The tavern seemed unusually quiet. Perhaps all the drinkers have gathered somewhere else tonight. The three feel disappointed that the gates are not flung open to welcome them. With the absence of lights, a night in the countryside is much darker than in the city. They shout and bang on the gate.

"Sell booze!"

"Make money!"

"Customers!"

At last, among the many pieces of wood, each looking like a door or a gate, one at the very edge squeaks open and produces a man's head.

"Who are you?"

"You give us liquor, we give you money."

"Well, we don't sell liquor here. Try next door."

"What do you sell here?"

"This is an inn."

"Yes, that's right. I don't see the sign we saw this afternoon."

"Well, what about a sign saying this is an inn, then?"

"Oh, we take guests without a sign."

"But you should at least leave the front gate unbolted."

"We have no customers after the last bus leaves at nine."

"Aren't we customers?"

"No, we aren't. We are customers to the next house, not to this one."

"I would rather be a customer here. I want to sleep."

Mr. Kim is already walking through the gate. The other two are taken aback.

"Hey, student! Student!"

But he does not look back. The inner yard lies pallid

in the dark. Beyond it lies the dusty veranda, then a lighted screen door. The door opens and a small kerosene lamp emerges. He walks toward it with long strides and sits down on the edge of the veranda. The boy hangs the lamp on the pillar and starts cleaning the room.

"Can I come in?"

Mr. Kim comes up on the veranda without waiting for an answer. He finds it harder to stand up than to walk. It grows quiet outside. The tax official and the school teacher have apparently gone to the tavern. The boy gathers up the littered books and comes out of the room. The stump of a broken pencil is visible under the dim lamplight. Stooping at the doorway, Kim enters the room with unsteady steps. The inside is dark and has a strong smell. The boy follows with the lamp and hangs it on a peg on the wall. The tin shade makes a slight clatter against the glass chimney of the lamp. The boy goes out. Kim sits leaning against the wall opposite the lamp and lights a cigaret. He blows out the smoke. After an instant the lamp gives a flicker.

The boy comes back with a mattress and quilt and spreads them on the floor. As he stands up, a medal shines on his chest. Kim bids him draw nearer and takes a look at it. It is round with "2nd Room, 5th Grade" written across it and the word "Monitor" written vertically. It is cheap vinyl.

"I see you are a good student."

"Yes, sir, I was the first in my class last time, too."

Oh, this is too brazen faced for a homely lad in shabby clothes!

"Is this your house?"

"No, sir. It's my aunt's. My home is in Wŏlch'ulli, about ten miles from here."

A poor college student. A rattling tramcar at night.

Weary passengers. The raucous sounding of a whistle. At the terminal the tramcar opens its jaws at both ends and spits out people. They become submerged in the surrounding darkness. The dull lights from the peddlers' booths rescue their shapes. They bury their heads in their chests and gradually become lost in the darkness again. And then, privately, in ones and twos, they disappear into their own alleys. In front of the college student looms a gate. He stops, facing it; he looks behind him and hesitates. Ah, if only there were a gate he could bang on without hesitation at such a time! He loosens his fist. With the flat of his palm he gently shakes the gate as if caressing it. He shakes it once more. The sound of dragging rubber slippers on the ground. The maid servant's slippers have a humble sound. He feels relieved. The feeling of relief sinks down to his stomach.

"You go to school here in Kunhari, then?"

He raises his heavy eyelids with effort. The lowered light of the kerosene lamp flickers before him; the boy is gone already. The ondol floor feels warm. The liquor seems to be rising to his head more and more. Without taking his clothes off, he pushes his hands and feet underneath the quilt. I must take off my necktie, he thinks, and closes his eyes.

"Tops in the class, eh? That's good. Just study hard. There is no end of opportunities. America, England, France—you can go anywhere. You can get government money or some other scholarship. You don't have to have a penny of your own. Oh, no, don't worry about not having the money. Scholarships are abundant. All you need is the brain and the effort. Yes, work hard, study hard, and have confidence!"

But nobody listens. And nobody could, for he has been mumbling to himself without opening his mouth.

And as soon as his words are done, in spite of the dizziness there arises in his mind each phase of the process by which a genius is transformed into a dullard. Yes, you are now the prodigy of the entire school, no doubt. In middle school you will be only an "excellent" student; then a "good" one in high school; about middling when you get into college; then you gradually turn into a dullard and come out into the world. In short, it was to become just this dull mediocrity that you have labored all those years with such persistence. How infinitely better for you to have fled, while still a genius, ten miles back into the woods and become a woodcutter among the hills! It is not at all pleasant to make the discovery that the glittering word *genius* stands for nothing but a figment of the ignorant imagination of country bumpkins. They did not know that a genius, after a protracted struggle against poverty, quietly turns into a dullard one fine day. Not everybody can set the Thames on fire, after all! The middle-school boy who walks to school for hours each day in frayed, outgrown pants. Plenty of sympathy and some admiration. The college student who makes his rounds of aunts', uncles', and cousins' houses, who walks back late at night from the library with a heavy, antiquated leather bag under his arm, tightening his belt over a hungry stomach and absorbed in thinking about the tuition fee for the next term. And so, in due course, you find the genius gone with the wind; instead there remains a servile, worn-out, yet arrogant bit of human failure. He is ready to do anything to get on. Nothing is more important than winning the recognition of his senior professor. Not a single opportunity of going abroad passes unattacked by him. Hence the probability of his succeeding is very high; he needs to hit only one among the innumerable marks. And the point is not whether he will hit or miss, but that it makes no difference whether he hits or misses. Whatever the outcome, he must find himself far removed from where he thought he would come to when first setting out. Ah, that it should be the loss of what cannot be regained!

He writhes a little. He sits up without opening his eyes and wriggles out of his overcoat and jacket in a single movement. Now he lies down more comfortably than before. Soon he starts snoring.

"What makes you a beauty?"

"What makes me a hag?"

"Money makes you a beauty,/ And lack of money makes me a hag!"

"Hear, hear!"

With the table set in the middle, the school teacher is lying down on one side and the tax clerk sitting up on the other. The barmaid is seated between the two. The teacher shouts into the ceiling: "Hear, hear!"

She yawns. The clerk grabs her wrist. She resists, giggling. But he is strong.

"You had a good time with Mr. Pak in the bus. Now it's time to flirt with me."

Mr. Lee takes her into his arms. She struggles out of his embrace. He pinches her on the thigh. She shrieks, pulls up her skirt, and examines her bare thigh. The lamplight, its wick turned up high, flickers from its place on the wall.

Mr. Pak is lying on his back and staring at the ceiling. He is full of hatred for Mr. Lee. The clerk is a dandy and a good dancer to boot. One day when he offered to teach Pak's wife how to dance and put his arms around her waist, Mr. Pak expected her to become furious, but she only giggled and ran from the room and seemed far from offended. In order to sound her out, he said to her, "Mr. Lee is quite a fellow," and she answered, "He really is." He was keenly disappointed. He can trust Mr. Kim, the old student, however. First of all, Kim does not care how he looks, does not like to mix with people, and never talks much. He is the only one of the three who can spend a whole day cooped up in his room. Left alone, he will spend not only a day but even a whole week just sprawled on the floor and tossing about.

"I guess Mr. Kim must really be sleeping."

Mr. Pak casts a noncommittal glance over the table at Mr. Lee, who now has his hand under the woman's sweater, over her breast.

"Oh, really, what happened to the other gentleman?"

This Lee sure is shameless! Granted that he has a right to think himself handsome and attractive, he doesn't have to show it to everybody. Whenever there is a female around, he confidently puts on what he obviously considers an irresistible smile. Whether it is irresistible to her or not, to another male nothing can be more contemptible and nauseating. This is an emotion quite distinct from jealousy. And Lee never stays home, except for sleeping hours. He returns from the office quite late, usually saying something like: "You sure feel fresh after a round of billiards," or "I ran into Mrs. Chang and we had a turn." Apparently he thinks it's something to be proud of if he spins round a dance hall with another man's wife. At such times Kim merely blinks his eyes and looks at the ceiling or the wall. He has no desire to argue about the rights and wrongs of someone else's behavior. They call him a man who can live without the law. Mr. Pak likes him. No one can dislike him.

"Why don't you go and fetch the college student?" Mr. Lee says to her.

"What, a college student!"

"Yes, the gentleman who was sitting next to me in the bus. He sat merely looking out the window all the way, but he is a deep one. He is next door, he must have had a good snooze by now. He won't mind your waking him. Let's have an all-night party."

She listens attentively. Mr. Pak, too, is listening without saying a word. His eyelids are growing heavy. As the woman stands up quietly, Mr. Lee, who was leaning against her, slumps down on the floor and falls asleep. She goes out, opening and shutting the door quietly. The lamplight flickers.

Outside, she is surprised. She puts on her rubber slippers and walks to the middle of the courtyard. Snow has fallen white on the ground and is still falling silently. She turns her face upward and looks at the sky. It is thickly dotted with the dark flakes of snow. The cold flakes touching her face give her a keen pleasure. She opens her mouth wide to receive them.

"Oh, how happy the bride must be. They say snow on the wedding night brings you riches. How lucky she is!"

She blinks her eyes. Countless flakes of snow appear and disappear before her. She has never seen the bride. But it seems to her as if all brides would have one identical face. The face of happiness, expectation, trepidation or perhaps something that means all of these at once —she drops her head. Keeping her legs straight, not bending the knees, she drags her slippers to make two parallel lines on the snow. She goes round and round the yard. Swiftly, swiftly, the snow flurries land on her hair. All of a sudden she stops dragging her shoes and moves to the gate. Then, quietly, like a cat, she opens it and slips out.

The street, too, is covered with snow. She walks with her eyes on the tips of her slippers as they make virgin marks on the fallen snow, walks as if she would walk for miles and miles. The fresh snow makes no sound under her tread. The whole world is quiet. She goes to the side gate of the inn. She slips her hand through the hedge and easily opens the brushwood gate. Flurries like cotton flowers fall from the gate. She enters the yard. Of the two guestrooms, one has a light on. She hesitates a moment, then goes up to the lighted room. She climbs onto the veranda and peeps in through a hole in the paper screen. In the dim lamplight a man is lying in an uncomfortable posture. She shrinks back. Then she goes toward the next room. With her lips to the paper door, she calls the boy. No answer. She shakes the door a little. Again no response. She goes back to the lighted room and opens the door.

Mr. Kim is sound asleep on the bare floor, lying on his side, all four limbs stuck underneath the quilt, his body bent over like a shrimp. She looks into his face. He is the very man she saw in the bus. And a college student! Softly she pushes his shoulder and lets him lie more comfortably. He shakes his chin left and right, apparently hampered by his necktie. Tut, tut, he didn't even take off his clothes, poor man! She becomes a sister, a mother! She unties his tie, pushes off the quilt to remove his trousers, takes off his shirt, straightens the mattress—he makes an abrupt movement as if to get up, but again creeps in underneath the mattress. It angers her. She pulls out his limbs forcibly and manages to lift him on top of the mattress. Then she covers him with the quilt and places the pillow under his head. Lying on her stomach she peers into his face. A college student!

The kerosene lamp hisses. She gets up, picks up the

clothes scattered about the room, and hangs them on the wall. The lamp is dark with soot. She bends down and, through the opening at the top, gently blows out the lamp.

Outside, the snow continues to fall, covering with white the tracks she has made.

The Author

Sŏ Chŏngin was born in Sunch'ŏn, South Chŏlla, in 1936 and was graduated in English literature from Seoul National University. He made his literary debut in 1962. Currently he is teaching English at Chŏnbuk University. "The River" was first published in the journal Ch'angjak kwa Pip'yŏng in spring 1968.

In his early works, Sŏ dealt with the solitary man's challenge to the irrational world and of man's relationship to time. An escape from here and now takes the form of nostalgia for the past, which results in disillusionment. Sŏ Chŏngin is not a prolific writer, but his mature stories, characterized by wit and humor and a keen ear for prose rhythm, demonstrate insight into gloomy life in a small city and the frustration of the educated, as in old student Kim's ironic comment on the world he inhabits.

Notes

Introduction

1. Figures based on Andrew J. Grajdanzev, *Modern Korea* (New York: John Day, 1944), chap. 5, and Han Woo-keun, *The History of Korea* (Seoul: Eul Yoo, 1970), Part 7.

2. The Korean unit of currency; worth 41 cents U.S. in 1925.

3. In *Der Soldat Tanaka* (1940), a play by Georg Kaiser (1878–1945).

4. *See* Im Changguk, *Ch'inil munhak non* (A study of collaboration literature during the Japanese occupation, 1966). Cf. Donald Keene, "Japanese Writers and the Greater East Asia War," *Journal of Asian Studies* 23 (1964): 209–225.

5. Uwe Johnson's third novel, *Zwei Ansichten* (1965), translated as *Two Views* by Richard and Clara Winston (New York: Harcourt, Brace & World, 1966).

6. *Character and the Novel* (London: Chatto & Windus, 1965), p. 24.

7. Ibid., p. 25.

Potato

1. A-frame: a back pack in the shape of the letter A, with which Korean workers carry heavy loads.

2. The chŏn is the Korean cent.

3. Kija (Chi Tzu in Chinese): the uncle of the last monarch of the Shang who fled to Korea in 1122 B.C., when the Shang were deposed by the Chou, and built a capital at P'yongyang. Traditionally the dynasty lasted until 194 B.C.

4. *Nyang:* an old Korean dime.

The Buckwheat Season

1. In the original, distance is given in the Korean measure, *ri,* which corresponds to one-third mile. In most cases, the mile is used.

Wings

1. "Blouses" in translation stands for *chŏgori* ("tops"), the Korean jacket worn by both men and women and tied in front.

2. In 1936 one wŏn was equivalent to 18 cents U.S.

Portrait of a Shaman

1. *The Complete New Testament.*

2. The Tonghak ("Eastern learning"), as opposed to Western learning, was a popular movement, emerging at the end of the nineteenth century. A composite of Confucianism, Buddhism, Taoism, and a belief in a heavenly father, its adherents sought to remedy administrative chaos and agrarian discontent and to combat the spread of Christianity at that time. Full-scale rebellion broke out in 1894, and when the government sought Chinese help, Japan sent soldiers into Korea. The presence of the two armies eventually led to the outbreak of the Sino–Japanese War.

3. One of the tutelary gods of Buddhism who resides in the Palace of Correct Views on the summit of Mount Sumeru in the Tusita Heaven and watches over the East.

The Last Moment

1. On February 15, 1953, the unit of currency *wŏn* was changed to *hwan* (100 wŏn to one hwan); and on June 9, 1962, hwan reverted to wŏn (10 hwan to one wŏn).

The Rainy Season

1. In 1953 $1 U.S. was equivalent to 6 wŏn in August and to 18 wŏn in December.

Flowers of Fire

1. "Blade of disgrace": the outbreak of the Korean War on June 25, 1950.

2. *Chusa:* a general term for a lower official of a bureau in the traditional administration. Here used as an honorific.

3. In the original, *Myŏngsim pogam,* a collection of Confucian maxims or sententiae, compiler unknown. The former Royal Library has two seventeenth-century editions (1637, 1664). There are modern translated versions in Korean.

4. Carl Sesar, tr., *Takuboku: Poems to Eat* (Tokyo: Tuttle, 1969), p. 27. Takuboku's dates are 1885–1912.

5. A learned allusion to political rhetoric in ancient China: the deer or stag is a symbol of the crown and its power in the *Tso Commentary* and the *Historical Record* of Ssu-ma Ch'ien.

6. In 1940, in an attempt to assimilate Korea into the Japanese empire, Koreans were ordered to change their names to Japanese style.

7. *Manyōshū,* a collection of 4,516 ancient Japanese poems, compiled around A.D. 770. *Hagakure,* or *Hagakure kikigaki,* a handbook on the way of the samurai, compiled by Tashiro Tsuramoto in the beginning of the eighteenth century from the conversations held between him and Yamamoto Jōchō (1659–1719). See Mishima Yukio, *Hagakure nyūmon* (Tokyo, 1967), p. 50 ff.

8. This is a lecture delivered in 1879. Thomas H. Green (1836–1882), *Works of Thomas Hill Green,* ed. R. L. Nettleship (London: Longmans, Green, and Co., 1911; 3 vols.), II: 308–333.

9. A popular prophetic book dating from at least the eighteenth century. Rebel leaders often invoked it to justify popular uprisings.

10. By "contractors" the author means agents contracted by a political party or a power group to do its dirty work, to act in behalf of their superiors and not out of their own convictions.

11. On October 19, 1948, instigated by the Communists, part of the national defense force stationed in Yŏsu revolted. The rebellion spread to other cities, but the Second and Fifth corps of the Korean army recaptured Sunch'ŏn and Yŏsu and quelled the uprising. The rebel remnants fled to the mountains and became guerrillas.

The Ducks and the Insignia

1. *P'yŏng:* an area measure of about 3.3 square meters.

The Young Zelkova

1. *Ondol:* the Korean heating system that utilizes beneath-the-floor flues through which hot air circulates from a fireplace outside the room or the building.

The Heir

1. *Hongp'ae:* a certificate on red paper given to those who passed the second civil service examination, held in the capital. The certificate was inscribed in black ink with the candidate's name and grade. In the original, *taekwa,* the literature section of the civil service examination. The successful candidate became part of the civilian corps of the government, in contrast to the military corps.

2. *Tori jade:* jade rings or beads worn only by those in the senior and junior first ranks in traditional Korean civil service.

3. *Okkwanja* or *okkwŏn:* jade rings or beads, carved or uncarved, on the two strings on either side of the headband of a horsehair hat worn by officials. Other beads are made of gold, horn, or bone.

Bibliography

General Background

Grajdanzev, Andrew J. *Modern Korea*. New York: John Day, 1944.

Han Woo-keun. *The History of Korea*. Honolulu: East-West Center Press, 1971.

Henderson, Gregory. *Korea: The Politics of Vortex*. Cambridge, Mass.: Harvard University Press, 1968.

Kim Se-jin. *The Politics of Military Revolution in Korea*. Chapel Hill: University of North Carolina Press, 1971.

Lee Chong-sik. *The Politics of Korean Nationalism*. Berkeley: University of California Press, 1963.

Oh, John K. C. *Democracy on Trial*. Ithaca: Cornell University Press, 1968.

Reeve, W. D. *The Republic of Korea: A Political and Economic Study*. London: Oxford University Press, 1963.

Studies in Korean

Chŏng Hanmo. *Hyŏndae chakka yŏn'gu* (Studies of modern Korean writers). Seoul: Pŏmjosa, 1960.

Im Chongguk. *Ch'inil munhak non* (A study of collaboration literature during the Japanese occupation). Seoul: P'yŏnghwa ch'ulp'ansa, 1966.

Kim Pyŏngik et al. *Hyŏndae Han'guk munhak ŭi iron* (Theory of contemporary Korean literature). Seoul: Minŭmsa, 1972.

Kim Sangsŏn. *Sinsedae chakka non* (A study of the new generation). Seoul: Ilsinsa, 1964.

Kim Ujong. *Han'guk hyŏndae sosŏl sa* (A history of modern Korean fiction). Seoul: Sŏnmyŏng munhwasa, 1968.

Paek Ch'ŏl. *Sinmunhak sajo sa* (Trends in the new literature), in *Paek Ch'ŏl munhak chŏnjip* (Collected works of Paek Ch'ŏl), 4 vols. Seoul: Sin'gu munhwasa, 1968. Vol. 4.

Yi Chaesŏn et al. *Han'guk kŭndae munhak yŏn'gu* (Studies in modern Korean literature). Seoul: Sogang University Institute on the Humanities, 1969.

ANTHOLOGIES

An Sugil et al., eds. *Shin Han'guk munhak chŏnjip* (An anthology of the new Korean literature), 51 vols. Seoul: Ŏmungak, 1970–.

Han'guk munin hyŏphoe, ed. *Han'guk tanp'yŏn munhak taegye* (An anthology of twentieth-century Korean short stories), 12 vols. Seoul: Samsŏng ch'ulp'ansa, 1969.

Paek Ch'ŏl et al., eds. *Hyŏndae Han'guk munhak chŏnjip* (An anthology of contemporary Korean literature), 18 vols. Seoul: Sin'gu munhwasa, 1965–1968.